Thirty Pieces

The Lost Templar's Secret

By

Gregory Valentine Flis

To My Wife Wanda,

In all things she has supported me

With love and trust,

I could not have done this without her.

To Sarah Freeman,

For always pointing me

In the right direction.

Table of Contents

Introduction

It was not long ago that the Glasgow School of Modern Art suffered a devasting fire. This was reported throughout Britain, and worldwide; the tragic loss of art and rare books. The Glaswegian cultural icon suffered huge losses mainly in the school's library. 8,000 books along with period furniture and some 90 irreplaceable paintings; in particular, two by Charles Rennie MacKintosh, the founder of the school were destroyed.

These headlines appeared on Friday, March 13th. It was only later did I connect the date to the events that were to unfold. To the Templars and the Masonic Order, Friday the 13th is an ominous date. It was on this date back in 1314 that Jacque de Molay, the last Grand Master of the Knights Templar, was arrested, charged with heresy, and after torture, a mock trial, and lengthy imprisonment was burned at the stake. At his execution, he cursed both the Pope and the King of France, predicting an early untimely gruesome death. In both cases, the curse was fulfilled. Jacque de Molay went to his death vehemently denying the charge of heresy. The reason for his arrest, execution, and destruction of the Knights Templar to this day is shrouded in mystery. What did the Knights Templar have that was so dangerous to their existence?

To this day I am still amazed at how these mysteries revealed themselves to me and the dangers that surrounded them.

"Glasgow School of Art reveals full toll on fire."

I remember reading the article in our local paper and the following description of the fire; I was shocked; this is disastrous, one of our local Glaswegian icons, a national treasury of art, and irreplaceable books. My friend Richard is the Director of this School; this must be heartbreaking for him. I must give him a call. I returned and read the full article.

"Scotsman" Newspaper article Friday, March 13, 2015

AROUND 8,000 books and journals, were lost in the devastating blaze at Glasgow School of Art, bosses have admitted.

Almost 20 percent of the institute's rare book collection was lost when the iconic Mackintosh library was destroyed. The blaze also hit some 90 oil paintings and nearly 100 items of furniture.

Two paintings by Charles Rennie Mackintosh, who designed the Glasgow School of Art, an A-listed building; one work by Joan Eardly and several by former director Francis Henry Newbery were among those destroyed.

It struck me as I reread the Scotsman's newspaper headline that Friday, March 13, was a memorable date. Considered unlucky to some but to those ancient Templars and today's Masonic Order, this is a most ominous date. It was on this date, I recalled, Friday, March 13, 1314, that Jacque de Molay, last Grand Master of the Knights Templars, was arrested, charged with heresy, and burned at the stake. At his execution, he cursed both the Pope, the King of France, and all their descendants with an early painful death. In both cases, the curse came to fruition with the gruesome death of both King and Pope. Jacque de Molay went to his death vehemently denying the charge of heresy. His arrest, death, and the destruction of the Knights Templar to this day are shrouded in mystery. I have always wondered, what did the Knights

Templar have that was so dangerous to their existence? Was it their wealth or something far more devious? Could this fire on the anniversary of the demise of the Knights Templar have anything to do with the secrets held by them or, just a coincidence? A whimsical thought, probably not. Everybody loves a mystery.

As I read the headline, thinking, poor Richard, this was his life's work. Richard McMillan is the Director of the Glasgow School of Art for quite a number of years now; he was also a dear friend. The School has been his life. This must be heartbreaking for him. So many treasures lost. I never thought that this would affect me other than the sympathy for a dear friend. I never even dreamt of the correlation between the School and the Knights Templar.

 I should introduce myself. My name is Gregory Flint. I have a Ph.D. in theology, nothing special, no real accolades, just a regular working guy, bit of a mundane life' but content. I have a wonderful wife and good friends. I'm not particularly religious, more spiritual, but I do give thanks for what I have, how I wished for the mundane to return in the days to come.

 I have nothing to do with the Knights Templar, nor am I a Mason, other than just historical interest. As I said, I am not particularly religious. How I was dragged into the mysteries of the Masonic Order of the Knights Templar I never in my wildest dreams thought would happen to me. How I would be part of solving one of their greatest mysteries, with the help of the Vatican, still amazes me to this day. I was dragged naively into this dangerous and mystifying episode. However, something was found that should not have been there. Now years later, back in my own country and safe at home, I can tell you the story behind this devastating fire, how I was drawn into it, to eventually reveal one of the world's most changing discoveries of the twentieth century. It started with a phone call.

The phone had just started ringing when I picked it up. I recognized the voice, "Richard, that you?"

"Yes, it's Richard," the voice on the phone answered. "How are you, old friend? I trust better than I am. I am up to my ears in such a mess."

"I know I have just read all about it. I'm so sorry," I commiserated. "Is it as bad as the paper reports?"

"It's worse," Richard responded, "I am barely making a dint."

"Anything I can do," I offered.

"Not really," a dejected Richard answered, "but I do have something a little odd that you might be able to sort out. Greg, can you come over to my office and take a look at something I think you may be able to help me out with."

"Anything I can do, I will; where are you," I inquired. "Are you still at your office?"

"Yes, Greg, I'm at my office now. I know it is a bit of an imposition, but can you come over right away? I need some help."

"Yes, I should be able to; I thought you were still in the middle of cleaning up from the fire. It is all over the news. I am so sorry for all the destruction."

"I am, and what a bloody mess. It is heartbreaking, a terrible loss. I've got workers, reporters, fire investigators, insurance people, restorers, and police all over the place. On top of that, I have a small army of students I am trying to organize into some sort of cleanup crew. I have started at least twenty things, and I still have twice that amount I haven't even looked at yet. Most of the library is gone. I don't know whether The Glasgow School of Art will ever recover from this."

"Don't say that," I tried to assure, "you will recover. What are the police doing there? I didn't think this was a criminal case. At least there is nothing in the papers suggesting that. What's the latest, anything new?"

"Not really," Richard responded, "the police say it is due diligence, covering all the bases, plus stopping the occasional looter from digging around. I have heard a rumour that the police feel a little suspicious about the fire. It started with an explosion and then the fire. The sprinkler system did not engage. They also feel there may have been a break-in, but the alarm system didn't go off. So, they are still guessing. Now the insurance people are nosing around."

"Suspicious fire; maybe a break-in and looting, really? Sounds like something out of an Agatha Christie mystery novel."

"I don't know," Richard sounded weary, "but whenever the insurance people are here, you know the police will be on the scene. Keep this little information to yourself for the time being. You know what the papers can be like if they get a whiff of this. "

"What do you want me to do, Richard? Is there anything I can do to help you clean up or organize? I've got some time as I am on a bit of a vacation. Jennifer is up north in the Highlands with an art painting group, so I am on my own."

"Not in that way, Greg, I have enough help in that area, I'm tripping over people. No, what I want is for you to look at something I found, or I should say someone found. It is a little leather-bound prayer book, maybe medieval. It is handwritten in Latin, not my strongest forte, but you read Latin. Could you come over and see how I should categorize it? Don't think it is quite the book for our library, but it was found here in the rubble under a cracked flooring flagstone. Maybe it was left by Charles Rennie MacKintosh; I don't know."

"Ok, you've got me intrigued. A medieval Latin prayer book does sound a little late for a Victorian-era school. Give me thirty minutes; I'll be right over."

The Glasgow School of Art was about twenty minutes away by car. It was midmorning and still drizzling a light rain as I drove over. The traffic was sparse. I drove through the rain and was over there in less than thirty minutes. I was stopped by a policeman as I parked the car in the School's parking lot. I told him I had a meeting with the Director. Once he had checked, he let me through. I dashed in, out of the rain. I called up to Richards's office on the intercom; there was a private entry code which I didn't have to let myself in. Richard buzzed me in, and from there, I went upstairs to his office. The smell of smoke and dampness pervaded everywhere. It looked like the aftermath of a World War II blitz, not that I had been in one. Everywhere was a beehive of activity. I said hello to Marge, his secretary, and just walked into Richard's office. Richard had a young student with him.

I popped my head through the door, "Hi Richard."

"Greg, come in," Richard called as he dismissed the student. "Please have a seat, just move those books over to the back desk. Leave your coat on; the heating isn't much at this time, as they are still trying to fix it. This is so good of you. I hope I have not put you out. Now, where did I put it, and first of all, where did I put the key? Oh yeah, key in the first draw, envelope in the second draw. " Richard reached to the side draw and unlocked it. "Here it is," as he took out a small envelope. "This is what I wanted you to have a look at," as he handed me the envelope.

I opened up the envelope and pulled out a small old leather-bound book or what could be a little prayer book. "Looks quite old," I glanced at some of the pages, "and it is handwritten in Latin on vellum. The Latin is archaic, and so is the writing. It's also interspersed with some French. This one is going to take a bit of time to translate. First, the actual script, second the Latin, and lastly the French. I'll have to make notes as I translate. Would you mind if I worked on it in my office at home?"

"No, go ahead; I have enough to do around here. I thought you would take it home to work on it. This place would not be the best place to do some academic work. It would be better if you took it home. Let me know what you find."

"Give me two or three days, and I should have it translated. The book does not look like the type for this School, too old; it looks medieval. I would have thought your library would be a little more contemporary, not any older than Victorian. Do you want me to sign out for it?"

"No, nothing like that. I would not know where to start to find a sign-out log. You are right, though, it does look a little out of place here. That is why I wanted you to look at it and advise me on how to categorize it. I don't read Latin. Don't lose it. We have lost enough around here. "

"Don't worry, I won't, I'll take great care of it. You look like you could use a break, want to get out of here and have some lunch with me? There is a nice pub just around the corner, The State Bar. We have been there before."

"I can't I'd love to. I'm up to my eyeballs, but thanks for the offer. My housekeeper packed me a sandwich and a thermos of tea. I'll be alright; I'll see you later, Greg, thanks again."

"Won't have any trouble with the police taking this out?" I asked.

"Sorry Greg, I forgot, I already had this letter made out, I'll just sign it. Should clear you through, have them call me if there is a problem."

"Alright, see you soon," I could already see Richard had his mind on other things as he gave me a quick wave goodbye. I left the school showing my clearance to the police and headed home.

Once home, I got out a pad and pencil, made myself comfortable. I was on my own as Jennifer, my wife, had rented a cabin in the Scottish Highlands for a personal art workshop. I put on a pair of white cotton gloves and started reading the little book. The vellum pages were stiff with age. It was difficult. It was in an ancient script, which I was having a hard time deciphering. The Latin dialogue was undoubtedly not contemporary, plus it had archaic French thrown into it.

This was a real headache. I worked at it well into the night, past midnight, but I was not putting it down. What I was translating, to the best of my ability, had me dumbfounded. It seemed to me what I could translate, that this was a confession. A confession by Jacque de Molay, the last Grand Master of the Knights Templar. There was a lot I was missing and could not figure it all out. I needed help; this was a bit beyond me. I decided there and then to get help, and I knew who to call. I would call my old friend Peter. He was an expert in this field, but by now it was after one o'clock in the morning. I would call at a more civilized hour later this morning.

It was now nine o'clock in the morning when I called Peter. "Good morning Peter. Sorry to trouble you at this hour, but I need some help with a translation."

"What's up? Can't make out a parking ticket or your doctor's prescription?" Peter humorously replied.

"Wish it was that simple. I have something that is quite mystifying, and I am having a lot of trouble translating what I have. I think you will find it interesting. Don't want to go into it in great detail over the phone. Can you come over later this afternoon? I'll cook supper, and we can have some wine. Stay the night; Jennifer is away up in the Highlands with her art break; also I could use the company. No reason why we cannot enjoy ourselves at the same time."

"Wine, huh, ok, you have got me intrigued. I'll be over after lunch. You did say wine?"

"Yes, some excellent red wine. I found something wonderful, one of my bargains, but it is excellent, and I am going to make a decent beef stew."

"Ok, sounds great, see you tomorrow. Is there anything I can bring?"

"Toiletries and pajamas, you know. See you tomorrow."

"Looking forward to it, you already have me intrigued," Peter hung up.

I looked at the little book again before I went to bed and thought, you are a little mystery.

The weather in Arkansas was getting warm, and pleasant, as he walked through the large modern stadium church. He was a large man, over six feet tall, well-muscled, tanned, with a close shaved scalp. The man had a determined walk of authority. There was a hard look to him. One did not want to confront him in a dark alley. Meanness glared through cold eyes. This man was unmistakably dangerous. The church that he strode through could comfortably seat five thousand people and had one of the most modern sound systems money could buy. Everything spoke of a well oiled, lucrative church. He made his way to the office behind the podium altar and knocked on the door, and walked in.

"Come in, come in, Jed, sit down. I have been expecting you," the southern Arkansas drawl of Reverend Andrew Ducane was thick but relaxed. "What have you got for me?"

 "We think something has come up," the southern drawl was just as thick, "I thought you would want to know right away. We think we know where it is, and it matches the description."

Jed entered the Reverend's mahogany-paneled office of the Grand Evangelical Church of the Savior and sat in front of the sumptuous rosewood desk. The Reverend was seated in a luxurious dark burgundy red high back leather chair. Everything in the office spoke of power and wealth, the power of the Lord, through one of his most ardent followers. The only hint of piety was the worn black leather-bound Bible on his desk and the plain brown wooden cross on the wall over his chair. The Reverend was dressed in a dark black suit, impeccably tailored with a crisp white collar, indicating a member of the church. Around his neck, he wore a silver chain and again a small wooden cross almost identical to the one hanging in his office. On his left hand, he wore a large gold ring inscribed with a cross, inlaid with diamonds. There was a hint of a very expensive wristwatch just under the white cuff of his shirt. The Reverend Andrew Ducane ministered in one of many very lucrative Grand Evangelical Churches of the

Saviour. Not only were the churches lucrative with their flocks, but the TV broadcasts more than tripled their tax-free income.

 Wealth was in the multi-millions. Their belief in the Bible was absolute and would brook no change; it was the sacred word of God. Any suggestion of change was blasphemy to the church and the monetary bottom line of their believers.

"Is it what we have hoped for? After all these years, we have finally tracked down Charles Rennie MacKintosh and where he hid it. After forty years of patient work, infiltrating the Rite, and finally, after seven hundred years, we will be able to silence that heretic Jacque de Molay on the anniversary of his arrest, Friday, March 13." The Reverend leaned over and gleamed, "did we not destroy the library where MacKintosh hid it, once and for all? I gave you all the information that finally led to the Glasgow School of Art and left this in your hands, Jed. Maybe we showed our hand a little early, setting the fire on March 13, but we wanted to put the fear of the Lord in them. We are still here and powerful enough to attack those bastards right in the heart of their territory. I was just reading the report of the fire on my laptop yesterday. Have we really done it ?"

"We are sure. Most, if not all, of the library, is destroyed. We were able to override the alarm system. Our inside contact gave us the code, so it didn't go off," Jed replied. "They believe it was an accident. We set it up nicely; heat lamp on an old gas cylinder, plus stuck a dead bird in the sprinkling system. It cannot be traced. Quite a nice explosion, I was told. If, as you said, it was in the library, it would have been destroyed. But now, with the restoration, it seems, something was found under a flagstone while repairs were underway. What we do know is one of our contacts at the Glasgow School of Art witnessed the find; a small metal box was taken to the office of Director Richard McMillan. A small ancient leather-bound missal was inside. We think he still has it but does not understand what he has. We do know that it is ancient and written in Latin; that according to our contact at the school.”

“Jed, how long ago did this happen?” snapped the Reverend as he pounded his desk. “If this is what we think it is, and it sure sounds like it. We must retrieve it at all costs.”

“Two days ago,” replied Jed, “from the time it was found until our contact called. As to what it is, we are still guessing, but they sure made off with it in a hurry. We feel it has left the school. It must be vital to them, and Bob Findley is with them. Our contacts at the Glasgow police advised us Findley arrived yesterday. Our team from the Glasgow police followed them to the Scottish Highlands, a place called Ardlui. We thought we had them there, but they gave us the slip. Don’t worry; we will catch up with them; we have good contacts in the Glasgow police force.”

“Jed, the description fits, and if Findley is there, I guarantee it is ‘the confession.’ We must get it here or have it destroyed. We know this confession will lead to a more revealing secret. If they have found the confession, they will have the directions to a greater and more dangerous revelation. At all costs, this, we must obtain, and Jed, watch out for that bastard Findley. We have had a run-in with him in the past. He is one tough well-organized asshole and has the Masonic Order of the Knights Templar behind him. He knows we have infiltrated their organization to some degree and may know who they are. We must keep our Bible pure for our God-fearing flock and keep those dam Masonic Templars, Papist Catholics, and Jesus killing Jews in their place. They would have Our Lord with that prostitute as his wife. Who knows what else they may use to try and desecrate His teachings and our church? No, Jed, this must not happen; our flock would be outraged. Jed, I am placing this sacred trust in your hands.”

Jed Cassidy was one of the Reverend's right-hand man when it came to using more than spiritual persuasion. Jed ran his own highly organized militant White Supremacist group, well-armed, well placed, and well-financed. Money motivated Jed more than any scriptures, much more. He couldn't give a shit about Holy Scriptures, but Reverend Ducane paid very well, and he enjoyed the work.

"Who have we got over there?" questioned the Reverend.

"We have our contacts at the school, and through your people, we have infiltrated into Scottish Rite Masonic Lodge. We are well-positioned with people in the local Glasgow police constabulary, some at the highest levels." Jed offered. "We are working on it right now to retrieve it. Also, I have a team on the continent if we need them, but they cost more."

" Jed, I want you over there today. You are to take full control and do whatever you need to either destroy or garner this manuscript. I'll call my contacts in Scotland within the Scottish Rite. Whatever it takes, do it; money is no object !" ordered the Reverend. "We have some very powerful allies watching us, do not let us down."

"As I said, we are on to them right now. We know where they are and are about to pounce. We could have it in our possession at this very moment," Jed bragged. "I'm off to Scotland this very day."

That day Jed was on a late-night business class flight to Glasgow, Scotland. He had a fake Canadian passport, driver's license, hospital card, and credit cards. No one would ever suspect he was just one of many businessmen entering the UK.

Two days before Jed's meeting in Arkansas with the Reverend, one thousand miles to the northeast, Bob Findley was boarding a 10:00 AM flight at Washington DC, Dulles International Airport for Glasgow,

Scotland. He had been picked up at 5:30 AM that same morning and whisked to the National Knights Templar's Lodge in New Carrollton, Maryland. He'd been summoned to the home of the Grand Commander. The Grand Commander and Bob were old friends; both had served with distinction in the Marines, Bob, with the rank of Captain.

Bob was immediately taken into the Grand Commander's study. A second gentleman was seated there. "Bob, good to see you; I think you know David Silver, CIA."

"Yes, we are well acquainted both in the field and at Lodge in Texas," replied Bob. "Hello David," they exchanged a warm masonic handshake," great to see you again. I think I know why you are here. Wherever there is trouble," Bob looked at the Grand Commander, "he shows up."

David smiled back as he held Bob's hand, "Not much gets by you when it comes to the Knights Templar and their history. You already know about the fire in the Glasgow School of Art. The Glasgow Constabulary believes it was an accident, but they have their doubts. A propane cylinder exploded after overheating. Now it's rumoured something of value was revealed, and it's a mad race to see it gets into safe hands. We have been listening to quite a bit of chatter with our white supremacist friends. The director of the Glasgow School of Art was roughed up and ended up in hospital. Nothing serious, but his office and home were ransacked. The police are now suspicious. Whatever they were after was not found. This is too much of a coincidence, first the fire, then the break-in, and lastly, the date of the fire Friday, March 13. The date was what piqued my interest. "

"We have known for years, through the Scottish Masonic Rite, that the founder of the Glasgow School of Art, Charles Rennie MacKintosh, a devout Knights Templar's Mason had been entrusted with a highly controversial ancient document and one of the original Molay confession. Something to do with the original Knights Templars, going back to the thirteenth century. There are maybe half a dozen people within the US Rite that know of its existence and our copy of the confession. We were told that the Scottish copy would also lead to something far more important. I've been asked to intercede on two counts. First, to see that no harm comes to anyone, and If I can, I will try to retrieve the document. I will not be alone; there is an excellent team there to help. We feel it will have great consequences for our order and Christianity in general. So what's the CIA connection to this?" Bob asked.

"Militant White Supremacists. Our Reverend Andrew Ducane is in league with them and helps finance them. We intercepted some chatter that leads us to believe he may have had something to do with the arson at the Glasgow School of Art. Nothing we can pin on him. He is mixed up with some pretty dangerous characters. We don't know who his contact is, but we are sure he will use them to do his dirty work. If they go overseas, that is our business, and we think they are there already. Bit of bravado on their part in setting the fire on March 13. They have shown their hand."

"This is their first mistake, a little overconfident. Is MI5 aware of your investigations?" Bob queried.

" Yes, we have informed them and also advised them we are not interceding on British soil unless an American national is intercepted or eliminated. They are fine with this and will work with us. We have an excellent working relationship with the British Secret Service. Right now, this is of little importance to them, and they are leaving it up to the local police force. You are on your own at the moment, Bob. If we can do anything at this point, we will, but we will not admit to anything."

"Well, that is reassuring; how about at least a lift to the airport," Bob asked, " I've got to get my flight arranged."

"Already taken care of my friend," the Grand Commander cut in. "Here is your ticket, and the car is waiting for you outside. David volunteered to drive you to the airport. Be careful; we have our own homegrown dangerous fanatics."

"Thanks," Bob shook the hand of the Commander, "I'll keep in touch as soon as I learn anything."

David Silver drove Bob to the airport.

 Before they arrived, David advised Bob, "Once again, Bob, this is in strict confidence; we are not overly concerned with what has been found. We are more concerned with this white militant supremacist group. They are extremely fanatical and dangerous. We know they have been behind a lot of criminal actions in this country. We want to expose and destroy them. At this point, it looks as if our roads coincide. I, off the record, will offer you as much help as I can, but there is only so much I can do, and then you are on your own. Take care."

 David pulled up to the departure gate and let Bob off," Bon voyage, my friend, take care."

"Thanks, David, I will try not to be a burden, but you know me, I like to work alone, and I am pretty good at it. I will call and let you know my progress. You do have a reputation for showing up just when I need you," Bob waved his friend goodbye.

I called Pete to come over this afternoon. Not the best weather, a cold, wet March Sunday, typical of a Glaswegian, Scottish winter. Windy, damp, and cold that just penetrates the whole body. What they call a lazy wind, rather go through you than around. Peter arrived at about 5:00 pm.

"Hi Greg, I'm chilled to the bone in this awful weather," he called, as I greeted him at the front door and took his wet raincoat. "I'm soaked, and I only walked from the car."

I hung his drenched coat in the mudroom to dry, "I'll be right with you."

 "What's this great mystery," he asked, giving me a huge bear hug, his usual greeting. "Something smells good."

"Come in, come in, you'll see."I offered him a paper towel to clean off his glasses. "Just going into the kitchen. I've opened a bottle of wine it's on the table; pour both of us a glass, I have to check the roast."

"I thought you were going to do a beef stew?" Peter took a large swallow of wine.

"Yeh, changed my mind," the roast was perfect; the aroma drifted through the house. I turned off the oven and left the lamb covered on the sideboard to cool a little.

"I've got a fire going; let's sit in front of it and warm yourself up. Bring that wine with you." I made him sit comfortably in front of the fire. We cheered, and both took a generous sip of wine.

"Wonderful, that warmed me up a little bit," Peter smiled, "probably could do with a little more warming."

"The wine cellars full, don't worry," I laughed, "and supper is nearly ready. I decided against beef stew as I didn't have any beef. Forgot we had already used it up. Instead, I did a roast of lamb, roast potatoes, peas, and gravy. I thought we would have an early supper if you don't mind. We might be working late, I think, so I want you in a good mood first. Jennifer is still away up north in the highlands on her art break, so we have the place to ourselves. We'll eat in the dining room; supper is about ready now."

"I'm always in a good mood," Peter smiled back, "especially if there's good food and wine."

Peter sat himself down at the dining room table while I carved the lamb. "Look at this, just right, a little pink in the middle," as I sliced generous portions for the two of us.

We both tucked in, charging our glasses with additional wine.

"There is mint sauce if you want it," I offered.

"Mint is not my favourite. So are you going to enlighten me as to your mystery?" Peter queried as he helped himself to potatoes, vegetables, and a generous ladling of gravy.

"Well, I received a little something from our friend Richard over at the Glasgow School of Art. Let's finish supper and then retire back to the sitting room and sit in front of the fire. I'll show you what I have."

"Richard?" Peter queried, "I hear he is in one hell of a mess, poor bugger. One nasty fire, most of the library destroyed. I called him the other day at work but could not get a hold of him."

"Yes, that is what this is all about. I'll get to it once we have finished supper."

It was not long before we finished, tidied up, and then headed back to the sitting room. I opened the second bottle of wine and stoked the fire.

"Ok, I've been waiting long enough," Peter was getting impatient as he stretched out in front of the fire, "let's see what you have got."

"OK, just a minute, but first put these on." I handed him a pair of light white cotton gloves. "What I am about to give you is ancient." I then handed him the leather missal, the reason why I had called him over.

Peter put on the gloves, took the missal from me, and delicately examined the article.

 "So, what do you think, Peter?"

Peter, comfortable in front of the fire, took another warming sip of wine, gingerly examining what I had handed to him. "Well, it's quite small, almost looks like a prayer book; it's old, vellum pages, leather-bound, and handwritten in Latin. Probably five hundred years old. It smells smoky. Guess it is from what's left of the library."

"Try seven hundred years old, and yes, you got it right, it does smell smoky, and it is from what remains of the library. "

"Greg, I am intrigued, but there are probably thousands of these old books locked up in museums, libraries, and monasteries all over the world. You have seen enough of them. Just exactly where did you get this one, and what is so special about it?"

"You remember a couple of days ago, the fire at the Glasgow School of Art. The MacKintosh Library burned down; forensic archaeologists and workers have been trying to salvage what they could for days now. This little book was just recently found by accident by a workman under a cracked paving stone in the flooring."

"Are you sure? The Glasgow School of Art is a relatively contemporary library. This book should never have been there."

"I know, that is why Richard gave it to me. Richard does not read Latin and was just as perplexed as to why it should be found there. He doesn't know what to do with it or how to classify it, so he gave it to me to sort out."

"So, why are you showing it to me?"

"Peter, I am a Theologian; I read Latin and have read what you call the little prayer book. I have some historical background, but you have far more background in this than I do. I need your help. The script, the Latin, and some of the French are archaic and a little beyond me. Another thing this must be kept very confidential. Do you think you can help me?"

"Very confidential? It sounds very cloak and dagger. Not like you to be so mysterious, Greg. What do you want me to do, and what do you think you have got?"

"First of all, I know you are joking about the cloak and dagger, but there were indications the fire at the Art School may have been set. The sprinkler system may have been tampered so it wouldn't engage. There were also signs of a break-in, but no alarms went off. An explosion started the fire, a propane tank, I think. Richard told me this in confidence, so let's keep it quiet. "

"What, why would anyone want to do that!? What's to be gained? That is utter madness. Theft I can understand, there were a lot of valuable books there. Vandalism like this is unthinkable. "

"Nothing yet has been proven, but there are other signs. Thank God this was saved. Just remember, books and libraries were always one of the first things to be destroyed by people afraid of the truth. We have seen this in the past with the Nazis. The destruction by the early church of one of the greatest libraries the world has ever seen, Alexandria. Maybe this was behind it? Are you sure you are not exaggerating a little? We are not in Nazi Germany; this is twentieth-century Scotland, the United Kingdom. These things don't happen here, but now you have me intrigued. Let's have another look at this little book. Well, it is a monastic, handwritten in Latin, with some archaic French. It is leather bound with vellum pages. A small book from the Cathedral and Monastery of Sens. You say it is probably seven hundred years old. Where is Sens?"

"Burgundy, France," I answered Peter.

"It is according to the intro," Peter added," witnessed and sealed by the Archbishop of Sens, Phillipe de Marigny, and scripted by the Abbot Henri Champs in the year of our Lord 1307. To be strictly held in confidence by only the above mentioned, on pain of death. "

I knew already this was pretty heavy stuff, but I wondered if Peter had yet put two and two together. Peter Osiek had his Doctorate in Ancient and Medieval History from Oxford. Peter read French, Latin, Greek, Aramaic, Persian, and Egyptian hieroglyphics. He always amazed me at the daily connections he could make to the contemporary with its historical background. Simple things like patterns we take as contemporary, or sayings we feel are modern; all have some ancient connection. Peter, at the moment, was on a sabbatical doing a historical and financial study on the relationship of the Euro currency to the first Euro of King Canute minted around 1010 AD. Peter was also very down to earth; he wanted the bare facts. Gods, myths, and fairies were not in his making. Peter was an atheist. Peter was also my oldest and most trusted friend. Both our fathers had been friends during the Second World War serving in the RAF.

"Philip de Marigny, Archbishop of Sens cathedral; why does that name ring a bell? Ah, he supported the Avignon Pope Clement V at the time of King Philip IV of France. There was a schism between the Pope in Avignon, France, and the Cardinals in Rome got a little nasty, and I could do with another glass of wine."

"Yes, Peter, go on. What other world-shattering event happened between the two of them?" I recharged both our glasses with wine. Peter took a deep sip and thought, staring at the little book.

"The Knights Templar were destroyed by King Philip and Pope Clement." Peter remembered, "Jacque de Molay was arrested on Friday 13 and later burned at the stake, accused of being a heretic. If I remember correctly, Archbishop Phillipe de Marigny tried to intervene with the help of Pope Clement, to give a fair investigation and trial. King Philip forced Pope Clement to decline the offer, or he would lose his support if he did not leave the investigation to him. There was a schism between Rome and Avignon for the Vatican crown. King Philip supported Pope Clement in Avignon and if he succeeded in gaining the throne of St. Peter, Philip would gain a lot of kingdoms in Italy. Turned out to be a kangaroo court, condemning Jacque de Molay. I believe Jacque de Molay confessed to some trumped-up evidence and was sentenced to life imprisonment. Later he recanted, but as a recanting apostate, the penalty was execution by burning at the stake. Am I on the right track so far?"

"You are bang on Peter; also, the full date of Jacque de Molay's arrest was Friday, March 13. The same date as the fire at The Glasgow School of Art. Now, what if I told you this ancient tome is the last confession of Jacque de Molay, as heard and written by Abbot Henri Champs. It was his last request that it should be written down and given to his friend, the Archbishop Phillipe de Marigny, to be kept in safekeeping. This is his confession knowing he was going to be burnt at the stake, after recanting."

"Do you think that this is what someone was trying to destroy? The date of his arrest and the fire is too much of a coincidence. Are we safe having this in our possession? Who could possibly find this dangerous and want to destroy it?" Peter asked. "It is just an ancient confession."

"First things first, I have read it. I have gone over it, but a lot of it is archaic and a bit beyond me. Are you alright to stay the night? I think this is going to take some time. I still have some more wine, a couple of good bottles of red, a French Rhone. If we are still hungry, there is still plenty of roast lamb for some sandwiches, and I'll stoke up the fire. The spare bedroom is ready if we go too late. Have you got anything on tomorrow that is important, or more important than this?"

"Not really," Peter answered, "let me call Pat and let her know I am staying over. What about Jennifer?"

"Jennifer, as I told you, is away, north of Loch Lomond in the highland wilds, on a winter painting session for a few days. We are both on a month's vacation, but instead of heading to warmer climes, I decided to catch up on some things at home. She wanted to do some painting and won't be back until next Saturday."

"Ok, let's do it," Peter offered, "I'll stay the night. You have me intrigued."

Peter called Pat to let her know he was staying over.

"Pat's fine with this. I think sometimes she likes to have me out of her hair," Peter laughing reported. "So, let's begin."

We settled down in front of the fire, and with a glass of wine, Peter started to translate.

It started; I, Phillipe de Marigny, Archbishop of Sens in the year of our Lord 1314, have ordered the written last confession of my fellow brethren Jacque de Molay, Grand Master of the Poor Knights of the Temple. This last confession was requested by Jacque de Molay to be written and saved by his Confessor Abbot Henri Champs the day before he is to be executed as a heretic on the orders of King Philip IV of France. The only other copy resides with Pope Clement in Avignon and one additional copy held by what remains of the Poor Knights of the Temple. We are all sworn to secrecy, and if this fell into the wrong hands, our lives surely would be forfeit. Even the Crown does not know of this confession and our lives would be in mortal danger if found out.

I start now my confession in the presence of Abbot Henri Champs. I have asked him to script truthfully my last confession, Jacque de Molay, Grand Master of the Poor Knights of the Temple.

I, Jacque de Molay, Grand Master of the Poor Knights of the Temple on the date of March 17, in the year of our Lord 1314 do ask Henri Champs, Abbot of Sens, to record my last confession. I know I am to be executed tomorrow. There must be a record left for my Order and the honour of the men that served faithfully under my command. May God have mercy on my soul and protect what is left of the brethern Knights now in hiding. I am a broken man in body, but not in soul. I have confessed to much under unspeakable torture by order of King Philip IV. I have confessed to devil and idol worship. I have confessed to having renounced the Church of Rome and our Savior Jesus Christ. I have confessed that my knights and I submitted to licentious acts. All this, I retract under pain of eternal damnation. We have never abandoned our service to Rome and love of our Lord and Savior Jesus Christ and his beloved wife and most cherished disciple Mary The Magdalene Canaanite priestess. It was she who brought the Gentiles into the light of Jesus with his blessings.

Under our tenure of nearly two hundred years in Jerusalem and the Holy Lands, we have learned much of our Savior that is omitted by our Church. This, we kept quiet only divulging these secrets to the highest office in Rome. In turn, the Vatican gave us the sacred trust to keep these secrets unto ourselves.

We first learned of this with the discovery of the ossuary of John the Baptist, cousin to Jesus. He was the first of the Essene prophets, as it states in the Bible. John the Baptist was the forerunner of the Essene Messiah, Jesus Christ, his disciple and, what our Church describes as the beginning of Christianity. This was not the beginning of Christianity, but the Essene movement through John the Baptist and Jesus Christ, to bring the Judean religion back to its' original roots through God's first anointed King, the Pharaoh of Egypt, Amenhotep, and his Prophet Abraham. This history follows through to the last of God's anointed Pharaoh Akhenaten and his holy temple housing the Ark of the Covenant. Through his bloodline, Moses, Prince of Egypt, his high priests, and the Judean ancestors of Abraham and Jacob fled the wrath of the priests of the revived old religion after the death of Akhenaten. Thus started the Exodus with only the priestly Essene holding to the original precepts of the Arc of the Covenant.

We held to the Essene holy law of lavations and emersion to render us clean in the sight of God. We kept the blessing of bread and wine as did Jesus, as thanks to God. We hold to the secrets to rebuild the Temple of Solomon, to the law of the Pharaoh Akhenaten and his prince Moses, this we hold most sacred. We are the spiritual free masons committed to rebuilding of this temple from the time of the pyramids to Solomon, as was the Essene Messiah Jesus Christ.

The Gentile , Mary The Magdalene , the priestess of the Goddess Artemis converted to the God-fearers of Judea before her marriage to Jesus. It was Mary The Magdalene that brought the Gentile God-fearers into the light of Jesus , our Messiah. It was through Mary The Magdalene and James , Jesus ' brother that the church continued after the crucifixion of Jesus Christ bringing in both Judean and Gentile God-fearers . It was our beloved Mary the Magdalene that brought Judean and Gentile together, starting the early Christian religion. We have also kept secret from the church , our evidence proving that it was Imperial Rome that condemned and crucified Jesus and not the Sanhedrin.. This we kept to protect the Pope and Rome.

"So he still tried to protect the Pope and his church, after all this," I butted in. I could imagine the aged Grand Master crippled with torture as he stoically recited this confession. "You know, Peter, that they tied his feet to a brazier and roasted his feet until he confessed.

"It would seem so," Peter added as he continued his translation, "no one could withstand that torture."

We hold many of these secrets, but the most telling is the written trial of Yeshua ben Yosef, the Judean name of Jesus Christ. This was written by the scribe of the high priest, Annas, and translated to Latin at the request of the court of Pontius Pilate. We also keep in secret the additional written trial of Jesus before the court of Pontius Pilate. These scroll s we have held in secret for over a hundred years. These secrets, and our great wealth , have already been spirited away for safekeeping until the time we are expunged of these dreadful accusation s. King Philip IV will not steal these secrets to pressure the Pope to his misadventures and empire building. Neither will we give these up to the Pope until the church expunges the lies perpetrated on us.

I go now to my death and my maker in the knowledge that I have been true to our Lord and Savior, Jesus Christ, and his beloved wife Mary the Magdalene. I have been true and faithful to our Church in Rome. I call upon all the prophets and God to bring down retribution on King Philip and all those who bore false witness against us and for the injustice and cruelty they have perpetrated.

Jacque de Molay, Grand Master of the Poor Knights of the Temple.

"My god, Greg, this is quite the confession," whispered Peter, "and you say this was found at the Glasgow School of Art. It doesn't make sense. Why would this be held there in secret? Who would have put it there? It comes right out declaring Mary Magdalene as Jesus' wife and cofounder of the Christian religion. It also states the Templers' kept secrets that could undermine the Catholic Church. No wonder it was so powerful. We could be rewriting history and the very Christian religion. Does this not allude to Moses being a true prince of Egypt and not an adopted Hebrew. Also, it does state that it was not the Pharaoh Ramesses that they fled from, but the predecessor of the Pharaoh Akhenaten, that would probably be the Pharaoh Smenkhkare. After the death of Akhenaten, all his historical existence and religious beliefs were expunged from Egypt. If this dynasty was the beginning of monotheism, and after his death, the old religion came back, one can see the need to flee the wrath of the new regime. There has never been a historical connection of Ramesses to the Exodus, as stated in the bible. The Exodus now seems to be at a much earlier date. I believe I read a new premise that states this in the 'Copper Scrolls of Qumran.' Now here is something new; who were the God-Fearers, Greg?"

"The God-fearers were an early religious movement that started not too long before the birth of Christianity. They were monotheists, pseudo-Judean Gentiles that followed some of the Judean traditions but not circumcision or the dietary laws. As for Mary Magdalene, it has long been held," I answered, "in the Gospel of Timothy and the Gnostic

Gospels that Mary Magdalene was his wife. It is also well documented that she was held by Jesus as his most important and intelligent disciple. It is no wonder she brought in large numbers of her followers into Jesus' flock. The recent finding of the Chronicle "Joseph and Aseneth" details in coded Gnostic script of their meeting, marriage, and her conversion from the Canaanite worship of the Goddess Artemis to the Judean God-fearers. Just remember, most of these Gospels were destroyed by the early church and also anyone who held to these beliefs. Over a million Cathars were murdered as heretics for holding the belief that Mary Magdalene was Jesus' wife. The church did its best to eradicate her importance, denigrating her to a reformed prostitute. Sad to think that Jesus' most beloved wife and principal disciple was debased in such a fashion."

"But, why?" queried Peter, "what harm would it have done?"

"Don't forget that the recognized church teachings at the Nicene council were the Pauline version. The Nicene gospels were also the recognized version of the Church of Rome. Paul only preached salvation through the death, suffering, and resurrection of Jesus. There was no duality of man and woman as preached through the eastern church of the Gnostics. In the Vatican's defense, they have recently put forward that there is no evidence the Mary Magdalene was a reformed prostitute but, neither have they recognized that she was the wife of Jesus or his most important disciple."

"The confession also alludes to further secrets of Jesus' trial. It also states that King Philip IV wanted to use these secrets to blackmail the Pope to bend to his purposes. What secrets could the trial of Jesus hold?" Peter asked.

"If these secrets told of other truths that the church at this time did not adhere to or was trying to hide," I added, "it could have terrible consequences to the church. Again remember the Cathars and the bloodshed it produced. Just remember knowledge is the guardian of truth, subdue the knowledge, and you can control what is perceived as the truth."

"If I remember correctly, did not the Vatican, under Pope Clement finally pardon the Knights Templar?" Peter asked.

"Good memory Peter. Yes, Pope Clement did eventually pardon them, but it did not save Jacque de Molay, he was burned at the stake. The pardon, which I believe was called the 'Chinon Parchment' came much later after the Knights had disappeared along with their fortune and secrets. Most historians believe this was a ploy to try and get the Knights to go back to the church with all their wealth and knowledge. The 'Chinon Parchment' still exists to this day, but it did not work."

"Was there anything else accompanying this?" Peter asked." Did Richard intimate there was anything else?"

"Not that I know, this was all he gave me. The book was found in a metal box; there could have been more pieces. I think we should visit him tomorrow and find out if you're up to it."

"This could be the find of the century," Peter added, "if it turns out to be authentic. Of course, I am coming with you. Richard has no idea what was uncovered?"

"No, that is why he gave it to me," I answered, "who would have thought?"

We sat sipping our wine deep in thought, entranced with the translation. The fire was starting to burn down. It was well past ten o'clock. We sat quietly for a while, finishing our wine. As Peter decided to stay over, we both went off to bed with more questions than answers swimming around in our heads.

The phone shattered my sleep early the next morning. I fumbled to answer it, "Hello, what, where? Ok, I'll be there."

I scrambled out of bed and ran to Peter's bedroom.

"Peter, wake up!" I called urgently.

"Jesus, what's the matter!"

It was already after eight o'clock Monday morning. The sun barely up and hidden by another damp, cloudy February day. I had not slept well after all the thoughts swimming around in my head from the previous evening. The phone call came from Richard's office at the Glasgow School of Art. That morning his secretary told me that Richard had been attacked and was now in the Royal Infirmary Hospital in Glasgow. He was not in serious condition but was ruffed up enough to put him in hospital.

"Richard is in hospital, his secretary Marge just called me. He was attacked. I'm heading down there right away."

"Wait," Peter called, "I don't believe this; let me get dressed. I'm coming with you."

"Peter, I'm not taking the manuscript with us. I feel I have to hide it somewhere safe." I looked around quickly and then saw my answer. We had a large front window; Jennifer had made all the curtains and framed the top with a balloon valance, which she stuffed with crepe to give it some body. I quickly stuffed the manuscript in the valance.

"Do you think that is necessary, and will it be safe there?" Peter asked.

"I don't know Peter, but I have a sneaking suspicion that our confession is behind all this attack on Richard. This little confession could be worth a small fortune, especially if someone wants to keep it quiet."

I called for a taxi, and just before 10:00 am we were heading into the Royal Infirmary and up to Richard's room. As we were about to come up, we were challenged by a uniformed policeman who would not let us enter until Richard had identified us.

Richard was sitting up in bed propped up by pillows, head bandaged, looking a little pale, but still pleased to see us, "hello lads."

"Richard, I'm so sorry, are you alright?" I asked.

A quick smile and a nod confirmed he was in no immediate danger. "Hello Peter, haven't seen you in a while and not the best circumstances now."

"I know, what a time to meet again," Peter answered, "are they looking after you?"

"They're lovely, couldn't be in better hands considering."

We sat down beside him. Richard had met Peter many times at parties at my place. "Now tell me everything. What happened?" I asked.

Richard explained, due to the fire, he had been putting in a lot of extra hours trying to sort things out, looking after restoration and repairs. I arrived at my office early around 6:00 am this morning, walked through my door, and was immediately hit on the head from behind. That was the last thing I could remember until I came to, with a terrible headache. I had managed to pull myself up on my chair and dialed 999 before I collapsed again. At that hour there was no one else in the building. When I came to, the paramedics had me on a stretcher asking me if I knew my name. It was only then I realized my office was completely ransacked. Now, my office is a crime scene, locked and taped off. The police have questioned me right here at the hospital but had nothing much to add. I was not in any condition to be that lucid.

"Richard," I interrupted, "Peter and I have a feeling we may know what this is about, but we must at this point keep this very hush, hush. Let me explain. First of all, was there anything accompanying the manuscript you gave me?"

"Yes," Richard replied, "It came in a small metal box the type you find in building cornerstones, left there for posterity. In fact, that is what the workman thought it was. The manuscript was in an untitled, tied, heavy manila envelope. There was also another handwritten sheet. I cannot remember what it said, and there was a silver ring bearing a skull. That was all."

"Do you still have it, Richard?" I asked.

"Yes, I think I left the metal box in the boot of my car when I headed home yesterday. I didn't think there was much value to it, and I had so much else going on I had forgotten about it. My car is still in the parking lot at the art school."

"That may have been the safest place at this point." I replied, "Whoever did this may have already broken into your home. Where are your car keys?"

"Shit, you don't think so?" Richard anxiously replied, "The keys are right here in the draw."

I retrieved the keys. Richard gave us the license plate and a description of his car. "Peter, we have to go and get the box. Sorry to leave you so soon, but we will come straight back. In the meantime, I will ask the police officer to come in and radio to have your house checked out and put your car under surveillance at the art school. Let them know you have permitted us to enter your car."

"Greg, do you really think this is necessary?" Richard asked.

"I don't know, we'll see, but better safe than sorry. Somebody wants something very badly. And I think we have what they want. Keep this confidential, tell no one until we come back later."

We left Richard with the policeman, Officer McKenna, and headed off, grabbing the first taxi that came our way. It was already twelve-thirty in the afternoon.

We watched through the rain as the city flew by. I turned to Peter. "A letter and a silver skull ring. So far, I am lost until we retrieve it."

"I think I know part of it," replied Peter. "The silver skull ring was a common insignia of the Knights Templar and Masonic organization."

"That does make sense Peter since it was a Templar confession."

The taxi pulled up to the Glasgow School of Art. We sited the car immediately. There was a police car parked and blocking off the entrance to the parking lot. We explained to the officer who we were and that we had Officer McKenna radio ahead for our clearance. We could see that security around the school was tight as they escorted us to the car. I checked the boot; the box was there. We took Richard's car and raced back to the Royal Infirmary, box in hand. We found Richard still in bed, but this time, with a plain-clothed officer with him. He turned to greet us.

"This is Chief Inspector Matthew Adam," advised Richard. "He has just informed me that my house was broken into."

"Oh no, Richard, this does not seem to get any better," I sympathized. "Did they take anything?"

"I am not sure," Richard sighed, "just ransacked the place, the police advised me."

The Inspector wanted to know our names and our relationship with Richard. Richard advised we were colleagues and friends. He still took down our names and where we could be contacted. At that point, the doctor came in and informed Richard could go home if he wanted. The x-rays showed he had a slight concussion but nothing more. Richard would probably have a bit of a headache for a couple of days, which a few aspirins would help. Docter advised Richard to stay at home for at least a week, no driving and also encouraged to make an appointment with his doctor. Since we had Richards's car, we volunteered to drive him home, which he gladly accepted.

"I may need to see you both at a later date," the inspector announced, "so don't plan to leave the city unless you give me a call first."

We both announced we would be at his disposal whenever he needed us. We waited for Richard to dress and collect his belongings, and with that, we took Richard and headed to his home.

Richard lived south of Glasgow, the house bordering on an area known as Pollock Country Park. The suburb was a little isolated, pretty, and very much upmarket. The police were there to greet us. The house had been ransacked, probably not long after Richard had left for his office. The police were about to leave. They asked Richard to make a list of all that was missing if anything.

Richard was a confirmed bachelor, living on his own for the last twenty years. He was neat and had a good sense of traditional decor. The place was a mess. Richard did have a couple of regular girlfriends that we had met, nothing serious, none that could or would do this kind of damage if crossed.

"Richard, shall I put the kettle on for a pot of tea?" I asked.

"Bloody hell, no! Look in the cabinet; there are a few good bottles of Scotch. I need a good stiff drink, and I hope you will join me and explain what the hell you believe is going on, but, first I have to call Marge my secretary, and let her know what's going on."

Peter poured us all a stiff drink while we surveyed the damage. Not much was broken, except the forced front door. Everything else was in an unholy mess. Drawers dumped out; books were strewn everywhere, cabinets open, pillows tossed, furniture moved and tipped; someone had been thorough.

We made room where we could and sat down. Richard came back from the phone and took a good belt of Scotch and slowly looked around, shaking his head.

"Oh, I needed that," Richard announced as he took another good swig.

"Everything alright at the School?" I asked Richard.

"Yeh, Marge told me the police are still there. I told her to carry on, that I would be convalescing for a few days."

"Richard, we believe this all has to do with the Latin manuscript you gave me." Between Peter and I, we related the confession of Jacque de Molay.

"I cannot believe it," Richard was dumbfounded, "and what was it doing in my school?"

Peter was now going through the contents of the box which we retrieved from Richards's car, "One string-bound heavy manila envelope and the silver skull ring. The ring is definitely a Knights Templar Masonic ring, but it is not old, probably turn of the century, by the silver marks." Peter started to untie the manila envelope and pulled out a handwritten letter. It read:

McLellan Galleries

Sauchehall Street,

Glasgow

August 5, 1871

Dear Brethren Iain McLellan,

As you are aware, the Brethren have already taken the manuscript from Mother Kilwinning and placed the trial manuscript safely with the Queen's Cross. It is imperative the enclosed confession must be kept together. Our most sacred secrets must be held on the pain of death. As you found it, so shall it be the most sacred place.

Your Brethren,

Charles Rennie MacKintosh

August 5, 1872

" So," Peter stated, " at the time of this letter, August 5, 1871, or 1872, the trial manuscript of Jesus Christ still existed and placed somewhere with the Queen's Cross. Queen's Cross, what could that mean, and who is Mother Kilwinning? There are crosses throughout England honouring Queen Eleanor of Aquitaine, wife of King Henry IV, but that is too early for this historical content. King Philip IV was married to Joan of Navarre, but I cannot see a connection there, especially when Philip was the one to destroy the Templars. Our Queen Elizabeth, not likely. I think Queen Victoria would also be a dead end but, who knows, she would be contemporary to our letter."

"And this doesn't make sense," I pointed out, "I wonder why the two different dates on the letter? Bit of a dead end. The only clue I do understand is Mother Kilwinning. Mother Kilwinning, if I am correct, is one of the oldest Masonic Lodges in Scotland. So something was taken from there and placed at Queen's Cross."

"Speaking of dead ends," Richard piped up, "are we safe digging around in this mystery? Let me correct that, as to what has happened to me, I do not think we are. Should we not just leave this up to the police?"

Peter jumped in immediately, "I don't know what the police could do. Confessions of the Knights Templar's, Jesus' trial, this is a bit beyond them. Would they know where to look for the trial of Jesus? The three of us right now have more insight into the mystery than the police. Let us see if we can find the trial of Jesus first. Once we have it, then we could hand it over to the police. Another thought, what do we think the value of Moray's confession could be? Richard, you would probably have the best idea of all of us."

"I didn't even think about that, but if it turns out to be genuine," Richard cautioned, "it could be priceless. You could easily be looking at a starting price of at least £ 500,000.00, and that depends on who wants it badly enough. We could be looking at the Vatican, the Masons, French Government, a myriad of museums, or libraries. Right now, it is still the property of the Glasgow School of Art, but I don't think it is safe there."

"Look, right now, until the police come up with something," I cautioned, "the only solid piece of evidence we have is the confession of Jacque de Molay. The confession I have hidden in my house. I think we should retrieve it and put it somewhere safe. I'll take it to my solicitor. I think we should leave it there in their safe. In the meantime, Richard, could you look into this letter and see if there is any connection between the McLellan Galleries, Charles Rennie MacKintosh, Mother Kilwinning, and the Queen's Cross. Are we agreed to this?"

The consensus, reluctantly, at the moment, was to agree to my suggestion. I also asked Richard if, once again, I may borrow his car. Richard agreed as the doctor didn't want him driving. He was not going anywhere with the headache he had and the mess he had to clean up. We agreed to meet back at Richard's later that evening.

Peter and I headed back to my place. "What's on your mind, Peter? I know that look when you get quiet."

Peter glanced over, "Well, I think someone wants what we have and is pretty desperate to get it or destroy it. That's probably why they set the museum on fire. So far, we have had a lot of property damage and one assault. I do not think that whoever hit Richard wanted him dead, but how far will they go? I think we had better go back to Chief Inspector Matthew Adam and at least advise him of what we have."

"Maybe you're right, but I have an idea. First, we retrieve the confession and leave it with my solicitor as we agreed. We then instruct the solicitor that if anything happens to any one of us, he is to call Chief Inspector Matthew Adam and give him the confession of Jacque De Molay. We will also make two copies of the confession at the solicitors and give one to the chief inspector when we meet back at Richards'. What do you think, Peter?"

"Yes, for the moment, you seem to have all the bases covered. When we get back to your place, let's not park in front of your house, just in case we are being watched. Park a couple of blocks away, and we will walk in and enter through the back laneway to your back door."

We arrived in my neighbourhood just after 3:00 pm; parked the car some distance away and walked in through the back lane. I have never felt the need to be continually looking over my shoulder as we approached the house, but now, I know I was doing this a lot. It didn't seem that anyone was following us, not that I could see. All appeared quiet as we entered the back door. Nothing inside had been touched all looked as it should, and I breathed a huge sigh of relief. I retrieved the manuscript from the curtain valance and put it in my briefcase.

"Ok, let's go, Peter. I want to get this thing put away safely as quickly as possible."

"Just a minute, Greg. Come here, don't move the curtains and have a look outside. Can you see anything untoward that looks out of place?"

 I secretively peered out and scanned the street up and down. All looked normal as far as I could see.

"I can't see anything, Peter. All looks normal."

Peter pulled me back, "That's what I thought, except, look to your left on the other side of the road. What do you see? Careful, don't move the curtains."

"There is only a green Land Rover and a blue Ford, so what? What do you see?"

"Look at the Land Rover again", Peter prompted.

"Green Land Rover, probably this year's model with two men sitting inside; oh, with two men sitting inside. I see what you mean. Could be nothing, but then again, it also might be the police."

"Could be the police," Peter mused, "and that might be the least of our problems. What if it is the same people that came after Richard?"

A cold chill crept right up my spine, "let's get out of here, Peter."

Peter didn't want to take a chance. He suggested that we could find that out later with our meeting with Chief Inspector Matthew Adam if they were staking out my place. In the meantime, we quickly made our way to our car as fast as we could. We left by the back door and into the back alley. A few houses down, we turned onto the main road and into our car. There didn't seem to be anyone following us, but we could still see the green Land Rover.

We drove to my solicitor. We asked to use their copying machine and made two copies of the manuscript and letter and left the original with my solicitor. He immediately put it in a sealed legal envelope, had me sign a receipt, and deposited it in the company's safe. I then advised him that Chief Inspector Matthew Adam or his second in command, to have access to the manuscript if anything happened to me. I informed my solicitor that we would also advise the Chief Inspector of this arrangement. My solicitor made notes of our agreement, which he would file and only retrieve if necessary. My solicitor looked worried and asked if we were in trouble. I just advised him we were handling some ancient documents from the fire at the Glasgow School of Art. The insurance company asked us to keep it safe with my solicitor and inform the police of its whereabouts. Not quite the truth, but he seemed satisfied with my explanation.

We drove the same route back to Richard's, constantly looking behind us to see if we were followed. There was no incidence, no green Land Rover following us. We pulled into Richard's driveway, much relieved.

The house had been straightened and tidied. Richard stated he could see nothing that had been stolen. In itself self, this seemed very odd. He stated this in the stolen items report and handed it to the on-duty constable, for Inspector Matthew Adam. Richard had a housekeeper, and he had called her over to help clean up. She had also made sandwiches and coffee for all of us before she left. I had forgotten that I had not eaten all day. I was famished; it was already 5:00 pm. Peter and I blessed his housekeeper and dove into her much appreciated spread.

"What did you tell her," I asked, mouth full of a ham sandwich.

"Nothing, really; that it was probably kids that broke in and most likely high on something," Richard responded. "I think she believed me as she knew of several incidences in her neighbourhood all involving young kids."

"Look, Peter, and I feel we should call Chief Inspector Adams over and tell him what we think is going on and what we have. What do you think?"

Richard was in full agreement and went ahead and called, only to find the inspector was not in. Richard asked that he call him as soon as he got his message.

"How's the head?" Peter inquired of Richard.

"The painkillers helped, the Scotch dulled the anxiety, and I have had a bite to eat, but I feel worn out. I'm going to have an early night and get a good night's sleep. Oh, by the way, I did a little bit of research on the McLellan Galleries and Charles Rennie McKintosh. It turns out......"

Just then, the phone rang. Richard lunged and grabbed it.

"Chief Inspector Matthew Adam, you wanted to talk to me?"

Richard put on the speakerphone, "Yes, inspector. Greg, Peter, and I are here and would very much like you to come around to my house. We have a lot to discuss as to what we think is going on; do not want to talk on the phone just in case. When do you think you could come over?"

"It is after 6:00 pm now. I could be over in about two hours. By the way, I have your stolen items report, and you say nothing is missing, rather odd, isn't it? Look, I know I said I could be over in about two hours, but something has come up. Can this keep 'till tomorrow morning? I could be there at about 9:00 am.

We all nodded quickly, and Richard agreed, "That would be okay."

 It was already dark outside, and I suggested that maybe tonight, we should all stick together until we had talked to the inspector tomorrow morning. Richard's house had four bedrooms, so there was plenty of space. We all agreed. I went off to make some more sandwiches while Peter poured us all a stiff drink of Scotch. Peter called Pat to let her know he was staying a second night.

"Didn't tell Pat what had happened to Richard. I didn't want her to worry," Peter confessed. "Told her we were helping Richard with the mess at the School, not quite the truth, but she would only worry."

"Probably the wisest thing to do at this point," I agreed with Peter.

When I came back with the sandwiches, Peter asked Richard what he had found out regarding the McLellan Galleries, Charles Rennie MacKintosh, and Mother Kilwinning.

Richard replied, "Did a little bit of research on the internet plus some of my knowledge. The McLennan Galleries was taken over by The Glasgow Government School of Art around 1845. After that, it moved to Renfrew Street in Glasgow, renaming itself the Glasgow School of Art, my place of work. This happed around 1869, also at this time, the building had additions added. The architect for this expansion was none other than Charles Rennie MacKintosh. The building was considered one of his masterpieces. It was his library, in this building that the fire broke out in. I already knew this, so nothing new here."

"What about the Queens' Cross?" Peter broke in, "anything on that?"

"As a matter of fact, yes." Richard beamed. "The Queen's Cross refers to the Queen's Cross Church right here in Maryhill, Glasgow. It didn't dawn on me that the letter was referring to the church, built around 1896. It is the only church Charles Rennie MacKintosh built, and it was considered to be his most mysterious project. Due to the connection with MacKintosh and the Glasgow School of Art, we take our students there quite regularly. I know the vicar, a Reverend William Bowen. A very engaging and pleasant man. As for Mother Kilwinning, it and the Aberdeen lodge are the oldest Masonic lodges in Scotland, probably dating back to the late fourteenth century. These are the lodges that probably had the closest ties to the Scottish Knights Templers and the Sinclair Lords. There is documentation that the Templars hid in Scotland with the help of the Sinclairs after their banning. With their help, there is evidence that Robert the Bruce defeated the English at Bannockburn. The Knights then blended into the Masonic movement with all their secrets. One of which has been uncovered and is now in our possession. I piped in immediately, "The letter states that the trial manuscript has maybe in that church, but where in the church? That has to be our next visit, and I think tomorrow."

We all agreed, and with that, we decided to call it a day and make our way to our assigned bedrooms.

I was up early the next morning and scrounged through Richard's fridge, finding eggs, bacon, some black pudding, and a loaf of bread. I had breakfast well on the way, with a pot of coffee brewing when Peter and Richard came down.

"Nothing like the smell of frying bacon and fresh coffee to wake one up," Richard announced. "Thanks to a good night's sleep, I am feeling a lot better, and the head is only a little tender with a little bump."

We had all slept well, and nothing untoward had happened through the night. A quick check of the road found no green Land Rover. We had also decided not to mention Queen's Cross Church to the police until we had something a little more definite. We ate heartily and had just finished when the Chief Inspector called promptly at 9:00 am.

"Good morning inspector," Richard had greeted him at the door, "Come in, Inspector, coffee? Just made."

"That would be lovely, "Chief Inspector Adams entered, followed by a second gentleman. "I would like to introduce Inspector Stephen Bliss. Stephen is with our antiquities and fine arts fraud department. I thought it was time you met him. He has been working on the library fire."

Inspector Bliss was a man in his early forties or late thirties, tall, fair, and looked fit. He shook hands with everybody with a firm and surprisingly strong grip.

We offered coffee to both visitors.

 "Yes, please, cream and one sugar," Adam answered, but Bliss declined with a shake of his head.

As soon as we got the Inspectors seated, I asked, "Did you have anyone following us yesterday in a green Land Rover?"

"No, none of our people, why do you ask." The inspector answered.

"Probably nothing, maybe a bit of overreaction after all that has happened. Anything new with the fire at the library?"

"Not until we get a full report from forensics and Steve. There was no weapon as to what hit Richard. By the way, how are you feeling, Richard?"

"A lot better today. I have a nice bump on my head. I have made an appointment to see my physician."

"I'm glad you are feeling better. Now, gentlemen, enough of the pleasantries, why did you call me?"

We laid our cards on the table, omitting nothing except Charles Rennie MacKintosh's letter and the reference to the Queen's Cross Church. We gave the inspector a copy of the confession, which he handed over to Inspector Bliss. We advised them the original was safe with my solicitor, locked away in their safe, and would only be released to the police if anything untoward was to happen to me.

"What do you think this confession is worth in today's market?" inquired the inspector. "If it is valuable, you may have found our motive."

We didn't want to let too much out, so Richard pretended to look dumbfounded, and we played along. As academics Richard stated, this was a purely historical and theological find. We had an idea of what the monetary value could be. As a national treasure, it could be worth millions. Could it be that this is what it was all about? And what about the indication that there was a further manuscript relating to the trial of Jesus Christ? Our find could even be far more valuable.

"Inspector, we had never thought about the value of the manuscript. It could be worth millions," Richard offered.

Inspector Bliss, at this point, looked up from the manuscript. "This is amazing. I have not seen anything like this, and its implications could be very far-reaching. This is a very dangerous and precious document, and you are correct, in the right hands, it could be worth millions.

"Can you read it?" I inquired of Inspector Bliss.

"Oh, yes, I can read Latin, Greek, Hebrew, French, and a little Arabic."

My estimation of this man skyrocketed. Inspector Bliss was not a man to deal with lightly.

Chief Inspector Adam replied, "I'm wondering if leaving it with your solicitor was the wisest thing to do. Should it not be back at the library?"

Richard answered, "After what has happened to the library and my person, I do not think we are ready for that undertaking. I don't think it is safe there."

"Look," replied Inspector Adam, "I'll pay a visit to your solicitor just to let him know the manuscript is under investigation. For the time being, the manuscript will be left with your solicitor until I deem it needs to be moved. With that gentlemen, I will be on my way, unless there is anything else. I cannot say you are out of danger. Let me know if anything happens that you feel is not quite right. I don't want any more bumps on the head."

"Will you leave a police presence here?" Richard asked.

"I don't think it is necessary now. They found nothing in your office or your home. If you are being watched, they probably think the police have the manuscript now. I think the pressure is off you."

With that, Richard saw the inspectors to the front door and thanked them for calling. It had just turned 10:00 am.

As Richard returned, we all knew the next step. Richard picked up the phone and called his friend Rev. William Bowan at Queen's Cross Church. "Hello William, it's Richard, I know it is short notice, and I do apologize. I have a couple of friends with me who would love to see your church. Would it be alright to pop around this morning? Yes, good, we will see you in about an hour."

Richard hung up the phone," Well, we are on gentlemen; we are getting into this deeper and deeper. Now is the time to either back off or full steam ahead."

"I think we are all in this together."Peter mused. "In for a penny, in for a pound, or maybe millions of pounds?"

 Peter drove us all in Richard's car. We arrived at Queen's Cross Church on Garscube Road around 11:30 am. The only church that Charles Rennie MacKintosh built, and to say that the church was one of his most mysterious buildings was quite an understatement. It looked foreboding, dark red stone, more like a medieval fortress castle than a church. What gave it the appearance of a castle was the watchtower where there should have been a steeple, a most ominous building.

"Listen, Richard," I suggested, "if we find anything, we must keep it quiet. You will have to use your art school connection if we have to remove anything. I want to keep this as small as possible; just among ourselves until the time warrants going public or handing it over to the police."

"Ok," Richard answered, "Greg, I agree, are we all of like mind?"

Peter nodded in support as we entered the church, "that's if we find anything. I hope we are not a little too optimistic. If we do find something, I'm with you, let's keep this as small as possible. We don't want the Reverend getting a nasty visit like our friend Richard."

"I never thought of that Peter," I remarked, "but the more we keep this amongst ourselves, the less risk we are putting on anyone else."

 We met Reverend William Bowen, Richard's friend, inside the church, a pleasant, engaging man who extended a warm greeting to all of us.

"Well, Richard, you have come to see my church again. I don't know what all the fuss is about; I find it quite a plain Jane as churches go. It's not that it's Westminster Abbey. You must get bored seeing it over and over again. "

"You're right. I should be doing all your tours," Richard answered.

Richard introduced all of us and explained we were interested in the history of the church and its' architect Charles Rennie MacKintosh. Would he mind us taking a tour?

The Reverend explained, "I've got a few things to do, but you feel free to examine the church on our own. Richard, you have been through the church so many times you don't need me. You probably know the church better than most. I'll catch up with you later."

We first made our way to the altar, as the letter stated, 'the most sacred place.' It was a heavy ten-legged wooden table, very spartan, as was the rest of the church knave, but full of symbolism. The symbolism was contemporary, almost fantastic, but as Peter pointed out, it did have connections with the past.

"Look at the front of the altar," Peter pointed out, "a square table, squaring the altar, very Masonic. It could be coincident, but I do not believe in coincidences. The stained glass diamond above the altar could almost be Rosicrucian. I cannot see anything under the altar as indicated in the letter; it is just a table, a bit of a dead-end. I guess it wouldn't be that easy, would it?"

I tapped the altar to see if it was hollow, nothing but solid oak. I further checked all the sides to see if there were any draws or secret latches, again nothing.

"Any ideas as to what the church symbols are indicating; are they showing us the way to the manuscript?" I asked Peter.

"Damned if I know," answered Peter, "so far, I am drawing a blank."

"What about the bottom of the altar under the legs, Peter?"

Peter crawled under and peered at the underside of the altar, "no, there is nothing here either. It is solid, a heavy wooden carved table."

We meandered further, still not knowing what we were looking to discover. Again Peter pointed out an elaborate circle pierced by what looked like a sword.

"I have seen something similar to that at the church at Rennes le Chateau in the south of France." Peter advised, "a church dedicated to Mary Magdeline, supposedly Jesus' wife. And over there, the stained glass window has a green glass tee cross. Again that could be very Masonic. The Masons maintain Jesus was crucified on a tee cross, what they call a tau cross, not the traditional crucifix."

"Still not helping us. If the initial find at the art gallery was under a flagstone, maybe we should be looking for something similar," offered Richard.

"That's not a bad idea." I replied, "There are a lot of flagstones and a lot of areas here to cover. Why don't we split up, we will save some time investigating all these flagstones? We'll meet back here in front of the altar. Say an hour? "

We met back at the agreed time, but to no avail, our search had revealed nothing. I checked under the altar again but found nothing that would indicate a hiding place. We were sitting at the base of the altar, pondering our next move. At that moment, we were joined again by the Reverend.

 "Well, have you enjoyed your walkabout?" the Reverend asked.

"To tell you the truth, we are looking for something that ties the church to Charles Rennie MacKintosh, other than the architecture, something that would connect him to the Masonic Order."

"He was a Mason; I do know that," the Reverend answered, "but as for the church, a lot of people see Masonic imagery everywhere. Myself, not so much."

At this point, Peter asked Reverend Bowan, "Did he leave any blueprints of the church, and are they kept in the church?"

"Now, as a matter of fact, he did. Where have I seen them? Of course, the rectory records. Is this what you would like to see?"

"Very much," I replied. "Anything that may enlighten us."

"Come this way; I just remembered they are not in the church rectory records. They are not kept in the church at all but in the vicarage office."

We followed the Reverend out of the church to the vicarage and into his office. Reverend Bowen produced a set of keys from his desk and unlocked an old filing cabinet.

"No one has been in here for donkeys," offered the Reverend, "probably since the place was built. Now let me see, ah, yes, here they are."

Reverend Bowen proceeded to lay out a set of six old fashioned blueprint drawings and placed them one on top of the other.

"These originals have to be well over a hundred years old. They are still in pretty good condition. You should have a copy of these at the Glasgow School of Art, Richard."

"If they have not been burnt in the fire," Richard replied, "things are in such a mess right now."

"I'm sorry to hear that," offered the Reverend, "was there much lost?"

"More than I would like to admit," Richard announced. "Everything is on lockdown right now until the cleanup is finished."

"If you like, I could donate these to the Glasgow School of Art," the Reverend suggested. "I feel that is where they belong anyway. You are the first to want to see them since I have been here."

"That is a very kind offer," Richard added, "and I think we will take you up on that."

We huddled over the drawings, studying each one, and found nothing that could indicate a hiding place until we came to the last plan layout.

"Reverend, this last drawing shows there is a basement or crypt. Is anyone buried down there?"

"As far as I know, nobody is buried down there; it is mainly a storage area. There once was a coal furnace and coal chute, but that has long gone. I have not been down there for years, and I do not remember any burial tombs. Do you believe someone is buried down there?"

 "I don't know," I answered, "would it be an imposition to go down there and have a look, we might find something of importance?"

"No," the Reverend answered, "what do you think you will find down there? I think you are grasping at straws. Is it that important?"

"Anything new that will tie it to Charles Rennie MacKintosh," I answered. "We have lost a lot with the fire."

"Ok, let me grab a couple of torch lights first, I do not know if the electrics still work down there. There are also keys we will need."

"Bring the drawing with you; it may help," I added.

We found the trap door entrance to the basement at the bottom of the stairs leading to the church's tower. Reverend William unlocked the door and pulled the heavy oaken door up, groaning and squeaking the whole time. Once opened, the trap door exposed a stone staircase leading down into a black hole. It smelt musty and damp. The cold air rushed up to meet us. Not the most cheerful greeting, almost as if it was saying beware of what you might find down here. The Reverend shone his torch down the entrance to reveal a set of stairs about ten to eleven feet deep.

"Well, gentlemen, shall we?" the Reverend offered.

He led us down into a cavernous, cold, damp basement with pillars and arches holding up the roof and church floor as far as we could see. Reverend William shone his torch onto the wall and found an electrical switch, which he proceeded to turn on. The illumination was dull, but at least we could now see our way. Everywhere there were boxes of all sizes, old furniture, and discarded building materials all covered in thick dust and cobwebs.

"As I told you," the Reverend stated, "I have not been down here for many years. I don't think anybody has."

"Is there not a furnace room or maintenance utility room?" I queried.

"No," the Reverend replied, "as I said that is gone some years ago and is not here at present. The furnace is now in the rectory basement. Used to be coal down here, and there was a huge coal-burning furnace, but now it has been converted to natural gas."

"Let me see the building blueprint for the basement." I still needed the torchlight to see clearly. "May I ask Reverend why you had to come down here?"

"Initially just curiosity, but also we keep old records down here. It is the only room in the basement."

"Well, let's start there; it is as good a place as anywhere. Lead on Reverend," I proposed.

The Reverend led us through about a dozen pillared archways until we reached a heavy wooden door at almost the end of the basement. He unlocked it, and the door swung fully open, moaning the whole way. He then turned on the lights to expose a room of about twenty by twenty feet. Most of the walls were covered in shelves holding bankers' boxes. The older the boxes, the more dust. A quick guess, there could be at least a hundred boxes.

"Reverend," I asked, "Where in location to the church is this room situated?'

"I believe the altar is exactly overhead," he answered.

"Christ, where do we start? Excuse me Reverend," Peter offered.

"Let's split up," I suggested, "We will each take points of the compass."

 After an extensive search for over two hours into every box and every shelf we were no further ahead, just boxes with annual running costs going back at least a hundred and fifty years.

"Was there anything else in the letter that could indicate where the location might be?" Peter inquired. "It was the letter that led us here, was there anything else accompanying it, Richard?"

"No," Richard replied, "I gave you everything."

"What letter are you referring to?" inquired the Reverend.

I hated lying to the Reverend, especially in his church, but I wanted to keep this among Peter, Richard, and myself. I also knew that this was dangerous and did not wish the Reverend involved.

I evaded the question and replied, "The letter was found in an old metal box while they were clearing the ruins of the fire at the Glasgow School of Art. We are trying to retrieve as much history as we can when we put the library back together. But it looks like we have reached a dead end."

By this time, it was getting on for 2:00 pm. I was getting hungry; none of us had eaten, so I suggested a lunch break.

"Reverend, would you mind if we came back after lunch for a further look around this room?" I requested. "And please join us for lunch."

Reverend William advised us he had to get ready to visit some parishioners and would not be able to accompany us. He would let us have the keys if we locked up after ourselves and returned the keys to the rectory. We could drop them through the rectory letterbox.

Even on a dull February day, the brightness hit us as we left the church's dim and oppressive basement. We still watched to see if there was anything untoward following us. Richard knew the neighbourhood and soon had us seated at a little restaurant not far from the church. We all sat quietly, meditating as our food came. We ate in silence and washed it down with a couple of pots of coffee.

Still sipping our coffee, I asked, "Any ideas?"

Richard replied, "I am at a loss unless there is something back at the School we have overlooked."

Then Peter interjected, "Let's see the letter again, Greg."

I still had my briefcase with a copy of the manuscript and letter. I handed the letter over to Peter. He read it out loud.

McLellan Galleries
Sauchehall Street,
Glasgow

August 5, 1871

Dear Brethren Iain McLellan,

As you are aware, the Brethren have already placed the trial manuscript safely with the Queen's Cross. It is imperative that the enclosed confession must be placed with it. Our most sacred secrets must be held on the pain of death. As you found it so, it shall be the most sacred place.

Your Brother,

Charles Rennie MacKintosh

August 5, 18, 72

He read it out loud again, then said, "The letter is short, and to the point, he knew the Queen's Cross was the church. Nothing devious there, we know that the manuscript was hidden somewhere in the church. Why does he not give any clues as to its location? He knew where it was, and by the letter, Iain McLellan knew where it was. What does he mean, 'as you found it so shall it be,' the most sacred place?"

"Is it a Masonic saying or greeting code?" Richard offered.

"Not that I know of," I replied.

"As you found it so shall it be, the most sacred place," but what was found? Is he referring to the Templar confession?" Peter ruminated.

"Yes, Peter, I think you have it. Jacque de Molay's confession was found under a flagstone. We were looking at boxes and shelves and not the floor. If it fits, there it should be under the most sacred place, under the altar. Come on; we may have got it."

We headed off back to the church, almost racing, and soon found ourselves back in the dingy basement room looking at approximately one hundred, two-foot by two-foot, flagstones.

"Where do we start?" Richard inquired, "We can't shift them all, and we need tools."

"I saw that there are some old shovels down here, where the old coal storage used to be. Richard, come with me. I think they are near the stairway."

We shone the flashlight to find the stairway and there propped up against the wall were several shovels and an old wheelbarrow. They were filthy and covered with dust and cobwebs.

"These haven't been used in years; in fact, they look Victorian. Thank God they didn't make throw away tools. These are solid and still in good condition."

Richard had a small package of tissues that we used to clean the tools off as best we could, and we took them back to Peter.

Peter had not been idle. "The most sacred place. This room is exactly below the altar. I think this is the flagstone right below the altar, indicating the most sacred place. Give me the shovel."

Peter gently tapped several flagstones to discover a hollow sound beneath one of the flagstones. Placing the edge of the shovel into the seam of the stone, he tried to pry it up, and slowly up it came.

"Give me a hand boys, I can only pry it up so far; it's damn heavy," Peter requested.

Richard and I both took a corner and lifted it. There beneath the two-foot by two-foot flagstone was a small safe set in the concrete. The safe door sat flat with the floor looking right at us.

"Well looks like we have it, but we have another problem," piped in Peter.

I saw what he meant; the safe was a combination safe. We all looked dumbfounded, where do we go from here?

"Do you think the Reverend has the combination?" I offered.

" I don't think so," Richard replied, " he doesn't use this area, it was only curiosity that brought him down here and by his own statement that was years ago. I doubt even he knows this exists, and if he did, he would have told us."

"Let me see the blueprints again," Peter requested, "maybe they show the safe and some clue as to the combination or where it might be."

We laid out the drawings again, but nowhere did it even show that a safe existed.

"There must be a clue we have overlooked," Peter countered, "It was the letter that lead us down here, was there anything else accompanying it, Richard?"

"No," Richard replied, "I gave you everything. There is a manufacturer's plaque. We could contact the safe manufacturers to see if they could open it if they still exist."

"That would be messy and pull the church into it. We should keep this amongst ourselves if possible," I countered. "It was the letter that gave us the location. There must be another clue we have missed. Let's have a look at the letter again."

McLellan Galleris
Sauchehall Street,
Glasgow

August 5, 1871

Dear Brethren Iain McLellan,

As you are aware, the Brethren have already placed the trial manuscript safely with the Queen's Cross. It is imperative that the enclosed confession must be placed with it. Our most sacred secrets must be held on the pain of death. As you found it so, it shall be the most sacred place.

Your Brother,

Charles Rennie MacKintosh

August 5, 18,72

I read it out loud again, word for word, then said, "The letter is short and to the point, he, Charles Rennie MacKintosh knew the Queen's Cross was the church, his church. We know the manuscript was deposited in the church, and we think we have found the location as per his clues, which he gave to Iain McLellan. If this is the location and safe, he would have known the combination and would have given it to Iain McLellan in this letter. This letter is the only clue."

"Greg read out only the opening date and the closing date of the letter," Peter asked.

"The opening date is August 5 comma 1871. The closing date is August 5, comma 18 comma 72. They don't jive and why all the commas in the closing date? The dates don't match. I think that one of them could be the actual letter date, and the other may be the safe combination, as it has broken the year up to 18 comma 72. You would not normally write the year in that manner."

Peter replied, "I'm game, let's try. We have nothing better at this point."

Peter tried the opening date combination, 5, 18, 72, "there is no 72. I'll try 5,18,7,2." He then pulled on the safe handle, nothing, it wouldn't budge.

"Damn, I thought we had something," Peter growled, "let me try the reverse 2,7, 18, 5."

But again nothing, the reverse combination did not work, the handle would not budge.

"Peter try the closing date, 8, 5, 18," I offered.

"Why 8?"

"August is the eighth month."

Again we were stumped; it would not open. This time Richard suggested all five numbers 8,5,18,7,2.

Peter let out an enormous sigh, blew on his fingertips as if he was one of the world's greatest safecrackers, and slowly worked the combination.

"Clockwise to 8, back to 5, clockwise to 18, and back to 7, clockwise to 2." Peter was talking to himself as he pushed down on the handle. The handle clicked open, "Bloody hell, it worked!" Peter yelled.

The handle gave way, and the door clicked. Peter pulled the safe door fully open to reveal its' only contents, a large leather cylinder approximately sixteen inches long by six inches in diameter, with a leather cap at one end. We all looked dumbfounded, no one wanting to make a move. What had we found?

 Finally, Peter gently lifted it out, "You little bugger, finally got you, and you are heavy!"

I looked at Peter and Richard, "what do we do now? We can't open it here."

Richard answered, "We have a fairly good library lab back at the Glasgow School of Art. It came with the Charles Rennie MacKintosh Library to help preserve some of the Victorian and Georgian manuscripts and books. We also have done some restoration of older paintings. It has been upgraded recently and was not damaged by the fire. I suggest we take it there and try to open it."

"I thought it was destroyed in the fire," Peter queried Richard.

"Not the lab," Richard answered, "it was an afterthought, and not placed in or near the library."

"Well, come on then, let's get out of here," Peter insisted.

"Will we have any trouble getting in?" I asked, "I mean, with all the police, insurance agents, and workers?"

"No, leave that to me, they don't stop me," Richard answered. "I have carte blanche, it's my Gallery, and it is away from the fire damage. Give me the tube."

Richard reached over, his hands trembling a little, and took up the leather tube. To his great astonishment, it was heavy, exceedingly heavy, about at least ten pounds or more."My God, what have we got here, you should feel the weight of this thing."

"I know, I did tell you," Peter answered.

We closed the safe door and put the flagstone back in its' place. I brushed a little dust back over the stone. All looked normal. We left the gloom of the basement, to everybody's relief. We locked the door and made our way to the rectory. The clouds had now broken, and the sun was shining as we dropped the keys through the rectory letterbox. The contrast between the dark, repressive basement and the now bright sunny afternoon seemed worlds apart, and it was so welcome. There didn't seem to be any connection to our world of intrigue and the glorious sunshine. But even with the sun beaming down, we still nervously scanned around to see if anyone was trailing us, nothing. We piled into Richards' car. Richard driving, we headed to the Glasgow School of Art.

"Peter, do you see a green Land Rover following us?" I inquired.

"Nothing yet," answered Peter.

"What do you mean by a green Land Rover following us?" Richard nervously asked.

"Just a bit of nervous speculation, we saw one earlier at my place, but so far nothing," I answered, trying to calm the situation. "I think I am getting a little paranoid, seeing spooks around every corner."

Peter then interjected, "If there is a dangerous third party and most probably there is, they probably have surmised that there is nothing more to be gained at the Art School. Furthermore, they did not find anything at Richard's place, and I don't think that as yet, they have connected myself and Greg. I have a feeling that they most probably are watching the police, in particular Chief Inspector Matthew Adam.

We may have bought ourselves a bit of time. Once we have found out what we have, we should bring the Inspector back into the picture."

To this, we all agreed, and the sooner, the better, but Richard interjected, "Who do you think they are, the people who attacked me and ransacked my house?"

"At this point, I don't know," I answered, "but they are taking every measure to get a hold of our discovery, and the measures are not nice. It is either the monetary value of what we have, which is great, or something more devious. I tend to think it is more devious. The Glasgow School of Art is full of valuable items; if this was an organized theft ring, they could have easily taken far more things of value and disappeared by now. No, they were definitely after something different, and I think it is what we have found."

"So you think it is the content of what we found rather than the monetary value," Richard asked.

"I have a feeling it is that," I answered.

"I agree with Greg," Peter added, "this could have profound consequences to many religions. Some good some bad. It is not the good I am concerned with."

After a short drive, we finally arrived and parked at the Glasgow School of Art, just after 4:30 pm. Richard showed his ID to the police guards and then guided us down to the basement lab. It was a windowless, brightly lit large room divided in two; the dividing wall was all made of glass. Two sealing doors lead through the glass partition. Inside the glass-walled room was an array of electronic equipment and two large working tables. Richard explained the lab was all atmospherically controlled and particulate free.

"Luckily, there is nobody here. I closed the school down until all the damage was assessed and cleared," Richard announced, "the only people here are the restoration workmen and the police."

Richard put the leather cylinder on the table and stood back, looking at us all.

"Richard, this is your field of work. Do you think you are capable of opening it?" I asked.

"I think I will need all of your help, but first put these on," Richard handed us white cotton gloves. He then proceeded to examine the leather tube. "Peter, there is a digital camera over there. Could you be the cameraman and take shots as we proceed?"

Peter started taking pictures of all sides of the tube.

With that, Richard started, "well, the first part is easy," as the top cap of the leather cylinder, although tightly on, slid off with just a little bit of effort. Richard then gently turned it upside down. Inside a grey metallic second cylinder wrapped partially in vellum slid out onto the table. Richard, with much care, unwrapped the vellum sheet, which was no more than ten by twelve inches. The vellum appeared to have Latin inscriptions.

"Greg, go into that cupboard, you will see some clear plastic folders. Get me one measuring about 20 x 20 inches," Richard requested.

I found what Richard was looking for and handed it to him. He promptly slid the vellum sheet in it and took it over to another machine and sealed all the edges of the plastic encapsulating the vellum sheet.

"Now that is safe and hermetically sealed. We can now make a copy of it." Richard instructed.

Richard promptly made three copies of the vellum sheet. He then turned his attention to the metallic tube.

"Whatever we have here," Richard remarked, "is in lead sheeting and is completely sealed. No wonder it is so heavy. By its weight, the lead cylinder is also hollow."

"By its marking, it is also Templar," Peter interjected, "do you see the skull imprint on the top of the cylinder? That was one of their standard symbols."

We all saw the distinct skull imprint. "The dots are beginning to line up," I observed. "We seem to have discovered a Templar mystery."

"How are we going to get into that lead tube?" I asked Richard.

Richard gingerly handled and examined the tube, turning it over and over again.

"This one is a little out of my scope. This problem is more for the likes of the British Museum. I think we should put it back in its case, hermetically seal it and give it to someone more experienced".

"Are we all agreed?" Richard asked.

"So, we give it to the police and let them take it to the experts?" Peter asked.

"Yes, but on the proviso that we accompany it," Richard added, "Is that what we want?"

We were all in agreement with handing it over to the police, as no one else had the experience to open it. Again with a small vacuum pack machine, Richard sealed the leather tube containing the lead cylinder and its contents.

"Now gentlemen, we have to interpret what we have, but I don't think here. I'm not comfortable staying here with what has happened," I suggested, "also, we must get the scroll to a safe place. Again may I suggest my solicitor with a copy of the vellum to Chief Inspector Matthew Adam. It is too late now, but first thing tomorrow morning. I won't feel comfortable until we do this."

"Where should we go?" Richard inquired, "It is just now turning 7:00 pm."

Peter suggested as he lived the closest to the Art School, that we go to his place. "It also may be the safest at this point. I don't think it is yet on the radar for surveillance. Is there a phone? I'll give Pat a call to let her know she'll have company."

We left the Art School again, very wary of our surroundings. All was quiet, nothing to be seen. As we drove to Peter's I had the cylinder, original scroll, and copies in my briefcase sitting on my lap. I had never felt so uncomfortable and yet so elated in my life. Soon we arrived at Peter's and were greeted at the door by Pat.

"What have you lads been up to?" Pat inquired with a very quizzical stare.

"I'll tell you everything, but first, we are starving. Let's have supper." Peter pleaded.

Pat ushered us into the dining room, "Well, on such short notice, I have defrosted some of Peter's spaghetti sauce. The pasta is cooking as we speak. The table's set, so sit yourselves down, and I will bring everything in."

Soon we were all seated. A steaming terrene of spaghetti sauce and a large bowl of pasta were placed on the table. Pat had tossed up a salad to accompany the pasta. Peter came in carrying two bottles of red

Chianti wine. Peter is an accomplished cook, and his sauce is exceptional. We were digging in with garnishings of grated parmesan, homemade garlic croutons, and ground red hot peppers. I took a couple of good gulps of excellent wine and, for the first time, today felt somewhat relaxed. We were all now replete and ready to relate our story.

We sat around the table and told Pat everything from start to finish holding her to the same secrecy we all committed to keeping.

"My God," Pat exclaimed, "Should you not let all of this be handled by the police?"

"The police are well involved in it and by tomorrow will have everything. We just have to interpret the scroll and then hand that over. The originals will be in safe keeping until we decide what to do with them. Without the three of us, this would never have been found," I explained.

"But," Pat interjected, "just how much are the three of you in danger? Richard has already been attacked."

"So far, it has just been Richard, and not to make light of it; I think the main concern of whoever has done this, their priority now has to be with the police. They know by now we have had contact with them and probably given them all the important evidence," I offered to Pat. "Tomorrow, we will give them the rest of our finds."

"The sooner, the better," Pat advised.

"Look, it's after 9:00 PM, we can't do anything until tomorrow, so let's bolt the doors tonight and all stay put," offered Peter. "We have four bedrooms, and I think I can rustle up enough sleepwear and toiletries to refresh all of us. What do you say?"

We were all in agreement, the three musketeers, more strength together than apart. It felt safe, at least we thought.

"One thing before we turn in," I asked, "We must take a look at least at the copy of the vellum sheet. My curiosity is killing me, sorry, maybe wrong choice of words."

Peter interjected, "I was about to say the same thing. I'm wide awake and won't be able to sleep anyway."

I pulled out one of the three copies and handed it over to Peter.

"Peter, will you do the honours again?" as I gave him the text.

Peter started, "Well again, it is in Latin, and entitled Order of the Poor Knights of the Temple."

Order of the Poor Knights of the Temple

Kingdom of Jerusalem

Grand Master Hughes de Paynes

Seneschal Robert de Craon

Dated February 1, 1129, Ano Dominus

Inventory List From the ruins of Solomon's Temple Jerusalem

Inventory Number 1998 of 4993 Items Found

Description of Inventory

One Latin Papyrus Scroll Copied From Hebrew For the Administrative Office of Pontius Pilate

Minutes of the Trial of Yeshua ben David, Jesus the Essene of Nazareth Conducted by The High Priest Caiaphas and Council Priest Annas

Second scroll papyrus minutes in Latin of the trial of Yeshua ben David, Jesus, conducted before Pontius Pilate.

These scrolls are only for the eyes of the Grand Master, the Seneschal and the Holy Pope in Rome on pain of death.

These minutes we have sealed in a plumbum tube.

"My God, Peter, this is part of an inventory list," I exclaimed. "It gives both names of Jesus. Jesus, the Greek translation and Yeshua ben David the Aramaic of Hebrew translation."

"Yes," Peter interrupted, "Yeshua ben David was his proper name in Aramaic, although we know it as Yeshua Ben Yosef. Also, this shows that the Vatican knew about this trial scroll over eight hundred years ago and knew it was hidden with the Knights Templers. What we see here is much earlier than the time of Jacque de Molay."

"So they knew an original exists," I added. "I'll bet they would love to get their hands on this one."

"To save it or destroy it?" Richard asked. "Do you think they could be behind the break-ins?"

"Who knows, they seem the most likely. I have never heard of this document existing anywhere, let alone the Vatican." I answered. "Tomorrow, we will put it safely away."

"I know this is part of an inventory list, 1998 of 4993; what the hell did they find," queried Pat.

"It is intimated, treasure and knowledge that made the Knights Templars more wealthy and powerful than the Vatican and most kingdoms in Europe," answered Peter. "Or so, the story goes and also probably their demise. Some people say they may have found the Ark of the Covenant and even the Ten Commandments. I think that is a little fanciful, though. They were wealthier than most European kingdoms at the time, had their castles and standing armies. The only entity to have a trained standing army. They pretty well ran the Middle East at the time. Their banking system was the envy of the world, trusted by Christian, Jew, and Muslim alike."

Pat left for the kitchen and, in a short while, brought in a large pot of tea. We all helped ourselves and settled in for the evening. It was getting on for 10:30 PM. Pat excused herself and headed off to bed. I gave Peter the copy of the trial inventory scroll while I made myself comfortable with the second copy.

 "Listen, lads; it's late, I'm ready for bed. In the morning, we will all head over to the solicitor and get this scroll safely locked away and then head over and see Chief Inspector Matthew Adam. Again are we all in agreement?" I asked.

There was no dissenting voice. Peter poured us all a nightcap of fine scotch. We sat quietly and sipped until we were finished.

Peter looked at us all and said, "we have a lot to sleep on right now. My biggest question is, where do we go from here?"

"Let's decide that after a good night's sleep," I suggested.

With that, we all headed off to bed, hoping for a good night's rest.

Morning came soon enough. I was up just before 7:00 AM and dodged into the empty bathroom for a quick clean and shave. I headed downstairs; Pat had already laid out breakfast, and Richard was already helping himself to bacon and eggs.

"Good morning," I offered, "where is Peter?"

"You know your friend," replied Pat, "mornings are not his best, but he should be down soon."

At this point, we all turned to the hallway as an earth-shattering yawn echoed through the house. Enter Peter, a little worse for wear, but still presentable and hopefully ready for the day.

"Good morning," a very audible greeting from Peter, followed by, "coffee?"

"What time does your solicitors' office open?" inquired Peter.

"Usually 8:00 AM," I answered, "but I am not sure if that is the time he will be there. It is after eight now, by the time we arrive, he should be there. I'll call to let him know we are coming."

"He is in, I just talked to him, and he will be expecting us," I came back to the kitchen table.

We all finished a hearty breakfast and were ready to take on the day. All three of us were soon heading for Richard's car, quickly scanning up and down the street, again no green Land Rover or anything else suspicious. The morning was one of those rare winter Glaswegian mornings where the sky was blue and bright, not a cloud. Nothing could go wrong on a day like today; it was beautiful.

We arrived at my solicitors' just before 9:00 AM.

"You two stay in the car, I won't be a long time. Keep an eye out for anything suspicious."

My solicitor saw me immediately and showed me to the vault where the original material was stored. He had also set up a safety deposit box within the safe, handed me the key, and watched me deposit the vacuum wrapped scroll together with the confession. He also gave me a passcode number for the deposit box. The deposit box had a double lock and could only be open with my key plus my solicitor. I also gave Richard and Peter legal access to the safety deposit box. Safe as houses as the saying goes. I felt comfortable that all was safe.

I explained to Richard and Peter what had transpired, and both felt comfortable that all was above board and safe. Nothing untoward had been seen by either Peter or Richard, so we headed back to Peter's house.

It was now just after 10:00 AM as we parked in the driveway of Peter's house.

"When we get inside, I'll call Chief Inspector Matthew Adam and tell him we are all coming around to see him," I said. "The sooner we get this into their hands, the better."

"I don't know if this is the best procedure," Peter interjected. "Should we not be giving this to, say, The British Museum or the Archbishop of Canterbury or even the Crown?"

"Yes, we should if all was ok and we were not being pursued, especially as was Richard. I still feel the best direction for us is to let the police handle it; at least they will subdue the criminal element. Inspector Stephen Bliss of the antiquities and fine art fraud department should be able to get things going and put us in the right direction," I added.

"Yes," Richard agreed, "I would feel a lot better if we handled it this way."

"Ok, let's see how it goes," replied Peter. "I think we are on the right track."

"So, we are all in agreement?" I asked. "I know I keep asking this, but I want to make sure we are all on the same page."

There was no dissent, and we headed back into the house, feeling we had a load off our minds.

"We're home, Pat," Peter called.

"I'm in the sitting room," Pat returned.

Pat was sitting on the settee on the far side of the room. We all walked over, ready to relax, and join her.

Something was wrong; she didn't look right; she looked frightened. She sat ridged starring at Peter, and just as I was to inquire about whether she was alright, a voice came from behind her.

"Would you please all sit-down? Don't make a sound and just listen," the stranger demanded. He held a gun.

Pat interjected immediately, "I'm alright Peter, no harm has come to me, all he wants is for us to listen. Please sit down."

We all sat down immediately. I felt like all the energy had drained out of me as I starred at the gun. Had our enemies finally caught up to us, were we so stupid and blind?

He was tall, about six foot, slightly tanned, salt and pepper hair, well built, fit, spoke with an American accent. He held the gun quite casually on his lap as if he was quite knowledgeable and relaxed around firearms. He slowly looked us up and down with piercing steel gray-blue eyes as we all sat there. He moved over to the other adjacent chair so he could see us all in one glance. He held the gun loosely; barrel pointed to the floor. I went cold, like an icy knife penetrating your heart. I felt paralyzed even though my only thought was for Pat. He turned and scanned us as he spoke.

"My name is Robert Findley; I am not your enemy. I have come to give you as much assistance as I can."

"What assistance are you talking about?" Peter snapped. "I don't get a warm and friendly feeling about you with that gun on your lap."

With that, he promptly put the gun on the coffee table, turned the handle towards me, and pushed the gun in my direction within easy access to me. He then sat back away from the gun. I could have picked it up quite easily and turned the tables. I declined. My heart was racing. I have never even handled a gun.

"Could we put that away?" I asked, looking at the gun.

"You can put it away, or I can put it away, but I feel we may need it in the future," Robert Findley answered.

Richard broke the silence, "are you the one who attacked me and broke into my office and home?"

"No," the intruder answered, "but I have a pretty good idea who did. Will you at least listen to me?"

"I would rather go to the police," I countered.

"So would I if they were not compromised," the intruder answered back.

"What do you mean?" I asked. I was starting to calm down.

"They pulled Chief Inspector Matthew Adam's car, near South Street, out of the River Clyde last night. This morning they fished his body out of the Clyde. You have not been watching the news. And again, I did not do it, but I have a pretty good idea who did."

"Peter, can you put the TV on," I asked.

Peter looked at the intruder. He nodded his head in agreement.

Peter put the TV on. It wasn't long before the news station confirmed that Chief Inspector Matthew Adam had drowned in the Clyde under suspicious circumstances.

"Oh, my God," Richard exclaimed, "this just gets worse and worse."

"Alright, who are you and how do you fit in all of this," I asked.

"May I?" answered the intruder as he pointed to the gun.

"Yes," Peter answered, "please put it away."

He picked up the gun, depressed the magazine button, the magazine fell out. He then cocked the breach ejecting the last bullet. He slipped the bullet back into the magazine and pocketed them both in his jacket. He did this as if he had done it a hundred times like a well trained professional.

"Again, my name is Robert Findley; my friends call me Bob. I am American from Texas; I am also a Mason, Knights Templar, Scottish Rite. I know that means something to you. I am fifty-two years of age and was a Captain in the American Marines. I have seen active duty but never thought I would be involved in something like this. What I do know has nothing to do with the American Government or any of its agencies. We, the Masonic Knights Templar's, have a good idea what you found after the fire at The Glasgow School of Art. Correct me if I am wrong, but it has to do with Jacque de Molay, evidence exonerating him and compromising the Catholic Church and maybe all of Christianity. The Masonic Order has known this document existed since the time of the Templar's demise. We know how it was secretly passed down through the ages until it came to Charles Rennie MacKintosh and Iain McLellan. From there, it got lost. Am I on the right track?"

"Suppose you are Mr. Findley," I answered.

"Please, your name is Greg, you are Peter and you Richard are the Director of The Glasgow School of Art, and you are Pat, Peter's wife. Please call me Bob," he interrupted.

"Alright, yes, Bob, you are on the right track. We did find the Moray document, and it does sum up what you have eluded to," I answered.

"Is it safe?" Bob asked urgently.

"Yes, it is very safe and protected," I replied.

"Good, but you are not. I believe they feel there is no more to be gained with Richard. I do not think they have made the connection to you and are still concentrating on the police," Bob replied. "I think you have bought us some time, but not much. What you have discovered is extremely valuable. They will stop at nothing to acquire it or destroy it, at any cost, including anyone that gets in their way. It is, at this time, not safe even in the UK, let alone in Scotland. "

Then Peter leaned forward and asked, "who are they?"

"They are also a breakaway sect of Masons, Knights Templers, Scottish Rite, but they also belong to the Grand American Evangelical Church of the Saviour. They are a huge, wealthy Midwestern radical Christian Church with connections to militant white supremacists. They have probably since the end of World War 1 infiltrated our organization in America with the sole purpose of destroying the Moray document. These are the people who broke into your office and home and accosted you, Richard. They probably have something to do with the circumstances surrounding the demise of Chief Inspector Adams. "

Again Peter queried, "but why?"

"If they knew there were documents dangerous to the existence of their church and could destroy it and Christianity as they teach it, would they not take great measures to destroy it," Bob answered. "There is also the monetary bottom line. This organization pulls in millions of tax-free dollars that support a lot of radical organizations, any loss to their bottom line would be disastrous. They cannot allow this."

" But it is only the confession of Jacque de Molay," I said, not wanting him to know just how much we had recovered, " that surely could not be of such a threat to them ?"

Bob was quiet for a moment and then said, "the confession of Jacque de Molay may have clues to an even greater secret and threat to them. This is very well documented within the higher levels of Masonry that a document exists that could change the course of Christianity. We feel quite certain that Charles Rennie MacKintosh had this document in his possession. Your find we feel certain will lead to this further document."

I quickly gave a slight nod to Peter and Richard not to divulge anything more to Bob.

"Are we being followed by a green Land Rover with two men inside?" I asked.

"So you have seen them," Bob replied, "they are part of the team that broke into Richard's office and home and assaulted him. They are the enemy, and as you can see, they are dangerous. I believe they think you have given all documents over to the late Chief Inspector Matthew

Adam. That is why I think you have bought yourselves some time, but not a lot. I believe they have infiltrated the Glasgow constabulary. Your tail in the green Land Rover is part of the Glasgow police force."

"So, what is your plan?" I asked."How do we fend them off?"

"First, we have to get you all to a safe house before they realize you have the document. I want you four to stay together. Second, once you are safe, we must get the document safely picked up and moved to a location overseen by one of my colleges, the Crown, the Vatican, and or Scotland Yard. I also want you four there as well if you are willing to trust me. "

"The Vatican!" Peter looked startled, "I thought you lot were not on the best of terms with the Catholic Church."

"Believe it or not, we have always had contact with the Vatican at the highest levels. Some of our brethren have been members of the Vatican at the highest levels. This association was kept very quiet as our membership does not reject you if you are of the Rome Church. The main requirement of the Masonic movement is that you are a man of good standing, believe in a higher deity, and recommended by another Mason. You're thinking is a little out of date, old history; the church today is far more liberal and open-minded as seen with the recent Pope. We have a good working relationship with the Vatican. The Vatican will have documentation to support the legitimacy of your find."

 We all looked a little stunned at the revelation.

"I would also like the press there when we make the document public, say the London Times," I added.

"Good idea, we will all see to that," answered Bob.

Pat broke the silence, "how do we know you are not just setting us up?"

"Good question, all I can say is I do not want the original document. I have not asked you for it. You keep it safe until you are comfortable to release it. I have been open with you and told you all I know regarding the Molay document. Now it is up to you to decide to trust me," Bob replied.

"Why do we not go to Scotland Yard right now?" I proposed.

"We could, but I guarantee that the first thing they will do is work through their Glasgow office. I do not know how compromised that office is, but it is compromised. We have just lost Chief Inspector Matthew Adam to very suspicious circumstances. It could be dangerous, and we could be bogged down with them for months." Bob formulated. "By the way, who have you made contact with at the police station?"

"Chief Inspector Matthew Adam, Antiquities and Art Fraud Inspector Stephen Bliss and   another Officer McKennan." That's all I offered.

"I knew of Chief Inspector Adam only through my contacts in Scotland. I believe he was above board, and I think his death proves it. Inspector Stephan Bliss, also I think he could be trusted, but I don't know of him that well. I hear he is a stickler for proper procedure. As for the other officer, he is unknown to me," replied Bob.

"One thing I don't understand Bob is why you have not asked to see the documents we have?" I asked.

"I know what you have, and I have seen it. A copy of the confession by Jacque de Molay, as he stated, was sent by the Archbishop Phillipe de Marigny to Pope Clement. That copy still exists in the Vatican, and I have seen that one and had it translated to me. We, the Masonic

Knights Templars American branch, also have in our possession since colonial times a copy of the confession. It is a duplicate to the one in the Vatican, and as I told you, we are now on good relations with the Vatican. What you have here is the original, kept with the Templars when they escaped to Scotland under the protection of the Sinclair Lords. Your copy, though, we believe, has further clues to a greater secret."

"Look, Bob, do you mind if we have a private conversation among ourselves? We have a lot to consider," I requested.

"Of course not, go ahead. I'll go into the kitchen; by the way, I am starving."

We had a short meeting while Bob waited in the kitchen. The consensus, we would go with Bob, although we would still hold back what we had found, the trial of Jesus. His plan seemed sound plus he had an air of openness and confidence that we felt comfortable with, like the State that he hailed from. We called him back.

"Ok, Bob, we are all on side with your plan," I offered. "How do we start?"

"It is just after 12:30 PM; I want to get you all to a safe house as soon as possible. You will have to pack some clothing and a change, and as I said, I am starving, how about the rest of you?"

"I'll put some lunch together," Pat volunteered.

Pat put out a hearty lunch of potato soup, bread, ham, cheese, pickled onions, and sweet chutney. Peter brought out several bottles of Innes and Gunn beer. We all dug in, in silence. Pat announced there was also coffee if we wanted it.

Peter broke the silence and said to Pat, "you and I better pack a few things. How long do you think we will be away?"

"I would pack for at least four to five days." Bob then asked, "Do you have somewhere safe to stay while I organize things? I don't want you staying around here."

"My wife is on an art painting break north of Loch Lomond. She has rented a cottage in a small village. I think it is called Ardlui. I must give her a call anyway," I replied.

Bob replied, "that's good, give her a call. Play it low key, do not alarm her. Make use of my mobile phone; it is untraceable. I will meet you there later. I'll give you my mobile phone number, call me when you arrive, just say arrived do not give any indication as to where. At this point, I do not want to be seen with you. I don't want to give them a connection with me. Greg and Richard pack up some clothing and leave together for the Highlands, as soon as possible. I'll meet you there."

I called my wife Jennifer up in the Highlands and asked her to make ready for myself and Peter and Pat. We were just coming up for a visit. I didn't mention Richard as I told her it was just a bit of a get-together. The cottage Jennifer had rented had four bedrooms, so there would be room for all. I did not want her worrying until we were together, and I could explain everything. She gave me the address, directions, and local phone number if we needed it.

Bob left after giving us his mobile number. We watched him walk down the street. He had parked quite a distance from the house so as not to put us in jeopardy. He turned into another lane and disappeared. No one seemed to be following him.

From there, we headed to my place in Peter's car to pack a few things and then onto Richards'. We had decided to take Peter's car as it was the only one we thought our adversaries had not seen. Once we left Richard's, we headed over to pick up Peter and Pat. We packed up the car as quickly as possible, always keeping an eye open for anything untoward. We saw nothing, and with great relief, we headed to the Highlands.

 It was getting on for 2:30 PM as we headed away from Peter's, to our highland destination. We were now fugitives in our own country. How did this happen? We were in the bastion of democracy and civility. Not only was I a fugitive, but Richard, Peter, Pat, and now Jennifer. Were we making the right decision? Did we really trust Bob Findley? All I could rely on was that we had made the decision together. The die was cast.

 The trip to Ardliu should only take about one and half hours. Traffic getting out of Glasgow wasn't too bad and we soon found ourselves north of Glasgow on the A82 heading towards the highlands and Ardlui. We headed up the western side of southern Loch Lomond. The loch was dotted with small green forested islands and the beautiful Trossachs Highlands starting to unfold before us. Although it was winter, the countryside was still virtually green. We could see in the distance the snow capped summit of Ben Lomond looming before us. The grandeur of the highlands was unfolding; it felt like nobody could find us in this wilderness. So far, our escape had gone off without a hitch. We still nervously watched behind us for any sign someone was following us, so far nothing.

We had not gone much further when Peter indicated, "There seems to be a road block up ahead. I think I can see flashing police car lights."

"Oh no, what now?" Richard nervously lamented.

We all looked ahead and could see police cruisers lights about two dozen cars in front of us. We had the Loch to the right of us and no turn off to the left, just heavy forest. Behind us, we could already see about four or five cars. We were stuck.

Peter and Pat were riding in the back of the car, Richard turned towards me and said, "What are we going to do now? Do you think it is us they are looking for?"

"Let's not lose our cool, we don't know what they are looking for and I don't believe it is a car full of holidaymakers," I added.

We inched forward and after what seemed to be an eternity, we finally arrived at the roadblock. There were half a dozen police cars blocking both sides of the road. A policeman approached our window.

"Good afternoon sir," greeted the officer, "may I see your driver's license?"
I took out my wallet and handed it over to the officer, "is there a problem constable?"

"Where are you headed?" asked the officer. "Is this your car?"

"No, the car belongs to my friend who is sitting in the back. We are heading to Ardlui, the Caisteal Lodge, just a few day's getaway with friends," I answered, "what is going on?"

"May I see your hotel reservations please and car ownership," demanded the officer.

I had no reservations, but thinking quickly I added, "My wife is already there, she made the reservations under her name, Jennifer Flint, my name is Gregory Flint. I'm sure if you called the lodge she will verify our reservation. Is all this necessary, what is the problem?"

"Could you open the boot of the car, please?" the officer demanded.

I flipped the handle to the boot to open it. The officer was already there peering into the boot. There was nothing there but our luggage.

Peter asked Richard to look in the glove compartment for the car registration and ownership. The officer came back to me and I gave it to him.
"One minute sir, I'll be right back," answered the officer ignoring all of our questions.

"I guess he was checking our luggage to see if our story held out," Pat added.

"Shit, I don't like this at all," answered Peter. "Mind If I take off for a stroll through the forest?

"Peter sit still and calm down," Pat admonished.

We sat dead quiet watching the policeman head over to his car and radio ahead. We waited about fifteen minutes when he headed back to us.

"Shit, what if Jennifer is not in, what then," Richard was anxious. " I never thought I would be afraid of our own police force."

"I'm sure the hotel will have the reservation," I tried to calm Richard.

The policeman headed back to the car and handed the license and car ownership back, "Thank you, sir, it all checked out. Sorry for the inconvenience you may go."

Again Peter asked again, "What is going on?"

"Just a routine check," answered the officer, "please move along".

 We drove slowly off.

"That was close," Peter nervously added. "I think I still need that walk in the woods to take a poo."

"Pat, do you think we could leave him in the forest," I asked jokingly.

"Yes, but he wouldn't stay. What do you think, was this due to the death of Chief Inspector James Adam?" Pat asked, completely ignoring Peter.

"Most probably,but they weren't looking for us,a carload of tourists heading for the highlands,"Peter answered."Looks as if Bob was right we have bought ourselves a bit of breathing space."

We continued north up the west side of Loch Lomond without further interruption. The beauty of the Highlands revealing it's self at every mile. Even in the winter, the greenery was everywhere, from the dark green of the evergreens to the softer greens of the bracken. Up ahead, the massive snow-capped peak of Ben Lomond stared down at us. We finally arrived at Ardlui and pulled into the parking lot of Caisteal Lodge. I called Bob and left a message, as he had requested, that we had arrived, just the word arrived. Jennifer had been watching for us and came down to greet us.

"Hi Pat and Peter," Jennifer welcomed us; "this is an unexpected surprise, and now Richard as well. Greg did not tell me you were coming."

"It was last minute, just a little getaway for a couple of days," Richard answered, "I need a break from all the mess I have. I hope it is not an imposition?"

"Of course not it is lovely to see you all. Did you know the police called here to verify you are staying here?"Jennifer asked."What's going on ?"

"Yes. Sweetie," I hugged her to me and kissed her lightly on the lips, " we were stopped at a roadblock just outside of Glasgow," I answered, " there has been a high profile murder of a police inspector in Glasgow. I think they were checking for suspects."

"How horrible," Jennifer interjected, "how did it happen? I'm a little out of touch up here. With the mountains, TV reception isn't the greatest."

"We'll tell you all when we get settled." I countered.

The lodge chalet complex was modern and comfortable with beautiful views over Loch Lomond and adjacent marina. We headed into the cottage. Jennifer directed us to one of the three bedrooms assigned to us and there we dumped our luggage.

We gathered in the little sitting room, Jennifer had prepared a pot of tea and advised us she had made reservations at the nearby Ardlui Hotel for six o'clock. It was now getting on for five o'clock. The hotel was just a short walk away.

"So what is this I heard? Something about the death of a high ranking police officer. All I heard was it looked like a car accident," Jennifer said, as she poured the tea.

"I wonder if that is how the police are reporting it for the moment," I added. "Maybe, at this point, we are the only ones who know the truth. Jennifer, we are all involved in this."

"I know, the police called here when you were at the roadblock to confirm your booking," Jennifer said.

"No, Jennifer, listen, we are actually involved in the murder," I said looking her straight in the eyes.

"What! No, you couldn't be. That is impossible, what do you mean? " stammered Jennifer. "Please tell me you are joking."

"Sit down, it is a long story," I began to relate everything from the fire to Richard giving me the ancient confession. I told her that Richard had been attacked, his office ransacked and his house broken into. I went on to tell her of our finding the letter by Charles Rennie MacKintosh which led to the Queen's Cross church and the recovery of the second ancient relic. I told her we did not have the artifacts with us, and that they were being held safely with our solicitor. And finally, the death of

Chief Inspector Matthew Adam and our meeting with Bob Findley, who advised us to get out of Glasgow and join you.

"We are being tailed by dangerous people who would do anything to get our find. Bob will explain further, he will be meeting us here later," I explained. "He feels the police have been compromised and could be a threat to us."

"My God, Greg, how could this happen," Jennifer replied, "I've only been away for four days. It just doesn't sound possible. Now, you are telling me you are not leaving it with the police."

"Well, we did at first, none of us liked it and now we have to make the best of it, trusting in Bob Findley. I'll tell you the police connection during supper," I answered. "Now, speaking of supper, we are all hungry. I suggest we make that 6:00 pm supper reservation at the hotel."

We all walked over to the hotel and settled down for a much needed supper. Jennifer was quiet; I could tell this had been unsettling for her. The food was good and plentiful. We washed it down with a couple of bottles of very nice wine. We were starting to feel a little relaxed. I told Jennifer we felt that the police had been compromised and on Bob's suggestion it was better to get out of town and let things settle down. Not quite the truth but I would let Bob explain that one.

"Who is this Bob Findley, how is he involved?" Jennifer inquired.

I told her of our meeting with Mr. Findley and his connection with the artifacts, "I know it is a stretch but we have put our faith in him for the moment."

"How do you feel about this Pat?" Jennifer asked.

 "Much the same as you, totally overwhelmed, but we are sticking to the plan, we have all agreed to this and to tell you the truth I don't know what the alternative is. Bob Findley will fill you in on the rest. I do get a good feeling about him."

 It was now getting on for eight o'clock and all we wanted now was to get ready for a good night's sleep. We all chipped in and paid for the meal with cash as Bob suggested. No credit cards to trace our movements. We headed back into the lodge.

"I'll put the kettle on for ....!" Jennifer stopped in mid sentence. She was staring at a complete stranger sitting in our little living room.

I held Jennifer back by the arm. "Jennifer this is Robert Findley, the gentleman I was telling you about. Apparently, doors and locks are of little concern to him. He has a habit of doing this."

Bob stood up smiled and offered his hand to Jennifer. "Please forgive me, I have asked everyone to call me Bob. Sorry for the dramatics but I like to make as little fuss as possible. I didn't think it was the best approach to come knocking, so I snuck into the back. I do apologize for alarming you."

"Anything new?" I asked Bob.

"Not much," he offered, "Inspector Bliss has made an arrest, or should I say holding someone of interest. I think it's a lead on the arson at the library. I don't think it is a real solid lead. With Chief Inspector Adams gone I think they are scrambling for anything."

"Have the police made it known to the public that Chief Inspector Matthew Adams was murdered?" I asked.

"No not yet, just saying the accident is still being investigated," Bob replied.

"We were stopped at a police roadblock just outside Glasgow. The police were quite mum about what was going on," Peter interjected.

"I know," added Bob, "I was also stopped. I told them I was heading on to Inveraray. I have a reservation at the George Hotel. I told them I was touring the highlands on a scotch tasting, at different distilleries. After he lectured me about drinking and driving he let me through."

"So what's our course of action now?" I asked Bob.

"First of all I want to go over everything with Richard, from the time he found the Molay confession to being attacked at his office. Everything, names, and any small details you might have missed or not thought important," replied Bob. "Let's start with the finding of the confession."

"Well, the metal box with the confession was brought to me in my office by one of the restoration people after the fire. I don't know his name," answered Richard, "but he worked for the Lannard Construction Company. They won the contract. We have worked with them on other occasions."

"Was he the only one that found it?" asked Bob.

"Yes, well no, there was another standing just outside the doorway to my office. One of our students, what was his name, Brian, Brian McMell, yes Brian McMell," added Richard. "Is that important?"

"Maybe, what else?" as Bob made notes.

"I remember him, Brian McMell, asked if he could take the box down to the inventory storage. He seemed rather insistent," Richard added.

"Good, good, anything more?" Bob asked as he was scribbling down more notes.

"I opened the box and tried to read what I thought was some sort of missal. It was Latin and I couldn't make it out so I locked it in my desk. The next day I called Greg as I knew he could read Latin and asked him to meet in my office. Greg suggested the pub, The Tartan, for lunch. I declined as I was up to my neck in everything and did not have the time. I gave Greg the Latin document to translate. I don't read Latin. I'm starting to repeat myself, aren't I? Well anyway, Greg couldn't stay, he asked if he could take it home and decipher it. I agreed and gave it to him and we departed rather quickly. Oh, one other thing, I gave Greg a pass slip for the missal to show the police guard outside. I do not know that officer's name."

"Was there anything else in the box?" Bob inquired.

At this point, we all looked rather sheepish. Richard looked at me waiting for me to respond.

"Go ahead Richard tell him," I responded. "In for a penny, in for a pound. We must apologize we have been keeping things back."

"There was a silver skull ring, silver markings showed it was Victorian, and a letter from Charles Rennie MacKintosh asking Iain McLellan to secret away the Molay confession. It also alluded that there was a further manuscript hidden at Queen's Cross. I later gave this to Greg. The police were asking the same questions, was there anything else in the box? We did not tell the police of our further findings," Richard confessed.

I butted in at this point, "Bob, we have not been quite upfront with you up until now, but really can you blame us? Here is a copy of the letter."

Bob read the letter and then again read the letter out loud. "Do you know what this means? Any idea what the Queen's Cross refers to?"

"Yes," I answered, "Richard figured out that one. The Queen's Cross refers to the Queen's Cross Church in Glasgow, the only church Charles Rennie MacKintosh built. In that church, we found what states there may be the scripted trial of Jesus before Caiaphas and Pontius Pilate." I handed him the copy of the vellum Templar's inventory sheet, Peter translated the Latin for Bob.

I gave a slight nod to the group indicating that was all we were going to reveal. I did not tell Bob that we also found a tubular leather case that may contain the actual trial.

Bob was stunned at our discovery. He couldn't take his eyes off it, finally he turned to us.   "This could be the discovery of the century, maybe the greatest discovery of the last two thousand years. This is immense. Are you sure you have it safely secured? Do you have any idea as to the whereabouts of the the scripted trial?"

I lied and advised Bob we thought that it was probably still hidden somewhere in the church.

I did assure him that what we did have was safe and that it could only be released to us or the authorities if anything untoward was to occur to Peter, Richard, or myself. After that, I related the rest of the story up to the point when we met Bob.

"Alright," Bob interjected, "this makes it even more imperative that we get you all to a safe and secure place. I said you were in danger earlier, this only confirms that all of us are in great peril. Getting back to youRichard, can you remember anything more the day you were attacked in your office?"

"I got to my office just before 6:00 AM. I had been doing that for the last three days trying to clean up some things after the fire. It was most overwhelming. That day, the same as usual I parked in the school parking reserved for staff."

"Anything unusual around the school that morning or the parking lot?" Bob inquired.

"No, not really, wait, there was a van. I thought it belonged to the restoration fire crew. I remember thinking they are in early," Richard added.

"The van," Bob prompted, "what colour, advertising, size, license plate, anything?"

"Now I remember, it was a small van with Hertz rental advertising. Is that important?" asked Richard. "I didn't get the license plate number as I didn't think it was important at the time."

"Could be, any clue, could help," responded Bob. "Now relate to me anything you can remember entering the building and your office."

"I punched in my entrance code and entered the front door, all was quiet, nobody about and then I started up the stairs to my office. Again, nobody about as I came to the second floor, my office is on the second floor, all was quiet, no wait, I did hear voices a muffled conversation. The voices were brief; I didn't think much of it at the time. I started to unlock my office door, it wasn't locked. That was odd, I always lock my door. I walked in, bang, bright lights and I was down for the count. I must have been out for about twenty minutes, when I came to I dialed 999. I had a terrible headache and the office was in a terrible array, books, draws and papers flung all over the place. Is this of any help to you?"

"Yes, I think this was partially an inside job. Who had the code to open the main front door and how did they get the key to your office door? The men in your office, there must have been more than one as you heard a conversation. I believe they were outsiders but someone let them in. Also, we can follow up on the van rental now that we know it was a Hertz rental. Also, I have a name to follow up, Brian McMell. We will just have to see where this all leads. Do the police have this information?" Bob asked.

"I'm ashamed to say that what I have related has only come back to me now, so no, the police will not have all this information," Richard answered awkwardly.

"That's normal after a very stressful incident, especially a head injury," Bob added sympathetically. "I have a bit more information. I'll have to leave you for a couple of hours. Just stay put, I will knock three sets, first two knocks, then three, three knocks, and then the third, four knocks. Do not open the door to anyone else and again no phone calls and no credit cards."

With that, Bob left into the darkness of the evening. He was gone as quickly as he had arrived. It was already after 9:30 PM.

Jennifer piped up, "Well, do we go to bed or wait up for Bob to return?"

"You all go to bed," I said, "I will stay up and wait for Bob. I think we need to get a good night's sleep."

I made myself comfortable while everybody else went off to bed. I turned off all the lights and sat in darkness. Peter came back into the sitting room.

"I'll wait with you," Peter offered, "I can't sleep. There is some red wine in the cupboard would you care for a glass?"

Peter poured me a glass of wine and one for himself. "What the hell have we got ourselves into?" I asked Peter.

"I think we will see it through to the end," answered Peter. "The girls are acting very brave, not a complaint from either one."

"We have got damn good wives and we have put them in danger," I added.

"We haven't put them in danger, it is events that have put us all in danger," Peter consoled. "I think once the police have this sorted this out we can all go home. I don't think we will be here for long."

We sat up and waited. I nodded off to sleep for about twenty minutes waking up abruptly.

"It's alright," Peter quietly spoke, "I have been watching, nothing untoward."

"Thanks, Pete I didn't think I was so tired."

"When do you think we should tell Bob of the trial find?"Peter asked.

"I don't know, but I think events will eventually dictate that," I replied.

Just then three knocks followed by another three knocks and then four knocks. Peter was up first, slowly opening the front door and letting Bob in.

"Don't turn the lights on. We have to go," Bob spoke urgently, "I think our cover is blown. The green Land Rover is parked over by the Hotel. They probably think we are booked over there at the main hotel. They are probably already checking it out. Get everybody up and packed. I don't know how long we have. Peter get your car, bring it around to the back. We must be packed and ready to leave from here as soon as possible."

Peter went out to his car and brought it around to the back. I roused everybody to pack and leave immediately. Bob was back in about fifteen minutes.

"I bought us a bit of time. I think they are going to be a bit annoyed, I jumped started someone's car and parked it right behind them, they are blocked in. It will take at least a couple of hours to sort that one out. Are we ready to go? My car is parked beside yours Peter, it is a grey Jeep Cherokee. You will be following me back down the A82 then turning right on the A83 straight through to Inveraray. It will be about an hour's drive. If for some reason we get parted I have booked four rooms at the George Hotel in Inveraray under the name James Morton. I know the hotel and the people, we will be well looked after and protected. As you leave, no headlights on the car until we are away from the hotel. No point signaling our departure."

We headed out of Ardlui, it was dark, I could see the green Land Rover with a car parked right behind it. No one was around it but it could go nowhere until the car behind it was removed. I had to chuckle at Bob's deviousness, looked like the act of some discourteous person. We headed back down the A82, lights finally on, once we were out of sight of the hotel. The countryside was pitch black. Thick dark evergreen forests on either side, only our headlights picked out the road ahead and Bob's Jeep. We found our turnoff and followed Bob onto the A83 through some of the loneliest countryside in Britain. A quick check showed there was still nobody behind us.

Soon we were coming down out of the highlands to the broad sea Loch Fyne. The salty air hit us almost immediately and then the cozy lights of the harbour of Inveraray broke the inky blackness of the night. The harbour twinkled with the lights reflected from the town onto the sea. Little fishing boats were safely moored all over the harbour. It was tranquil and the air was mild, a most welcoming site. We followed Bob along the harbourfront road and soon found ourselves parked in front of the welcoming George Hotel.

Bob was waiting for us and advised us we should park behind the hotel and then meet him in the lobby. "Let's not advertise we are here."

Bob was waiting in the lobby and advised us, "Your rooms are ready, I suggest we book in and try to get a good night's rest. We will meet in the hotel restaurant for breakfast at say 9:00 AM tomorrow. I believe we have shaken off our tail and it will take them some time, at least two to three days to figure out where we are, so you are safe for the time being."

We found the George Hotel warm and charming; the air was scented with the warm fragrance of wood fires. The Hotel was full of old world ambiance and there was a lovely glowing fire in the bar lounge. We booked in and true to his word the hotel was ready for us. Soon we were ensconced in very comfortable rooms, ready for a good night's rest. It was already 1:00 AM.

"Are you all right, Jennifer?" I asked.

"I'm tired and afraid; I just need a good night's sleep. Just come to bed with me and hold me tight," she pleaded.

"That is exactly what I had in mind," I answered smiling, with my arms around her.

Just then a gentle tap on the door, three, three, and then four. Bob was knocking. I answered the door.

"Just came to see you were all comfortable and have everything you need," Bob queried. "I've just checked up on everybody. It has been a bit of a harrowing night."

"Yes thank you, Bob, we are just off to bed," I answered. "Everybody else ok?"

"Yeh, everyone is fine, see you in the morning then. Don't worry, plans are already in place for our next leg of our journey. " Bob answered and left.

"I have a good feeling about him," Jennifer added, "now come to bed with me.

"I wonder what the next leg of our journey will be?" I mused.

Jennifer cuddled in tight to me, resting her head on my shoulder. I held her close and she soon fell into a deep restful sleep.

After a good night's sleep and a refreshing shower, we met the next morning for breakfast. Bob was already there and so was Richard. We made ourselves comfortable at the table and soon Peter and Pat arrived. We were all famished. Breakfast was sumptuous as only a good British breakfast could be. Ayrshire bacon, eggs, black pudding, kippers, grilled tomatoes, and fresh warm baked bread. We ate our fill. Finally, the table was cleared leaving only our coffee service of two large silver coffee pots and one pot of warmed cream.

"First things first," Bob started, "I gave Richard's information to my contacts before we left Ardlui. I have heard back this morning and my contacts are confirming the Glasgow police have been infiltrated. Inspector Bliss has followed up on the van rentals and has some new leads. We think Inspector Bliss can be trusted. He has also put a tail on Brian McMell your student. Bliss has also requested help from the Edinburgh constabulary as he feels the Glasgow constabulary has been compromised, but to what degree he doesn't know. This is being done all very hush, hush."

"Are we safe here for the time being?" asked Richard. "Do the police know of our whereabouts?"

"Yes, for a couple of days at least and that is all we need," answered Bob. "We have a lot of friends here in Inveraray that are looking out for us. And, to answer your last question, no the police do not know of our whereabouts. I want to keep it that way for the time being."

"So what is the plan now?" I asked. " First, we need to get some fresh clothes and toiletries. There are a couple of nice shops in town that I am sure can accommodate us. Get yourself some good warm clothing.

The hotel can clean what we have on at the moment. I have all the cash you need, don't use credit cards, they can be traced. Once we are ready to travel again I'll give you the rest of the plan. Shall we meet for supper here in the hotel say six o'clock this evening?"

It was nice to get out and walk in the harbour town. Inveraray was bordered by the highland mountains and dark evergreen forests. Everything seemed so normal after the last three days on the run, but I still could not get out of the habit of checking to see if anyone was following us. Peter seemed as nervous as I was. As it turned out nobody was following us. We soon picked up everything we needed including a couple of changes to supplement what we had packed. The monies Bob gave us was more than enough to cover our needs. Nothing untoward happened that day. We had a light relaxing lunch at the Argyll Bar. We sat taking in the stunning views of the surrounding countryside. The weather was still mild, it almost felt like we were on vacation. We soon found ourselves back at the George in our rooms. Time to relax for about an hour. Just before 6:00 PM we freshened up and headed down to the lounge bar. The bar was polished wood paneling and stone, in the fireplace there was an inviting warm fire. Bob was already there, sitting at the bar sipping a fine Scotch.

"One of my small weaknesses, a good scotch and of course I am lost for choice here," Bob beamed. "This one is only eighteen years old, just a baby."

It was probably the first time I had seen Bob look a little relaxed.

We joined Bob at the bar and ordered our favourite aperitifs. I was also given all the monies that were left over from our shopping, which I handed back to Bob.

"Keep it, Greg, you can be our purser for light expenses. If you need more just ask. I trust you found everything you needed in the town."

We all agreed we had and pressed Bob for more information as to our next destination.

"First let's have supper, I have taken the liberty of ordering this evening's menu," Bob added, as the waiter came in and indicated our table was ready. He led us to our table in a little private room.

We were greeted at our table by the wonderful aromas of a carved medium rare Black Angus prime rib roast. There accompanied it was roast potatoes, roast parsnips, brussel sprouts marinated and sautéed in sweet cider, and finally golden roasted miniature Yorkshire Puddings. There were pots of horse radish and gravy boats full of steaming wild mushroom gravy. Bob had also selected three bottles of Californian Merlot. We were all instantly famished.

"Before we eat," interrupted Bob, "something a little appropriate for the occasion and where we are."

Bob started, "Some have meat and cannot eat, and some that want they have none. But we have meat and we can eat and so the Lord we thank him. We also ask him for protection and safe passage to our destination."

We all said amen, cheered, and clapped.

"Well done Bob and thank you," I offered, for the traditional Robbie Burn's, Scot's grace.

"Now let's tuck in," Bob added, as he offered the beef to the ladies first.

"I feel like this is the last supper for a condemned man," Peter added nervously.

"The last supper here," Bob answered, "but we will talk about that after dessert."

We soon finished our supper which was outstanding. We were feeling quite replete when dessert was served, a steaming sticky pudding with Sauce Anglaise. It was light as a feather and believe it or not we had room for it as well.

"Bob, on behalf of us all," I offered, "thank you for a wonderful evening and supper."

By this time we were all feeling quite comfortable and trusting with Bob. He was turning out to be a reliable and trusted friend, so we hoped.

Bob thanked us for the vote of confidence and then directed us to a little snug bar with a warm glowing log fire and comfortable deep cushioned chairs; we were finishing off with fine scotch and liqueurs for the ladies. We were feeling very comfortable and relaxed, almost safe, after the harrowing events.

I turned to Bob and asked, "How did all this hatred for what we found start?"

Bob sat staring into the fire, he took a moment and sighed, "Where do I begin? The political foundation of the original thirteen colonies really started with the English Civil War that deposed King Charles. Parliament under Oliver Cromwell was to rule the British Commonwealth without a monarch. Unfortunately, this went south after Cromwell died and his son took over and did very badly. The country was in an uproar and finally, King Charles II was reinstated as monarch. The royalists were back in power. So, where did the protestant parliamentary survivors go? To the colonies, this started the beginning of New England, the Thirteen Colonies or should I say the beginnings of the United States. The original colonies were founded on the principle to be a new protestant elected Parliamentary commonwealth, although much of this was hidden. The Masonic movement played a pivotal part in its early development. As you may know, George Washington was a mason as were many of the founding fathers. There was a real hatred against the Papist Church of Rome and the colonies felt threatened by it already. Catholic New France was to the north while Catholic Spanish Hispaniola was to the south, two countries Britain had already terrible wars with. With New France conquered by Britain, that threat was thought to be diminished, but Britain guaranteed the religious rites of conquered New France. The colonies felt betrayed by the crown and still threatened by Rome. The colonies were ready to unite into a commonwealth for self preservation and defence. Britain countermanded this making the colonies feel further threatened. Now at this time before the overthrow of King Charles I, New England Masons had in their possession one of the copies of the confession of Jacque de Molay and knew that there was a further Templar document in Scotland. They wanted to release the document and by doing so, they thought, it would condemn the Church of Rome. They thought it would cripple the Church and start a renaissance with the Protestant movement. Mother Killwinning Lodge, the oldest Masonic lodge in Scotland plus the Aberdeen Lodge, voted against this revelation as Britain was having trouble with their Stuart Catholic Kings. Time wasn't right politically. There was a sect within the New England Masons that still wanted to go ahead and reveal the confession. With the civil wars in Britain with the Crown and Cromwell, the time politically was still not right. After Cromwell, the Stuarts were brought back. Would Britain be Catholic or maintain its' protestant stance? Again not a good political situation to start destabilizing the crown. The New England colonies were under more pressure now with France pushing up the Mississippi River from New Orleans. They felt surrounded, New France to the north, Spain to the south, and now France cutting them off to the west. Bitterness was fermenting especially since Britain would not allow the colonies to unite against this threat; so, the movement for independence was born." Bob stopped for a moment staring into the fire taking a sip of scotch. "Then came the Hanoverian Monarchy and Parliament banned the Church of Rome from having any political say in Britain, that sparked the Jacobite rebellion in the Scottish Highlands, to put a Catholic Stuart on the throne. More turmoil and again not a good time for the Masons to release their secrets. When Britain defeated the French in Canada, they guaranteed their Catholic religious rites plus maintaining Indian land treaties, thwarting westward expansion. This threw the New England colonies into revolt."

"Are you saying, Bob, that this was the beginning of the American Revolution and not taxes and the Boston tea party?" Richard asked.

"This more than anything, not taxes. Don't forget the colonies were founded by the Puritans, the Quakers, the Baptists, the Methodists, and the Masonic movement. George Washington was a mason, so was Ben Franklin right up to Roosevelt. The colonies had enough of the religious turmoil in Europe. They wanted a Protestant region free from Rome and Europe. The Revolution solved their problem, they were free and free to expand."

"So why the continued hostilities?" Richard again asked.

"The American Revolution was more a civil war, Englishmen against Englishmen. George Washington considered himself an Englishman. Brother against brother, family against family, this is where the bitterness really started. Some within the Masons still wanted to destroy Roman Catholicism even though the revolution had founded a Protestant nation. They had the Templar confession and knew that a further far more damaging evidence existed in Scotland. The destruction of Rome with the release of the Templar evidence was a double edged sword. The breakaway Masons knew in destroying Rome with their evidence it would also have drastic effects on their biblical beliefs. They knew even then that the evidence they had was so powerful it would rewrite the bible or destroy theirs. So the best course, destroy the evidence. This has been going on for over two hundred years. This finally comes to a head with the Second World War. There were literally thousands of Americans on UK soil, so a little bit of undercover work has led to where we are today. One camp for openness and truth, the other to destroy and hide. This is where we find ourselves today. Money also plays a huge part. Some religions in the USA are a huge multimillion charitable entities, all tax free. The religious group in the United States that are after us is huge, both in numbers and money. Any challenge to this, resulting in loss of congregation, would have detrimental effects on the bottom cash line."

"My God such an ancient grudge," Peter added.

"Yes, pushing us onto the next leg of our journey," answered Bob. "We are leaving tomorrow by boat, a small boat, for Brodick on the Isle of Arran."

"Why by boat," I asked the slightest bit alarmed.

"We can't go back the way we came. They are probably looking for us up north, so we cannot go there. It will take them a few days before they start looking west and we don't trust going south back to Glasgow. That leaves us to go further west and west is the Mull of Kintyre peninsula. To get off the peninsula we need a boat and by boat, we have multiple destinations. Should throw them off for at least a week," Bob responded.

"Are they that well organized?" queried Richard.

"Yes they are," answered Bob. "They have been setting this up for a long time. They infiltrated us back in the USA and here in the UK. The Glasgow police have been compromised. Richard was attacked and we have one murder, Chief Inspector Matthew Adams. They knew exactly when the Molay confession was discovered and acted on it immediately. They were able to set up the break-ins and almost stole the Molay document. They are very well organized and dangerous. On the plus side, Inspector Bliss has tied the van rental to two arson suspects and probably the break-in at your office and home, Richard. Brian McMell your student that was there at the discovery of the Moray document has gone missing and is now considered a suspect. We have clipped their wings a little bit."

"What about our cars?" Peter inquired.

"As I said earlier we have a lot of friends here in Inveraray. This is the ancient domain of the Dukes of Argyll, again friends, high ranking Templar Masons. Your car will be safely hidden away until you can safely retrieve it," explained Bob. "You don't have to worry about that."

"What about me?" Richard asked. "They will be wanting to know my whereabouts at the School."

"Inspector Bliss has taken care of that, advising your head injury will still need time for convalescing," Bob advised.

"Arran is an island," I added, "we will still need a boat to leave from there. Where are we going from there?"

"You're right Greg; from there at least we will have a bigger more comfortable boat to get us to our next destination. Where that destination is I don't know. We are trying to keep this as secret as we can. The fewer that know the less chance of being compromised. I will get instructions once we arrive in Arran. We will be leaving first thing in the morning at 5:00 AM. That is the usual time the fishing boats head out and we will look like one of them. No one will suspect. It will also be dark so less prying eyes," Bob explained. "So I suggest we head off to bed as we have an early start. We'll meet at reception at 5:00 AM."

"One other thing, Bob," I interrupted, "are the police aware of what we are doing?"

"No, as I advised earlier, not at this point. They are aware that I am with you and have a plan to keep you safe. They want to find the mole in their organization first so nothing of our whereabouts is leaked out. Now I suggest we head back to our rooms and get a good night's sleep. See you in the morning."

We all made our way back to our rooms. The thought of leaving this gracious and comfortable sanctuary was not pleasing, but I knew we couldn't stay here.

"I love this place." Jennifer announced, "When things settle down and are back to normal we have to come back here for a real holiday."

"Yes, we will make a plan when this is all over, I promise. I just wish it was all over now. Now I am just tired, better get to bed, we have a very early start."

"Me too," Jennifer agreed, "the bed looks so comfortable."

I don't remember much after that, we just put our heads down and we were gone in deep slumber.

Jennifer and I were up at 4:00 AM the next morning. After showering and dressing we met everybody down at reception. Bob led us dockside and introduced us to Alex. Alex loaded our luggage and helped us board a small gig. Bob assured us this was not our transportation to Arran. Alex ferried us out to a small fishing boat. It was a chilly morning and still very dark. There were at least two dozen fishing boats getting ready to head out. We looked like just another fishing boat heading out. Bob had said the fishing boat would be small and he was right, only about a forty footer. We were helped aboard by the captain, Roy, and first mate Andrew. That was the crew.

"This is our captain, Roy," Bob informed us, "and while on board he is in charge and then after that the first mate Andrew. If all else fails then you will defer to me."

"Not as ominous as it sounds," Captain Roy interjected in a broad highland accent. Captain Roy looked hale and hearty, with a ruddy complexion as red as his hair. "Trip will take four to five hours depending on the weather. We have a crisp westerly, but we are sailing in sheltered waters, I don't forecast any problems. Make yourself comfortable below. Bob had the hotel make some sandwiches and hot tea for the voyage. If any of you are prone to sea sickness we have motion bands you can put on or, motion sickness pills. There is foul weather gear you can put on if you're feeling cold. Now excuse me, as we will get on our way."

The engine started up and Andrew released us from our mooring buoys. It was still dark as we started to leave Inveraray. Those welcoming lights of the harbour and town were drifting away. The only comfort was that we were part of the fishing flotilla heading out to sea; their lights were all around us. In the distance, we could just make out the dark silhouette of the hills against the starry skyline. I had made up my mind, once this was over, Jennifer and I would return to this little sanctuary.

"Come down and have some breakfast, "Bob shouted up over the drone of the engine." Who needs motion sickness pills?"

Pat, Jennifer, and Richard requested motion sickness pills. Jennifer preferred the sea bands as they had worked for her in the past. There was a brisk sea wind and the salty smell drove the diesel smell away. Bob had also laid out the sandwiches and was starting to pour the steaming hot tea from the large thermos the hotel has supplied. It was most welcome and for a while, we sat in silence eating our breakfast while the boat gently undulated in fairly calm waters.

"Bob, do you believe the police suspect anyone of us?" I asked.

"I don't know," Bob answered, "but I think if we turned ourselves in, we would certainly be held in custody and interrogated. They may find our story too fantastic and until we can prove ourselves we will have opened up ourselves to our enemy. If they got Chief Inspector Matthew Adam they can get us. We will eventually turn ourselves over to the authorities but I want to do it on our terms. Are you still with me?"

"Yes, Bob, I have to admit I am," I confirmed with him, "you haven't led us wrong yet."

"Are you all in agreement?" queried Bob.

We all looked around at one another and one by one we all nodded in agreement.

"I think we should tell him," I looked around at the others.

We all turned to Bob and silently nodded in agreement.

"Well go on Greg tell him," Richard pushed.

Bob gave us all a quizzical look, "Tell me what?"

"Peter has never been to sea," I quipped."And we are all worried about him."

"Oh, now you are worried about me," Peter chimed in. "What happened earlier when I was feeling so fragile?"

There was a momentary silence followed by a chorus of belly laughs that lasted at least five minutes. The quizzical look on Bob's face didn't help either, but it broke the tension.

"Sorry Bob, we needed a little light hearted banter, but, on the serious side, we think we found at Queen's Cross, Charles Rennie Mackintosh's church; the last part of this riddle. What we found in a safe, buried under a flagstone in the churches' cellar a leather cylinder containing a description in Latin. The Latin inscription described that the lead cylinder contained the original manuscript of Jesus' trial before both Caiaphas and Pontius Pilate. We do not know for sure as we do not have the expertise to open the lead cylinder. The cylinder does have the Templar's skull imprinted on it."

"My God you people never fail to astound me. This is huge if what you have found turns out to be genuine. I had no idea this existed, but some within the Masonic Templars believe documents do exist that confirm your find." Bob exclaimed. " Is it safe?"

"Bob, it is with my solicitor in his safe, held in a safety deposit box. Right now it is as safe as it can be."

"Good," Bob replied. "But I will tell you now, nothing is safe in Scotland. If these people cannot get it they will destroy it by whatever means they can, even destroying your solicitor's office. Somehow we must retrieve these precious items and take them with us. Let me think on this and I will put a plan together and let you know."

"Christ," I exclaimed, "I had no idea at the time that I would put my solicitor in danger."

"I doubt they will be that stupid at the moment," Bob responded. "They may suspect, but I don't think they will show their hand that openly, but, we must get it back. They probably think that we have it with us at this moment."

"Bob, I feel like we have been stupid, but at the time we didn't know," I pleaded."No one was to know until I came on the scene," Bob calmed us. "And maybe I was a little late."

Richard then turned to Bob, "After what I have been through and I know we all feel like escaping refugees, but I feel safer in your hands than anyone else at this time. I think we all feel that way."

"Thank you very much, it is very humbling to know you have put so much trust in me. I will do my best to live up to that reputation and not let you down. You must remember also that it is not just me, there are many people putting things in place and looking out for us."

"What are we doing on Arran once we get there?" asked Peter.

"All I know is that we are booked into the Auchrannie Hotel in Brodick for one or two nights. I have been out of contact with my people since we left Inveraray as we are trying to keep mobile phone use down to a minimum or not at all. They are too easy to trace," Bob warned us.

After our briefing with Bob, Peter and I headed up on deck. By now the sun was just starting to come up. We could start to see the heavily forested hills on either side of Loch Fyne and to our starboard, we were just passing a group of small islands.

"That's Lachlan Bay and those islands have been a grave to many a boat in the spring high tides," our captain offered as he made his way forward. "The tide is so high and swift it submerges some of the islands and drags boats onto them. But I think we are all right now. We can see the islands and the tide is taking us out. It's not the first time I have sailed this way and it is certainly not springtime."

"He didn't sound too convincing did he," Peter whispered to me.

"That's the highland way. They never overstate things and it's awfully hard to ruffle them," I tried to reassure Peter.

"Have you ever been to Arran?" I asked Peter.

"No never been to Aran; up until now never been to Ardlui, Inveraray, and certainly never sailed down Loch Fyne. If it wasn't for the beauty of the place don't know if I would want to do it again. I just want to go home," Peter confided to me.

"So do I, Peter. I do think we are doing something monumental and I think we are doing the right thing."

"I don't know," Peter replied, "do you think in a hundred or two hundred years' time it will make any difference? Maybe our religions will have run their course, maybe they will be obsolete. So what will it matter?"

"You may be right, but to subjugate the truth and commit murder while doing this is definitely not right. We must try to stop them," I replied. "I truly believe we are doing the right thing."

"And with any luck at all we will," replied Peter. "I just hate what they have done to all of us. To me it is personal."

The sun was up now shining through the clouds over the green forested hills in the east. We turned to port as the loch opened up to a much wider expanse and the waves became a little more choppier. Peter and I headed back down to the warmth of the galley and poured ourselves some more hot tea. We sat comfortably with the girls, the sea gently rocking us. I think I even drifted off for a while until I was awakened by Bob.

"Come on people, you don't want to miss this," Bob called from above on deck.

We came up on the starboard side of the boat. Bob indicated to the right hand side of the shore.

"There lies Skipness Castle ancestral home of the Clan MacSween, imposing enough but look over the sea to what their view is," Bob indicated pointing across the sea. "That is the Isle of Arran."

The castle was imposing, but the view of the Isle of Arran was magnificent. There set in the green sea was this beautiful island, crowned with snow capped peaked mountains. Thick dark green forests cloaked the mountainsides down to the sea. Mists crept through the upper mountain valleys. Here was an enchanted island and we watched her spellbound.

"We will be docking soon," Bob announced breaking the spell. " There should be a car waiting to take us to the Auchrannie Hotel. All the rooms have been reserved under

different names. We will sort it all out in the lobby," Bob informed us. "For the moment we are all using aliases."

It was now 11:00 AM as we motored up to the dock. With the help of a shore man, we moored to the dock. We all disembarked and as Bob informed us there was a van waiting to take us up to the Hotel. The driver helped us load our luggage. Bob sat in the front, the driver handed him an envelope, and started to drive to the hotel. Bob opened it and quickly read it.

"It seems that I am assigning your rooms under the guise of a tourist director. The hotel staff are friends and are aware of our predicament. They will do what they can to help and protect."

"Is there anyone you don't know?" Pat asked Bob. "I am utterly amazed at your organization on such a short notice.

"Well, as I told you, we have a lot of friends here in the Western Highlands and most of them are connected to the Lodge," Bob informed us.

We were soon in the lobby of the Auchrannie Hotel. Bob had received our keys and assigned us our rooms.

"We'll meet for lunch, say, around 1:30 PM," Bob directed, as we headed off to our rooms.

The rooms were spacious and most comfortable. We had a view of the gardens and the mountains in the background. It always amazed me that in these northern climes, the gardens had a large collection of subtropical plants. I flung myself on the bed and just stretched out. Jennifer came and sat down beside me. I pulled her to me.

"Just a minute Mr. Flint, we are not on holiday we must maintain a serious disposition," Jennifer twinkled at me.

"I'm very serious, just come here and I'll show you how serious I am," I coaxed her and pulled her into my arms.

For the next hour, we forgot about everything except the intimacy of ourselves. After, we lay there embraced, totally relaxed, and even drifted off for about an hour's nap. Finally, we washed and dressed and then started down for lunch.

"You know we loved Inveraray," Jennifer was looking out the window, "but this island is gorgeous. I don't know which to choose."

"When the time comes, my love, we will do both. You live in a country all your life and don't appreciate the beauty that is right on your doorstep. I think it is time we started exploring." We all met for lunch at the appointed hour. The restaurant was very attractive and the staff made us feel very welcome. We had a light lunch and Bob informed us that his people knew were now safe on Arran. Our next move was being planned at the moment and we would probably know by this evening.

"I have some further news," Bob announced, "the van rental has been found and Inspector Bliss has the van at their forensics lab. It did have trace of explosives and a fire accelerant. The renters of the van were caught on in-house video at the rental office and have been identified. A couple of local no goods, police have them in custody. The trouble is they are both dead, strangled."

"Shit!" Peter hissed, "Three murders now and right under the nose of the police."

"They're getting desperate," Bob added, "I don't think they wanted things to get so out of control. This is when they will make a mistake."

"I'm lucky I'm not the fourth," whispered Richard. "Anything further on the student Brian McMell?"

"Not on my watch, Richard, I'm here to look after all of you," assured Bob, "and no nothing yet on your student. I suggest now we go back to our rooms and stay there. If I need you, I will come and knock on the door; the same code knocks. Make sure we are fully organized for our next move. If nothing else happens we will meet for supper at 6:00 PM. I should have further news and our next move."

"Bob I don't know about the rest of us but Jennifer and I could do with a walk around the grounds just to unwind."

"Alright, not a bad suggestion," Bob replied, "just stay close to the hotel grounds. Keep to yourselves as much as possible."

We all went back to our rooms and unpacked. After, we took a leisurely walk around the extensive hotel gardens. It did us the world of good; the weather was pleasant and the scenery magnificent. The mountains climbed up to snow peeked tops that contrasted the dark evergreen forested slopes. We didn't meet anyone on our walk, but then again, at this time of the year, the hotel was nowhere near full.

"I could stand here all day and just take the scenery in," Jennifer sighed. "We will one day I promise, but we better get back to our rooms."

After that, it was just a matter of waiting and resting until supper. Jennifer had bought a couple of magazines plus the Scotsman paper down in the lobby. I read the paper thoroughly but, found nothing relating to what we were going through. After that, I put my feet up and watched a bit of television. I think we both nodded off for a bit; with all the stress we needed it. Finally, Jennifer and I headed down to supper. We met in the lounge, Bob was already there sampling a fine Arran single malt.

"Hello," he called over, "come and join me. I can highly recommend this Arran scotch."

"Don't mind if I do," I answered, "how about you Jennifer?"

"I'll have a sip of yours, Greg, but I think I would rather have a glass of red wine," Jennifer requested.

Our drinks came just as the rest of our party entered the bar. Peter and Richard ordered the same scotch while Pat had a glass of white wine.

"Any news?" Peter asked after his initial sip of scotch.

"Yes," answered Bob, "but, let's enjoy supper first and get down to business afterwards. I have ordered supper again and they are ready for us."

Supper was wonderful, and again, was served in a private room. We started with a creamy potato soup, followed by grilled salmon and roasted pheasant. The salmon had a lovely sweet and sour white gooseberry cream sauce while the pheasant was served with a spicy Cumberland sauce. There was a medley of roasted carrots, parsnips, and baby potatoes accompanied by buttered sweet peas. This we washed down with three bottles of a fine Australian Chardonnay. Nobody really wanted dessert but, we were coaxed by the staff to have a little raspberry sorbet. After that, Bob ordered a couple of carafes of coffee with pots of warmed cream.

Once we had been served the coffee Bob got down to business, "We are staying in Arran overnight. We will be leaving early, 7:00 AM tomorrow morning. The van will be here and pick us up at that time and take us down to the dock. From here we will go by boat to France. We will also have some backup aboard; won't tell you who until we have boarded but, they will be traveling with us. Greg, I want you up much earlier tomorrow morning. We are going to take a quick trip back to the mainland and retrieve your precious articles from your solicitor. Meet me tomorrow morning at 4:00AM. I want you to phone your solicitor this evening. Do not use the hotel landline, use my mobile, it is untraceable, tell him to meet us at five thirty am at his office. A matter of life and death. Tell him to put the extra time on his bill. I will look after that, just give it to me."

"France!? Is that necessary?" Richard asked.

We were all taken aback by this latest news.

"Why not London and Scotland Yard?" again Richard asked.

"It was considered," Bob replied, "but they will be looking for us there first and by boat it will be faster to go straight across to France. We know the Glasgow constabulary has been compromised. It would not be difficult for them to place someone in London if they have not done so already. Sailing to France should buy us extra time and completely throw them off our track. This we feel will be the best plan. Greg and I will head off early to the mainland tomorrow and be back for our 7:00 am departure."

"Now, are we all ok with the next step?" Bob asked, "Any questions?"

There were none, as by now, we were completely in Bob's hands. I called my solicitor and after cajoling him with the importance of the meeting plus the added fee, he agreed. I advised him of the importance that he tells no one of our meetings. I explained we were transporting ancient antiques to the Glasgow Hunterian Museum. God, it was getting too easy to lie. Once I had informed Bob, we headed off to bed for an early morning rise, especially for me.

Both Bob and I were at the dock at 4:00 am the next morning. I should have been tired but the adrenalin was flowing and I was pumped. I told Bob about my conversation with my solicitor and he was not too happy about it. I explained it was a matter of extreme importance and secrecy. I told Bob that I had advised my solicitor not to speak to anyone about our meeting as we were taking ancient articles to the Glasgow Hunterian Museum for safekeeping until the Glasgow School of Art was ready. He did eventually come around as I told him to put it on my bill as overtime.

"Good," Bob replied, "I doubt he would suspect anything other than what you told him plus he will be out of harm's way once we have the articles."

 We made our way down to the dock and were greeted by what was to be our captain for a fast trip back to the mainland. He led us down to the end of the jetty to what I can only describe as a cigar boat. It was still dark, black as coal and the boat was also black as coal.

"We should be there and back within two hours. Now, all aboard," Our captain commanded.

"How fast will she go?" I asked a little nervous, "And how can you see where to go?"

"She will easily cruise at 50 knots, but can easily open up to over 80 knots," our captain offered, "just depends on how calm the waters will be. As for navigation, it is all GPS. We could be blind as bats and it will still get us there within five feet. Now buckle yourself in."

be. As for navigation, it is all GPS. We could be blind as bats and it will still get us there within five feet. Now buckle yourself in."

Bob and I buckled ourselves in. We gently cruised out into the open sea about one nautical mile, then, all I can describe as a rocket launching herself into the heavens. I sunk back paralyzed with "G" forces into my seat. I felt like an astronaut being rocketed into outer space. The twin engines growled like satanic monsters being released from the bowels of the earth. We cruised with no running lights, which made me even more nervous as the boat was black as coal and literally invisible.

"We have no running lights," I yelled to Bob.

"I know," Bob replied, "just a little illegal precaution. No one can see us, but we have a very advanced GPS and radar system. We can see everything."

 In less than an hour as we drove through the pitch black night. We were debarking just west of Langbank, a small wooded area on the Clyde. We were met by two men who helped us get to shore.

"More friends of yours?" I asked Bob.

"Yes, we put in a call from Arran to arrange all this. Put these on," Bob announced before we left the boat. "We are now officially UPS men."

Both Bob and I were dressed in UPS overalls, peaked UPS caps, and sure enough a brown with gold lettering UPS van awaited us.

"We want to be as inconspicuous as possible when we pickup at your solicitor's," Bob revealed. "What could be more inconspicuous as a UPS delivery, especially if your solicitor may be under surveillance?"

"I hope I have not put him in jeopardy," I prayed.

"Don't worry," Bob replied, "I doubt they will show their hand there."

We were soon driving down the M8 motorway on our way to my solicitor's in Glasgow. It was almost 6:00 AM, still dark. Bob pulled up outside the office and parked. He handed me a large cardboard box.

"Have your solicitor place the items in this box. If we are being watched it will look like an ordinary UPS delivery and pickup. Nothing out of the ordinary, just in case the place is under surveillance. I'll wait for you here, now, take this envelope; the monies inside it should cover his inconvenience. Walk in and out casually."

"Bob, look down the street, there is that same green Land Rover. What do we do now and how would they have known? Do you think they might recognize me?"

"Do the same as I told you, casually walk in as any UPS agent. I doubt they are inside your solicitor's office. As for how they knew to watch your solicitor, it only confirms the police have been infiltrated. The information came from the Glasgow Constabulary. You go in and don't worry I've got your back. Is there a back entrance to your solicitor?"

"Yes, at the back parking lot. It should be open, as my solicitor parks there. His office is on the right hand side as you walk in, front office."

"Ok, I am going in the back way. When you have the articles hand them to me, I will return to the van via the back," Bob ordered. "You walk back via the front door with just your pouch containing a signed invoice of delivery. If you are intercepted you have made an early call to deliver important transcripts for a court hearing today, got that?"

"Yes," was all I could say.

"Don't worry you will be ok," Bob tried to calm me. "Take this UPS ID. You are now John Brown from Motherwell. Take this as well, it is a collaborating driver's license with the same name."

"You really do think of everything," I answered.

"Hopefully, now go," Bob ordered as he pulled down my peaked cap covering more of my face. "There, it is hard to see your face now in this light. Don't worry, I'll be there watching every movement."

I walked into my solicitor's office, the sweat trickling down my back. I thought for sure they would see how nervous I was. The transaction took no more than fifteen minutes, although my solicitor was taken aback by the costume. I told him one day I would explain everything, but for the foreseeable future, keep this very confidential. We went to the safe which he opened and then with our keys we opened the safety deposit box and retrieved the contents. I settled with him his billing as Bob walked in. I told my solicitor not to worry as he was a friend. I handed the box and contents to Bob and left the office. I started to slowly walk back to the van. As I got to the street I was intercepted by two men.

"Morning sir, out early?" One of them asked.

"Yes, you startled me," I answered. "We have a twenty four hour service when needed. Can I help you?"

"Just a routine police check," the other answered. "We have had some suspicious movements in the area. Do you have some identification?"

"May I see your police identification first? You can never be too careful these days," I answered, not knowing where the courage came from.

"Sorry sir we should have done that right away," they both showed me their Glasgow police identification cards. One, a Sergeant Black, and the other a Sergeant Mike Crothers.

"Thanks, I feel much better knowing you are police," I handed them my UPS identification card.

"Mr. Brown is it?" One of them asked.

"Yes, John Brown," I answered not trying to look too nervous.

"I see you have a partner in the van. It takes two to make a delivery?" the officer asked.

"Yes, company policy when delivering at night," I answered, thinking quickly. "We have had break-ins at night."

"Can't be too careful these days, can we? Well Mr. Brown may I ask what you were delivering?"

"I believe they were court transcripts for a hearing today. Apparently very important as you can see by the hour of the delivery" I answered.

"Do you have a receipt for the delivery?" the one called Sergeant Black asked.

"Yes, signed by the solicitor. It's right here," as I showed it to the policemen.

"Very good sir, sorry for any inconvenience, but we do have to check things out."

I turned and walked to the van as casually as I could hoping they would not see the trickle of sweat running down my back.

Bob was waiting outside the van casually leaning on it and smoking as if he had no care in the world.

"Everything alright?" Bob queried.

I nodded my head. "Solicitor was still a little upset wanted to know what was going on but I think I calmed him down. He did happily, except payment for the inconvenience but there is

still quite a bit of money left in the envelope. Bob, they were our own Glasgow constabulary; Sergeant Black and Sergeant Crothers, I can't believe it. I can now really see the danger we are in. Anything untoward out here?"

"No, if we are under surveillance they certainly are not suspecting us. I made sure no one saw me come back to the van. One of the officers did get out of the car after I came back from the office, but when he saw me smoking casually by the van he started walking back. That's when you came out. A little bit of bravado nearly always pays off. Saw them talking to you, but you seemed to handle it very well. Nice bit of detective work getting the police names. That will come in handy. They are making little mistakes, to our advantage. Anyway, let's get the hell out of here."

"With pleasure," I answered, "one thing though, I didn't know, you smoked."

"I don't," Bob answered. "It makes a great prop. You would be amazed what the offer of a cigarette will get you."

Soon we were cruising back down the M8 motorway, nobody was following. The green banks of the Clyde came into view. The sun was just coming up. It did not take long before we were back in Langbank. We were helped out of our overalls and into our speedboat, carefully securing our precious cargo. We cruised slowly down the Clyde for approximately five nautical miles, past Greenock, and then we let fly. We were cruising through a calm sea at just over fifty knots an hour. It wasn't long before Arran came into view and we were docking at Brodick harbour. It had just turned five after seven am. All this had transpired in just over three hours. It felt much longer and it was good to see the rest of the crew waiting at the harbour.

"Our next leg of our journey; on to France," Bob indicated, "now that we are here all safe and sound I am asking you to entrust our precious cargo with me. It will be traveling with us all the way under lock and key."

I looked at everybody and could see no dissenting nods. "So we are all in agreement?" I announced.

Both Peter and Richard said yes, with Richard adding, "You have taken us out of harm's way so far and brought us safely here. We are in your hands."

We arrived back at Brodrick harbour just after 7:00 am. The sun had not quite risen, still dark and chilly. The rest of the crew were waiting for us there. Much to our dismay, there was the little fishing boat that had brought us to Arran. Everybody looked nervous and quizzical.

"Bob, please tell us we are not sailing to France in that little dingy?" I begged.

"Have patience, all will be revealed, just have faith, but no, we will not be sailing to France in that," answered Bob, "trust me, I said we would be sailing in comfort. I think there are a few blankets on board to keep the morning chill off."

It was cold, dark, and there was a damp mist hanging over everything. Bob's answer didn't raise the morale, and we glumly boarded, wondering what was ahead of us. It reminded me of the old saying, "The beatings will continue until the crew's morale improves." Captain Roy and First Mate Andrew were there to greet and help us aboard; they seemed in a much brighter mood. Once safely onboard, the motor started up, and the shore man cast us off. We slowly motored away from Brodick harbour, out to sea, and then headed south. We passed an island to our right, which put the island blocking Arran from us. The wind was brisk but light, it was still dark and chilly, but the sea was calm. I was wondering why Bob had not come down with the motion sickness pills. We were all huddled down in the cabin to keep warm, and yes, there were blankets that we snuggled in together. Still heading south for about an hour, we kept the shoreline of the island in view until we reached its southern end; Holy Isle Bob informed us, a small island just off the coast of Arran. From there, we seemed to be heading back inshore, cruising north between the mainland and Holy Isle.

Bob called us up deck side, "Come and see this. I think you will find this interesting."

We came upon deck and could see directly in front of us, about half a mile away, was another much larger ship anchored at sea. We watched as we got closer and closer and the ship became bigger and bigger. She looked sleek and fast, a beautiful ocean cruiser.

"That is our transportation to France," Bob beamed. "She is a Cape Hatteras Motor Yacht out of Chesapeake Bay, on loan to us from some very dear and powerful friends. We have renamed her at present to blend in with local shipping, 'Highland Spirit,' and she's sailing under the British ensign. Three diesel engines with three props; one hundred and fourteen feet long and as much comfort as you could want. From here to our port in France is approximately six hundred nautical miles. Once aboard, cabins will be assigned; then, we will meet for a briefing in the main salon. I trust you are happy with your accommodations."

As we got closer, our spirits soared, she was a beauty, sleek, and rakish. We pulled alongside; bumpers lowered; we stopped at the stern of the ship. A rigid ladder lowered; Andrew helped us disembark while other crew members welcomed us and helped us and our luggage aboard.

Captain Roy came aboard, while Andrew gave a quick goodbye and departed in our little fishing boat.

Once all on board, Bob announced, "The crew will take you down to the lower deck to your assigned cabins. Your luggage should be there already. It is now 8:30 am; we will meet again up here on the main deck salon at 9:30 am. Breakfast will be served at that time."

We were all speechless as we were escorted to our cabins, this was luxury only dreamed of. Teak paneling and polished brass fittings everywhere. We had a luxurious queen-sized bed, a full, ensuite shower bathroom, a spacious closet, a small settee plus a wet bar with a small stocked fridge.   It also made me wonder what other connections Bob had. This luxury was overwhelming. At that moment, we could hear and feel the diesel engines startup. We were slowly moving.

"What do you think of this, Jennifer?" I asked.

"I just wish it was under different circumstances," she answered, "but it is lovely. It does make you wonder about Bob's connections. Wherever we are going, we are going in style. By the way, how did your meeting with the solicitor go?"

"We got everything we wanted. We were in and out quickly and back to the launch before we knew it. Our solicitor was very accommodating but a little perplexed. I did calm him down," I answered. I did not want to make Jennifer worry about our close encounter with the police.

"So, no trouble at all?" Jennifer quipped.

"No, not really, I was nervous, but Bob handled everything," I lied.

"Well I'm hungry, let's get us settled, and then we will go and have breakfast," I started putting away my clothing. "Plus, I'd like to hear what Bob has to say and who all this extra help is."

We settled into our sumptuous teak paneled cabin complete with a queen size bed, en suite bathroom, and lounging settee. We had a peek at our little wet bar, complete with a generously stocked small fridge. There was also a small writing desk. I could get used to this, just sit back and relax, but no, we set off to meet in the main salon above deck. As we made our way upstairs into the main salon, I was surprised to see Inspector Stephen Bliss and Captain Roy accompanying Bob at the table. Bob got up to meet us.

"Bit of a surprise, Greg?" Bob greeted me, putting up his hand to stop my questions. "Let's have breakfast first. We have a lot to talk about."

I walked over to Inspector Bliss and offered my hand, "I'm surprised to see you here, Inspector. Taking some time off, holidaying, and sailing south with us?"

The Inspector got up from the table and shook my hand warmly and smiled, "It's Chief Inspector now I'm sad to say, I will miss Matthew Adam. I wish it were something as simple as a sailing holiday down to the Cornish Rivera or the Channel Islands. My wife is always after me to come down this way, but this will do nicely. I don't know about you, but I'm starving. Let's have some breakfast; all will be revealed afterward."

One of the crew members led us over to the table. Richard was already seated, so were Captain Roy and Bob. Jennifer and I sat down just as Peter and Pat came up. Now there were eight of us. One of the crew came around offering seasickness pills or sea bands. Another crew member started putting out trays of scrambled eggs, fried bacon and sausages, grilled tomatoes, mushrooms, and warm soda biscuits. Tea or coffee was available along with orange juice. We all tucked in as we felt the ship pick up speed.

Bob started the conversation, "You know Captain Roy McMillen, as before, while onboard he is in charge. Our Captain is ex SBS, for anyone who doesn't know, that is Special Forces Boat Service, one of Britain's most elite and secretive special military units. You are in good hands with our Captain. Except for the ladies, we all know Chief Inspector Stephen Bliss. Stephen will have something to say after I have finished. As I said earlier, we will be on board for about 30 hours. We left early this morning from behind Holy Isle so that no prying eyes could see us board from mainland Scotland. Once we dock at Brest, France, we willhave additional help from the Swiss Guard and Interpol. I'm going to turn the meeting over to Stephen now."

"Well, as you are aware, things have not gone very well for the Glasgow constabulary. We have a mole, and we are going to flush him or them out. This is very personal for me; Matthew was not only a mentor to me but a very dear friend. We have three suspects. I have given each of these suspects different travel plans to meet up with us at a different location. One, I have given plans that we will meet up in a safe house in Glasgow. For the second suspect, we have given plans for a safe house in Edinborough. And the last one, a setup with Scotland Yard's safe house in London. I have in each travel plan a dummy team posing as us, whichever dummy team is intercepted will confirm the mole. The safe house in Edinburgh was the only place that came under attack, so now we have our first look at with whom we are dealing. We staged a fake retreat and got away. No arrests were made; they are not aware we are onto them. Scotland Yard is well aware of my plan, but not all of it. They are keeping it on a need to know basis, keeping those in the know as small as possible. Scotland Yard has supplied backup where we need it. I know this is dangerous. I may have guessed wrong as to who the mole is, but at least we are ready and forewarned. I think this is putting us at the least risk. This boat has a crew of six plus Bob, Captain Roy, and me, all highly trained in anti-terrorist tactics. In Brest, we will also have the aid of the Swiss Guard, who are already stationed in Brest waiting for us, plus Interpol will be shadowing us. When we arrive in Brest, our team will impersonate you and go ashore. We have two highly trained female police officers impersonating Jennifer and Pat. We are providing additional protection just in case somehow they have followed us to Brest. Captain Roy and two other policemen will stay and guard you onboard if our team of impersonators is attacked onshore, Captain Roy will spirit you off the stern of the boat to another high-speed motor launch supplied by the Interpol. From there, we will take to a safe house where we will all join up. Any questions?"

"We have intercepted them at the fake safe house in Edinburgh," Richard pointed out, "why not just swoop down and arrest the whole lot and end this?"

"We only have some of the tentacles," Inspector Bliss answered. "The head and remaining tentacles are still out there. We want the whole organization, which is in the USA, Scotland, and we now know on the continent. Those we uncovered, will lead us to the rest. Then we will end this."

"What if we are attacked at sea?" Peter inquired.

"Highly unlikely, but Captain Roy can best answer that," Stephen answered. "Captain Roy?"

"As Stephen pointed out, there are nine of us all highly trained and very well armed if we are well equipped to handle the situation. We also will have two highly armed speed boats just out of sight, one trailing and one leading us when we sail into French waters. These have already left Brest and will stay with us there. They will be out of eyesight but can be here in fifteen minutes to assist. We agree with Bob that we have bought some time and I doubt they know we are sailing or where we are sailing. I hope that alleviates some of your worries."

"Bob, do any of the enforcement agencies in the USA know what is going on?" I asked.

"The FBI does know, and it is watching The Grand Evangelical Church of the Saviour. They feel this organization is playing it low key in the USA. They feel this group has all its' gang in the UK and on the continent in place. The Grand Evangelical Church of the Saviour is part of a loose-knit paramilitary group in the USA. The FBI is aware of this and has plants in the organization. They are just waiting for them to make a mistake. The FBI only has authority in the continental USA. They have made contact with Scotland Yard. I think Stephen will confirm that," informed Bob.

"Yes," Stephen replied, "that is correct, and as you can see, we are gradually pulling a large net around these people. We are the bait, but now we have become the hunters that are ready to spring the trap on those who hunt us. The hunted have now become the hunters."

"For the time being," Bob announced, "unless there are any more questions, you can enjoy the cruise. Weather looks alright to France. We may pick up some strong headwinds in the Irish Sea just south of Ireland, but nothing to be overly concerned. Lunch will be ready in the main salon at 1:00 pm. One more thing, ladies and gentlemen, could we all meet at the stern, on the flying bridge in about one hour. Wear something warm; you will be outside. Are there any further questions we can address?"

"Where are we heading once we land in France?" Peter inquired.

"That is on a need to know basis," Bob answered. "Even I am not fully informed; it keeps the circle of people in the know small. Less chance of the enemy finding out. Anything else?"

There were no further questions.

"Before we head down, could Richard, Greg, and Peter stay here with me for a few private moments?" Bob requested.

Everybody left except Richard, Peter and me.

Bob lifted from under the table the UPS package we had picked up at my solicitor's and put it on the table.

"This is what we are guarding with our lives," Bob looked at us all.

It was at that moment; the truth came home; this was exactly what we were doing, putting our lives on the line to save something significant for posterity.

Bob proceeded to open the box. With great reverence, he placed the confession on the table first, then the leather cylinder, the inventory sheet, and Charles Rennie Mackintosh's letter. "This is amazing. I have never seen or handled any of these. We being entrusted with a great treasure. Some will hold it as sacred others profane, some enlightened, and others hazardous and damaging. There lies the danger. I trust all we want is the truth."

The articles, as we had placed them, were still all vacuum packed. Bob then brought to the table a large valise. "This is almost bulletproof, and I would, with your approval, store these items in this case. We will then store in the ship's safe, combination, and key given to whom you approve."

We looked at each other, then Peter spoke, "I would be happy with you, Bob, and Richard having the combination and key."

I agreed instantly, and Richard quietly nodded his head in agreement.

"Again, thank you for your confidence. Richard and I will deposit this in the ship's safe. We will all meet as previously discussed on the flying bridge."

 I returned to our cabin to pick up our coats. Jennifer was waiting for me.

"What was that meeting all about," she asked.

"Just wanted to make sure that we were all happy with the security and safety of our find."

"And were you?" Jennifer added.

"Yes, very much so. We are putting a lot of well-deserved trust in Bob and our team. We had better get off; Bob is expecting us up on the flying bridge."

"I wonder what he wants us for on the bridge," I mused.

"I don't know," Jennifer replied, "but let's go."

All of us were on the flying bridge ten minutes later. The sea was choppy but relatively flat. Bob and Steve joined us. It was a little chilly with a steady breeze, but we had a bright blue sky, and we were all dressed warmly. There was a large table to the left of us on which lay five pistols and five, what looked like flak jackets.

"Not to alarm you," Bob announced, "this is just a very last precaution. This is only for onboard; once we leave the ship, these will be returned unless otherwise stipulated. We want you to have some knowledge of firearms. Does anyone have any experience with firearms?"

We all looked dumbfounded nobody had any experience with firearms. We just stood there, shaking our heads.

"Fireworks!" Peter called out with an enormous grin. "I've shot off a few of those."

Bob just shook his head, "where did you find him, Greg?"

"He does come in very handy at times," I laughed.

"I had a Roy Rogers cap gun and holster when I was little," Peter added. "Does that count?"

"So no, Peter," Bob replied, again shaking his head. "Ok, I will take Greg and Jennifer. Stephen will team up with Richard, Peter, and Pat. The first lesson is how to put on a flak jacket. The jacket will stop most rounds from a hand pistol, so make this your best friend. Hopefully, it will never have to be put to the test."

The flak jacket was easy enough, a big body bib vest that covered the full front and adjusted and fastened at the back like a bra. Bob made us put it on and take it off at least a dozen times until we could do it in the dark. Once he felt we were proficient with the jacket, he picked up one small automatic pistol.

"This is a Walther P22 semiautomatic pistol, carries ten rounds 22 gauge, and weighs one and a half pounds. It fires with very little noise and recoil. It is simple to aim and accurate. Before we start to teach you how to shoot, I want you to be able to load, unload the weapon, and be conversant with the safety lock, slide, and cocking procedures. First and most important, whenever handling a firearm, always point the weapon down at the floor and keep the safety lock on," Bob instructed.

Bob made us familiar with the magazine, how to load the magazine, and then load the actual magazine into the pistol. He showed us how to engage the safety and, finally, the slide and cocking procedure, making the weapon ready to fire.

We went over the procedures from 10:30 am right through to lunchtime. Both Jennifer and I were quite proficient, but I must say Jennifer was the better student, even helping me.

 We stopped for lunch, potato, and leek soup followed by a medley of egg salad, ham, and smoked salmon sandwiches, washed down with a lovely steaming hot aromatic coffee. Both Bob and Stephen gave glowing reports to the crew about our introduction to firearms.

"You are catching on nicely; I am pleased with your progress. Now that lunch is over, it is time for target practice," Bob announced. "Everyone up to the stern on the flying bridge again."

We all met up on the flying bridge at the far end at the stern of the boat. Two large target boards were floating about fifty feet away secured by rope to the stern of the ship. On a table were five side holsters containing our Walther P22 pistols, next to the firearms were five ammunition magazines.

"Please pick up your holsters, they are all the same so don't worry which one is yours. Remove the pistols and put your holsters on," directed Bob. We adjusted the shoulder holsters until we were comfortable with the fit. "Now, Jennifer, pick up your pistol and check to see if it is loaded."

Jennifer picked up her pistol, checked to see that the magazine was empty, engaged the slide of the gun to see if there was not a round in it.

"No, it is not loaded," replied Jennifer.

"Good, excellent," Bob answered, "now load it, engage the slide, cock it, and put the safety on. Always point the gun down to the floor when not in use. Now, come and stand by me. Your target is on the right-hand side. Turn the safety off, and keep your trigger finger outside the trigger guard. Lift the gun with your right hand, with your left-hand cup, and support your right hand. Extend both arms keeping your elbows slightly akin bow, and look down along the barrel to the sight, take a deep breath hold and aim at your target, squeeze the trigger, and fire."

Jennifer took her first shot, the kick and firing noise was minimal, she was off by about six inches, not in the least bit nervous. She was enjoying it, grinning from ear to ear.

"Excellent, considering it is a moving target!" exclaimed Bob, "now do the same firing all nine remaining rounds."

Jennifer beaming, fired off the remaining rounds, two hitting bull's eye, the rest no more than five inches away from the center.

Bob was exuberant, "We have a natural shooter. Top marks for Jennifer; now, let's see if Greg does as well."

We practiced all afternoon, even reloading the magazine, we finally stopped at 4:00 pm. Pat and I did almost as well as Jennifer, but Peter needed a little bit more practice.

"It's me eye, Jim boy, no sense of depth, ever since I've had me patch," Peter complained in a Long John Silver accent. "Anyway, me farts are more powerful than this pea shooter and more dangerous. Now give me a flintlock, a cutlass, and some pickled eggs I'll show ye what I can do."

Well, that broke the discipline and tension; everybody was bent over in laughter.

Bob added to the moment, "All right me hearties, down to the main salon for grog. It's time to splice the main brace."

We all headed down, in good humor, to the main salon for happy hour. The bar was well stocked, and Bob did the honours as the barman. We all had a libation and soon felt very relaxed.

"Supper will be at 7:00 pm this evening," Bob announced, "so I suggest we head down to our cabins and get freshened up and relax a little. I want you to get used to wearing your firearms, so keep them on. Also, take your flak jackets and keep them in your cabin."

The sun was starting to set as we headed down. The wind was brisk and the sea a little choppy, but not uncomfortable. All in all, an enjoyable day. We headed down to our cabin.

"Well, how is the champion shooter?" I asked Jennifer.

"I really enjoyed it, but I don't feel very comfortable wearing this thing," Jennifer complained.

"I think you look sexy," as I hugged her to me.

"Oh, you do, do you? Are you just happy to see me or is that a pistol in your pocket?" teased Jennifer as she pressed close, kissing my lips.

"You're a naughty girl, but right now, I want a shower and stretch out on the bed. It has been a long day," I pleaded.

"All right spoilsport, we will swab the decks," she giggled.

We smelt of cordite, and I could feel the sea salt on my skin. A shower was most welcome and relaxing. After we dried and changed, we lay down together and soon fell asleep for about an hour. I awoke first.

"Sweetie," I roused Jennifer, "it's nearly six-thirty, time we made ourselves presentable and headed up for supper. Are you hungry?"

"As a matter of fact, I am starving. I wonder what culinary delight the cook has served up this evening?"

It wasn't long before we were groomed and dressed. We headed up to the main salon and joined Bob, Stephen, and Richard, who were already there sitting at the table. Peter and Pat were right behind us. We started with a light cock-a-leekie soup followed by fish and chips with mushy peas done in ham aspic. The fish was fresh flounder, picked up early that morning from the local Arran fishermen. The fish fried in the lightest of batter. We were all drooling. Bob had supplied a sparkling dry cider and also a marvelous Scottish ale, Keith and Gunn. We sat back and relaxed. A little later, the cook brought in a Scottish Highland desert. He called it Athol Brose, a wonderful concoction of Scotch, Drambuie, strained porridge, honey, clotted cream, and raspberries. We finished it off with an 18-year-old Arran scotch and later coffee. There was also Drambuie for the ladies if so desired. It was desired.

"Must thank the crew for looking after us and a marvelous supper," I said to Bob.

"The crew know the risk you are all taking," Bob replied, "that in a way is thanks enough; they are here to look after you. They are extremely loyal and trustworthy. You could not ask for better people."

"We owe them nothing else but the same," Peter added.

"Any further news?" inquired Richard.

"No, nothing until we reach Brest," Bob answered. "We want to keep radio silence as much as possible. Marine short wave is the easiest to eavesdrop. We have a team waiting for us in Brest plus our Swiss Guard contact. Interpol is also shadowing the operation, although they are keeping a low key, keeping things small. There will be a prearranged password when we arrive. We have tried to cover all bases. Right now, we are about halfway there, somewhere off the coast of Southern Wales. It is now just after 9:00 pm; we can relax up here or if you wish head down to your cabins.

We all decided to keep each other company and stay in the main salon. The sea was still a little choppy, but nothing uncomfortable. For those that needed them, the sea bands were abating the motion sickness. It was getting on to 10:30 pm when we decided to call it a day and head down to our cabins.

Jennifer was in bed first and calling me to hurry up, "Come here, sweetheart I need a little cuddling. We both cuddled into bed and with the gentle rocking of the boat, it wasn't long before we were rocking in sexual unison with the motion of the ship. Our bodies entwined to a sweet climax, a gentle moaning coming from my wife.

"That was lovely," she whispered, "we should go to sea more often. All of a sudden, I am sleepy and ready for a good night's sleep, how about you."

"Yes, you have worn me out, you little minx. I know I will sleep like a log. Are you alright?" I asked.

"Yes, just cuddle up to me, and could you rub my back a little?" Jennifer murmured.

I kissed her shoulders and gently caressed her back. It was not long before I heard her gentle breathing in a deep relaxed sleep. We were now both in a deep relaxing sleep, but not for long.

"Jennifer," I gently prodded her, "wake up."

"What is it? What time is it?" she answered.

"It's 4:00 am, someone is knocking at the cabin door." I got up, slipped into my robe, and staggered to the cabin door, nearly losing my balance, the ship was heaving heavily, "Who is it?"

"It's Stephen, are you decent, may I come in?"

"Hang on a minute," I fastened my robe, struggling to keep my balance.

I opened the door and let Stephen in holding onto the cabin wall for balance. We seemed to be in very rough weather.

"Please get dressed," Stephen demanded. "We have hit some bad weather. Come up to the main deck, also put on your life jackets; they are under the bed."

"Are we in danger?"

"No, not yet, at least, we will probably just ride it out, but it is best to be all together. It is on Captain Roy's order."

We got dressed as quickly as possible; being tossed about in the cabin didn't help. Eventually, we managed and headed up to the main deck.

 Everybody was there, including our Captain Roy. One of the crew inspected our life jackets to see that they were correctly attired.

"We are heading into some easterly gale force winds," Captain Roy announced, "probably up to seventy miles an hour. This storm has developed out of nowhere. At present, we are about forty nautical miles northwest of the Isles of Scilly. We are off the south coast of Cornwall. I do not want to go between these islands and the mainland of Cornwall; it won't give us much room to maneuver. We are going to skirt these islands to the west and then head into the storm. Once we have passed these islands, we will turn east into the storm and push on into the English Channel. The reports say this gale will last at least twenty-four hours. I have decided to make for the Carrick Roads, a deep safe, sheltered harbour in Cornwall. There we will dock at Falmouth. It should take us seven to eight hours. Keep seated up here, in the main salon; try to make yourselves as comfortable as possible. It is going to get a little rough. Are there any questions?" Nobody spoke. "None, good, I am now heading up to the bridge, and don't worry, we will ride this through. I have been in far worse."

Bob added, "Make yourselves as comfortable as possible on the salon couches. Use the pillows to brace yourselves in."

We were just over an hour into the storm when the winds picked up to 65 miles an hour. The ship was slammed with thirty-foot waves breaking over the bow. The crew had supplied seasick bags which were being generously used. Storm cables had been erected around the ship to help navigate through the companionways. We were holding on for dear life. The winds were now howling, and the rain was blowing in almost horizontal. Visibility was down to about thirty feet. Everybody was hanging on to each other, pale, nervous, and quiet. I don't know how he made it, but Bob had managed to come down from the bridge. He was wearing yellow foul weather slicks, but as yet, he was still dry. Bob was almost thrown into one of the club chairs, which were secured to the deck.

"I've been in worse. This Hatteras motor yacht was built for this kind of weather, and you could not ask for a better crew." Bob shouted. "How is everybody holding up?"

"Don't you mean how is everybody holding it in?" replied Peter. "I don't know which orifice is going to give out first."

"Here, little sips at a time, it will help," Bob yelled as he passed around a small bottle of rum.

We all took a little sip, and it did seem to help, warming us up.

"Captain Roy has changed course. The easterly wind is pushing us away from the Isles of Scilly, so we are going to let the wind push us west of the islands. Once past the islands, we will then turn east into the storm and head along the coast of Cornwall. We will steer south past the Lizard and then head up to Falmouth. The storm will get worse as we head into the English Channel. It's still dark but, the GPS shows we have just past Saint Agnes and Saint Mary's Island, part of the Isles of Scilly. We have at least fifty miles until we pass south of the Lizard."

Just as Bob had finished his update, a huge crashing wave hit us broadside starboard. We all lurched to the left, the bottle of rum went flying, as the ship leaned dangerously over. She soon came up and righted herself. Now the howling wind was directly in front of us. The rain lashed into us, obscuring any visibility. We were heading straight into the storm.

"Believe it or not," Bob yelled, "it is better to be heading directly into the storm. It will slow us down, but we have better headway control."

"I know which orifice gave out first," yelled Peter as he covered his face with the seasick bag.

 We were all pale as sheets, hanging on to one another, but believe it or not, Peter broke the strain and got us all laughing again. He even crawled on all fours and retrieved the rum. Moments later, two of the crew members were struggling down from the bridge with Inspector Stephen between them. Bob went over to help and brought Stephen down on one of the lounges. He had a nasty bleeding gash on the side of his head.

"That last wave threw him for a tumble," yelled one of the crew. "There is a first aid kit over on the bar. Can you look after him? We have to head back up to the bridge."

Bob lurched over to the bar and found the first aid kit. The wind was howling now. The ladies had already got Stephen lying down as Bob struggled to return with the first aid kit. Pat had medical training and started to clean and bind the wound. Stephen was conscious but in pain. Pat got Stephen comfortable, placing an extra life jacket under his head while Jennifer tucked a blanket around him. Bob stayed long enough to see Stephen was being cared for and then returned to the bridge. The wind was just as strong, howling like a banshee. Now we were on a full headwind, slowly gaining ground towards our destination. Around 7:00 am the rain started to let off. The sun was beginning to rise in the east just under the cloud cover spreading the sky with crimson red. Red sky in the morning sailor take warning flashed through my mind, but just as quickly, the sun disappeared behind the clouds turning the sky from crimson to slate grey. The wind was still howling, pushing twenty-foot waves into our bow. We could just start to see Lizard Point on the Cornish coast. We were dangerously close to a rocky shore, and the wind was pushing us closer.

"How are you feeling now?" I asked Stephen.

"The head is still sore, but I will be alright," Stephen answered, he was sitting up now. "It's going to leave a beautiful bruise."

"I don't think you have a concussion." Pat reassured Stephen, "But I think it would be better if we keep you sitting up now. I don't want you lying down, try, and stay awake."

"I don't think I am going to sleep in this storm," announced Stephen. "My stomach is all over the place, but thanks for the first aid."

The sun had buried itself in the stormy horizon. The clouds were dulling the daylight. It was still raining hard, and again the winds were still howling, blowing the rain in intermittent sheets. One minute you could see the coastline, the next minute obscured; every time the coast came into view; we seemed closer. We sailed with a heading wind for another hour. We were being heaved into deep green watery troughs burying the bow in boiling waters, then throwing us up to thirty to forty feet on hills of breaking green waves. We all held on for dear life.

Bob lurched down the stairway from the bridge announcing, "we are heading north now using the Cornish headland to shield us from the worst of the easterly gale. It will be rough for the next twenty minutes or so until we are out of a starboard broadside wind. So, hold on!" With that, he returned to the bridge.

We could feel the boat strain turning to port as the wind hit us full broadside. We lurched dangerously over to port. The Captain was gunning the engines for all they had trying to make northern headway. The coastline was closer than ever, but eventually, it was shielding us from the worst of the storm. Things started to calm down a bit. The waves and the wind were not as strong but still dangerous. We all let out a sigh of relief and kept our fingers crossed.

One of the crewmen almost flew down the stairway and announced we would be entering the harbour in one hour. The closer we came to our destination, the calmer the sea. Eventually, we slowly eased into the Carrick Roads, one of the deepest harbours in England. Now we felt safe and let out a rousing cheer. The twin medieval castles of Pendennis and St. Mawes greeted us. One castle was on the right side of the harbour and one on the left, guarding the entrance to the harbour. We slowed and cruised toward Falmouth and finally dropped anchor just off the town; it was now 9:30 am. It was raining gently but the seas were calm in this deep sheltered harbour. I never felt so safe as in this beautiful green banked harbour sanctuary.

Bob and Captain Roy came down to the main salon.

Captain Roy announced with a smile, "Well, that was a wee bit of a bother, wasn't it? Needless to say, we are now safe and sound apart from that nasty bump Stephen received. Are you all right, Stephen?"

"Yes, I am fine now," answered Stephen, "no serious injury, the ladies took fine care of me."

"Good," replied Captain Roy, "the boat received no severe damage, but we pushed her to the limit. I want to do a full diagnostic of her engines before we leave for France. Maintenance should only take a day, provided we find nothing untoward. I'll take my leave and let Bob take over; he has a few things to review."

"Looks as if we will be here today and tomorrow," Bob announced. "I think we will be quite safe here in Falmouth, but before we go ashore, I would like to introduce you to your alter egos. Come with me up to the bridge."

We followed Bob up to the bridge. Our legs were a little wobbly from the strain of the storm, but we did alright, looking like drunken sailors. Bob did the intros, "I would like to introduce you to Mary, Susan, Dennis, Harry, and Fred. Susan and Fred are Americans and are part of my team. Mary, Harry, and Dennis are part of Stephens' team handpicked from the Edinburgh and Glasgow constabulary. These are all highly-trained people who are your decoys when we disembark in Brest, France. Once you are all safely ashore, they will leave and head back to Britain. I will stay on with you and join up with my Swiss Guard contact; When we are ashore, your weaponry will be handed over to our Swiss Guard contact, he will have diplomatic immunity. Once we are away from marine customs, we may give them back to you. That's all, for now, other than to say, we will all go ashore as a team. I suggest we have lunch dockside at a nice little pub I know called the Chain Locker. I recommend it. It will be close to lunchtime once we get ashore. Do not take your guns ashore."

"One thing," Peter asked, "Swiss Guard, why Swiss Guard, that sounds like a Vatican connection."

"He is part of my volunteer team." Bob countered, "We have worked together before. He is one of the best. Let's just say he is on loan to us. Now, how about that lunch?"

Moments earlier, Bob privately pulled Captain Roy aside.

"Ok, Roy, we are going ashore. You know the plan; if our informer is aboard, he will surely try to make contact once ashore. Are your men ready?"

"Aye, Bob, everything is in place," Roy answered. "We will have two teams in dinghies motoring around the hull. It will just look like a regular maintenance check of the hull. They will be in radio contact with a lookout on the bridge, once you and your people are ashore the dinghies will discreetly follow all who come ashore. My lookout on the bridge will direct them. These men know what they are doing; no one will see that they are followed."

"Great, let's hope they play their hand," Bob replied.

It was just Bob, Peter, Pat, Richard, Jennifer and I went ashore in the ship's launch for lunch. We all still had sea legs as we wobbled ashore to the Chain Locker Pub. The pub was right on the dockside, had been around since the mid-sixteenth century, and had a beautiful view of the harbour. It was a friendly stop, lots of locals, warm and inviting. We sat beside the glowing fire, next to a large bay window overlooking the harbour. The harbour was full of ships and boats of every description, from pleasure crafts to a Royal Navy frigate. Over to the far side of the harbour the beautiful green Cornish countryside tumbled down to meet the sea. Lunch was light. I had delicious fresh crab sandwiches. I sat there in an unreal reality; we were surrounded by laughter and good humour of the locals. The thick Cornish accent, sometimes understandable, while other dialects flew over our heads. I didn't want to leave, I felt safe, this was my Britain, but I knew for the safety of the whole group this couldn't last. Almost instantly, as if he was reading my mind, Peter turned to me.

"I don't want to leave, why can't we lose ourselves in the Cornish countryside," Peter lamented.

"I know," Bob answered. "If only it would be that simple, but you know they would find us, putting us all in jeopardy. We will get through this, don't worry."

"Don't worry, Bob," Peter replied, "I'm with us all until the bitter end."

 We were all quite unsettled, having battled through the gale. Although we hadn't eaten, we consumed little. Only Bob tucked into a hearty meal of Cornish pasties followed by a good tot of scotch.

"A walk through the town," suggested Bob, "just might be the thing to get rid of your sea legs."

The gale by now had subsided, leaving blustery winds blowing clouds across a blue sky. The weather now was mild. We were quite surprised to find quite a variety of subtropical vegetation growing around the town, including palm trees. After walking for a good hour, we felt much refreshed. The girls stopped at the local Marks and Spencer's and picked up a few more pieces of clothing. Falmouth was a charming seaside town; little winding narrow streets that nearly always opened up to lovely views of the harbour and the green banks and pastures that bordered it. After a while, we stopped at a little local cafe for a pot of tea, fresh scones, clotted cream, and strawberry jam.

Only Peter balked at the clotted cream, "I don't think I could keep that down. Still feeling a little woozy. Just tea for me."

"Tell me more about your Swiss Guard contact?" I asked Bob.

"His name is Pierre Godet, forty-seven years old, Swiss national. Was training to be a Jesuit priest but decided instead to join the Swiss Guard, rose to the rank of Captain in the Swiss Guard, spent five years on loan with Interpol. Since then, he has been with the Swiss Guard at the Vatican. He speaks German, French, Italian, Arabic, and English perfectly. I trust him highly, and you would be surprised as to whose confidences he shares around the world. I consider him an excellent friend."

"How did you meet him?" I queried between mouthfuls of cream tea.

"In what was then West Germany. I was with the Marines investigating a cold war military murder. Pierre was very helpful; he was working for Interpol then. The two of us slipped over into East Germany several times undetected until we solved the murder. A good man to have in a tight spot. He got us in and out without being spotted."

"I know you will be staying on with us in France. Will this Pierre have a team with him to help get us through?" Peter asked.

"Probably," Bob answered, "but I don't know for sure, and I don't want to know. He knows what he is doing. He is a one-man team all by himself. The less known, the less chance of being infiltrated."

It was now after 3:00 pm as we started back to our launch and ferried ourselves back to the ship. Bob was quite capable of driving the boat. We were met by Captain Roy, who informed us we would be ready to sail by about 7:00 am tomorrow. The ship has had a full diagnostic; there were no problems. Tomorrow morning the weather will be fair. The crossing will take about 11 hours; we should be docking in Brest by 6:00 pm.

"We are sending ashore for fish and chips and Cornish pasties as all hands had been occupied with the ship. You will not get any fresher fish and chips anywhere better than here, and the pasties are quite tasty. Supper will be ready at 6:00 pm." Captain Roy informed us.

One of Stephen's men, Dennis, went ashore to pick up our supper.

After our light lunch and not to mention cream tea, the hunger pangs returned quite healthily. Must have been the sea air. True to his word, Captain Roy's description of the local fair lived up to its reputation. The batter was light and crisp while the fish was fresh off the boats that afternoon. We devoured our supper with relish, washed down with a local best bitter and cider. We even had room to try the local specialty, Cornish Pasties, which consisted of half-moon flakey pastries filled with beef, turnip, peas, and a light gravy. As we ate our supper, we heard the twin engines come to life. The crew was busy casting off lines, and slowly we started to move out into the harbour of the Carrick Roads. It was then that Captain Roy appeared and announced, "We are just heading over to refuel, top up the water tanks and pump out the bilge, will take a few hours, but our departure is still at 7:00 am tomorrow. The weather is holding for a fair crossing to Brest."

After supper, we retired to the ship's salon, still sipping on our beer.

I turned to Bob and asked, "There is still one thing that is bothering Peter and me."

"What is that?" Bob answered.

"We still cannot fathom a relationship or partnership with the Swiss Guard, which is the Vatican and the Masonic Order. The Masons and the Church of Rome. Can you explain that one to us?"

"First of all, you must understand that the Masonic Order is not anti-Catholic. We have had many high-ranking members of the Catholic Church as Master Masons. We do not want to be ruled or dictated by Rome or any church. All are welcome in the Masonic Order as long as you believe in a Supreme Being and are a person of good conscience and standing. Our aim has always been enlightenment through the truth. The Church of Rome has been moving in the same direction for quite some time."

"Doesn't seem that way," answered Peter, "when you look at what is happening within the church."

"I know," Bob replied, "the Church is going through its own evolution. That is why it is reaching out to find the truth. There have been so many discoveries in recent times, uncovering lost religious history. Dead Sea Scrolls, Gnostic Gospels, Gospel of Timothy and Philip, Qumran Copper Scrolls, the coded Gnostic Gospel of Joseph and Aseneth, and many more are just the tip of the iceberg. They are all pointing to a far different history of Jesus Christ, his disciples, and his marriage to Mary the Magdalene. It is not that the Catholic Church did not know of these secrets as we also knew, but now, this cannot be kept from the public and media any longer. The Church is losing ground in the western world. It must go through its second renaissance and reinvent itself and reveal a new truth. We as Masons understand this and support it."

"And what secrets will be revealed in the trial of Jesus?" I added.

"Who knows, but I think it will be earth-shattering. The Christian Church is on the verge of a huge change." Bob added, "Some want it while others would do anything to stop it. They are trying to do it now. We are still in grave danger."

"Can you trust all factions within the Church of Rome?" Peter asked.

"We have been working with the Church for a long time now. Our greatest setback was the assassination of Pope John Paul I. The cover-up was supposedly financial. Remember the Banco Ambrosian? Pope John Paul was ready at that time to announce the acceptance that Mary Magdalene was Jesus' wife and his most revered disciple. Remember, it was not too long ago that the Catholic Church renounced its decision calling Mary Magdalene a reformed prostitute. There was, at no point, any proof that she was ever a prostitute. We all ran for cover at that time, and very slowly we have been working back up. We think we know all the suspects behind the assassination of Pope John Paul and have neutralized them."

"You think?" Peter queried again.

"As far as the Swiss Guard and the Jesuits are concerned and our investigation." countered Bob.

"Do you think the faction that assassinated the Pope is in league with the people we are trying to avoid?" I asked.

"Yes and no, the assassination of Pope John Paul has been uncovered, and persons brought to justice. The people at the top who organized this have been dealt with and are gone. Are there still groups sympathetic? I'm sure there are, but they have so weakened they will not show themselves unless we fail." Bob answered.

"So, they are well established in the USA. They almost caught us here in Britain, and now you are telling me there is a faction within the Church. What kind of odds are we up against?"

"10 to 2 in our favour." Bob replied and added, "I am pretty sure we have outmaneuvered them here in Britain, and I am positive they do not know our whereabouts now. I think they may know we want to get to France. If I were in their shoes, I would be watching all ports of entry to France from Calais to Bordeaux. That's a huge area, so right now, the odds are in our favour. Doubt they will be reaching out to any contacts in the Vatican as they are too weak and could jeopardize their plan."

"If I were them," Peter pressed," I would be looking for all entrances from Germany to France. If that is where they think we are going."

"You are right, Peter," countered Bob, "and that's where we have the greatest advantage. I think they will run themselves very thin, looking in all directions."

At that point, we heard the ship's engines start up again. We were slowly moving out of the refueling area to dock out in the Carrick Roads harbour. The ship slowly came to a halt and dropped anchor rattling until it hit bottom.

"Why couldn't we sail all the way to the south of France?" Pat added.

"We could, but that would take us through the Straits of Gibraltar. That would be the easiest place to spot a ship. And once they spotted us there at sea, we would be the easiest to intercept, board, or sink once they had found us," Bob explained.

"Sink!?" Richard exclaimed.

"One surface to surface missile, and we would be done. No, it is better we change the mode of transport and keep them guessing." Bob replied.

"Bob, do they have that capability, a guided missile?" I asked.

Bob took me aside and quietly advised me, "I don't know, probably, that is why it is best for us to keep our mode of travel changing as much as possible. The one thing I can tell you in strictest confidence, we know who we can trust and who we cannot, that is all I can tell you. Do not breathe this to anyone."

It was now getting on for 10:00 pm. We had no more questions and decided we would all turn in for the night. Jennifer and I headed off to our cabin.

"I don't like that missile comment, Greg. These people are a lot more dangerous than I thought. They are not just thugs but highly trained, organized, and lethal,"

 Jennifer added. "I am afraid."
"I know," I answered, "how did we get ourselves into this mess?"

"We got into it because we know we are doing the right thing. Do you still feel confident we will make it?" she added, squeezing my hand.

"I'm confident in Bob's decisions. He has got us here, and once we land in France, there will be reinforcements. I don't know what the plan of attack is once we disembark. The decoy team will leave first; if all goes well, we go next. And yes, one thing I do know is we are doing the right thing. I also know we can rely on Peter, Pat, and Richard. Funny how heroes come out of nowhere."

"Why can't Interpol take over from here?" Jennifer asked.

"If these people can infiltrate the British police force, what makes you think they cannot do the same thing with Interpol? Bob wants to keep it as small as possible, trusting only those we know. I'm tired of thinking, right now, I just want my bed and my wife beside me."

"Alright, sweetheart, let's get to bed. I am sure things will look brighter in the morning," Jennifer kissed me.

The stopover in Falmouth had been most welcome, but we were still weary. The storm had taxed us physically and emotionally; we both finally bedded down for the night. I nodded off, wondering what tomorrow would bring. We both slept soundly and at the exact time of 7:00 am, we were wakened by the low throttle of the triple engines firing into life. We heard the rattle of the anchor lifting, and slowly we felt the ship moving forward. We were on our way to France.

We both washed and dressed quickly and raced up to the main deck. To the aft of the ship, we could just make out the twin castles of Pendennis and St. Mawes that guarded the harbour, our last glimpse of England, Britain, and home. It looked so green, comforting, and civilized, but it was hiding a nest of vipers.

"Come on, you two," Peter called out, "Breakfast is served, "Probably be our last British breakfast for a while."

We sat down to a hearty breakfast of bacon, eggs, sausages, kippers, fried mushrooms, tomatoes, black pudding, and toast. Our meal was all washed down with a lovely Twinning's English Breakfast tea. As we ate, we watched the rugged English coastline slowly disappear, to be replaced by a golden sunrise over a calm sea.Bob called us up after breakfast to the stern of the main deck for gun practice. We spent the whole morning going through the entire cycle of loading and unloading our Walther P22 before he had us do our target practice. We all found it enjoyable, and it took our minds off the danger. I doubt anyone of us thought we would ever have to use our firearms.

After target practice, lunch was called in the main salon; we dined on ham sandwiches, Melton Mowbray pie, and cheeses ranging from Shropshire Blue, Cheddar, Lancashire, and Cornish Brie. With this, we drank a lovely local dry sparkling Cornish Cider. We were feeling very relaxed.

Bob broke us out of our relaxing revelries. "We will be arriving in Brest on time, 7:00 pm this evening. There we will meet up with Pierre Godet, our Swiss Guard. I don't know what plans he has for us. I do believe your doubles will disembark first, if there is nothing untoward, we will disembark next. Then it is up to Pierre. Just remember our plans are flexible and can change with the situation. One other item, this must be kept secret. Nobody is to talk about it at all. I cannot emphasize this enough; we know who the mole is; he blew his cover in Falmouth. That is all I can tell you at this time."

"Who else knows other than us?" I asked Bob.

"I cannot tell you that either. One thing I can say is it puts us in a commanding position."

"Will you be staying on with us after we reach Brest?" Richard asked.

"Yes, you won't be getting rid of me that quickly. Now I suggest we get ready and pack up. See you all here at approximately 6:30 pm."

It wasn't long before we sited the French coastline. It had been just over five days since we left Glasgow. We were now into March, and I could not help thinking, "Beware the ides of March."

"What the fuck have you guys done," Jed Cassidy was furious. He was addressing a group of five men.

"How in the hell could you kill a cop?" Jed's anger dangerously boiling over. "Is this how things are done in fucking Scotland? I thought you cops were some of the best in the world and not just an ordinary cop you bumped off but the Chief Inspector. Who the fuck did it?" Jed yelled, "Now we have the whole Scottish constabulary breathing down our throats plus Scotland Yard."

All five men were silent. They could not even look Jed in the eye.

"Who was the idiot who did it?" again, he demanded.

Begrudgingly one man moved forward. "I did it. I knew he recognized me and saw me use the entrance code to the school. He must have realized I should not have had the entrance code; he would have blown our cover. When he drove away, I had to stop him. I followed him in my car. It was dark when I drove behind him along the Clyde bank. I made sure nobody was around, then I sideswiped him and drove him off the road into the Clyde River. It happened so quickly; I don't think he realized what was happening. I waited to see if a body surfaced, none did. Later it was confirmed he had been fished out of the river dead. They reported it as a car accident, a hit and run."

"What the fuck is this shits name?" Jed yelled, "Instead of a quiet, clandestine operation, we now have all of Britain's best hunting for us. Makes our job so much god damn easier, doesn't it you ass hole."

"This is Mike, Sergeant Mike Crothers," Sergeant Black spoke. "This should not have happened; it was a mistake. Mike's hands were tied; he is one of our best insiders in the Glasgow police force. Without him, we would be lost; he is our insider as to the police force movements. With Mike, we are still well-positioned in the police force; nobody knows. They have no idea or leads as to the death of Chief Inspector

Adams. Mike is our best contact in the Glasgow constabulary. He has several men inside working with him.”

“Are you sure they do not know who we are and what we are after?” Jed demanded.

“I don’t think they know that we are working with orders from our Masonic group here in Scotland and the USA,” Sergeant Black answered. “Even if they do, they are unaware of us. That is why Chief Inspector Adams had to go. He was probably the only one that could have put the connection together.”

“Let’s fucking well hope so. Where are the artifacts now?” bellowed Jed.

This time it was Mike that spoke, “We don’t know. We thought we had them in a safe house in Edinborough, but they gave us the slip and apparently made it back to the west coast of Scotland. ”

“Shit! This gets better and better,” Jed spat out, “what the fuck do we know?”

“We know now they fled up north,” Sergeant Black reported, “ into the Highlands to a place called Ardlui, from there we lost them. They either went west or east. The road north and south from Ardlui we had watched, we would have seen them on either route. They did not turn up. We think they went west, as later, we think their car was seen in Inveraray, but it was not a positive ID. The car disappeared.”

“How did you lose them in Ardlui, and what the fuck is your name again?”

“Andrew, Sergeant Andrew Black, we thought we had them there. Followed them from the restaurant to their cabin, from there they left. We were after them, but somehow we got blocked in the parking lot. Some idiot parked in front of us. It took the hotel over an hour to track down the car owner. The idiot protested that he had no idea how his car moved to block us in.”

“Well, Sergeant Black, that is one of the oldest tricks in the book. The idiot was you lot,” Jed was livid, “Do we know how many they are?”

“We think there are either five or six, two women, three or four men.”

“You don’t even have a positive ID. Is there anything positive?” Jed snarled.

“We know one of them is Richard McMillan, the director of the Glasgow School of Art. We think one of the other persons is Greg Flint. He is a friend of Richard McMillan. We saw him around the school after the artifact turned up, but we are not sure he is with them,” Sergeant Andrew Black offered.

“I will tell you this one for free; one of the group is Bob Findley, an American, ex-Marine, and a Knights Templar Mason. He is tough, well trained, organized, and financed. He is one fucking headache and the reason they seem to be one step ahead of you lot. Now, do we have anything else helpful?”

“We also have this. It just was received today,” Mike offered a letter, “the letters postmarked Falmouth, Cornwall, three days ago. We have a mole in the group on board. All it says, fled Scotland by boat to Falmouth, from here we are sailing to France, Port of Brest. They have the confession, and something else discovered. It was in a leather cylinder. Only got a glance at it, do not know what it is, but seems very important to them. No mobile phones and radio silence. Sorry for the letter, the only way.”

“Once we received the letter, we sent a team from here to Brest to watch all entries and try and make contact with our mole on board,” Mike added.

"A letter, why not a delivery boy on a bicycle? That was three days ago, they probably have disembarked already," Jed snarled. "Do you guys have any fucking idea where they are going?"

"Not really, but there are limited choices," Mike answered. "We are dealing with religious antiquities. If it were me, there are only two choices, Lyon, France, headquarters of Interpol. They are probably the world's best in dealing with international antiquity crime. My second choice would be Rome if what they have is to be religiously verified and shown to the world. They could also hightail it back to the UK and sail right up the Thames to London; I think this would be their last choice."

"Ok, let's see if we can get this right." Jed was starting to calm down a bit and thinking things through. "I also think London would be their last choice, having run into the constabulary here in the UK. We still have good contacts there in London, although, since this death, they will be harder to use. I think either Lyon or Rome would be their best bet. What would be their route for either destination?"

"Probably, Brest to Bordeaux and then on to Lyon. If it is Rome they're heading for, it would be Bordeaux to Montpellier, Marseille, and Nice; then over the border and on to Rome. Through France, they would probably follow the coast road on their way to Rome," Mike answered.

"Why the coast road," Jed inquired.

"Don't forget they still have a boat and could keep on sailing right down the coast to the river Landes and up to Bayonne. If they followed this route, they probably would not be going to Lyon."

"Shit! All I wanted, was a quick snatch here in Scotland and then I could be back to the US of A. Now we are in France, we have nothing set up there," Jed was frustrated. "I'll have to figure out that one, and that will be costly."

"Look," Mike answered back, "we have infiltrated their group. It won't be long until we know where they are going. We will get them. We already have a team in Brest."

"Ok, if it is Rome, why not just sail right up the Tiber to the Vatican," Jed countered.

"They could if they were going to the Vatican," Mike offered, "but then they would have to pass through Gibraltar. We would spot them a mile off. I think they will keep us guessing and do an overland route. We still do not know their final destination."

"Get me a goddamn map of France and Italy. We do have one?" Jed accusingly asked.

A large map of southwestern Europe was spread out on the table.

"So far," Jed growled, "we still have our contacts in the Glasgow constabulary intact, right?!"

Mike nodded in agreement, "Yes, plus our team in Brest."

"What about Scotland Yard?" Jed queried.

"They are all over the place in Glasgow, helping the investigation into the murder of Chief Inspector Matthew Adam. I know this is not what we wanted, but at least we know what they are up to," Mike replied. "We are getting reports all the time from our people inside, and they are giving them a lot of dead-end leads."

"So we are agreed, with the UK constabulary partly compromised we don't think they will return to the UK and if they do, we will know," Jed offered. "So our choices are either Lyon or Rome, and you don't think they will be sailing right through the Straits of Gibraltar onto Rome."

" We did think of that, but it would take over three times the length of time to get to Rome, and it would be easy to intercept them at sea and sink them," Mike responded, " we believe that speed is of the essence to them."

"We have that fucking capability to sink them at sea?" Jed questioned.

"Yes, we could easily arrange that," Mike answered. "Helicopter and a handheld missile, they would be toast."

"Why did we not blow them up at sea when they left Scotland?"

"We had absolutely no idea where they were at that time," Mike responded, "and we were told not to harm them and get the artifacts in one piece."

"We know who is running their show. As I said, it is very professional and not short of funding," Jed mused. "Who is running the show with the Glasgow lot?"

"Right now, all we know is they have a team from the Glasgow Constabulary. We believe Inspector Stephen Bliss is running that show. Our mole, as of now, is planted in that team. We did guess that there is an American involved somehow. Our people followed them north through the Scottish highlands; we advised them there was an American in their company. Registration at the lodge at Ardliu did not show any name except Jennifer Flint, that's why we believe her husband Gregory Flint is part of the party. We do not have a visual ID on him yet," Mike explained.

 "Well, now we know who the American is, that bastard is Bob Findley. We have run into him before. He is one fucking tough bastard, and as I said, well connected and financed. You have to be very careful with him. I have run into this son of a bitch in the past. That is one I would love to eliminate at any cost. When will we get any news from our team in France?" Jed asked.

"They should be arriving at any moment if they are not there already. Our team will phone from France the moment they disembark. There has been total radio and mobile phone blackout on board their ship," Mike offered. "We have not been able to track them at all. Our mole is the only information we are getting, and that is limited. The last contact, as I said, was Falmouth, England indicating they were on their way to Brest, France."

Jeb banged the table, "I want a second team and myself in the Bordeaux ASAP. I'll get a hold of Claude De Bose in France; he is one of my team. Claude will help us co-ordinate things over there, one of my best men, professional soldier. He has a few of the French Police Nationale on his payroll. Hopefully, he will do a better job than you idiots, no more fuck ups. I want the items retrieved. You can be as rough as you want, but I want them alive. Once we have the item, you can do with them as you like, but quietly. I don't want it broadcast as you did here in Scotland. Do you understand? Now is that all? "

Sergeant Black answered, "The two arsonists, we got rid of them."

 "What do you mean, we got rid of the arsonists?" Jed asked.

"They were dispensable, plus the Glasgow office had identified their van. They were about to pick them up. We wanted no loose ends, so we terminated them. They also kept upping the ante for more money. Eliminating them was not in the plan originally; no one can tie it to us. This was carried out before Adams' death."

"Jesus, I thought the UK was fairly calm, not violent. You guys are like a bull in a china shop. Why could you not pick a more reliable team? I hope you left no evidence. I don't give a dam about them, but now we do things my way."

"Bodies were left in a rough part of Glasgow. We did it quickly, strangulation. No traces were left," Mike answered.

"You better be fucking right on this one," Jed snarled.

"Jed, we have just received a call. They have landed in Brest, looks as if they have all left the ship. The ship is sailing under British colours as the Highland Spirit," Sergeant Black announced.

"Was it them or their doubles?" Jed snapped back.

"There were eight of them, no positive identification yet. Nothing confirmed yet," Mike answered. "One other thing, do we have any contacts at the Vatican if we need them?"

"Yes, but nothing reliable. Things have been pretty tight there ever since the attempts on the lives of two Popes. I do not have direct contact with them either. So, forget about them, plus we won't need them," Jed informed them. "Now, let's get going; I have a helicopter at my disposal. I can be in France in approximately three hours. When we get confirmation that they have disembarked in Brest, I can make for Brest. If not, I will get the Brest team and fly us all to Bordeaux. You keep things under control here. Keep me informed on anything that comes up. No more screw-ups."

"Jed, my boy, what news have you got?" The Reverend inquired.

Jed had called through to the Reverend Ducane on his disposable mobile phone. "They have arrived in France by some luxury power cruiser. Something called the 'Highland Spirit' sailing under UK colours. We have been advised that they have just docked in Brest and gone ashore. They have doubles to put us off. We have a team in Brest to make a positive identity.

"What if it is not them that have come ashore?" the Reverend butted in.

"Don't worry, we will find out," Jed replied, "If it is not them, we believe they will sail onto Bordeaux. They won't slip by us; we will be there to greet them."

"Are you sure they have what we want?" Ducane snapped.

"Yes, Reverend," Jed snapped back. "They have the confession and something else they are guarding very closely. Our mole says it is a leather cylinder. That's all he knows, only had a quick glance at it."

"So two pieces," the Reverend excitedly repeated. "This is it; I am positive. We must retrieve it at all expenses. Jed, you cannot fail us."

"I'm on it, don't worry," Jed bragged. "They won't get away."

Two hours later, Jed was more than halfway to Brest. Two hours after that, Jed and the Brest team of four men were on the ground. The team was in place if they had to fly further onto Bordeaux, France; they had the people ready and were throwing the net wide.

"Cannot raise them on the short wave," yelled Captain Roy. "They are maintaining radio silence." It was 6:30 pm and already getting dark as we approached Brest, still about ten kilometers from shore. Peter, Richard and I were all standing at the stern of the boat, packed and ready to depart. All looked calm as we peered towards the approaching shoreline until Bob ran up yelling.

 "Get down everyone, quick, flat on your bellies," Bob yelled, "arm yourselves we got visitors, get your guns out, on the ready, safety off. Remember your drills".

 "What's up?" I yelled, already down on my stomach. I couldn't believe my reflexes, and I don't remember doing it, but my gun was in my hand, safety off.

 "We are being intercepted by a high-speed motorboat on the port side," replied Bob.

We looked off to the port side to see what looked like a customs patrol boat bearing down on us at quite a speed. By now, we were all down, guns out at the ready. Our hours of training had paid off.

 "Where are the girls?" I scrambled on my belly over to the port side where Bob was crouching, gun at the ready. "Who are they; can you make them out yet?" I asked Bob.

"No, I cannot make out who they are. The girls are safe below. Right now looks like we have a high-speed French Customs boat intercepting us, but why are they coming out here?" Bob was nervous. "I don't like it."

 "Is everybody armed and ready?" yelled Bob back.

"Everybody is ready," called Inspector Bliss.

"Are we going to open fire on them," I blurted out to Bob. I could feel my inners' turning over like jelly. My hand shaking and sweating as I held the Walther, "Not until we see the whites of their eyes," answered Bob calmly. "Just hang on."

"I'm not looking into anyone's eyes, "shouted Peter, "that's a little too close for me. I'm going to wave; if they don't wave back, I'm shooting."

"Easy, Peter easy," Bob shouted back, "hopefully there will be no shooting at all. Just breathe deeply slowly in and out; it will steady you."

 Just then, Jennifer appeared scrambling over on her stomach to my side.

"Sweetheart, what are you doing here? You should have stayed down below."

"I know, but I couldn't," she answered.

"Are you alright?" I answered her back.

"No, I'm scared shitless, but I'm ready, and I'd rather be with you."

I had never heard Jennifer use an expletive like that; it almost made me giggle.

"How about you, Peter?" I managed to call over.

"My mouth is so dry I can hardly spit, and my bowels are so fluid they wish they could trade places. Other than that, I think I am doing quite well. What do you think, Greg?"

"You're my hero Pete; you'll do fine. Richard, are you ok?" I called over.

"Yes, no, I'm sweating like a pig, and it's running into my eyes. I can barely see, just tell me where to shoot. I'm hoping the noise of the gun will scare them off."

I wasn't sure, but I think I heard Peter chuckling to himself.

What a bunch we are, I thought to myself.

Just then, Captain Roy yelled down, "Stand down, it's Pierre Godet, our Swiss Guard. I can see him through my binoculars."

With great relief, we engaged the safety and holstered our sidearms.

Peter broke up the tension yelling, "I didn't pack enough underwear."

"Trust Peter," Bob chuckled, "I never know when to believe him."

It wasn't long before the customs boat had rafted on our port side. Pierre and another gentleman were scurrying up on a rope ladder to our deck. Bob was there to greet them.

"My apologies Bob for the dramatics, but I thought it best to board out here away from spying eyes in the harbour and no radio contact."

"Good to see you, Pierre," Bob grinned, grasping Pierre's hand. "I feel a lot more comfortable now that you are here. Who is your partner?"

"Ah, yes, this is Inspector Jurgen Muller from Interpol. We have worked together, and I would trust this one with my life." replied Pierre.

Jurgen smiled broadly, extending his hand, "That's only when he is drinking."

"Welcome aboard; I would like to introduce you to Richard, Greg, and Peter. They have been the main movers in discovering the ancient manuscripts," offered Bob. "Also, this is Jennifer Greg's wife, one tough cookie."

We shook hands with Pierre and Jurgen. "You are the only reason we are here," Pierre advised. "We are here to protect you and your precious cargo and get you to safety. That we will do and don't believe Jurgen about my drinking."

"I guess we are in your hands now." Bob interrupted.

"Only if you are comfortable with that," Pierre replied. "Is there somewhere private we can all meet? I just want you, Richard, Greg, Peter, Inspector Bliss, Captain Roy, and Inspector Jurgen Muller. "

"Yes, we can use my cabin, the master suite on the main deck. Follow me," Bob indicated, leading them on.

"I need to tell Pat that I am alright," Peter implored.

"Ok," Bob replied, "Steve, can you get one of your men to let her know everything is alright."

"Right away," Steve answered.

We ended up in Bob's cabin. It was a little crowded, but we all managed to find seating either on the berth or on the floor. Pierre was the only one standing.

"As you know, you have a mole in your group here on the ship," Pierre started the conversation. "I will let Inspector Bliss take over from here."

"Yes, it is Sergeant Dennis. I had my suspicions earlier when we saw Dennis send off a letter in Falmouth. I had been watching him for some time. Once we knew, we wanted to use this to our advantage. Bob and I wanted to use the mole, so we had some control as to where the interception might take place. Bob contacted Pierre from Arran as to where we would be landing in France. At that point, we didn't know who the mole was."

"What are we going to do with the mole, or should I say, Sergeant Dennis?" I queried. "I don't get an overall comfort feeling having him around."

"It's alright. He has served his purpose and will be leaving the ship here in Brest with one set of the doubles. I'm pretty sure he doesn't know he has been compromised, but Inspector Jurgen's people will take him down very quietly. No one will know, and I am going to become Sergeant Dennis. I will be our mole in their organization," Inspector Bliss replied. "He does not know that the rest of us will stay on and sail down to Bordeaux."

"Will, they not recognize that Inspector Bliss is not Sergeant Dennis?" I queried.

"No," Inspector Bliss answered, "we have accounted for all of the Glasgow Constabulary that are working for the enemy. What they have in France is a team not connected to our department; these are Jed Cassidy's men, paid French mercenaries. Black and Crothers will stay in Scotland feeding Jed information that we will have intercepted unbeknown to those two."

 "So you can calm yourself, Greg. As far as Sergeant Dennis is concerned, we will all be departing here at Brest. I have also let it out that the women will be sailing back to the UK for their safety. We will do it under the cover of night. He will not know we have not left and when he has figured it out, if he does, it will be too late, Jurgen's men will have taken him down. We will make out he is officially debriefing the case. He will not realize he has been compromised," Bob added.

"What happens when Sergeant Dennis does not turn up in Glasgow? Will they not smell something fishy?" I asked.

"Again, no, Greg," Inspector Bliss answered, "once the doubles reach the UK, they will all be held for debriefing, and that should take four to five days, in complete isolation; no phones, no mobiles. We will be in

Rome by then. If Sergeant Dennis doesn't suspect anything, he may try to make contact either with the Glasgow constabulary or Jed Cassidy's team, and we will be watching, and by then, it will be too late. "

"The doubles will leave at midnight and have been told we will leave an hour later at 1:00 am. I even have transportation ready to further make him believe we are leaving the ship." Pierre stated, "Bob has advised them the ship will leave and sail back to the UK. At this point, nobody knows our plans."

"What will happen to the mole and the others that are acting as our doubles?" Peter interrupted. "Will they be in any danger?"

"Jurgen brought over a team from Interpol; the mole will be held by Jurgen's team first. He will finally be taken back to England for a supposed debriefing and then on to Scotland, where he will be eventually arrested. We will hold him long enough so he will be of no assistance to our enemies. I doubt he will know we are onto him until we reveal he has been compromised. We are hoping he will give us information as to the plans of the ring leaders," Pierre added. "We can be very persuasive."

"If we have discovered and dismantled the enemy, why do we not just hand everything over to the authorities now?" Peter asked.

"We don't know for sure," Pierre answered, "we think we have all bases covered, as the Yanks say, but again if we can keep this small, we have more control and fewer leaks. Cassidy's team in France is still unknown. We are working on that right now."

"Now be discreet with this info, do not tell anyone until we are on our way to Bordeaux. Not even your wives at this point. I would suggest we head back to our cabins and go through the motions of packing," Bob

interrupted. "It will take us approximately 48 hours to sail onto Boudreaux."

We retired to our cabins and went through the motions of packing.

"Greg, I don't like this," Jennifer complained, "we'll be sitting ducks out there being ferried ashore."

"I'm sure that Bob and Pierre know what they are doing. Don't worry; we have got to finish packing."

We finished packing and decided to rest as it was now after midnight.

"I don't know how you can be so calm and relaxed," Jennifer murmured as she tried to stretch out."

I stretched out and put my arm around her and cuddled her close to me. I could hear her breathing start to slow down, and I was sure she would have dropped off if it wasn't for the knock on the door.

"It's me, Bob; you can relax now. We will be underway in a minute. You guys can get a good night's sleep. See you for breakfast."

"What's he talking about, see you for breakfast?" Jennifer had sat straight up in bed, "I thought we were leaving, now where are we going?"

"We are staying on the ship and sailing on to Bordeaux. Our doubles have left the ship to convince whoever is after us that we went ashore. It's a clever divergence. We should arrive in Bordeaux in about 48 hours. We can get some shut-eye and be well rested for tomorrow."

"You knew about this all along, didn't you and let me worry? I think you are enjoying this and turning into an undercover agent right before my eyes," Jennifer pushed her inquiry at me.

"Believe it or not, I hate this, and I hate having put you in this situation. I wish this had never happened. We did this on the advice of Bob and the police. If we all behaved too calmly, someone might have suspected something." I put my arms around her and held Jennifer tightly.

"Don't worry, I know you will always do the right thing," she whispered and kissed me hard. "Come on, let's get some shut-eye and maybe a little bit of cuddling."

Cuddling was Jennifer's code name for a little extra sweet intimacy.

The turbo helicopter was cruising at 250mph at 15,000 ft on its' way to Brest when Jed received a call.

"Jed, this is Mike, we have just received a call from Sergeant Dennis in Brest. It looks as if they have come ashore," Mike reported, "we got a call from your team ashore in Brest that they have left the ship. Our contact reports they may have doubles."

"Is it them, or is it their doubles?" Jed snapped. "Who has come ashore?"

"Don't know for sure. Dennis thinks they have come ashore. He feels the doubles were just a precaution if they were intercepted. They also have an escort ashore to cover them plus transportation. Three black Mercedes SUVs," Mike answered.

"I want a confirmation ASAP, but carefully, no slip ups, but most of all, I want these people alive so that we can confirm they have the goods. We must be able to take them down where we want. They are no good to us dead at this point," Jed growled. "Once we have them, I don't give a shit what happens to them, especially Findley."

 "Now," Jed snapped at the pilot, "how long until we land in Brest?"

"We should fly in and land in about three hours." The pilot answered, "We'll be met at the airport and taken directly to the Port of Brest. We have weapons and transportation waiting there. The pilot was one of Jed's team in France, part of Claude's mercenaries."

"Ok, let's get this going, and once there, I want you to stick around until we confirm they have departed at Brest," Jed ordered. "If not, we are onto Bordeaux."

Jennifer and I woke early, whispering into my ear.

"Good morning, sweetheart," she purred as she slipped her arm around me, "I slept wonderfully. Any chance for an encore?"

"Yes, my little darling, but we have quite an intense day today. I think we better see what we are up to first."

"I know, it was just nice to forget about it for a while," she sighed, poking her tongue at me.

 We washed and dressed and made our way to the main salon. The sea was a little rough; we had to hang on to steady ourselves. We had our sea legs back and made our way up with little problem. As we came up to the main salon, the bright sun hit us, illuminating a beautiful blue sky and glaring white breaking waves. There was also a heady aroma of rich coffee and frying bacon mixed in with a tangy essence of salty sea air.

"Good morning," Bob called.

Bob, Pierre, Stephen, and Jurgen were already seated drinking coffee and examining charts.

"Where are we heading?" I asked as bacon and eggs were served.

"We are heading on to Bordeaux, actually a nice little harbour called Palmyre on the river Garonne, about hundred and seventy kilometers northwest of Bordeaux," Bob answered. "We will get off there quietly while the crew will take the ship onto Bordeaux. Keep them guessing if they have anybody there, which I doubt. Pierre has arranged transport from there. We will be traveling by car to Italy. We should be on board for another 38 hours, so one more night on board."

"Italy, so we are going on to the Vatican," I queried.

"Yes," Bob replied, "Pierre has it all arranged. Don't worry; we are in extremely good hands."

"Do you think they lost our trail?" Jennifer interrupted.

"Likely, but not for long," Pierre answered. "As soon as they realize we are not in Brest, they will probably have guessed we have sailed further on. They will fan out to the ports on this coast. They may already have people watching at different ports. My guess is they will."

Bob turned to me, "We are ahead of the game as far as I am concerned, and I think Pierre will concur with me. As long as we can be one step ahead of them, I think they will finally make a mistake out of frustration; then, we will have them and turn the tables. Now, you two get some breakfast, and after that some more target practice."

We sat down at the salon bar to have our first cup of coffee. In the morning sea air, it was heady and aromatic; an excellent pick me up.

"We'll all have a cup of that, smells wonderful."

I turned to see Peter, Pat, and Richard coming to join us for breakfast. As we drank and ate, I filled in the rest of our group with the latest. After a leisurely breakfast, we all met down on the main deck transom, pistols at the ready. Bob drilled us for three hours, loading, unloading, loading magazines, and finally, target practice. We had an abundance of tennis balls on board; Bob would whip them off the stern, and we would use them as a moving target. Jennifer amazed us all again, hitting three out of ten balls even though they were bobbing up and down in the sea. I was the only one to hit at least one ball. Peter said he was tired of shooting tennis balls, so he shot at seagulls and was convinced he had hit one. We all knew he hadn't. Bob thought it was a cleverly disguised white cresting wave. After, Bob had us dismantle the pistols, clean and reassemble them, three times.

"I hope we never have to use these," Bob was examining one of the pistols, "but as long as you keep them clean, they will serve you well."

After our to-do in Brest, we were taking our practice very seriously. That was too close for comfort.

 We spent another night on board. Supper was quiet as we all knew we were leaving our temporary home the next day. We had been safe and secure onboard; nobody wanted to leave.

 The following day we entered the mouth of the river La Garonne that flowed straight to Bordeaux. We promptly turned to port and headed into the little harbour of La Palmyre, which lay not far from the mouth of the Garonne River.

"This is where we get off," Bob indicated, "a little quieter than Bordeaux and far less traffic. There will be a team waiting for us."

"Where are they now?" queried Jed.

Jed had just been met by his contact Claude De Bose and his team at the airport just outside Brest. Claude De Bose was an avowed Neo-Nazi, he had worked with both Jed and the Rev. Ducane in the past. Claude was tough and mean, Foreign Legion trained. At six foot and two hundred and ten pounds of hard muscle, he had worked with the fringe elements in Europe for over ten years. Had a short stay in prison twelve years ago but now had managed to stay clear of the law, although partaking of many nefarious and shadowy dealings.

"They did come ashore last night about midnight," Claude reported, "but the boat did not dock. I seems it headed back to the UK; at least that was the story. We watched her from shore as she headed back across the channel."

"So, only one team went ashore?" Jed asked as he studied a map of France.

"Yes, that is what they are telling me," Claude answered.

"Doesn't make sense. Why would only one team come ashore, and the rest head back to the UK? If the real people got off the boat, why would they leave their protection behind, unless these are the doubles that got off to trick us? If the real personnel went back to the UK, why would the doubles stay here in France?" Jed mused. "This is a trick, I think, a sleight of hand. They are still on the boat and probably heading south."

"Probably Bordeaux or Lyon," Claude interjected, "if they are still aboard, it would be Bordeaux. They did have a team to meet them in Brest; maybe they feel this is enough. We also have eyes on all major airports."

"Ok, we will watch them in Brest, but I think they are heading south. That is where we are heading, Bordeaux, but I will keep a team here to follow the doubles. I want to know for sure if the boat has gone back to the UK. Also, I have a chopper to fly us down to Bordeaux or Lyon if necessary. You got that?" Jed ordered, "Do we have a team down in Bordeaux there already?"

"No," Claude answered, "but I can have one down there in twenty-four hours."

"Good," Jed replied, "I will have them contact Sergeant Dennis, our mole on board. He will be joining us in Bordeaux if that is where they are."

We waited the next day until dark. Bob advised us Inspector Jurgen had dealt with the port authorities on our behalf. It was 8:00 pm as we left the ship and ferried to the Palmyre dockside. The ride was quiet; we all spoke in hushed tones even though we were in an open boat. Bob had ordered us to keep our weapons coming ashore, Jurgen had arranged this with Interpol. Bob assured us we would not need to use them, although it did not make us feel any easier. We were greeted by four of Inspector Jurgen Muller's men.

Bob turned to Inspector Jurgen, "Did your men bring the special addition?"

Inspector Jurgen called over to one of his men, "Bernhard, do we have the special parcel?"

"Yes, chief," Bernhard handed Jurgen a black valise, "all is in order, you should not be able to tell the difference."

"What's all that about?" I asked Bob.

"Again, Greg, I am sorry, but this is only on a need to know basis," Bob responded. "I promise you all will be revealed to your satisfaction."

At that point, Inspector Stephen Bliss turned to us all, "This is where I leave you. I am now Sergeant Dennis. But, don't worry, I will still be behind the scene watching your every move."

"Where are you going?" I inquired.

"I will be joining the enemy in Brest. I know where they are, and they are expecting me. I should be meeting them in about two hours. I will still be feeding some misinformation to our mole in Glasgow. Put them off the track even more. This should give us at least twenty four hours before they head down here."

 We said our goodbyes, and with that, Inspector Stephen headed off to a waiting car.

We were now twelve. I thought how appropriate as to what we were protecting. There was Bob, Jurgen, Pierre, Peter, Pat, Richard, Jennifer, myself, and four of Inspector Jurgen's men.

"What is the attaché case?" Richard asked.

"Listen, people," Bob answered, "as I told Greg, right now what we have will be considered only on a need to know basis. Eventually, you will know everything. You must leave this with me for the time being. Now I hope we are all packing and loaded for bear. I hope we will not have to use them. I don't think so, but be ready."

"I thought we were out of that kind of danger," Peter queried. "You said we would not have firearms on land. Has something changed?"

"Yes," Bob answered, "we are now tightening the noose. We have become the hunters, and the plan has begun, but don't worry; I just want you to look the part."

"The only part I will look is green," Peter murmured. "They may think I am diseased and that might frighten them off."

"Bob, are we now under the protection of the French Gendarmerie?"I asked.

"It would be the Police Nationale if we needed them, and that would be the decision of Inspector Jurgen of Interpol. Right now, we want to keep things as compact as we can. So no, the French police are not working with us. In other words, too many chefs can spoil the broth. Now let's get going; we have no time to waste. We have a safe house here to regroup and rest for the night. Early tomorrow morning, we drive to our second safe house in Toulouse."

"Why do we not fly from here to wherever we are going?" Jennifer asked.

"Airports are busy places, too many watching eyes. I don't think right now they quite know where we are, and I want to keep it that way," Inspector Muller replied. "Inspector Bliss is going to put them on hold for twenty-four hours with some misleading information until he can confirm our mode of transport. We are starting to control the enemy."

We spent the night comfortably in a small house on the outskirts of town. We each had our bedrooms and enough bathrooms and toiletries to freshen up in the morning. Captain Jurgen supplied us with

EU passports, all with false names just in case we were inadvertently stopped. We also had return air tickets to Glasgow and hotel reservations for the south of France; these were just a ruse to look like tourists. Better safe than sorry, he pronounced.

It was dark the next morning as we all met in the kitchen for breakfast. Nothing fancy, just croissants and coffee, bless Pierre. I don't know where he rounded that up from, but it was good. After breakfast, it was still dark at 6:30 am as we and all our gear loaded into three large black Mercedes SUVs. It had started raining during the night and was still coming down. Bob, Captain Jurgen, Pierre, Richard, and myself were in the leading vehicle. Peter, Pat, Jennifer, and two of Jurgen's officers driving the middle vehicle. The rear vehicle had the remaining two of Jurgen's officers.

"Is that what I think it is?" I asked Bob. He had a black leather attaché case cuffed to his wrist.

"Yes, and it is going to be safe with me."

 "Where are we heading?" I asked.

"Five-hour trip to Toulouse. There Interpol has arranged a safe house," Bob explained.

"Who is this?" asked Jed as he stepped out of his private chopper at Aeroport de Bordeaux-Merignac.

"This is Sergeant Dennis, Glasgow Constabulary," Claude reported. "He has advised us that he has been our most vital mole traveling with them by ship since they left Scotland. It was Dennis who sent the letter from Falmouth."

"Well, Sergeant Dennis, what have you got to tell me?" Jed inquired. "I hope it is not as slow as the letter."

Inspector Bliss, aka Sergeant Dennis, ignored the caustic quip, "So far nothing resembling the description you gave us has entered Bordeaux harbour or Bourg harbour. If they were quietly trying to disembark at these places, I doubt that could be possible. So we are also looking further up the river at Royan and Palmyre. We should be getting a report at any moment. We are also watching the airports as well. We have transportation by chopper or car available at a moment's notice."

"Good," Jed answered, "we will be moving fast. Do they have the relics with them?"

"Although I have not seen it personally, I am positive they are carrying them."

"Alright, the game is on gentlemen," Jed responded.

We were cruising down the A62 to Toulouse; it was dull and raining. The traffic at this time of year was light. Inspector Jurgen was driving.

"We have a plan, believe it or not," Bob piped up, breaking the silence. "We are always at our weakest when we are on the run. We must force their hand, thus exposing them. That is when they are the weakest. I doubt they will catch up to us until Toulouse. Inspector Bliss, aka Sergeant Dennis, will advise them where the safe house is but will give us plenty of time to set things up. There will be two safe houses, one for them that they won't like and one for us, well anyway for some of us. They want this package in one piece, so we believe only minimum force will be used to retrieve it. In other words, they do not want to destroy it; this should work to our advantage.

"Just in," Sergeant Dennis announced the next day.

"What have you got?" Jed snapped.

"Our mole in the Glasgow Constabulary report they are on the way to a safe house in Toulouse. We have the address," Sergeant Dennis reported.

"Alright, I want our team in Brest, and all our people here to all converge on Toulouse. Claude, get us somewhere close to their safe house in Toulouse. I want a nice reception waiting for them. Now let's get back into the chopper and head down there. We should be there before the bastards arrive. Got the buggers now! I don't want any fuck ups, understand. You are all supposed to be professionals, so act like it."

"We will be leaving Jennifer, Peter, Pat, and a couple of police officers in our second safe house just outside Toulouse," Bob announced. "The rest of us will head to the other safe house in Toulouse and await our adversaries. I will need you, Richard, and Greg, with us."

"What could Richard and I possibly do, Bob?" I asked.

"Nothing, except you are possibly the only two they could identify. If you are not there, they may suspect something is wrong. You are our authenticity."

"Are we going to take them down there?" I asked.

"No," Bob countered, "If we try that, we may or may not be successful, and even if we get a few, they will send others. We will still be on the defensive. I want them to think they have taken us down, and then they will leave. If my plan goes well, it will be weeks, if ever, for them to catch up with us. By then, it will be too late. You and Richard will be a little bit of bait but don't worry; we will have you well covered. I promised Jennifer that."

We headed off in the dark in our assigned cars for Toulouse.

It was an uneventful drive from Bordeaux to Toulouse. It was still dull and raining harder, we could not see much beyond the edge of the road and the headlights illuminating the SUV in front of us and the approaching highway. The SUV in front, plus the rain was keeping the windshield wipers working at top speed. We were all tired, anxiety hung over us, and we were not much in the mood for chatting. I still wanted to know a little more about what awaited us. I still felt hunted.

"Bob, I know you have said from now on we will be advised on a need to know basis. Can you not at least fill me in a little as to your plan? I feel so unsettled."

"Greg, Jennifer, Peter, and Pat will be protected in the second safe house. Everything will go down in the false safe house that we will occupy. It will be a grand bait and switch. I have set up a carefully planned sting. Some of Captain Jurgen's people have already set up across the street from the false safe house. They will not make themselves known, but they will be there, and they will be watching us. We know our adversaries are almost here. We are ready to spring the trap. That is all I can tell you for now."

"You said that we are just coming along, to be no more than props," Richard announced. "Is there anything we should be doing?"

"No," Bob replied, "you will be directed into the house as normal. Just follow our plans that is all. Now just try and relax; we will be in Toulouse in about an hour."

"Easy for you to say," I tried to settle down and nod off, but no luck. I had an uncontrollable desire to throw my gun and my stomach contents out of the window but knew I might be depended on to help.

Calm yourself down, Greg, I repeated to myself, Bob has got us this far safely. I started deep breathing to calm myself down, and after a while, I did dose off for about thirty minutes. I woke up as we slowed down on the outskirts of Toulouse. It was still dark and had not let up raining as we drove further into the town; my anxiety only increasing.

"We will be at the safe house in about fifteen minutes. Jennifer, Pat, Peter, and two police officers will be leaving us for the second safe house in about five minutes. They will be safe, I can assure you. Captain Jurgen has some of his men already there," Bob tried to calm me. "Are you alright, Greg?"

"I can't say I'm the best. I'm a little frightened, sweating, my mouth is dry, and my heart is pounding a mile a minute. Oh, yeh, my bowels are gurgling nicely, and I am sick to my stomach. Other than that, I'm ok," I tried to smile as I replied.

"Oh no," Richard added, "I feel exactly the same way. I thought it was just car sickness."

"Good, I'm glad to see you're in tip-top shape. By the way, I feel the same, so you are in good company. Let's concentrate on being ready. Greg, let me see your firearm," Bob ordered.

I nervously handed my sidearm over to Bob. He checked it quickly, checking the magazine clip and then putting it on safety. "Goodman," Bob smiled, handing it back to me. "Now, Richard, let me see yours." Bob went through the same procedure and found Richard's in proper order.

"I won't have to use it, will I?" I asked nervously.

"Not if I can help it. Now start breathing slowly in through the mouth and slowly out through your nose," Bob advised and then handcuffed the attaché case to his wrist. "We are almost there."

"Oh, shit," kept repeating in my head.

"Are you sure this is the place?" Jed snapped. It was still raining heavily, and visibility was not the best.

"Yeh, yeh," Claude growled back, "311 Rue Saint Aubin. They said it was a cul-de-sac. This is the place. I have paid off a few cops to stay clear of the area. We should not be bothered."

"Good, nice and quiet now, check out the house, take two men with you," Jed ordered. "Looks as if the house is empty, but I do not want any surprises. Have one of your men check out the garage at the end of the cul-de-sac. See if you can open the garage door; check it out, no surprises When you have secured everything, station your men out of sight at the end of the cul-de-sac."

It didn't take long for Claude to come back. "The house is secure, Sergeant Dennis, your inside man, advised us there is nobody here yet. The garage is locked, and my men are out of sight, at the end of the cul-de-sac. "

"Ok, Claude, come with me and bring a couple more of your men with you. I want to talk to this Sergeant Dennis."

Jed, Claude, and two men entered the house. Chief Inspector Stephen Bliss, aka Sergeant Dennis, was there to greet them.

"I left as soon as I got the Toulouse info," Dennis announced, "chopper got me here about an hour ago. I'm your main contact at the Glasgow Constabulary, as you have been advised. I have been with them since they sailed from Arran. Sorry, no names were given. We wanted to make sure we were secure. Reverend Ducane told me you were in charge. I have secured the house. There is nobody here yet, just

Claude's men. Black and Crothers are supporting us from Glasgow. What are your orders?"

"When did you talk to Ducane?" Jed queried.

"Just before we made it out by ship from Arran. You guys made such a damn mess back there. I had to do a lot of covering up your mistakes."

"Fuck that; I wasn't there yet," Jed snapped, "most of the fucking mistakes were made by your guys."

"We didn't make a bloody mess of the fire and subsequent break-in," Dennis countered. "If that had been done properly, we would not be in this mess now, and you would be back in the good old USA with the goods. We had to go back into the school to follow up on your job, that's when Inspector Adam caught on to us, you know the rest."

"Ok, ok, this is getting us nowhere, but I'll tell you this, there is no way I wanted a hit on a cop. That was your boys who did that. I wanted it clean and quiet. In and out before anyone knew."

"So, what's your plan now?" Inspector Bliss, AKA Sergeant Dennis asked.

Before Jed could answer, one of Claude's men came back, "We have secured the garage. There was nobody inside. Had to jimmy the lock. The street is also secured."

"Good, Dennis, what are we looking at?" Jed ordered.

"There will be two vehicles, about eight men. One of them, Bob Findley, will have an attaché case chained to his wrist. That will contain the articles. Richard McMillan, Director of the Glasgow School of Art, and Greg Flint, are also with them. Richard was the one who found the confession. There is still no chatter on their mobile phones as they are not using them.

"I've been told," Jed butted in. "that there are two articles now. Are they both with them? "

"Yes, "Bliss answered," I have seen one of the articles but only a glance at the second. Whatever they have, it seems highly significant. They are keeping them together."

"I was told there were three vehicles," Jed countered.

"There were, but the women were sent back to the UK. They thought it would be safer that way," answered Bliss.

"Women, how many, and who did they belong to?" Jed asked. "I want no fuck-ups."

"Jennifer Flint, Greg Flint's wife, and Pat, Richard's girlfriend," Bliss had to think fast on that one as Peter was not known to them.

"Girlfriend, why the fuck would he bring his girlfriend along," Jed snapped.

"She knew about the break-in, also we feel she helped find the articles. I guess they thought she would be in danger if we caught up with her," Bliss lied.

"Would she?" Jed queried.

"If we could have got to her in Scotland, she might have had some interesting information," Bliss answered, "and we would have made her talk."

"Ok, our prime target is Bob Findley. If he gives us trouble, we will use the others as hostages until he plays our game. I want no bloodshed if we can help it, just clean in and out before they know what's happening," Jed Cassidy ordered. "I don't want another Inspector Adam."

"So, we are not taking any of them with us?" Bliss, aka Sergeant Dennis, asked.

"Fuck no, when we have what we want, there is no need. What I want now is one van at the entrance to this dead-end street ready to block any retreat. I want the other van in the garage at the end of the cul de sac ready to make a quick exit when we have what we came for. Your men, Claude, will also close the trap coming up from behind. The rest of us will be inside the house to take them down. I want them all in the house before we pounce. The object is to be secured, not harmed in any way. Again, I want this quick and quiet. I do not want a shootout at the OK Corral." Jed ordered. "Sergeant Dennis, I want you with me, can't wait to see the look on that bastard Findley's face when he sees you and realizes he has lost. They will have no idea their safe house has been compromised."

"The cops in the initial vehicle will probably come in first to secure the house," Dennis added. "If we can take them down right away, we will have hostages. They will have no chance but to surrender. I know Bob Findley, so may I suggest I take him and retrieve the relic? He may not give up that easily, so we must secure the rest as hostages. I have brought tools to break the lock and chain cutters for the attaché case."

"Ok, you do that. Now everybody knows what to do. Any questions? We have the element of surprise, and the night is on our side. Let's get ready and no fuck ups."

"And if and when they start shooting?" Claude asked.

"Then shoot to kill, but the relic must be protected at all costs," Jed pointed at all of them.

"We have arrived," Jurgen broke the silence. "Around the next corner will be Rue Saint Aubin. I have just received a call; my men are in place, and Cassidy's gang has taken the house. They also tell me Chief Inspector Bliss is with them and looks as if they have accepted him as Sergeant Dennis. Everything is running smoothly according to plan."

"Where are your men?" I asked Inspector Jurgen. "I don't want us to get too cocky."

"Very well hidden, so don't worry, my men are good."

We arrived at the first safe house. Coffee and a light late lunch were provided, but nobody had any appetite. Nerves were strained, and voices were hushed.

"We will be heading over to the second house at six-thirty this evening," Bob announced. "Inspector Jurgen's men have the place secured and are well hidden. Jed and his crew have shown up and occupied the house. We have been expecting them, and they have not disappointed. We are setting the trap."

Waiting for the last four hours was almost unbearable even though Bob, Pierre, and Jurgen were very attentive and kept us in conversation, generally about nothing. Finally, Bob signaled it was time to move out.

"Are you two ready and alright?" Bob prodded.

Richard nodded, "Yes, let's get this over."

Before I could answer, Jennifer had her arms around me, holding me tight.

Bob gently interceded, "Greg and Richard are our bait, but don't worry; we will look after them; they are our single highest priority. I promise you, Jennifer, we will bring them home safe and sound.

"We have come this far, my love. I feel we must see it through." I held her tight in my arms.

Jennifer kissed me, "Do what you think you have to do, I am with you. I know you will be alright and come back to me."

We headed off in the dark in our assigned cars, c'est la guerre.

It was not long before our SUVs pulled around the corner into Rue Saint Aubin. It was quite dark, and the occasional street light did little to illuminate. Drizzle was still falling, giving everywhere a slick soaked look. There was only one none descript vehicle parked at the entrance to the cul-de-sac, other than that the street was empty. We followed behind the first SUV and parked behind it. Bob got out and spoke to the officers in the first vehicle.

"We know, Jed and his crew are waiting for us, the plan is a go, let's do it," Bob then directed them into the setup safe house, and then walked back to our vehicle.

"Ok, let's get this over with. We all know what to do. Greg, Richard, you follow me in. We have the area well protected. Jurgen's men are concealed on the rooftops, left, right, and center. He knows what he is doing; they will never see them. He and his men can see all approaches to this road. All we have to do is play the part. Come on, let's get in and get this over."

All I could think of was, do or die, do or die, "let's get this finished."

"Don't worry, I'm watching you," Bob reassured me.

Bob walked in first with Inspector Jurgen. I followed next with Richard, Pierre, and the remaining officers behind me. Bob stopped so suddenly that I bumped into him, throwing him off balance, I proceeded to fall face-first on the floor. What happened next seemed like mass confusion. We seemed to be surrounded by armed strangers. There was a lot of yelling, telling us to drop our weapons. Bob regained his balance quickly and had his gun in hand, attaché case in the other.

"Findley, drop it; we have you surrounded. We have guns trained on all your people. One false move and it would be tragic," it was Bliss disguised as Sergeant Dennis ordering us.

"You fucking bastard, how much does a traitor cost these days?" Bob snarled.

I was still on the floor face down but had managed to draw my weapon, only to have it kicked out of my hand. I heard a shot and another command to surrender and drop our guns. I saw Bob swing the attaché case and knock Bliss sideways against the wall; Bob then made a dash through a door to what looked like the kitchen. Bliss took after him. From there, I heard Bob yell, "You bastard," followed by three shots and then silence. The rest of us had been subdued and disarmed. It seemed to happen in a flash. Something must have gone wrong was all I could think.

Then someone yelled, "Jed, you better come and see this."

I was on my stomach and could just see through into the kitchen. Bob was lying on his back quite still, blood covering his chest.

The one called Jed seemed to be the ringleader, he yelled at us to lay flat on the floor face down and not to move. He then walked to the kitchen. "Shit," he cried, "Claude, what the hell happened here!?"

"Looks like they both shot each other," Claude answered. "Findley has two in the chest and Sergeant Dennis right in the heart. All deadly wounds. What do you want to do now?"

"Findley must have gone berserk when he discovered Sergeant Dennis was the Glasgow Constabulary mole. Any damage to the attaché case," was Jed's priority.

"No, it looks ok. Should I put a bullet into each of them?" Claude asked.

"No, as far as the police will be concerned, they will have killed each other. Let's not leave any more evidence behind. Claude, bring me those bolt cutters and screwdriver that Bliss brought," Jed barked.

At that moment, one of Claude's men shouted through the front door, "Cop sirens coming this way, let's get the fuck out of here."

Jed worked quickly, cut the chain holding the case, and then proceeded with the screwdriver to pop the locks on the attaché case. He had it in his hand the Templar cylinder. Jed scanned it, weighing it in his hands, then putting it back in the case. I wondered if he knew what he had. All the trouble we had taken to keep it away from these villains lost. I could not believe we had lost Bob. We were all still lying face down on the floor. Everything had gone terribly wrong. Bliss had fooled us, but it had cost him his life and Bob's as well.

"Let's get out of here quick. I thought you had bribed the cops to stay away? Anyway, we've finally got the fuckers. They won't be able to follow us now," ordered Jed. "I've been after that bastard Findley for years. I wish I could dance on the fucker's grave."

"The cops may have been giving us a warning," Claude replied. "Jed, what about Sergeant Dennis?"

"He is no use to us or anybody now, just leave him. We have got what we came for now. Let's get the hell out of here. Did you slash their tires?"

"Better than that, Jed, those vehicles are going nowhere."

"Good, let's go," Jed ordered. "Anyone of you gets a bright idea will get a bit of air-conditioning through the head. Do you hear, no heroics? "

They all proceeded to quickly leave the house, keeping us face down on the floor. I could hear vehicles outside and also the police sirens getting closer. Car doors slammed, and finally, cars squealing away at high speed.

My heart was pounding as I raced to Bobs' side. His chest was covered in blood, and there was no movement.

"No!" I screamed, tears welling up in my eyes, "This can't be. I thought we had this all under control." I slumped down, covering my eyes, and wept. Bob and Bliss dead. Even though he had betrayed us, I didn't wish to see him like this.

I felt a hand on my head; it was Inspector Muller, "it's not as bad as you think, Greg. Bob, you can get up now; they have all gone, you to Bliss."

To my amazement, both Bob and Inspector Bliss rolled over and got to their feet. Both drenched in blood, but both very much alive and grinning ear to ear. My head was swimming.

Bob bent over and gently pulled me to my feet, "I told you we had to make them show their hand. That is when they are most vulnerable, especially when they thought they had us."

"What about the relic?" I cried, "They have it now. How will we be able to retrieve it?"

"They have what Jurgens' people made, an excellent duplicate. Interpol is amazing at detecting fakes and also duplicating them. Don't you think Jurgen? The real one is with the girls and their police guards," Bob answered. "Now, sit quiet, and I'll tell you the rest."

Bob started to unwind the plot, "we found out who the mole was within the Glasgow Constabulary. My friend David Silver, CIA, has been keeping tabs on the Reverend Andrew Ducane and his White Supremacist back in Arkansas. It was Ducane along with some very wealthy members of the Grand Evangelical Church of the Savior and, I hate to say, a few high ranking Masons that orchestrated this attack. They desperately wanted to retrieve or destroy what you and Richard discovered back in the Glasgow School of Art. The Masonic Order has long known that there was something significant to Christianity held by the Masons, particularly Charles Rennie MacKintosh, founder of the Glasgow School of Art. This relic supposedly will rock the beliefs and the tax-free wealth of Duane's church. These few turncoat Masons have worked along with the Reverend Ducane. Silver, along with Inspector Bliss, discovered who the mole was. With the help of a covert action under the direction of Inspector Bliss and a small cadre of trusted Glasgow constabulary, the mole was compromised without his knowledge. Rather than arrest him, we used him to feed some misinformation which passed onto Jed Cassidy, their head man in this affair."

"I thought we had screwed this up royally, you dead along with Inspector Bliss. Even I was fooled," I replied.

"No, I am not dead," Bliss reassured. "The mole in the Glasgow Constabulary did not know I had changed places with Sergeant Dennis. All Jed Cassidy knew I was just another trusted member of Reverend Ducane's team. I had to do some quick thinking, though when Jed Cassidy asked me if I had been talking to the Reverend. The only time that could have happened without Cassidy knowing was when we were leaving Arran. Cassidy was still in transit and organizing his plan of attack. I called him hard regarding his mess in Glasgow. He didn't like that, but it threw him off his chain of thought enough for me not to get further interrogated. Then he wanted to know about the women. I had to do some quick thinking there, as Peter was still an unknown."

Bob added, "We set Inspector Bliss up in this safe house to meet Jed Cassidy. Cassidy's team was given the address and date of arrival to this safe house through information we fed to the Glasgow mole. We also told him that he would meet one of Ducane's loyal members, that was our plant, Inspector Bliss. We had three of Jurgen's men from Interpol hidden up on the roofs just in case. All our people were on to it except you and Richard. Sorry to put you through it, but you and Richard were the only unknown as to how you would react. We still needed you and Richard as Cassidy would expect you to be with us."

"I almost shot someone, but my gun was kicked out of my hand," I whispered.

"No, Greg, do you remember when I asked you to check your gun and pass it to me?"

"Yes," I replied.

"Quick sleight of hand, I substituted a cartridge of blanks to keep you out of trouble. If you had fired, it would sound real enough, but with no effect."

"And sorry, Greg, it was me who kicked the gun out of your hand," Inspector Jurgen confessed. "I didn't want anyone from Cassidy's gang shooting you."

My head was still swimming, "what happened in the kitchen with you and Inspector Bliss?"

"As planned, I fired one shot into the floor, and Inspector Bliss fired two shots into the floor. At the same time, we had blood explosive capsules triggered to go off, looking just like deadly wounds. Even I was amazed at how much blood came out."

"It sure looked real from where I was, and it fooled Jed, he couldn't wait to get out. I think it shocked him," I added.

"I think more the fake police sirens," Bob suggested, "that was Inspector Jurgen's idea; nice touch."

"We thought that would panic them to move things along," Inspector Jurgen added.

"I think he was more concerned that the attaché case was not damaged." Bob mused. "When he discovered all was ok, he got out of there as soon as possible. After all, that is all he wanted. He had no concern for Inspector Bliss, aka Sergeant Dennis, whether he was alive or dead, supposedly a valued ally. A cold-hearted man. I am sure his reward for a successful operation would be substantial. He wouldn't wait for that."

"What will become of him, Bob?"

"We are tracking him as we speak. Nothing like what he sees as his success will blind him to everything else. He probably will be on the next plane to the USA, that's where the FBI will intercede. They will follow him to Reverend Ducane and take the whole lot of them down."

I had almost forgotten about Richard. He was sitting on the floor in the corner of the room, arms around his knees, white as a ghost. "Richard, are you alright?" No answer, "Richard, it's me, are you alright?"

Captain Muller moved towards Richard putting a hand on his shoulder, Richard flinched, "it's alright you are safe. It's all over."

Richard was pale and shaking, but managed a weak smile, "I know, I know, it was just too violent. I'll be fine."

Muller pressed a flask of cognac in Richard's hand, "Drink this; you'll feel better."

Richard took a mouthful, swallowed it, and then proceeded to take another three good gulps.

"Easy," Muller advised, "don't want you throwing up."

"Is it really over?" Richard asked; he was still shaking.

I went over and sat beside him, "yes, it is over we are safe, and we have won."

"Thank God, all I want to do is roll up in a ball and sleep for a week," Richard announced.

"We are safe, and a good night's sleep is all arranged," Bob told Richard.

"What I would love now, Bob is to see Jennifer. She is probably worried out of her mind." I pleaded.

"All arranged," Bob answered, "as we speak. The SUVs are waiting to take us there. Sorry, we still do not want to use our mobile phones, just in case they still may be listening."

"I thought Cassidy's men had disabled all of the vehicles."

"They did, we anticipated that, but Inspector Muller had backups waiting in the next street over."

I was still shaking as we drove for about twenty minutes. Captain Muller handed me the small flask of cognac, "Sip it; it will steady you."

The warmth of the cognac in my stomach did indeed settle my nerves. We were still in darkness as we drove, but the rain had stopped. Along the way, we passed the town's Cathedral, Saint Etienne, Bob advised. The Cathedral close was softly lit, the light reflecting off the puddles left by the recent rain. The tranquility was surreal, considering what we had just been through. We finally stopped outside the second safe house. We walked in; I was overwhelmed by such a feeling of weariness and wobbly legs.

Jennifer rushed over, threw her arms around me, and smothered my face with kisses, "I was so worried about you," she was trembling.

"Easy girl," I almost laughed as I held her tight, "the legs are still a little wobbly, but I'm alright darling, everybody is alright. I feel the worst is over. It should be smooth sailing from here on, but I could use another good belt of something and a good night's sleep."

Captain Jurgen again came to my rescue, handing me the flask of cognac. Smiling, he said, "Yah, keep it, finish it off, you have earned it."

I took another good swig and then handed it over to Richard.

Richard downed the lot, smiled, and said, slightly slurring, "Now I feel better. Where is my bed?"

At that point, Pat and Peter took Richard under their wing and helped him into his designated bedroom.

Peter called back, "You have to tell me everything, so don't go away; I'm coming back."

Then Jennifer got a look at Bob, his shirt bloodied, "Oh my God, are you hurt Bob? You look dreadful."

"A little bit of magic to deceive the enemy. Don't worry; we are all fine. I would suggest you take your man and get him a good night's rest. He and Richard were very brave. Your room is ready; all our rooms are ready. I think we should all turn in for a safe, good night's rest. We have a lot to plan tomorrow."

"Just a moment," Inspector Jurgen Muller produced another bottle of French cognac, "I thought we all might need this as he passed around."

"Bless you, Jurgen," Jennifer took a deep draught.

We passed it around, and all took a generous mouthful. It was heady and sweet. As soon as it hit my stomach, it warmed and calmed. I could not have thanked Inspector Muller more.

At that point, Peter came back down, "didn't take long for Richard to nod off, he's snoring peaceably. Now let's hear it, the whole story.

I passed the cognac to Peter, and after taking a good swig he returned it to me. I took a good gulp and then related the evening's events, a condensed version.

"Everything was so quiet; it was surreal. I thought it's not happening; we have the wrong date. After that, the first thing I remember was bumping into Bob and then falling flat on my face. From there, it was just a blur of shouting and gunshots. It was over before I could react. I did manage to get my gun out only to have it kicked out of my hand; I didn't know what I was going to do with it. I thought we had failed, and all was lost. The rest you will have to ask Bob. I am bushed, so pardon me, I'm off to bed."

Peter hugged me, "Sorry to keep you up; you go on up now. Take the cognac with you."

"No, Peter, you have it. All I want is sleep."

Peter took the cognac and handed it to Bob, "well, Bob, what's the rest of the story?"

Bob was now sitting and took a good swallow of cognac. "It was a classical switch and bait. Cassidy had no idea that Sergeant Dennis was Inspector Bliss, nor did he know we had switched artifacts. We had planned the bloody shootout. It all went so quickly that I think it even threw Cassidy off, especially when Inspector Jurgen arranged the police sirens. They couldn't wait to get out of there. The only thing I felt bad about was that Greg and Richard had no idea of the plan. We wanted it that way as their reaction was as real as it could get."

"Thanks, Bob, now I think I can sleep, good night," Peter headed off to bed.

We all had assigned rooms in the second safe house. The beds were all made up and looked very comfortable. I soon found myself cuddled in bed in my wife's arms. The cognac, and sleep quickly blessing me into profound oblivion.

"Jed, that you?" the southern drawl of Reverend Ducane sounded over the mobile phone.

"Yes, Reverend, we got it." Jed was elated, "It's ours."

"You got it?" Ducane sounded incredulous, "You really have it?"

"Yes, I have it with me at this moment. I am going to Paris right now and will board a plane to Nashville and then onto Memphis. Should see you in about forty-eight hours."

"Lord be praised!" Ducane shouted, "Did you have any trouble?"

"Bob Findley and the Glasgow Sergeant Dennis shot dead. It happened so fast couldn't be helped, a bit of collateral damage. I think Findley had a real hate for Black when he realized it was Black who betrayed them. Everybody else is fine, including myself. I doubt they will trace it to either you or me, I'm guessing. It could be a bit sticky with the Glasgow Constabulary. With Glasgow, it could also be a dead end as both high ranking officers have been killed. Everybody else has dispersed and well paid. Just need to get out of circulation and keep quiet for about a year."

"Ok, Jed, get here as soon as possible. You've done well, my boy. Done God's work. A bonus too, with Bob Findley out of the way. He has been a thorn in our side for years. I'll make sure you are well rewarded."

"Yeh, I'm so glad that bastard is out of the way," Jed countered.

 I was up early the next morning, considering what we had endured. There was a pleasant aroma drifting into the bedroom of coffee.

"Greggie, stay in bed just a little bit longer," Jennifer purred, "just a little bit longer."

"Alright, my little darling, what did you have in mind?" I whispered in her ear, already knowing and anticipating the answer.

"Something we will both like," as she pulled me close. "Maybe a little bit of cuddling? I need you close to me."

Jennifer came to me, and we passionately made love entangled in each other. We both needed to be close after the danger we had endured. We lay there in each other's arms content and oblivious to the outside world and wonderfully drained. If only this were the only thing that mattered, but finally, we both succumbed to the fragrance of coffee and fried ham.

"Come on, sweetheart, let's go and eat; I am famished," I coaxed Jennifer out of bed.

We washed and dressed quickly and headed downstairs. Pierre was cooking up a storm in the kitchen. Everybody was there, Peter, Pat, Richard, Bob, Jurgen and the rest of the police force. We all looked rested but did not dare to own up to the fact we were or so we thought, home free. Could anything else hit us?

"You alright, Richard?" I asked.

"Yes, the cognac knocked me out, and I slept like the dead," Richard answered. "Now, believe it or not, I am famished."

"Well, breakfast is ready," called Pierre, "my specialty, 'Croque Monsieur.'"

Croque Monsieur turned out to be the French equivalent of a grilled cheese sandwich, only with Gruyere and ham. I must say, very delicious. We washed this down with his excellent coffee.

"Bob has been filling us in on your nail-biting episode," Peter announced, "Bob has told us everything, quite a shocking account. Did you have any idea what was going on?"

"No, not at all, all I knew is that something had gone terribly wrong. I thought all was lost and we had lost Bob. I could have put up with the loss of our relic, but not Bob."

"Glad to hear it, Greg," Bob responded, "but all's well that ends well. Anyway, we are not staying here, just in case. We are now heading on to Narbonne to meet an old friend."

"Not before I say goodbye, and thank you for your confidence and bravery. You have gone through a terrible ordeal, but I think the worst is over."

All eyes turned around, and to our great surprise, to see Chief Inspector Matthew Adam walk through the door.

"I know, I am not dead, but the assumption I was, certainly worked to our advantage," the inspector grinned.

We were all dumbfounded except Bob, who walked over and warmly shook the inspector's hand.

"It wasn't for want of trying," Bob stated. "That was a close call in the river."

"Yes," James answered, "I went down with the ship, car that is. Waited until the car submerged, took a deep breath, and rolled down the window to equalize the pressure. I then opened the door and swam out. The only person I contacted was Inspector Bliss. I knew who had driven me off the road, it was Sergeant Mike Dennis, and as long as he thought I was dead, Inspector Bliss could shadow him and help expose the group."

"I guess Chief Inspector Stephen Bliss will not be impressed now that he has been demoted back to Inspector," Peter winked.

"Actually not, he will keep his promotion, and I have been promoted to Superintendent," Matthew bowed.

We all cheered and clapped at the good news, both that the inspector was alive and at his promotion.

"Frivolity aside," Peter broke in, "you must have realized earlier that something was amiss within the police force."

"Not at first, but Sergeant Dennis gave himself away when he let himself into the Glasgow School of Art using the security code. At first, it didn't click, but he knew I had seen him use the code. None of our force should have known the code. I was a liability whether I realized what he had done or not. He could not take the chance. I had to be eliminated. When he ran me off the road, it fell into place. From there, I swam underwater surfacing along the shoreline. I was freezing cold and could barely control the shaking. It was dark. I saw him scanning the shore, but he didn't see me. I waited until he left and then managed to get to a payphone and called Inspector Bliss. He came immediately wrapped me in a blanket and got me into a warm car. It must have taken at least a half-hour before I was somewhat coherent. We set the whole thing up, including my fake death, while sitting in the car. Once Sergeant Dennis thought I was out of the way, he continued his liaison with the gang. Later Bob contacted Inspector Bliss, but we didn't let him in on our setup till later."

 "So we set the net," Bob added, "to catch the moles inside the police force and trap Jed Cassidy and his gang."

"We didn't know the half of it," I responded," but now it is over. The only question is, how did you hide a fake body that didn't exist?"

"Again, that was Inspector Bliss," Adam replied. "We had a vagrant body posing as myself. The only other person that knew was my wife but in the strictest confidence."

"I'm not sure it is all over. Bob is now telling us of a meeting with an old friend," Peter added. "Now, what mystery have you got in store for us, and where is Narbonne?"

"Wait and see, all I will tell you is Narbonne is in one of the most beautiful parts of France. I think everyone will be well pleased, especially with the old friend."

It was still early morning, and we were now driving on our way in a large comfortable twelve seat van, courtesy of Interpol. There was a second SUV following with Captain Muller's Interpol police. Bob did relent and advised us Narbonne was on the south coast of France. It was early March now since we had made our mad rush out of Glasgow. We drove through rolling rocky countryside of vineyards and heavily wooded vistas. The sky was a dazzling blue, and the weather had that lovely touch of warmth. Spring was on its' way. I cannot say at this point we were feeling totally relaxed, maybe guardedly safe. The south of France seemed welcoming and calm, bursting with early spring wildflowers.

"We are staying at a small country hotel outside Narbonne," Bob announced. "Friends have booked the whole place for us for one night. A break that will give us a breather to refresh and get ready for the last leg of our trip, and as I said, we will be reunited with an old friend."

"What old friend could that be?" Peter asked again.

"Ah, I think you will be more than pleasantly surprised," countered Bob teasingly.

"I don't know if I can take any more surprises, Bob," I meekly added.

"Don't worry, Greg," Bob assured, "I know you will love this one."

"One thing I would like to know is how you duplicated the Queens Cross relic," Richard asked.

"I think, Richard," Bob replied, "Jurgen should explain that to you."

All eyes turned to Inspector Jurgen Muller.

"Well, Inspector Jurgen Muller of Interpol, how did you do it," Richard again asked.

"Certainly not by myself. We first got a look at the relic when Greg and Bob brought it aboard at Arran. While on your trip, it was photographed, weighed, measured all dimensions, and gave a description as to colour, material, and any markings. We knew what the leather cylinder was plus the lead tube inside. All this information plus photos were encrypted and emailed to me at Interpol, Lyon. We have quite the lab there dealing with antiquities and fakes. We have the ability to copy or restore most items there. We also have all the experts to detect forgeries and hidden paint over lost or stolen artifacts. Our team went to work, making a copy that was the exact twin of the original. As for Jacque de Molay's confession, the Vatican made that reproduction at Bob's request. Their copy was so good only an expert could tell the difference. I then brought it all aboard when you arrived in Brest."

"What did you put inside the lead tube?" Richard asked.

"I think it was a rolled newspaper, the Lyon Capitale." Jurgen smiled.

"They'll shit when they open it and only find a local paper," Peter added.

"Yeh, it's all in French. That will baffle them for about two seconds; by then, it will already be too late," Bob added.

"Bob, was it always your plan to use a substitute to deceive our adversaries?" asked Richard.

"Not at the very beginning. I didn't know what you had found. It was a plan in the making as we escaped. Once we knew, the substitute would be with me; the original was kept safe. I knew we would eventually be intercepted. We knew we had a mole amongst our ranks, that was then our plan. If and when we were compromised, I would use the fake. My plan later developed into forcing their hand so that we could plant the fraud. Use their interception of us to our advantage. We had a lot of help from our people in Glasgow, the USA, Interpol, and Masons, and still are helping."

"When we first met at Peter's house in Glasgow, I had wondered then how a single man could protect us. I had no idea how well connected you were." I remarked.

"We knew for many years Greg, even before my time," Bob answered, "that this relic would surface. There was always a plan. You are now all part of history in the making. What the relic will reveal we have always thought would be ground shaking and change Christianity forever."

"For the good, I hope," Richard added.

"Bob," I asked, "do you know what the cylinder contains?"

"There is more than one probability as to its contents. Let us just wait and see. We have gone this far; a few more days and we will see. We do know it is the recorded trial of Jesus Christ. Does it match what the New Testament states, or is there something quite different? My feeling is the trial will reveal a new slant on what we have taken for granted for the last two thousand years. I guess this is why the Knights Templar kept it so secret and guarded it up until the present time."

"Bob," Richard asked, "do you believe remnants of the Knights Templers still exist?"

"Very much so Richard, very much so."

"And their fabled treasure?" Richard added.

"Treasure comes in many forms. Need I say more?" Bob replied. "You may have found one of the greatest treasures of the twentieth century."

 I knew as we drove through the countryside, we were reflecting on yesterday's events and what would be revealed at the Vatican. I must say I still had my reservations about the Holy See.

As we drove further south, the countryside now took on the look of landlocked islands of gagged white limestone cliffs surrounded by densely forested valleys. Bob called this area Massif de la Clare. It soon opened up to beautiful views of the blue Mediterranean. The air was relaxing, filled with sweet fragrances of herbs, wildflowers, pinewood forests, and salt sea air. It was not long before we turned off the road to the approach of our hotel.

We drove down a private road that led to the hotel; it was a large two storey contemporary Mediterranean style villa, white stucco face with terra cotta roofing tiles. Semi-tropical gardens surrounded it, but it backed into a heavily forested area. The woods at the back climbed up to white limestone cliffs. The front entrance overlooked the Mediterranean Sea. It was an idyllic setting, the sun shining in a beautiful blue sky. The air was warm with a soft wind blowing. There were large shrubs of bright pink azaleas in full bloom, and Mediterranean palms lined the entrance to the hotel.

"Alright," Bob announced, "ladies and gentlemen, it is still early, grab your gear and stretch out and get some rest. The rooms are reserved under your names. I suggest room service for lunch; I will be tied up confirming some of our plans. Supper will be at six, see you later."

We were all entranced by our surroundings like troops returning from the front to find Shangri-La. The main entrance and lobby was bright and airy, potted palms and luxurious tropical plants greeted us everywhere. The staff was more than pleasant and accommodating. We were soon ensconced in our luxurious rooms. Jennifer and I both crashed onto our bed. Within minutes we were both fast asleep. I don't know how long we slept, but when we awoke, the sun was in the west over the Mediterranean Sea, it was flooding our room with sunlight.

"Come on, sleepyhead; I think we missed lunch," I kissed Jennifer," it's time we got up, and I am hungry, what about you?"

"Yes, I am ready for a bite to eat. What time is it?"

"Just after four, we have slept through lunch. Time enough to shower and freshen up before supper," the stress of the previous day had knocked us out.

We were down in the dining room at five-thirty. Everybody was already down there sitting at the bar. We met Peter and Pat, making their way at the same time as us.

"Well, this should be a bit of a celebration," Peter announced.

"We all hope so," Jennifer added," it should be clear sailing from here, I hope. Come on let's have a drink."

"What's everybody sipping?" Peter called.

"I've been down to the wine cellar," Bob piped up, "and found a few bottles of a delightful local Chardonnay. It is wonderful and served at cellar temperature. I find too often that Chardonnay, when served, is over chilled, but this one is spot on."

Bob was right; the Chardonnay was exceptional, lovely liquid sunshine with a buttery taste and a lingering complexity of mangos and pears. We were soon feeling quite relaxed and ready for supper.

"Alright, folks," Bob called, "the waiter is indicating our supper is ready. I have taken the liberty in arranging supper again."

We started with local fish soup with saffron, absolutely wonderful. There were plenty of warm, fresh-baked country loaves of bread and local butter; I could have stayed on this one all evening. The main course arrived, langoustines sauteed in a light garlic herbed butter and lemon. We were soon dipping our bread so as not to waste anything. Oh yes, the Chardonnay kept flowing.

"Before we get a little too relaxed," Bob interrupted, "I want to let you know we will be here for tonight and tomorrow night. We are awaiting confirmation as to the whereabouts of Jed Cassidy and his hired mercenaries. Inspector Muller has informed me they are tracking Cassidy, Claude De Bose, and his mercenaries. They have split up, Cassidy up to Paris; we think he will be flying back to the USA as fast as he can. We think the others are heading up to either Switzerland or Liechtenstein, probably to deposit earned monies in a numbered account. We want Cassidy in the USA; then, the FBI will track him to the Reverend Ducane. Once there, the FBI will take them down. Inspector Muller will bring us up to date as to what he intends to do with De Bose and his henchmen."

"As this was a well-planned sting, nothing actually was stolen, and nobody was eliminated or used as a hostage. We cannot charge them with much. We do not want to charge them as this will tip off Ducane and his people that something has gone wrong. Interpol is watching them very closely, and once Cassidy has been apprehended in the USA, we will swoop. It will not take much with these people to pin something on them if only illegal weaponry. That could put them away for at least ten years. Are there any questions?"Inspector Muller asked.

Peter was the only one to ask, "So you do not feel they may be following us?"

"That," Muller answered, "is a definite. I am pretty sure, thanks to Bob; we have pulled the wool over their eyes.

Some good-hearted cheers and claps went out from the team.

Bob then added, "Now, let's enjoy our dessert."

Cheers went up as plates of Crepe Suzette were passed around and bottles of a lovely sweet Muscat. With coffee, there were little chocolate profiteroles. Nobody said no. Just when we were feeling satiated, the waiter brought a bottle of Remy Marten XO that was offered to anyone who wished. We sat and sipped, conversation light, humorous, and frivolous exactly what we needed. We needed no rocking when finally, we wended our way back up to our rooms.

"Wonder what Bob has got up his sleeve this time?" Jennifer mused. "He's very secretive about this old friend."

"Whatever it is, or should I say whoever it is, we are all in his hands. He has not let us down yet. We have met the enemy, and he does not know he is defeated. That was genius on Bob's part. I have never trusted, so completely, a stranger that I have only known for the last couple of weeks," I concluded. "I will trust him to the end of this saga."

"He has become a dear friend," Jennifer added. "I hope, after this, we can still keep in touch."

"Yes, it would be ashamed to let the friendship end here, but I have a feeling it will not, and we will see more of him."

We were replete with food, wine, and a little fine cognac. I threw caution to the wind and opened our sliding terrace doors wide open to soft breezes and the sound of the sea. Our bed was inviting, large, and soft. Soon we were encompassed in all of its comforts. After sweet goodnight kisses, we were quickly in the arms of Morpheus. Fast asleep in seconds.

The next morning the sun was shining brightly through our terrace doors. The fragrance of pine, herbs, and the sea air wafted in on mild breezes. I stood there on the terrace, taking it all in. I felt like I had been reborn, regenerated. A touch on my shoulder brought me out of my meditation.

"Good morning, sweetie."

Jennifer laid her head down between my shoulder blades. Such a small gesture of love, but it felt beautiful. I turned and held her tight, kissing Jennifer on the cheek. She was so precious to me. She looked up and kissed me.

"We have slept a little late," Jennifer announced, "they are probably waiting for us at breakfast."

"You're right; I was just taking in this wonderful view. It just doesn't seem to connect after what we have been through."

"I know," Jennifer answered, "but, come on let's get some coffee and see what Bob is going to reveal."

It was just after ten am when we arrived for breakfast. Peter, Pat, and Richard were already seated drinking coffee.

"Have you guys eaten already?" Jennifer asked.

"No, not yet," Peter answered, and you should see what's on the menu."

Pat pushed the coffee pot towards us, "I'll bet you're ready for this."

"Yes, please," I pleaded. "What is Bob, Pierre, and Inspector Jurgen up to huddled over in the corner?"

"They have been over there ever since we came down," Richard commented. "Don't ask me about what. All I want right now is breakfast; I am starving."

We all walked over to the breakfast buffet. There was everything from fresh croissants, eggs Benedict, cold cuts, cheeses, scrambled eggs, and fresh fruit salad. We all dug in.

"Hey, leave some for us," Bob called as he and Pierre and Jurgen joined us. "We have news."

As we sat eating breakfast, Bob informed us of the latest. "Inspector Jurgen's men tracked Cassidy to Paris, where he chartered a private jet to Nashville with a connecting flight to Memphis. He has already informed the FBI of Cassidy's movements. As for Claude De Bose and his men, they have split up. We think De Bose is on his way to Marseille while the rest seem to be heading toward Croatia. I'll let Inspector Muller fill you in on that."

"As Bob advised, we followed Cassidy to Paris; once he is on US territory, the FBI will tail him. They will not make any arrests until he is with the Reverend Ducane. As for De Bose, we just might make him disappear for a while so that he is out of action. The others we will also track, but they are not of any danger to us. We will make life difficult for them so that they will constantly be on the run. All in all, we are out of danger."

Bob took over, "So folks we can take it easy and enjoy ourselves. Today will be our last night here, so relax, explore, and enjoy the grounds. Lunch will be here at 1:00 pm, and supper tonight will be served at 6:30 pm."

"Inspector Muller," Richard asked, "what do you mean when you say you will make life difficult for the rest of De Bose's people?"

"Most of his gang is known to us and have records of some sort. We will just give them enough rope to hang themselves, then pick them up for questioning. We'll drop a few hints that we think they were involved in some covert action in France. Then we will let them go; in a few days, we will pick them up again for questioning. We will have them running in circles. Eventually, we will arrest De Bose. If we catch him with illegal weapons and we probably will, if you catch my meaning, we could put him away for at least ten years. That gang is dead."

"So Bob," Pat now asked, "do we meet our old friend now, and could that be Chief Inspector Matthew Adams?"

"Not until tomorrow, now go out and enjoy the sun and scenery," Bob laughed.

"Come on, guys, Bob is keeping things close to his chest, as he always does. Let's go and sit in the sun," I suggested.

And that we did. The hotel faced due south, with the sun full on the front. We found a sheltered spot with plenty of garden chairs; we made ourselves comfortable and soaked up the sun. The hotel staff made themselves present and offered us a variety of beverages and canopies.

"I wonder what Bob has in store for us, and how are we now getting to Rome?" Peter mused.

"Well, we are not the ones hunted anymore, so whatever it will be, it will be a little more leisurely. I still think Bob will do something different just to throw any possible threat off," Jennifer suggested.

"Are you still worried, Jennifer?" I asked her.

"Maybe they have got a backup plan just in case," Jennifer mused. "I still can't believe we are safe."

"Even if they did," Richard countered, "it would take a long time to catch up to us, once they found the deception."

"They found us after we left Arran, not a small task," Pat countered.

Pat's comment kept us all quietly thinking. The warmth of the sun found me dozing off comfortably only to awaken for lunch.

Lunch was light, a lovely lobster bisque served with a cheese, and shrimp quiche washed down with freshly squeezed orange juice mimosas. We didn't see Bob, Pierre, or Jurgen. After lunch, Jennifer and I took a long walk around the hotel and the surrounding countryside.

"It is beautiful here, isn't it," Jennifer observed. "Do you think Bob planned it this way? Every time we are in danger, he manages to find us a little bit of heaven to cheer us up."

"Nice thought, but I don't think so," I replied, "his main plan is to keep us and our discovery safe so we can show it to the world. If there are other powers directing us, it is beyond him."

We took a long walk through the surrounding woods. Everywhere the signs of spring were bursting up, wildflowers by the myriad. Red poppies, white saxifrage, pink rhododendrons, purple geraniums, wild lavender were just a few that Jennifer could name. She picked an arm full, which we placed in a vase back in our room, the sweet perfume wafting over us. Both of us stretched out on our king size bed and gently dozed off. It was Peter and Pat that woke us knocking at the door.

"Come on, guys, it's 5:00 pm time for a cocktail, just enough time before supper, which is again at 6:30 pm," Peter hurried us.

"Ok, ok, give us ten minutes, we will meet you down there," I replied.

We met down at the bar; everyone was there, including Bob, Pierre, and Inspector Muller. We all ordered drinks. Jennifer and I kept to the delightful Chardonnay while Bob found an interesting scotch.

"I can update you on Cassidy," Bob announced after a sip of scotch, "as of 10:00 am this morning, Cassidy chartered a private jet and is now about to land at Nashville in about two hours. From there, he has made arrangements to fly on to Memphis. The stopover will be approximately three hours before he boards again for Memphis. He has booked an overnight stay in Memphis at the Airport Holiday Hotel. From there, he is driving to meet the Reverend at his church, all this, according to the FBI. By the time they realize they have been duped, we will be well on our way out of France to our next destination."

"Will the FBI make their arrest at the church?" Richard inquired.

"That I don't know. All I know is Jed, and the Reverend are being watched, and at the appropriate time, they will swoop and try and get as many of them as they can," Bob replied.

We were just finishing our drinks when we were all called to supper.

"This is our last night here," Bob reminded us, "so enjoy, we will meet tomorrow in the lobby at 6:30 am for the next leg of our journey."

"With an old friend," Peter yelled, "and who is that, are you going to let us know?"

"Patience Peter," Bob replied, "wait until tomorrow."

The hotel had prepared an excellent Bouillabaisse full of all sorts of fish and shellfish. Accompanying the dish were fresh warm baguettes and a lovely chilled white, bone dry Sancerre. Dessert was light; fresh strawberries served with crème fraises and an excellent Champagne. Everything was delightful. Finally, they offered us liquors; most of us declined as we were all stuffed.

"I would suggest an early night as we are heading out at 7:00 am, so be here at 6:30 am sharp," Bob commanded. "This is the last leg of our journey."

We headed to our rooms, replete, and totally relaxed.

"Well, something is going to be revealed tomorrow," Jennifer mused. "What do you think it could be?"

"I don't know; I'm baffled," I answered. "I've searched my brain and come up with nothing. Bob is not giving us any clues, except it is an old friend. That means an old friend that we all know, and that limits us to someone we all know, including Bob."

"No, I have gone through all the people that we have all met and come up with nothing except Chief Inspector Adam. He can't have meant future people as they are not acquainted with us. Well, we will find out tomorrow, and I am ready for bed," Jennifer announced.

We had enjoyed a relaxing day and what with the wine, good food, and company it was not long before we had drifted off into a deep sleep.

The next morning, we showered and dressed, meeting down at the main lobby at six-thirty am, all feeling wonderfully refreshed. We were all packed, ready, and eager to go. There was a lovely coffee, at least that we all helped ourselves to in the main lobby. We were all wondering what was Bobs' secret, and where were we headed now? The van and SUV were ready at the front door, and Bob directed us all into our appropriate vehicles.

"It's only a short run this time to a little place by the sea called Gruissan," he added, "and we will soon be on our way on the last leg of our journey."

We traveled down the valley towards the turquoise Mediterranean Sea. The sky was blue, and the ocean calm, just gentle undulating waves. We offloaded at Gruissan at a small busy marina, cries of seagulls everywhere. Bob directed us down one of the docks. There to greet us was a power launch that Bob directed us to board.

"But I must bid you goodbye," Captain Jurgen Muller announced, "you are in good hands and no longer need my assistance. I wish you a bon voyage. I will be watching your progress once you reach the Vatican."

With great reluctance and with many thanks, hearty handshakes, hugs, and kisses, we said our goodbyes to Jurgen and watched him and his men drive off. We then motored out to the open sea.

“Well, I told you we would meet up with an old friend. If you look out to sea, you will see her just over to port. That is our old friend, the ‘Highland Spirit’; she is sailing under the French Tricolour and renamed ‘Le Mar.’ Just an added precaution to throw anybody off, and I think that is a minimal chance. From here, she will take us onto Rome and the Vatican in three days.”

We couldn’t believe our eyes, but there she was. It indeed was like meeting up with an old friend. We were all thrilled.

 “I believe breakfast awaits onboard,” Bob announced.

We were soon aboard the 'Highland Spirit' now renamed, 'Le Mar.' Captain Roy was there to greet us warmly. It was wonderful to see him again and all our familiar crew. It felt like the Navy had come to our rescue, taking the troops home. Well, that is what it felt like, but the reality was just around the corner. Still, it was a very happy reunion.

"Same cabins," Captain Roy announced, "get yourself settled, your luggage should be there already. When you are unpacked, come up to the flying bridge for breakfast. I know you must be starved. Rumour has it that Bob doesn't feed you well."

"It's true," Peter chimed in, "I'm feeling thin."

"Now that's odd, you don't look it," Captain Roy headed off laughing.

 We all made our way back to our old cabins.

Jennifer and I felt like old hands as we made our way down to our cabin. The bed was freshly made up, and there were fresh towels in the en suite. All was as it was when we first boarded. I almost expected chocolates on the pillows. It was just too much to ask and too much to be true. We were exuberant.

Jennifer turned to me, "Do you remember when I said I would love to be aboard under different circumstances? Well, I think we have been granted our wish. Nearly three days of luxury and no longer hunted."

"Well, let's make the best of it and just enjoy," as I kissed her. "Anyone for breakfast?"

"Oh yes, but let's just get a little organized."

We stored our luggage and hung up most of our clothing then headed up to the flying bridge for a late breakfast. Bob, Pierre, Richard, Peter, and Pat were already there waiting for us. The crew had rustled us up a proper breakfast of poached eggs, bacon, sausages, fried tomatoes and mushrooms, and warm fresh bread, all washed down with either tea or coffee. The conversation was relaxed and jovial as we heard the engines come to life, and the anchor pulled up. She gently started to cruise out to sea.

"Somehow, I don't feel we deserve this. Can we now let our guard down and start to enjoy ourselves?" Peter piped up.

All eyes turned to Bob.

"Yes, I am sure we are in the safe. Jed and his gang think they have won but will soon realize they have been duped. By that time, we will be safe in the Vatican, but we still have some work to do."

A group groan went up.

Bob raised his hands, "sounds like a mutiny to me."

"Mutiny on the Bounty," Peter piped up, "but we have no island to desert to."

A good-natured laugh went all around, as Bob advised," There will be islands to come, but I hope there would be no mutiny."

"So you better treat us well," Peter laughingly interrupted, "or I am jumping ship."

"Look, I just want to say we are in good hands with Captain Roy and his crew, for the voyage, that part I will leave up to him. What lies ahead of us is crucial. We are about to release to the world what may change the way we see the founding religions of the Western world and the Middle East. When we get to the Vatican, who do we want to be present at the unveiling of your discovery? I want you to sit down and draw up a list of those establishments and people you want present. Also, we must draw up a letter of invitation to those invited. Do we invite only scholars or religious theologians or both? Once the invite has gone out, how do we vet those that the invited wants there? What happens if the press gets wind of this? Do we invite the press? These are all things we must consider. And finally," Bob added, "to whom do we give these artifacts to guard for posterity? Do they go back to the Glasgow School of Art or The Queen's Cross Church?"

Richard was the first to speak, "There is a lot to consider, my first thought though is it must go back to Scotland as all the artifacts were discovered there. It is part of Scotland's historical heritage."

"I tend to agree with Richard," I added, "I think we must put our thoughts together, let's meet up here say 2:00 PM, and draught up our conclusions."

"Are we not being premature?" Pat asked, "What if there is nothing new in our discovery? Shouldn't we look at our discovery before we take it to the world?"

We all looked a little dumbfounded at Pats' remark.

"She is right," Richard agreed, "So what do we do?"

"All of what we have talked about should be ready, but first, as Pat has pointed out, we should see what it is we have," I suggested. "With that in mind and as we are going to the Vatican, I think we should ask Pierre. Pierre is a Swiss Guard and a former Jesuit."

"Once a Jesuit, always a Jesuit," Pierre added, "but I do agree we should look at it first. We have all the necessary laboratory equipment to open and preserve. We also have experts to confirm authenticity. You will be in a protected environment, not that I see any unforeseen problems. So put your ideas and needs together. If this proves to be the ground shaking discovery, you think it is; you will be ready to move to the next step."

"Alright," Bob put in, "we have nearly three days to put this together. I suggest we get to work."

"There goes our mini-vacation, Jennifer. No rest for the wicked," I added. " Haven't heard from you, Peter. Care to add your two pennies worth."

"I'm not here I've jumped ship," Peter grinned at all of us. "I guess I'm not wicked."

"Not wicked enough, but we will need someone to record minutes," I added

"I'll volunteer," Jennifer announced. "We will need pads, pens, and could a laptop and printer be found?"

"Pierre, we will need you as well," I added.

"I'll see what I can rustle up," Bob volunteered and then disappeared.

With that, we all headed down to the main deck to put our thoughts together. As we started to put ideas together, Bob arrived with pens, pads, and a laptop plus a small printer. We asked Bob to stay on as he was as much of the team as we all were.

Richard was the first to speak, "As director of The Glasgow School of Art where the artifact was initially found, I think we are all agreed that all the artifacts from the Templar confession to the Queens Cross discoveries should all go back to Scotland. This find is Scotland's historical heritage."

There was a unanimous agreement, including Pierre.

Richard again spoke, "Pierre, who will meet us and work with us at the Vatican?"

"I trust I have not overstepped, but I have already arranged that. With your approval, we will be working with the Arivum Secretum Apostolicum Vaticanum, in other words, the Vatican Secret Archives. I have already contacted the Cardinal Archivist, Cardinal Jean, and the Archivist Prefect Bishop Page; he is also the Scientific Director. All these men are highly trained and qualified. I know this sounds daunting, and none of you are Rome Catholics. Still, if it makes you comfortable, Cardinal Jean has offered to allow any other people of training to accompany you in this discovery."

"I will vouch for Pierre, I trust him," Bob added. "I am also acquainted with Cardinal Jean. He is a man of science and truth. It will be an honour to have him on our team."

"Richard, are you qualified to dissect the lead canister?" I asked.

"Yes, I do have the training and background for the task. The lab at the Glasgow School of Art was not equipped to handle this. It all depends on what the Vatican has to offer. Pierre, can you shed some light on this ?"

"I can assure you our physical lab has all the most up to date equipment to handle this plus proper air conditioning and filter system to store and protect the items."

"Alright, let's get cracking and put together our requirements." Richard requested.

We spent the better part of the morning, lunch, and a couple of hours after that before we presented our requests.

Richard sat back and looked at us all, "alright, I think, these are the requirements we have all agreed to. First of all, we are still all in agreement that the artifacts will go to Scotland. The confession of

Jacque de Molay will remain at the Glasgow School of Art, and the object found at the Queens' Cross Church will be returned to that church. For the initial opening of the cylinder, we would like to have present the Director of Theology and Religious Studies from St. Andrews University. The director is an old friend of mine, Dr. John Harris. He is the only other person we would like to be present. I know he will come at my request. At this point, all we are going to tell him is that we have found an object that he will find of great interest. Plus I know he would love to come to the inner sanctums of the Vatican. Once we have discovered what we have and it proves to be of great consequence, we have decided on the following establishments."

Richard read off the following establishments;

The British Museum

St. Andrews University

University of Basel

University of California

Oxford University

Manchester-Sheffield Center for the Dead Sea Scrolls

Cairo Museum

The Open University of Israel

Harvard Divinity School

"We will send out the letter of invitation explaining what we have found. We asked Pierre if we could send it out on Vatican stationery. Pierre thinks that would be very acceptable. I don't know if they will all come, but I suspect they will and probably bring a team with them.

Ladies and gentlemen, I think we have everything in order. Are we all in agreement?"

"One moment," I added, "once these people are here, they will surely open it up to the media. Are we comfortable with this?"

"We may as well accept this," Bob replied, "and must be prepared for this, there is nothing we can do to stop it, and neither do we want to."

"One other item, can the Vatican house this number of visitors?"

"Pierre," Bob interrupted, "that is a question for you."

"That will be no problem. All will be most welcome and housed in comfort. Any overflow will be settled in comfortable hotels at our disposal within easy reach of the Vatican. After all, this is not only the Vatican but Rome."

"Good, now that's looked after, are we all in agreement?" Bob asked.

We were all in agreement with no dissenting remarks.

 "Good," Bob announced, "now let's have supper and then relax. I don't know about the rest of you, but I am starving. I believe they are setting it up on the flying bridge. Richard come with me, and we will call your friend at St. Andrews University."

Richard called from one of the ships' phones, with an untraceable line that Captain Roy supplied. Old habits die hard. Soon he was talking to his friend Dr. John Harris.

"John, yes, it is Richard. I know I have sort of disappeared, that is the reason I am calling. Just listen for a moment; I have found something ancient and significant to our belief and history in Christianity. I am on my way to the Vatican to have it unveiled and authenticated. I have had you invited to attend the unveiling. That is if you will come? Yes, you will, wonderful. We should be there in three days from today. Your contact there will be Cardinal Pace at the Arivum Secretum Apostolicum Vaticanum, here is his personal number. They will be expecting your call."

 At supper, Richard announced that Dr. John Harris would be thrilled to join us at the Vatican and could not contain his excitement.

"I did not tell him exactly what we had found, or what we had been through to get it here. I did tell him it would be extremely exciting and of great antiquity. I think though; I had him at the Vatican. He has never been there. Pierre has already called and set it up with the Cardinal."

Supper was a delicious chicken al a king, with fresh warm baguettes and that excellent chardonnay we had in Narbonne. For dessert, two large bowls of tiramisu were placed on the table plus to accompany it a lovely sweet Muscat that we had from the South of France. After supper, we retired to the comfortable lounge on the flying bridge to sip fine Cognac and coffee. We sat and watched the snow-white wake from the stern of the boat. The air was still mild, almost warm, and the sea was calm. The ship rolled gently; it was the end of a perfect evening. The stress from our escape from Scotland and France seemed like a distant memory and was slowly starting to evaporate.

"Anybody up for a game of cards, Shanghai Rummy?" Bob announced with two decks of cards in his hand.

We all looked dumbfounded, "what is it?" Richard asked.

"Doesn't anyone know how to play it ?" Bob asked.

"I do," Jennifer answered, "I play it with some of the ladies in my art clutch. It is a revolving game of rummy with changing hands with every play. It's easy and a lot of fun, but it gets harder as the hands progress.

There are two decks of cards, and the Jokers are wild, and you can buy cards to aid in your hand."

We all decided to play, with Bob and Jennifer explaining the rules. The hardest part was remembering what hand we were playing at each new round. The Cognac did not help either, but it was what we needed. We laughed a lot. I think Bob planned this for a little bonding, especially with Pierre, being the outsider. It certainly worked especially when the cards confounded Pierre, he turned the air blue as he reverted to French curses and then humbly apologized in English. We played till just after midnight and were now ready for bed. We were drained and totally relaxed.

 As we lay in our queen size berth, the boat gently rocking us to sleep, Jennifer announced, "I really enjoyed this evening, and for the first time I feel a little safer."

"Yeh, it was great fun. Now, I'm ready for a good night's sleep."

"Have you thought," Jennifer asked, "what our lives will be like once our discovery hits the world?"

"With everything that we have been through I haven't even thought about that."

"Time to sleep on it," Jennifer responded, "I think it will have quite an impact. There will be reporters everywhere. Our quiet lives will be exposed all over the world. There will be interviews, book offers, magazine offers, we must think about it."

"Or maybe it will fizzle out in a month," I countered, "after all, it is about religion, not a subject the majority of people get wound up about these days."

I did lie in bed thinking about it for about five minutes until sleep seduced me.

The next morning bright sunshine, aquamarine blue sea, and the heady smell of the salty sea found us all together again on the flying bridge for breakfast. The crew again made a hearty English breakfast but added fresh croissants.

As we were drinking coffee, Bob announced, "We will see landfall today as we pass between Corsica and Sardinia. We will be passing through the La Maddalena Islands, quite a pretty sight. Most of the islands are protected national parks. We should see them around lunch time. We will have one more night aboard before we reach the mouth of the River Tiber, and then on to Rome and the Vatican. Pierre has arranged that we will be met by Vatican river launches and ferried straight to the Vatican. Customs has also been taken care of as we are all now diplomatic guests of the Vatican. Pierre has also arranged visitor's apartments for all of us. I'll let him detail that."

"We will probably be staying in the Vatican for at least two weeks," Pierre explained. "First, of course, we must open the cylinder, photocopy what we find. We must then preserve the items found. Next, whatever we uncover must be translated and recorded. After that, the objects must be tested for authenticity and again sealed and preserved. Richard has advised me he is well aware of the procedures having done quite a number of these on rare books back at the Glasgow School of Art. He will have as much help as he needs plus all the necessary equipment the Vatican labs can supply. The Vatican has extensive labs for such purposes. It will probably take the better part of a day to see and familiarize yourselves with our laboratories. I think we are on the verge of a great discovery. Once we have determined what we have, then your invitations will go out to the various institutions you have selected."

"Pierre," I asked, "can they also advise us as to how to deal with the publicity if this is as great a discovery as we think it will be? Jennifer brought this up last night, and to tell you the truth, I have not given it any thought. Our lives could be completely changed by this, for good or for bad."

"As a matter of fact, they will be able to advise you. The church has had many years dealing with exactly this sort of thing. All you have to do is ask."

At that point, Captain Roy announced over the PA system that lunch was served on the flying bridge. Trays of sandwiches, ham, cheese, salmon, pate' and egg salad followed by platters of fresh fruit and assorted cheese. Two samovars, one of coffee and one of tea, were also procured. At the same time, Bob announced we were starting to pass through the Maddalena Islands. As we got closer to the islands, the raucous calls of seagulls inundated the skies.

"To the north, that island is called Cala Santa Maria and further north is Corsica. To the south on our starboard is the island of Maddalena, and further south is Sardinia," Bob informed us. "I wonder if it was called after Mary Magdalene, supposedly Jesus' wife? It would be very pertinent, wouldn't it?"

"I can help you out there," Pierre piped up, "as a matter of fact you are right on. There was much veneration in the early church for Mary Magdalene, with many holding to the belief she was the wife of Jesus and that she fled to Europe via the Mediterranean after the crucifixion of Jesus. She may have very well visited this island. Legend says she settled and died in the south of France."

"I wonder if our find will confirm that?"Pat questioned.

"That and many other things, I am willing to bet," Richard added.

The islands were rugged sundrenched islands set in crystal turquoise blue waters. The rocks and hills were almost bleached white, defying the vegetation to grow. There was, though, much greenery and tropical pines in abundance growing throughout the island. Captain Rob announced there was a pod of dolphins off the starboard side. We rushed over to see them; they kept us entertained for over an hour, surfing in our wake before they disappeared.

We soon left the islands and were out into the open sea, wondering if Mary Magdalene's sad voyage had brought her to these islands.

I turned and approached Peter and Richard, "Meet me in my cabin in about fifteen minutes. Nothing alarming, but keep it quiet."

We were soon all seated in my cabin.

"I didn't bring it up, but how do you now feel working in the heart of the Roman Catholic Church? Do you feel they will try to hide whatever we find if it is too controversial?"

"Do you feel that way, Greg?" Peter asked, "And how about you, Richard."

"The Vatican is world-renowned for its research in biblical and ancient historical research. It would be hard to hide something this big if it turns out to be what we think it is," Richard answered, "plus they have allowed my colleague Dr. John Harris to be present. I doubt they would be doing this if they wanted to hide our find."

"Whatever happens, I put my trust in Bob," Peter added his approval.

"And so do I," I confirmed, "I just wanted to see that we were all on the same page. Sometimes I feel like a small cog in such a large machine. Whether we like it or not, we are being swept along with little control on our part. I feel so inconsequential. "

"I think we all feel that way," Peter added, "but don't forget it was our effort that deciphered the mystery and found the artifacts."

At that moment, Jennifer walked into our cabin.

"What's going on here?"

"We were questioning, or at least I was, as to how we felt being under the control of the Vatican."

"And how do you all feel about it?" Jennifer asked.

"Basically, we have put our faith, sorry for the pun, in Bob," I answered, "but we don't feel there is anything nefarious going on with the Vatican."

"I think you are right," Jennifer added, "but do you not feel Pierre has been very open and obliging? The Vatican has also been very accommodating, asking your friend Richard, Dr. John Harris, to be a witness at the opening of the cylinder. Why would they go to all this trouble to double-cross us and especially Bob?"

"You are right Jennifer, we also came to the same conclusion." Richard answered, "I think it all comes down to our faith in Bob."

"And speaking of Bob, "Jennifer announced, "he would like to see us all on the flying bridge."

We made our way up to the flying bridge to meet with Bob.

" Listen, people," Bob greeted us, " I know I have drilled you up and down with the use of your Walther P22, but I think it is time we put our guns to bed. I feel we are quite safe and have no need for them anymore. Unless there are objections, I would like to collect them. What do you say?"

We had almost forgotten that we were still wearing firearms. Bob had drilled us with their use and handling to such a degree it had become second nature to be carrying them.

Pat was the first to hand over her firearm, "I'm so glad to get rid of this. The thought of using it gave me nightmares."

"Me too," added Jennifer, "although I did not mind the target practice; in fact, I quite enjoyed it."

We all handed over our pistols quite happily, although I shuddered at the thought I had almost used mine back in Toulouse.

"Do you really feel we are out of the woods, Bob?" Richard questioned.

"Yes, I think we are good, and tomorrow we will be under the protection of Pierre and the Swiss Guards. I do not think they would want you running around the Vatican armed. Tonight we will celebrate our last night aboard. I suggest we go and relax in our cabins and refresh ourselves. Put your feet up and arrive totally refreshed for our celebration."

We were all in much agreement and headed down to our cabins. Jennifer and I just plunked ourselves onto the bed and stretched out. The sea was gently rolling, rocking the ship, and our bed to a relaxing calm.

"Our big adventure starts tomorrow," Jennifer mused, "unveiling what we have found."

" Well, not exactly tomorrow. I suppose we will be introduced to our hosts and then escorted to our accommodations." I answered. "The following day, it will be setting things up in the labs. Will you join us to see what happens ?"

" After all this, I won't miss it for the world," Jennifer nuzzled closer.

We relaxed for a couple of hours in our cabin and then headed above decks to take in the sea air and the early spring sunlit Mediterranean.

We found a spot with a couple of lounging chairs on the starboard side, which was sheltered and quite warm.

"We've had quite an adventure, haven't we?" Jennifer questioned. "Did you ever imagine this could happen to us?"

"Never in my wildest dreams could I have imagined this, and it is not over yet. I'm just wondering what we will uncover in the Vatican. My feeling is this will be something monumental, earth-shattering. People have killed over this. We have been chased down the length of the British Isles, across the channel to France, through France, and attacked in Toulouse. Now we are sailing to Italy and the Vatican. So much effort to destroy either us or what we have. I can now understand the terrible religious wars of our past when we have lived through this."

"Do you still feel in danger, Greg?" Jennifer asked.

"More like battle shock. I know we are safer now than we have ever been during this episode. I have great confidence in Bob, plus Interpol, our crew, and now Pierre's Swiss Guard. Our police force back in Scotland finally did an amazing job of flushing out the enemy. I will feel a lot better once we are in the Vatican. I still keep looking over my shoulder just in case. Our enemies are still very potent."

At that moment, Peter stuck his head around the corner, " found you love birds. Supper is almost ready, but Bob would like a word with us."

Everybody was up on the flying deck, seated at our table. Bob was already there waiting for us.

"Ladies and gentlemen, confederates and dear friends. You are all that and more to me. You have been brave, resourceful, and supportive, more than what I had ever hoped for. You have trusted me, and for that, you have my deepest thanks and admiration. As they say in the movies, 'I think this is the beginning of a wonderful friendship.' Today will be our last night onboard, and I have arranged a little celebration."

With that, the crew started uncorking bottles of Champagne and poured liberal glasses for all of us.

"To our success now and the future discoveries in the Vatican," Bob proposed the toast.

We all raised our glasses and cheered.

"And if I may," Richard interrupted, "to all those that brought us here safely, from the Glasgow constabulary, Captain Roy and his crew, Inspector Jurgen Muller and his Interpol, Pierre, and the Swiss Guard, and most of all to you Bob."

This time a thunderous cheer went up. The girls embraced Bob with hugs and kisses.

"That is the first time; I think I have seen Bob blush," Peter announced.

"Please!" Bob raised his hands, "Enough praise or you will have me blushing. Now let us enjoy ourselves."

Soon trays of hors-d'oeuvre were being served; oysters on ice, scallops, angels on horseback, Burgundy pate' with truffles, smoked salmon, jumbo prawns, and prosciutto-wrapped melon. What a feast, and the Champagne just kept coming.

"Bob," I asked, "who are your friends and how do they finance all of this? I don't know whether we deserve this."

"Don't ask, just enjoy. All of the food served today came from our one day stay in the south of France. The day you all put your trust in me is now your reward. We have been waiting a long time for this going back as far as the Sinclair Templars of Scotland, and that is nearly seven hundred years ago. I truly believe we will be changing history. I also feel it will be a change for good and, therefore, a change for the better."

To that, we all raised our glasses to Bob again for all he had done. We had a wonderful time that evening. The food and the Champagne just kept coming. Someone brought up a decent stereo system, so we danced until after midnight.

Finally, Jennifer tugged at me, "I'm ready for bed. My feet are killing me from all the dancing and trying to keep my balance with the rocking ship. The Champagne hasn't helped either; I'm feeling a little light-headed."

" Ok, sweetheart, let's go." We gave our goodnights and off we went. Peter and Pat were of the same mind and ready for bed. I did manage to take a bottle of Champagne and two glasses with us.

"That was a wonderful evening," Jennifer announced. "I feel we should have stayed up and watched the sun come up, but I am dead beat."

I was already in bed when Jennifer cuddled in, "good night sweetheart," was the last thing I remembered.

That morning Jennifer was up just as the sun was starting to greet the day. I could hear her splashing water on her face. As she came back to bed, she let her nightgown slip off to the floor.

"Good morning, darling," she purred as she cuddled next to me. In a moment, I was naked, and Jennifer had, with a naughty little smile slipped on top of me. She plumped up both pillows and put them behind my head. I softly caressed her back with the tips of my fingers; I could feel her whole body shiver. We softly swayed with the undulating ship and kissed. In each other's embrace, we rocked to an intense climax while I gently held her to me. After that, we collapsed into each other's arms and slept till after ten am. A luxurious, shared shower soon brought us around. I toweled her off with soft thick white towels.

"Alright, sweetie, I think I am fully dried now," Jennifer laughingly complained.

"Are you sure I can still see a couple of water drops," I answered, "come here, I can gently wipe them off."

"Any more of that and we will be back on the bed."

"Yes, please, why not?" I pleaded.

"Come on now, we are late enough as it is and probably missed breakfast," Jennifer kissed me and gently pushed me away.

"Spoilsport, it was well worth the missing," But she was right, and we dressed and headed up.

"There's Italy in the distance, nice you could make it. We will be at the mouth of the Tiber River in about two hours. What took you so long ?" Bob queried with a knowing smile.

"Bob," Jennifer asked, "I never asked, is there a Mrs. Flint anywhere?"

"Not exactly a Mrs., but there is someone very special that I love dearly."

" And what does she do ?"

"She looks after me and does a pretty good job of that. Always good to have someone special that loves to look after you. Don't you think? Maybe one day I will pop the question."

"Don't wait too long. I hope one day to meet her and give her my personal thanks, girl to girl. Is she in Texas?"

"I have a feeling you will," Bob replied. "And yes, she is from Texas."

"Does she know what you are up to at the moment?" Jennifer inquired.

"Not exactly, but she has the same background as I, so I doubt this would surprise her," Bob replied.

We sat and sipped coffee and watched as the Italian coast came closer and closer. Within two hours, we dropped anchor three hundred meters off what Bob announced was the Porto Turistico Di Roma. A Vatican tender was heading towards us.

" Alright folks time to get your gear in order and depart the Highland Spirit. The Vatican has arranged that we all have diplomatic status, so no customs check. We will board the tender, and it will ferry us up the Tiber right to the Vatican. We will now be in the capable hands of Pierre and his Swiss Guards."

 Jed Cassidy had left Paris airport on his forged Canadian identification. He had no problem with it at all. Cassidy had packed the artifacts carefully in his luggage and had no problem getting them through customs, through the arranged private jet. Within eight hours, he had landed in Nashville, refreshed, and exuberant. Jed had treated himself to first-class. The private jet personnel had pampered him the whole flight, including at least six good hours of relaxation; Cassidy didn't sleep; he was too high on success. Once in Nashville, jet lag, and booze took over, Jed booked a room at the airport hotel for one night. The next morning he was on a business class ticket for a short commuter flight to Memphis. He then rented a car and drove down to Alabama and the Grand Evangelical Church of the Saviour.

Jed walked straight into the Reverend's office, suitcase in hand.

"Jed, welcome, my boy. I have been waiting for you for the last two days. Come in, come in, please let me see it," Reverend Ducane nervously waited. He was breathless and trembling in anticipation as he impatiently wrung his hands.

Jed unlocked the suitcase and removed the leather cylinder and the Molay confession.   "Doesn't look like much does it," as he handed it over to Ducane.

Ducane was trembling as he cradled the cylinder. "Jed, you have done the Lord's work here. He has blessed us with success. The Templars will no longer be able to hold this over us. The Bible will stay as it was intended, pure. Lord be praised."

" What are you going to do with it now?" Jed asked.

" Destroy it! And praise the Lord," Ducane prayed almost maniacally.

"Destroy them, are you crazy? It must be worth millions!" Jed pleaded. "We went through hell to retrieve it. Aren't you at least going to open it?"

"I will not blaspheme my eyes and mind. My soul will remain pure. What we have must never fall into anyone's hands; it is too dangerous to our cause. For us, this doesn't exist, and I will make sure it doesn't. You have been more than compensated for a job well done. Now it must be destroyed. We will give it a proper funeral. Jed, come with me. I have everything arranged."

The Reverend Ducane led Jed to the funeral chapel, which stood separate to the Grand Evangelical Church of the Saviour.

"We have our crematorium here at the chapel. I even have its' coffin to put it in. It will never bother us again, Jed. Everything is ready; the furnace is all fired up."

A full-sized silk-lined coffin was open, all laid out ready to receive the cylinder and confession.

"Jed, since your efforts brought it safe here, it is, I feel only befitting that you lay them to rest."

With much opposition, Jed took the cylinder and confession and bent over to place it in the coffin.

"I still think it is a waste," Jed answered; he had other ideas, "I don't think I can do it. We have millions of dollars here just for the asking."

"Jed, you and your people have been well compensated for your part plus the heavenly reward you will eventually receive."

Jed bent over the coffin and held the cylinder. He had already placed the confession in it.

 "I don't know Reverend; I don't know. I cannot do it; he held the cylinder tightly to his chest. We can make a deal and make millions."

It was the last thing he uttered. The Reverend Ducane came from behind and struck Jed on the back of the head with his pistol. Ducane always carried a gun holstered inside his jacket, he never trusted anybody, especially Jed's lot, Jed slumped forward. Ducane caught him and used the inertia of his body to tumble Jed and the cylinder into the coffin. He then closed, locked the casket, and activated the conveyor into the crematorium.

As the coffin moved into the open crematorium, the Reverend could hear muffled shouts and pounding in the coffin.

"He will suffocate or heat prostration will kill him long before the flames disintegrate his body. It won't be that painful. I won't be betrayed, no more corruption with money. He was betrayed with thirty pieces; it will not happen again. All is safe now, praise the Lord."

As Bob advised, we boarded the Vatican motor launch with no problems. The Swiss Guard was well prepared for us and very accommodating. They had our diplomatic status papers ready, so there was no delay with customs. Of course, Pierre was well known and greeted like a long lost brother. Pierre had us seated comfortably, and within a short time, we were motoring away from our port of entry.

I watched as our temporary safe home, Le Mar, or should I say Highland Spirit disappeared. She had delivered us out of two harrowing experiences, and now we must leave.

Jennifer touched my arm, "I know what you are thinking, look everybody has their eyes on her saying a quiet thank you."

We motored down the Tiber River for approximately two hours, passing through green farmlands, then gradually building up to the outskirts of Rome. The trip was pleasant; the weather was sunny and mild. We got to know our additional Swiss Guards. With Pierre, there were now four Guards, one Italian, and two German-speaking Swiss. They all spoke English proficiently and made us feel quite welcome. It wasn't long before we docked at the Ponte Vittorio Emanuele Bridge, deep in the heart of Rome and minutes from the Vatican. There were three large black SUVs with the crossed keys coat of arms to the Vatican to meet us. Pierre phoned ahead to let them know we would be arriving at the Vatican in ten minutes. We loaded ourselves and our luggage into the SUVs. From there, we were driven along the Via Della Conciliazione Boulevard to the Piazza Papa Pio XII and then onto the Via di Porta Angelica. The route took us straight through the Porta Sant' Anna into the Vatican. Pierre had informed us that we were to be taken directly to the Biblioteca Apostolica Vaticana, the Vatican Library. We pulled into the vast courtyard in front of the Vatican Library to be greeted by two priests, an elderly priest, and a younger one, both in dark suits. The older priest turned out to be a Cardinal.

"This is Cardinal Jean and his assistant Bishop Pace," Pierre informed us. "Bob, I believe you and the Cardinal are well acquainted."

"Yes, very well," Bob offered his hand to the Cardinal, "We have had a few adventures together."

Cardinal Jean came amongst us, his features grave. He had a heavy Italian accent but spoke English very well. He cradled Bob's hand in both of his, "Bob, you are most welcome and trusted; it is good to see you again. We have had some very interesting times, haven't we? I know you all have traveled through perilous ordeals to get here. Now is the time to feel safe and relaxed."

 Bob did the introductions; we were all welcomed by the Cardinal and Bishop.

"With God's grace," Cardinal Jean added, "you are safe here, and we will continue to protect and look after you. It will be Bishop Pace that will be working with you most closely, but now we will both accompany you into the library. Come, now you are most welcome."

Cardinal Jean and Bishop Pace escorted us into the library. We passed through their security into the elevator. The elevator took us down into their storage area, all hermetically filtered and air-conditioned. Bishop Pace informed us that the filters trapped 99.99% of particles while ultraviolet light filters destroyed nearly 100% of all bacteria. The air-conditioning kept the moisture to an acceptable level.

"This is where we keep our most fragile pieces," Cardinal Jean announced. "We also have a special vault for pieces given over for loan or inspection. You will have your safety deposit with a combination that only you will know to store your relics. I hope this will give you a sense of security as to how we value and protect your discovery."

We were soon inside the vault. We were met by the security officer who explained how the deposit box combination was set up. He then left us alone in the vault to decide what and who would have the combination.

"Bob," Richard asked, "you know the Cardinal and the Bishop?"

"Yes, they are both Jesuits, and I can tell you, you are in good hands, and they can be trusted. There is more to those two than meets the eye. One day when we have time, I'll let you in on a little of it."

"I always thought Cardinals wore red," Richard questioned.

"Only on very ceremonial occasions." Bob still had the attaché case handcuffed to his wrist, "well, what do we decide? The combination should be easy enough, but who is to have it?"

"We have put our faith in you, Bob, all this while so I feel you should be one plus Richard. The Glasgow School of Art owns these articles, and Richard is entrusted with them. What do we think, are we all in agreement?" I asked.

There was no disagreement; we all thoroughly agreed. Bob and Richard set the combination and placed the attaché in the deposit box.

We all walked out of the vault back to Cardinal Jean.

"Good, it is safe," Cardinal Jean announced. "I believe you know, Dr. John Harris from St. Andrews University?"

At first, we did not see him standing behind the Cardinal and Bishop Pace. Richard was the first to recognize John.

"So, you did come. I am so happy to see you. I was wondering, but really, I knew you would not be able to keep away," Richard warmly took John's hand. "This is my dear friend, Dr. John Harris Director of

Theology and Religious Studies, St Andrews University," Richard introduced John to all of us.

"Welcome to our team," Bob offered, "I hope you know what you are getting into?"

"Couldn't have kept me away," John answered. "I've been wondering what Richard had got himself into; it seems like in Scotland, he has fallen off the face of the earth. On top of that, a visit and stay in the Vatican, how could I refuse? But I am still in the dark as to what you are up to."

"That will be quite a long and detailed conversation," Richard answered," but I promise all will be revealed."

Cardinal Jean turned to Bishop Pace, "Now we must make our guest comfortable, but first we have identification cards for all of you. As you can see, they are to be worn like a necklace. Please wear them at all times in the Vatican proper. Now, Bishop Pace has apartments ready for you. If you will be so kind as to follow him, he will get you comfortably settled."

Bishop Pace took us back to the SUVs and our Swiss Guards. The drive was not far; we could have had a nice walk to what Bishop Pace called the Palazzo Apostolico.

"We have arranged apartments for you in one of the Popes' residences. I trust you will be comfortable." The Bishop escorted us up to our apartments.

The Bishop's statement was more of an understatement. We were in a palace where Queen Elizabeth would have been comfortable. It was quite overwhelming. We shared a large apartment, each with two adjoining bedrooms. All the bedrooms, much to our delight, were equipped with en suite bathrooms. Peter and Pat, Jennifer, and I shared one apartment while Bob, Richard, and John shared the second apartment. Our luggage had arrived, and as we started putting things away, there came a knock on the door. Two nuns greeted us at the door, delivering tea trays of sandwiches and pots of coffee. To this, we were most grateful, having almost forgotten we were starving. We tucked into it and finished the lot off. While we were sitting sipping coffee, a second knock came at the door. Bob, Richard, and John entered.

"It is time we filled in Dr. John Harris as to how we came to the Vatican," Bob suggested. "Are you up to it, Greg?"

"Please," Dr. John Harris interrupted, "I would prefer just John."

"John, it is then," Bob announced.

"Thank you," John replied. "Greg, the floor is now yours, if you are up to it."

"Well, of course, I will probably need some help if I miss out on some parts. First of all, what we found is now safely ensconced in a vault here in the Vatican only Bob and Richard know the combination. To this, we all agreed. These ancient items are to be revealed, translated, and verified as to their authenticity here in the Vatican."

"You feel they are that important?" John replied.

"After what we have been through with our lives on the line, you tell me," I countered.

"Your lives were at risk? Now you have all my attention, Greg." John replied, "Please start."

We poured ourselves coffee and got comfortably seated. I began with the fire at the Glasgow School of Art. Richard's call to me as to what was uncovered in the wreckage aftermath of the fire. The discovery of the confession of Jacque de Molay, the last Grand Master of The Knights Templar. There was also a subsequent paper intimating that a further document of even greater importance had been secreted away. There was also police evidence that the fire may have been arson. I added Peters' involvement in helping me translate the confession and what it contained. Then there was the attack on Richard and his hospitalization. Both his office and home were broken into and ransacked.

"Sorry, to butt in Greg, but Richard, I had no idea of this attack on you," John interrupted.

"Things happened so fast, and under a cloud of such secrecy, nothing went out to the public," Richard added. "We did inform the police at this point, and the school still thinks I am convalescing. The police wanted it that way."

I continued relating how we found the second relic at Queens Cross Church, the Knights Templar's leather tube, and what it contained. In it was a sealed lead tube with supposedly the written account of the trial of Jesus Christ. We had not the equipment to open it at the Glasgow School of Art. At this point, we knew we had to put the items in safekeeping and did so with my solicitor. Then there was the first meeting with Bob revealing that we were in great danger. His warning was confirmed with the murder of Chief Inspector James Adam of the Glasgow Constabulary.

"Shit!" John was absolutely amazed, "I did hear about that one, but had no idea you were involved. I can see now; you are in great danger."

"The attack was real, a close call. The supposed murder of Chief Inspector Adams was faked to flush out the culprits. It was kept a secret, known by very few. The attack on him was deadly real," Richard added. "He's another one of our quiet heroes."

"It was a cat and mouse chase from there on, escaping to the Scottish Highlands and from there by boat to Arran. From Arran by ship to France with a quick stop in Falmouth, Cornwall, due to a bad gale force storm. All this escape was orchestrated by Bob and some very mysterious friends."

"Don't forget we were sure the Glasgow Constabulary had been compromised with a mole or two. Later this was proved to be the case. The faked death of Chief Inspector Adams was instrumental in flushing them out. We could only trust a small group within the Glasgow Police. That is why we did not go to them," Peter added.

"We also had to make a quick stop from Arran to Glasgow, by an amazingly fast speed boat, to retrieve the relics," I added. "We were nearly intercepted in Glasgow."

The story continued with our deception in Brest and sneaking off to Bordeaux by ship. The meeting of Interpol and the Swiss Guard through Bob. From there to Toulouse and the deadly sting, replacing the relics with fakes. Finally, Narbonne and then by ship to Rome and then here to the Vatican.

"The sting setup was the most frightening. We came face to face with our deadly nemesis. Shots fired, and I thought we had lost both Bill and Inspector Bliss in a hail of gunshots. Inspector Bliss was Chief Inspector Adams's replacement. He was one of the few within the police we could trust. I felt lowest at this point; I thought all was lost, so convincing was the sting. We could not have done any of this without the help of Bob and his friends, a small trusted police organization in Scotland, the USA, Interpol in France, and now the Vatican," I added. "Quite an international escape plan."

"We were under attack from a radical Masonic splinter group in the USA that had aligned themselves with the American Evangelical Church of the Saviour. Their organization is directed and funded by the American Evangelical Church of the Saviour. Apparently, this is a very large and well funded Midwestern radical Christian group with ties to militant white supremacist groups. They knew this relic existed and what it contained, as they had infiltrated some parts of American Masonry. They were hell-bent on either destroying the relics, us along with it, or hiding them away in their organization. They felt it would radically change their teachings of the bible and, consequently, their view of Christianity. This could also have a huge effect on their monetary bottom line, which is multi-millions of tax-free money."

"Bob," John asked, "are you aware of what the relic contains?"

"As a high ranking Mason, I know we are aware both in the UK and America that this relic existed and had some idea of what it contained. No one has seen it since it was sealed by the Knights Templar, not even the Vatican. We know it was spirited away by the Knights Templar to Scotland into the hands of the Sinclairs. From there, it was handed down from generation to generation in secret, until it reached Charles Rennie MacKintosh. Even we didn't know that he held it. The last person that we know of, who knew the whereabouts, was this Iain McLellan, mentioned in the letter. Even he is a mystery to us. That is what we hope to uncover here in the Vatican."

"But," John asked, "the Masons and the Catholic Church? I didn't think there was much trust between the two of them."

" I know our history has not been the smoothest. As I explained, that has changed a lot in the last one hundred years. You would be amazed at the good and solid relations that exist today between us."

"This is a lot to take in," John announced, "What have you uncovered that is so dangerous that people will kill rather than have this revealed?

I cannot wait for the unveiling. Thank you so much for inviting me. I get shivers just thinking about it."

"Shivers, sweats, nausea, and diarrhea, I call it my Mexican vacation," Peter chirped, "and that was just Bob. I think I held up very well, didn't I?"

"Yes, Peter, you were the rock of Gibraltar," Bob answered, as we all giggled.

"Let me continue, once we have revealed what the canister contains," added Richard, "we have a list of leading experts in this field we are inviting to review our finds."

"Why was I invited?" John asked.

"We wanted at least another expert in this field to be present and particularly from Scotland. You were my comfort level," Richard explained.

"I feel very humbled at your confidence in me," John responded.

We sat and talked for over four hours. John was digesting everything along with the occasional further explanation or clarification. At this point, we were interrupted by a knock on the door.

A priest in a long black cassock announced that supper would be ready in two hours. He would be back to escort us there. Cardinal Jean and Bishop Pace would be joining us for supper. Also, not to worry, the attire was casual.

Casual or not, we all needed a bit of sprucing up. We retired back to our bedrooms to tidy up. At the announced time, the priest came back to take us to supper. Our apartments were on the third floor; we were led down to the first floor and then to the dining room. Our Swiss Guards were hovering not far behind. The dining room was an understatement;

this was a baroque palatial grand dining hall. It felt very intimidating. Cardinal Jean and Bishop Pace greeted us.

Cardinal Jean made us very welcome and laughed, "I know the place is a little overwhelming. I can tell by the looks on your faces. This dining area is all we have when guests stay with us. I trust you are not let down?"

At this, we all laughed. We were ushered and sat down at the end of a table that could seat at least forty people with Cardinal acting as host at the head of the table.

"Believe it or not, but this is one of the smaller tables for this room. We can add on to this one and double its' size."

"Does the Pope stay in this palace?" Pat asked.

"Yes, sometimes, he has three residences in the Vatican grounds."

"Will we meet him?" Pat added.

"Oh, I am sure you will, as He already knows of you and what you bring. He has had Pierre Godet brief him."

Terrenes of hot soup were now being brought in, at this point Cardinal Jean asked us to bow our heads while he gave a small grace and blessed us all.

"Now, please start. I know you must be hungry."

 Onion soup with little croutons, after that, steaming bowls of a delicious lamb ratatouille with warm fresh baked bread. We sopped up the last of the gravy and washed everything down with a very acceptable red Primitivo.

"I trust everything was acceptable?" asked Cardinal Jean.

We were all in agreement; supper was excellent.

"Unfortunately, there will be no dessert, a small sacrifice as we are now into Lent. I must take the blame for smuggling in the wine, and I ask the Lord's forgiveness, but as none of you are of the Rome Catholic faith, I took a little liberty."

"If you would like to take a little bit more liberty, "Peter grinned, "I'm not anything, so on my behalf, we could have some more wine. Besides, I hear Jesus liked wine, and I won't say a thing."

Cardinal Jean chuckled, "He did indeed, but I smuggled these in myself, and I do not have the gift of changing water to wine. I hope I do not disappoint?"

"No," Peter laughed, "everything was wonderful, thank you. Maybe that miracle of the wine might happen when you are Pope."

"Only if you convert Peter," I laughed.

"I know Peter that I will have to watch out for you. I shall take you under my special care," Cardinal Jean replied.

"Now what have I done," Peter shaking his head.

"You will have a very unenviable task," I added.

"But that is my mission in life," the Cardinal added, winking at Peter.

"If you can reform him," Pat added, "you will have my gratitude forever, Cardinal."

"I am up for the challenge, Peter and I will become inseparable," offered the Cardinal.

"Now, if I may," Cardinal Jean changing the subject, "what we have planned for tomorrow will be your introduction to our library laboratory. I was advised that both Richard and John are more than qualified to proceed with the opening of the relic. Bishop Pace will take you through the lab and place at your disposal all the necessary equipment needed. I think you will find we are well equipped with everything you will need. Tomorrow will be a familiarization of the lab and set up our equipment. The following day we will dissect the patient. We will film the whole procedure; I trust there is no objection to this?"

"No, that is excellent," Richard agreed.

John nodded his approval.

"Good, then I suggest an early night and lots of rest, "

We were more than ready to accept the Cardinals' suggestion. We were all tired, plus the food and wine had a further sedative effect. We thanked the Cardinal for a wonderful supper and said our goodnights. Cardinal Jean called for the priest to take us back to our rooms. As we left, our Swiss Guards were there waiting, always protective.

We settled into our apartment, "well, Jennifer, that was quite an introduction to the Vatican. They have gone out of their way to make us feel comfortable, welcome, and safe. We could not have asked for better hosts."

"Are you planning to convert?" Jennifer giggled as she put her arms around me and kissed me.

"Yes, I am planning on taking the vows of celibacy," I countered.

"Are you, well we will see how long that lasts," Jennifer teased.

"Probably just tonight, I am bushed. Too much excitement, come on, let's get to bed."

"I can show you a little more excitement if you want," Jennifer teased as she kissed me and dragged me onto the bed.

All my discipline vanished as we hungrily devoured each other. After, we lay there, now completely spent.

"That may be a first for the Vatican," Jennifer giggled, as she kissed me.

 The next day, wakeup was early, as breakfast was delivered to our apartments. We ate breakfast and were advised we were to be escorted to the Library Laboratories in an hour. We were more than ready before the hour was up; we could barely contain our excitement. When the knock came, we were all primed for the day's revelations. We were taken by the same priest that had brought us to supper. This time we walked to Biblioteca Apostolica Vaticana, the Vatican library. It was a pleasant day, the sun shining, and in the confines of the Vatican, it was quite warm. It would have been lovely to linger a little longer outside, but soon we were being ushered down to the underground Library labs. At this point, our Swiss Guards left us and stayed behind. White smocks were supplied to all of us plus white cotton gloves. We put these on and had our identification cards scanned and then taken through double climate-controlled doors into the lab.

"Good morning," Bishop Pace was there to greet us, " I trust you slept well, and breakfast was adequate."

We all agreed we did, and yes, breakfast was more than sufficient.

"Good, Richard, John, and I will be the main team to unlock the secrets of our relic. Are we still all agreed to this?" Bishop Pace asked.

There was no objection. We all felt we had the best team to undertake the opening of the cylinder.

Bishop Pace added, "Tomorrow, we will have a couple of university intern students to assist. Now I would like to acquaint you with our equipment. As Cardinal Jean advised, we will be filming the entire procedure. As you can see, we have three video cameras and 35mm high-speed cameras. Over there is our picture development room. We will be filming with two cameras, using our staff here to film. Over there is our X-ray room, and beside it is our sonar wave detection machine, much like a prenatal device. We have several types of copying machines for any documents and, of course, vacuum sealing devices. We have ultraviolet and infrared detection units. The adjacent room to your left is the chemical laboratory. On your workbench, over here, we have a myriad of draws containing every conceivable physical tool at your disposal. Of course, this lab is hermetically sealed and climate-controlled. The only apparatus we do not have is carbon testing that we will have to send out. May I ask what your procedure will be tomorrow?"

"We have already opened the leather cylinder," Richard stated, "to reveal a further lead cylinder plus a vellum sheet inside. The vellum sheet belonged to the Knights Templar dated 1129. The sheet is an inventory description in Latin describing the contents as the trial of Jesus Christ before the Sanhedrin and the Governor Pontius Pilate. This inventory sheet we had copied at the Glasgow School of Art. I think we should make additional copies here for the Vatican to keep on file. We are not any further than that. We know it is lead, and by its' weight, we know it is hollow. The lead cylinder is inscribed with the skull and crossed bones of the Knights Templar. Bob and Pierre have informed us that they have made you copies of Charles Rennie MacKintosh's letter, and you also have an additional confession of Jacque de Molay here in the Vatican Library identical to the one we have."

"Yes," replied the Bishop, "our investigations lead us to believe there were four copies made of the confession of Jacque de Molay at the time of his execution. We have one; you have one; we know where the third one is, but where the fourth one is, we do not know. The copy of the Knights Templar inventory sheet is completely new to us and very exciting."

"Tomorrow, we will take a tiny sample of both the leather cylinder and the Templar's' inventory sheet and have them carbon dated," Richard advised. "Also, tomorrow, we will initially take all the physical dimensions of the cylinder plus photos. Then we will open the lead cylinder to reveal its' contents. I have ascertained that all the necessary tools are available in the lab. I believe the opening of the cylinder will be conventional tooling, very similar to a plumber's pipe cutter. We cannot use heat of any kind or any tooling that will generate heat. Bishop Pace has advised us he will have everything set up today, and we will meet here at 9:00 AM tomorrow. "

"Now it is time for lunch, I have arranged this in the library cafeteria," the Bishop announced. "After lunch, I will set up all the necessary equipment in our library lab as per your request. You have the afternoon free, and I have arranged that Pierre will take you on a tour of the Vatican. I trust that is alright and enjoyable to you?"

We all felt that the change would be pleasant, especially viewing some of the wonders of the Vatican.

We had a light lunch in the cafeteria, and later Pierre joined us with his Swiss Guards, always present in the background. We all felt like high ranking dignitaries, although it was a little intimidating.

"Well, for once a pleasant task, I am to give you the busman's tour of the Vatican. I am at your disposal for the whole afternoon, but if you have any personal requests, I will do my best to fulfill them. It is not every day one gets a personal tour of the Vatican by the Swiss Guard. So, what do you think of Cardinal Jean and Bishop Pace?" Pierre asked. "You know that Bob is well acquainted with the Cardinal."

"Both the Cardinal and the Bishop have been more than helpful and, at the same time, most congenial hosts. Their lab is state of the art, couldn't ask for more," Richard replied.

"How do you know the Cardinal?" I asked Bob, "Plus, are we still in danger? We have your Swiss Guards following us everywhere."

"I'll leave that one to Pierre. As to the Cardinal and Bishop, yes, I do know both Cardinal Jean and Bishop Pace very well," answered Bob, "and we have been in contact with each other over the past ten years. When Cardinal Jean spoke of the four medieval copies of Jacque de Molays' confession, he enlightened us to the whereabouts of two of them. One we have brought to the Vatican and is now back with the Masons, one the Vatican has had for many hundreds of years. That left two, one of which we have now, and of course, there is the one we do not know where it is. That fourth one is still lost; we have no idea where it is. The one copy the Masonic Order of the Knights Templar in Maryland has, and it has been in its possession since 1634. What better place to hide it than in the New World? Cardinal Jean and Bishop Pace plus myself and members of the National Knights Templar's helped us verify its authenticity ten years ago. Both of them traveled to the Lodge and then invited us back to the Vatican. That is also where I met Pierre Godet. We have worked closely with them for many years, and I can tell you they are highly trained in their field. Men of great integrity. The Cardinals' title is Arcivum Secretum Apostolicum Vaticanum, in other words....."

Peter piped up, "The head honcho of the Secret Archives of the Vatican."

"Correct Peter and Bishop Pace is the Scientific Director of the Secret Archives. You have at your disposal two of the most learned men in the world in this field. We are quite honoured don't you think? Anyway, enough of this, Pierre, we are at your disposal for a tour of the Vatican, lead on."

Before Pierre could answer, Richard interjected, "Now we have one confession of Jacque de Molay that will be displayed back in Scotland. We have almost come full circle."

"Yes, quite right," Bob answered, "we have added to Scotland's history. We do believe the fourth copy is still hidden somewhere in Scotland."

"Greg, as to your question regarding our Swiss Guards," Pierre added, "they are here at my request. I do not think we are in danger. They are here as a comfort factor for you, after all, you have been through. If you feel uncomfortable with them, I can dismiss them."

"No, Pierre, please forgive me. I see boogeymen around every corner. Please let them stay, I'm just being a nervous Nelly," I answered.

"Alright then," answered Pierre, "I shall take you on the most intimate tours of the Vatican that most people never see."

We had a lovely afternoon, and yes, it was nice having our personal guard looking out for us. We felt like very special VIPs being escorted around the Vatican with our own Swiss Guard, passing through all the tourist queues. Again, the sun was out, making the sheltered parts of the Vatican quite warm. Everywhere was green, and signs of an early March spring were starting to show. Everybody wanted to start at St. Peters' Basilica, which was where we spent most of the afternoon. No long queues for us, we were ushered through everywhere we went, most satisfying. It was utterly amazing, and unfortunately, there was not enough time to take it all in. St. Peter's Square was breathtaking, with room enough for at least two football fields. One had the feeling the glory of ancient Rome was still present as we were surrounded by Romanesque columns leading to the Basilica. St. Peter's is humbling; one feels so small, almost as if in the presence of God. The magnificence of Michelangelo is everywhere. St. Peter's covers nearly six acres under one roof, the largest Christian church in the world. Pierre led us to one amazing site, the tomb of British royalty, James Edward Stuart, and his wife, Maria Sobieska. A little bit of Scotland here in the Vatican. He also took us under the Vatican, where most tourists never go. We saw what is reputed to be the tomb of St. Peter, Jesus' pick to lead the Christian community. The time flew by, and finally, Pierre advised us it was time to go back to our apartments and ready ourselves for supper.

"What did you think of our tour?" I asked Jennifer once we were comfortably ensconced in our apartment.

"It was overpowering for me. I think it would take a month for me to see everything. I thoroughly enjoyed it," Jennifer answered. "How about you?"

"The grandeur was utterly amazing. A little too much opulence for my taste. "I laughed,"

"Spoken like a true Scotsman." Jennifer giggled. "Give us our Presbyterian values and Spartan churches."

"One did not know where to rest one's eyes to meditate or pray," I replied. "It was like being in a grand museum."

"Well, this is the headquarters for the world's biggest Christian church. We should allow them a bit of show for the two thousand years they have been around," Jennifer added.

"Oh, I am not criticizing. It is just overwhelming. I have never seen anything like it to compare. I must say it was beautiful. Anyway, we had better get ready for supper in another intimidating room," this time, I laughed.

We quickly washed and changed. Our clothing from our voyage and the previous day had already been laundered and pressed all laid out on our bed.

"I could get used to this lifestyle so easily," Jennifer mused as she put our laundered clothing away.

It wasn't long before we were being led back to the palatial dining room. We were greeted again by Cardinal Jean and Bishop Pace and directed to the same seating as the night before.

This time it was Bishop Pace that said grace before our meal. Supper again started with terrenes of hot soup, a delicious Italian bean soup. To our surprise, the main course was Sheppard's Pie with gravy boats of lamb gravy with just a hint of mint. The mashed potato topping was grilled to a lovely golden brown crust, accompanied by young sweet peas in their pods.

"Our chef had a little more time to prepare something a little closer to home," Cardinal Jean announced, "I trust it will be to your liking? A little Chianti will enhance it to no end, don't you think? Again, a little indulgence for lent, Peter I hope you like it as there will not be a desert. I know there will be penance to pay for my sneaking wine to our table. I cannot get that one past the chef; he looks after our wine cellar as well. I lifted this wine from some private stock. Thank you, Bishop Pace, for grace to Our Lord for our bounty and your safe trip here to the Vatican."

"I hope you don't mind," the Cardinal blessed all that sat at his table.

"I can see a perceptible change in Peter already," the Cardinal winked.

"Only if it comes with wine," Peter laughed.

I felt a little inwardly embarrassed that I did not consider giving the same thanks in my daily rituals. Bob broke my thoughts as he tasted the Cardinal's selection of wine.

"Cardinal Jean, any of your Chianti will enhance. Your wine is superb," Bob complimented.

"Yes, it is," answered Cardinal Jean, "and this one is from one of our vineyards up north in the heart of Tuscany."

"It reminds me of the old saying, "Peter added, "water, water everywhere but nor a drop to spare."

"Peter, come back after lent, and I will take you on a personal tour of the Vatican's vineyards," Cardinal Jean offered. "As my guest."

"You're on, Cardinal, enough wine and I may convert," Peter beamed.

"Any improvement in Peter and I will convert," Pat added.

Peter and the Cardinal seemed to have started a light-hearted friendship and delighted in the repartee they shared.

"And the Sheppard's Pie was excellent," I added.

"You certainly have gone up in our estimate," Pat proclaimed, "You have made us so welcome, and if you can convert Peter, sainthood cannot be far behind for you."

"Now you have certainly made it a real challenge," Cardinal Jean announced. "Saint Jean of the Vineyards, I like it."

At that point Richard stood up and raised his glass of wine, "I would like to propose a toast to our hosts Cardinal Jean and Bishop Pace. I had my trepidations, but you have been nothing but wonderful and accommodating to complete strangers. To you, Cardinal Jean and

Bishop Pace, I hope we have a long and continued friendship. By the way, my money is on you if Peter takes the tour of your vineyards."

To this, we all stood, clapped a sounding cheer, and raised our glasses to the Cardinal and Bishop.

" I thank you, you have touched my heart, but now dear friends, we are all embarking tomorrow on a mission that may have monumental effects on all Christian faiths, and I dare say Judaism as well. Think well on what lies ahead and how we will pursue it, and with that, I will bid you goodnight."

We were led back to our apartments, and soon we were slowly getting ready for bed.

"So, what do you think now of our hosts, my love?" I asked Jennifer.

"I think they are men of science and wisdom, kind and accommodating with profound spirituality and love of the divine. A rare combination, don't you think?"

"You are absolutely right, my love," as I climbed into bed.

 Sleep, though, did not come easily that night. My mind was racing as to what we would uncover for ourselves and the universal effect it would have on tomorrow and the years to come.

We all met early the next morning in the library cafeteria. None of us slept well; the anticipation was too great. No one could eat much either, just coffee all around. The excitement could be bottled, even though we were all very quiet. Finally, Cardinal Jean and Bishop Pace arrived. We all stood at once to greet them.

"Well friends," the Cardinal and Bishop Pace greeted us, "I can see we are all ready to go. I hope you thought about what we may discover today. It never fails to amaze me even at my age, the excitement that always precedes a major discovery. Shall we proceed?"

There was no disagreement, and we moved together as if one unit united in our single purpose.

It raised a chuckle with the Cardinal at our eagerness, "alright, let's go," he called, "I can see I cannot hold you back."

We followed the Cardinal and Bishop Pace to the elevators, each of us presenting our identification cards to the security guards. We followed the Cardinal and Bishop down to the underground Library laboratory. Our intern students dressed in the working attire of lab technicians were there to greet us. They had white smocks, gloves, and surgical masks ready for all of us. To see the Cardinal and Bishop dressed as lab technicians was most unusual; science and theology united.

"Now you can see us in our working clothes," Cardinal Jean indicated, "which believe it or not is more the norm for us. Science being the workhorse to our theology."

We followed Bob and Richard to the vault. Both went in to retrieve the attaché case and bring it through the double airlock doors to the lab. Bob unlocked the attaché case and lifted the leather cylinder onto the lab counter. We all stood back and stared, such a little object with such great potential. Life and death had presided in its presence. Bishop

Pace, Dr. John Harris, and Richard took up their positions as if on an operating table.

"Well, Richard," spoke Bishop Pace, "this is your baby; how will you proceed?"

Almost as if talking to himself, Richard answered, "Very delicately, very delicately indeed."

We all moved in to watch the operation, almost holding our breaths.

Cardinal Pace indicated, "If you cannot see everything with the procedure, there are three TV monitors that will give an excellent view of the operation."

Richard removed the vacuum-sealed bag with a pair of surgical scissors. He discarded the bag and placed the leather tube on the operating table. Richard then gently slid off the leather cap and opened the leather tube. Laying the leather tube on its side, he slowly slid out the lead cylinder. From the weight of the cylinder, we knew it was hollow and had something inside that had enough space to move around. The lead tube was embossed with the Templar skull and crossed bones. The lead tube resembled a large pipe with a cap that fit over the tube top and the same for the bottom. The cap looked like it had been soldered on at the top and bottom, but on closer examination, we could see that instead of soldering, the cap on, small bands of lead had been jammed in between the cap and the tube with some kind of resin making it a solid air-tight fitting. The first task was to remove one of the lids.

"As this is lead, we cannot x-ray the tube, and lead is a little too dense for an ultrasound of any consequence. I cannot remove the seal with heat; it could damage the contents. I am not sure if we can pull the sealant out." Richard announced. "So I will delicately cut the cap off. We can vacuum pack it when we are finished. Do you agree Bishop Pace and John?"

John answered, and the Bishop agreed, "We cannot use heat; therefore, we must cut."

Richard gently placed the tube wrapped in a cotton cloth in a workbench vice. The jaws of the clamp were lined with soft rubber. He then proceeded to gently secure the tube just enough to hold it firm but not crush it. From the drawer, he took what almost looked like a large plumber's pipe cutter. He then proceeded to place the pipe cutter at the top of the lead cylinder just under the cap. Very gently, he tightened the cutting edge into the lead. He then turned the pipe cutter one complete revolution with John balancing the cutter as it turned. He kept repeating this procedure, gently tightening and rotating until the top of the lead cylinder came free.

"Believe it or not, this tool is almost an exact copy of a medieval drain pipe cutter. H'm, just as I thought," Richard murmured, wholly absorbed in his work, "there is a space between the lead tube and whatever is inside. The object does not fit tightly."

 Once the lead cap was off, we could see what looked like linen bandages wrapping an object inside the lead tube. Richard then took a pair of large forceps out of the table drawer and gently lifted the bandaged object out of the lead cylinder. The linen bandages were in surprisingly good condition considering their age. They looked almost brand new.

We were all silently transfixed at the procedure, barely breathing. Richard stood back, surveying the situation. He then examined the lead tube to see if anything was left inside; there was not.

"We cannot do a carbon testing on lead, but a sample can determine where it was refined and smelted, due to minute particulates in the lead." Richard gave a small sample from the pipe cutter to one of the students, who then put it into a sample vile and categorized it.

"Well, gentlemen, shall we unwrap the patient?" Richard proposed.

"Can you tell, Richard, what the wrappings are?" asked the Cardinal.

"I think it is linen sealed with beeswax. John, can you take a small cutting? We will have it tested."

John cut a tiny sample of the linen and a small sample of the beeswax. Bishop Pace held out a small vial for each and sealed it once the sample was contained. The samples were passed to one of the students to have them tested and cataloged.

Richard started to gently unwrap the remaining object using what looked like a type of hair dryer to melt the beeswax. The procedure was awkward and time-consuming so as not to destroy anything. The wrappings encircled the object about three times until it uncovered what seemed to be another hollow cylinder, this time wood.

"Do you smell it?" Richard queried, "Cedar, the fragrance is still there even after all these years."

The pungent sweet fragrance of cedar wafted up to all of us. We stood amazed.

"Could this be from the legendary cedars of Lebanon?" John questioned.

There was an additional fragrance, not as strong.

"I can again smell beeswax. It is there also," I added.

"Yes," Richard replied, "the top of the wooden cylinder is sealed with beeswax. I can smell it."

On further examination, the cedar tube was approximately fourteen inches long by four inches in diameter. The cap, which was approximately an inch thick, was wholly sealed with beeswax. The cap had been dipped into it. The top of the cap had the Templar's cross imprinted into the wax. Further down the side of the cylinder were carved two knights sitting on one horse, The Poor Knights of the Temple insignia.

Richard again took a small sample of the cedarwood and beeswax for further examination and testing. These were handed to the Bishop and John.

" A riddle within a riddle. What do you call those Russian dolls that fit one inside the other?" Richard offhandedly remarked.

"Matryoshka dolls," Dr. John Harris offered, "sometimes they conceal a bottle of vodka which I would not mind right now. Steady the nerves."

Richard then took from another drawer what looked like a box cutter with a very fine razor. He gently inscribed the wax at the cap joint until he had followed it around the whole circumference. Then he firmly twisted and pulled until the cap came off. At this point, he put the cylinder down and changed into another pair of clean white cotton gloves. We were all mesmerized as if watching open-heart surgery. What slid out next was what seemed to be a white cloth bag synched at the top with a bow knot. The material almost seemed pristine, considering the number of years it had been sealed.

"Silk," Richard remarked as he undid the bow and pulled out what looked like a Roman scroll tied up with a red ribbon. Along with the scroll, a small piece of plant fell out.

" What is this ?" Richard queried, looking at the vegetation.

Cardinal Jean was the first to speak, " I do believe it is hyssop."

" Hyssop, why would hyssop be added ?" Richard asked.

Again it was the Cardinal who answered, "Cedar, silk, beeswax, and hyssop were ancient elements of purification in the ancient middle east. Whoever put this together considered this to be extremely holy."

Richard gently placed the rolled scroll on the work table and undid the ribbon. The outer scroll, which was vellum came off in one piece. The scroll was written in Aramaic. There was an additional scroll, which was tied up with another red ribbon.

" Gentlemen," Richard commanded, " what we do now must be done as quickly as possible. We must photograph the contents and then return them to their original state. Although they look in good condition, we must keep them in that condition."

"How do we do that?" I queried, "We have already disturbed the wax seal and the lead casing."

"Everything will be returned back as we found it in situ, and then I will vacuum pack it." Richard replied, "We have the equipment here to do that."

Richard, with the help of the Bishop, transferred the scroll to a second work table and set up an overhead digital camera. After placing a section of the vellum page under a glass sheet, he took the first copy and kept repeating until all of the scroll had been copied.

"I've set it up to make three copies. The copies will be sent to our PC, which will then send it to the printer. John, watch the printer," Richard ordered.

At that moment, the first copy came through, followed by two additional sheets all in perfect reproduction.

The second scroll was written in Latin and was of a different composition.

"Papyrus," both John and Richard announced almost in unison.

Both the vellum and papyrus were in excellent condition considering their age. Both pieces were written on one side, which Richard commented would make our job a lot easier and faster. He also praised the people that had the knowledge to package and preserve the scroll so carefully.

"Alright John, so we will do the same with the second scroll, I will place the section under glass, and you photo it. I will lift the glass and John you will unroll the next section as I roll up the copied section. We will continue this process until the entire scroll is copied,'' Richard concluded.

Little by little and oh so carefully, we copied the entire scroll, which was almost six feet long. Every time Richard took a picture, the copying machine spat out three copies from the printer. It took us twenty minutes to copy the entire scroll and roll it back up to its' original shape. The vellum and scroll were then fastened with their original red ribbons, placed in the silk sack with the hyssop, and tied. It was then placed back in the cedar tube, the cap fitting tightly back, and then carefully bandaged in the original linen. It was then placed snuggly back in the lead container. Richard then took it over to another machine placed the lead top on the lead cylinder stretch wrapped the two parts together and then vacuum packed and shrink-sealed it in a heavy plastic bag. He did this twice to ensure the greatest protection. It was then placed back in its' original leather case.

After this, Richard had us collate the three copies into consecutive pages bound in legal size covers.

" Peter, since it was you who originally did the initial translation of the confession and got us into this mess, would you be so kind as to do the honours again ?" Richard asked.

"And get you into another mess you'd like to say. Once more into the breach, dear friends." Peter grinned and opened to the first page. " This is a great honour, thank you."

Peter methodically scanned the first page. "This is written in Aramaic," Peter announced and proceeded to translate.

Sanhedrin Temple High Council, Jerusalem, Tammuz, Yon Revii, 3791

"Peter, sorry, to interrupt," Richard asked, "but what is Tammuz, Yon Revii, and 3791?"

"I believe Tammuz is our equivalent of April, and Yon Revii is Wednesday, but I am not sure. 3791 would have been the current Hebrew year this trial took place."

"You are correct, Peter," Cardinal Jean assured. "Please continue."

Presiding Scribe, Priest Hedron

Charged by the Sanhedrin,   Yeshua Ben Dawid accused of blasphemy, sedition, and treason. Blasphemy by calling yourself God. Blasphemy and sedition bringing in the Canaanites and so-called God-fearers into the Temple. Treason, trying to overthrow the Kingship of King Herod and provoking revolution against Imperial Rome. Charges are laid by Priest Annas of this Sanhedrin Temple, Jerusalem.

High Priest Caiaphas presiding.

Priest Annas,   Bring forward the Essene Rabbi, Yeshua Ben Dawid of Nazareth

High Priest Caiaphas, who will act on his behalf?

Priest Annas, Yosef Ben Aramathia of this council, has proposed defense on his behalf, and the Pharisee Nicodemus has come forward as support in this matter.

"My God, Peter, have we stumbled onto the original transcripts of the trial of Jesus Christ? No wonder people wanted this destroyed or anyone who got in their way." I exclaimed, "But why, what does it contain that is so damaging?"

Cardinal Jean turned, and out of old habit, he blessed us all, "we in the Vatican were always told that this transcript existed, but probably lost. The Romans, Greeks, and Hebrews all kept extensive records on almost everything. What truth we have here and what it will reveal we don't know, but we are going to find out. I never thought I would live to see the day I would see it. I am in awe and wonder; I am blessed." Tears were welling up in the Cardinal's eyes.

"We, the Masonic Knights Templar, knew it existed, hidden away since the Sinclair Lords of Scotland. Everything at that time was verbal and memorized. Where it was hidden was lost, but we had our suspicions that, if it were found, was going to be earth-shattering in its revelation," Bob replied. "Please, Peter read on, let us see what further unfolds."

"Before you do, the trial script is calling Jesus, Yeshua Ben Dawid. Is this confirming that Jesus was a direct descendant from the royal house of David?" I pointed out.

"He always said he was," Bishop Pace answered. "This is the first written confirmation I have seen. Please, Peter, continue."

Peter continued with the translation.

High Priest Caiaphas, Let it begin, Yeshua Ben Dawid, you are charged with treason, sedition, and blasphemy against Imperial Rome, Royal Court of King Herod, and this Sanhedrin. You are also charged with conspiring with your wife, Mary, the Magdalene Priestess of the

Canaanite Temple to bring Gentiles and so-called God-fearers into the Judean temple; this is also blasphemous. At Passover, you entered Jerusalem and declared yourself King. You had the crowds lay wreaths at your entrance and declare you King. The Sanhedrin Council has the right to put you on trial as a blasphemous Rabbi calling yourself the son of God and on behalf of King Herod and the Protectorate of Rome, Pontius Pilate. If found guilty, the punishment would be death by stoning. What do you say?

"Again Mary the Magdalene, Priestess of the Canaanite Temple, Jesus' wife and God-fearers. What we are seeing confirms the confession of Jacque de Molay," Richard exclaimed. "Is this true?"

" Maybe you would like to take this one Cardinal Jean," I asked.

" There are many Gospels not included in the New Testament that allude to Mary Magdalene being the wife of Jesus or at least his most favoured disciple. Certainly, she was not a reformed prostitute; the Church corrected that a few years ago. There is also the Gnostic Gospel, written in code, of the meeting and marriage of Joseph and Aseneth, actually the code name for Jesus and Mary Magdalene. This manuscript describes that Mary Magdalene was a very powerful person in her own rite. She was a Canaanite priestess that converted to the teachings of Jesus before they were married. In doing so, she brought large numbers of Gentiles from her own Temple to Jesus. There was also a very large group of Gentiles calling themselves God-fearers. They believed in one supreme God, as did the Jews. Jesus' preaching of brotherly love and inclusiveness rather than dietary rules and circumcision was attracting large numbers of these God-fearers. This was the strength and persuasiveness of Jesus' preaching. Peter, please continue, let us see what else is revealed."

"It would seem in these recordings Jesus would not answer to these charges," Peter quoted. "Listen to this."

Yeshua Ben Dawid, Remains silent.

Priest Annas,   He remains silent as he knows he is guilty.

"Peter, I never understood why Jesus would not defend himself. Why did he remain silent ?" Richard interrupted.

"Don't forget," I answered, "that Jesus held himself higher than the Sanhedrin. He claimed direct descendant to King David, so he was not answerable to a false court or a false temple. He maintained that the Temple did not follow the Essene holy temple building plan. Remember the casting out of the moneylenders from the Temple? This, some scholars believe, was the first public denouncement of the Sanhedrin. We never really knew Jesus' true lineage. His foster father, St. Joseph was never mentioned in the gospels of Mark, the earliest gospel. Some believe Joseph was added later to coincide with the old testament of Moses' common birth. To be brought before the Sanhedrin certainly denotes that Jesus was a very powerful man. No commoner would be brought before the Sanhedrin. Again, this confirms when he is brought before Pilate, he would not hear the trial of a commoner. To be brought before Pilate also confirms Jesus held a lot of power. It has been assumed that Jesus was a backcountry illiterate preacher; this proves to the contrary."

"You are well versed, Greg. Your comment has always been a theory held by many," Cardinal Jean added. "Although now, Moses' common birth is being questioned and new evidence seems to suggest he actually was a real prince of Egypt. Please continue Peter."

Yosef Ben Arimathea: I would like to bring in before the high counsel my witness to these procedures, Judas Iscariot.

Priest Annas: Ciaphas, I must protest, this man has no bearing on this trial and is one of the accused disciples, anything he says will be biased in Yeshua Ben Dawid's favour.

Yosef Ben Arimathea: The Sanhedrin High Counsel has brought Yeshua Ben Dawid before this council. Judas Iscariot was instrumental in bringing Yeshua Ben Dawid to you. He has evidence as to why. He should be heard.

High Priest Caiaphas: Alright, I will allow it. Judas Iscariot, approach us, you may speak.

Yosef Ben Arimathea;   Judas, who are you to Yeshua Ben Dawid?

Judas Iscariot; My name is Judas Iscariot; I have been with my beloved Rabbi Yeshua Ben Dawid for over twelve years. I am his chief scribe and monies accounting for Yeshua and his disciples. I know Yeshua holds me in high esteem, and I love him dearly.

"Peter," I interrupted, "Judas was scribe and purser to Jesus' church?"

"This is also news to me," Peter replied.

"I think I can do some enlightening on this point," Dr. John Harris answered. "There has been found very recently a Coptic Gospel, the Gospel of Judas, describing the very same. In it, Judas is the scribe and what would be called an accountant to Jesus and his Church. It also suggests that he was very close to Jesus, and Jesus held him in high esteem."

Richard excitedly butted in, "I have never heard this. Cardinal Jean, has the Roman Catholic Church been aware of this?"

"Yes," Cardinal Jean replied, "we are aware of the Coptic Gospel of Judas, and so are most biblical scholars of today. It also makes sense why Judas was approached with the supposed bribe."

"But, was he not reviled by the other disciples and even called a thief in the New Testament?" Richard queried.

"Probably more jealousy than anything else," Bob quickly chimed in. "And what accountant has not been called a thief at one time or another."

"Amen to that," Cardinal Jean commented. "When you control the purse strings, you control people, whether they like it or not."

We were all quite suddenly quiet, silent, trying to take in this new revelation.

Peter broke the silence," Shall I continue?"

We almost answered as one, "Yes, please, please."

Yosef Ben Arimathea: Judas Iscariot, why did you point out Yeshua Ben Dawid to the temple guards while in Gethsemane?

Judas Iscariot: I was told the Sanhedrin guards were to bring Yeshua before King Herod, not your tribunal. Herod was to confirm who was worthy to be leader as the religious Messiah, Yeshua claims, and has proved he is of the family of Dawid. No other in the Sanhedrin can make this claim. They told me there was a group within the Sanhedrin that supported Yeshuas' claim. Nicodemus petitioned the Sanhedrin for the monies to pay the Royal court costs before King Herod. They paid me the money in silver, thirty pieces, to pay the court Chancellor and court costs of going before King Herod. I was to make payment at our hearing. Obviously, this did not happen, and I still have the monies. King Herod also supported Yeshua's claim as the Messiah. The Pharisee Nicodemus can confirm what I say is the truth. Here is the silver they gave me. I give it back to them; I do not want it. They tricked me and gave it under false pretenses so they could arrest Yeshua.

Priest Annas: That is a lie; we gave him no monies.

Judas Iscariot: Then where did I get this large amount of money? You have given me thirty silver pieces.

"Peter," I interjected, "I have always wondered the value, according to the Bible, of thirty pieces of silver. Here we have Judas indicating it is quite a large sum of money."

"It was a fair amount of money, probably Roman Denarii. In today's currency, about £ 1,700. Judas is telling us in this document that this is the amount needed to pay for court costs at King Herod's court," Peter pointed out. "Most court officials made their living this way, through bribes and fees. The more important the official, the higher the payment."

"It seems logical. Sorry to interrupt, please continue," I apologized.

Priest Annas: Did you not betray your leader by pointing him out with a kiss? Have you abandoned him because you knew he was false?

Judas Iscariot: Yes, I did kiss Yeshua but not to betray him. Yeshua knew I was the one to point him out. He told his disciples the one I will share my plate to dip his bread would be the one to bring about the starting of his heavenly kingship as Messiah.

"Here again is another riddle of the bible explained," Dr. John Harris pointed out. "In the New Testament, when Jesus offers his plate to Judas to dip his bread in it indicated that Judas was the betrayer. This revelation shows the exact opposite; Jesus is actually telling Judas to go ahead with the plans to make him the Messiah with the support of King Herod. It also takes into question why the disciples would ask Jesus if they were the betrayer. That never made sense to me; more likely, they were asking Jesus to make one of them the instigator of his Messiahship. What do you think, Cardinal Jean?"

"It certainly is pointing in that direction," Cardinal Jean answered. "Let us see what else unfolds. Peter, please continue."

Joseph Ben Arimathea: What did your kiss intend?

Judas Iscariot: When I kissed Yeshua, it was to honour him and to congratulate him. I told him we have won. You are to be the Messiah; there is enough support in the Sanhedrin to support your claim. King Herod has also given his approval. I did not betray Yeshua; I love him. This is blood money, and I cast it before this court. Lord Yeshua, I did not betray you, you know I did not.

" Peter, I can now understand Judas' suicide. He must have been devastated knowing he had been deceived, causing the death of Jesus, the man he loved above all else. Even I can feel his painful depression," I added.

"So, can I Greg, such sadness," Peter agreed. "It must have driven him mad."

"Doesn't the New Testament state in the gospels of Matthew, Mark, Luke, and John that Judas betrayed Jesus with a kiss?" Richard added.

"Betrayed or pointed out could be the interpretation, if it is pointed out, it conforms with this new evidence. The New Testament also points out that Jesus knew that he was to be pointed out to be the Messiah. If this proves to be true, "Cardinal Jean almost whispering," we will have to rewrite the New Testament as we know it. The reconciliation of Judas. This would also confirm the Gnostic Gospels. Carry on; please continue Peter."

 Priest Annas: Guards subdue that man. I will have no outbursts of this type in this Temple.

High Priest Caiaphas: Judas Iscariot, you will be removed from the court if there are any further outbursts.

High Priest Caiaphas: Guards pick up that silver. Judas Iscariot, who gave you this silver?

Judas Iscariot: It was the secretary of Priest Annas, Ben Zebulun that gave me the thirty pieces.

Scribe Priest Hedron: Presents to the court silver coinage in the amount of thirty pieces.

High Priest Caiaphas: This is temple mint coinage.

"Well, there is a different twist to the Judas betrayal," I remarked, "I have never heard of this one before. It also proves a point; the coinage was Sanhedrin Temple mint and not Roman. This also confirms it was the Sanhedrin that brought Jesus to trial as it was their coinage."

" It tends to be more believable, Greg," Peter answered, " It has always been hard to come to terms that one of Jesus' close disciples would betray him. Do you not agree, Cardinal ?"

"Yes, so far, I must side with what you are translating," Cardinal Jean answered.

Peter continued with the translation of the trial.

 High Priest Caiaphas: We will deal with this bribery later. This still does not address the issue of high treason; this court is still answerable to King Herod, Rome, and Pontius Pilate.

Yosef Ben Arimathea: The bribery charge is central to this hearing as it was to be initially heard by King Herod, but the monies did not come from the King, but from this court. I would now bring forward the Pharisee Nicodemus. He has much to say on behalf of Yeshua Ben Dawid.

High Priest Caiaphas: Bring forth the Pharisee Nicodemus.

Yosef Ben Arimathea: You have heard the account by Judas Iscariot; can you confirm his testament?

Pharisee Nicodemus: What Judas Iscariot has testified to is correct. I petitioned the Sanhedrin for court cost monies, to enable Yeshua to present his case to King Herod. King Herod, first wanted Yeshua Ben Dawid to present himself to the populace in Jerusalem. If they accepted Yeshua as their Messiah, King Herod would give him his support. Yeshua was declared Messiah in Jerusalem by the people. They laid palms at his feet as he entered Jerusalem. When King Herod heard of this, he put his support behind Yeshua Ben Dawid. Yeshua Ben Dawid was to present himself to King Herod and not this Sanhedrin. King Herod will vouch for this.

Yosef Ben Arimathea: We must petition King Herod for the acceptance of Yeshua Ben Dawid as Messiah and therefore accepts there is no treason in this appointment.

High Priest Caiaphas: My judgment is this hearing will adjourn until the petition is heard by King Herod. Scribe forward our petition and have the guard deliver our petition immediately to King Herod. We wish to have his council regarding the claims of Yeshua Ben Dawid that he is the legitimate Messiah of the Temple of Jerusalem. Also, I want the secretary Ben Zebulun brought to this court when we reconvene.

Sanhedrin High Court Adjourned at request by the High Priest Caiaphas.

"According to this, King Herod did support a spiritual Messiah Jesus while he maintained his corporal Kingship. The tradition goes back to the original Israeli and Essene concepts. King Saul had Samuel, King David had Nathan, and King Solomon, Zadok," I interjected. "Also, if Jesus was accepted as Messiah this would greatly diminish the power of the Sanhedrin, maybe eliminate it. I guess someone like Priest Annas would not be pleased. The scenario does make a lot more sense."

"We are into the second scroll now," Peter indicated.

Sanhedrin High Court is Reconvened, Jerusalem, Tammuz, Yon Revii 3791

Scribe: Priest Hedron

High Priest Caiaphas preceding.

High Priest Caiaphas: Bring in Secretary Ben Zebulun.

High Priest Caiaphas: Ben Zebulun, did you give Judas Iscariot these thirty pieces of silver?

Ben Zebulun: Yes, High Priest.

High Priest Caiaphas: By whose authority and under what instructions was this silver given?

Ben Zebulun: I was instructed by Priest Annas to give the monies to Judas Iscariot to pay for the court costs of King Herod's court.

Priest Annas: What does it matter how we brought Yeshua Ben Dawid to this court, the charges still hold.

High Priest Caiaphas: You have prejudiced yourself, Priest Annas, by bringing the accused Yeshua Ben Dawid to this court under false pretenses.

High Priest Caiaphas: We now have the answer to our petition to King Herod.

Guard presents High Priest Caiaphas with a royal scroll.

Royal Court of Judea

King Herod, Ally and Supporter of Rome, and the Emperor Augustus Tiberius

Petition of the Sanhedrin to accept Yeshua Ben Dawid as Messiah and to drop all charges of treason on my person and Imperial Rome.

After consideration, We have decided to defer judgement to the Sanhedrin and to the court of Rome, and it's appointed Governor Pontius Pilate.

There is too much change that the Glorious Emperor Augustus Tiberius

has to deal with in Rome; therefore, I defer to the Governor Pontius Pilate.

We do concede that there is no inferred treason on the part of Yeshua Ben Dawid to My Person or Our Royal Court

We hold Yeshua Ben Dawid in Our High Esteem.

"Well, this is something completely new," Peter announced, "an actual copy of King Herod's answer to the Sanhedrin. I wonder where the original is? It does look like Herod is covering his ass in this one. The politics in Rome at this time was quite tumultuous with the execution of Sejanus, supposedly the heir to the Imperial throne. Sejanus was trying to covertly overthrow Tiberius, making secret alliances all over the empire. Tiberius found out and had him eliminated; all those secret alliances were then under close scrutiny."

"Now we can start to see the politics," Cardinal Jean added. "This is what King Herod would fear."

Peter continued.

High Priest Caiaphas: The answer from King Herod is that he has deferred judgment to the Sanhedrin High Court and further to Rome's Governor Pontius Pilate. However, King Herod sees no inferred treason by Yeshua Ben Dawid against his person or court. Scribe Hedron add King Herods' royal scroll to these court proceedings.

Yosef Ben Arimathea: As you can see, there was no intended treason against Rome. All this is an internal Judean matter between King Herod, Yeshua Ben Dawid, and the Sanhedrin. King Herod wishes this court to decide upon the charges against Yeshua Ben Dawid. Yeshua Ben Dawid, you entered Jerusalem, your Judean, and Canaanite Gentile followers laid palm wreaths at your feet declaring you the Messiah King of Judea and Israel. Have you come to overthrow Herod and Rome and declare yourself King?

Yeshua Ben Dawid: Am I not of fourteen generations of the house of Dawid, son of Abraham? Am I not anointed through Moses Prince of Egypt and God's anointed King Pharaoh Akhenaten. I am the way and the light through holy scripture. I am his anointed Son of God. You know I have always preached this.

Priest Annas: You see, this is blasphemy; he calls himself a god; he has condemned himself.

Yosef of Arimathea: Yeshua Ben Dawid, when you say the Son of God, are you not proclaiming the title through Abraham and the Pharaoh of Egypt who gave to his anointed priest, The Son of God? And is this not the continuing tradition of the Essenes? Have you also many times proclaimed yourself the Son of Man?

Yeshua Ben Dawid: thou has said it.

 At this point, Peter interjected, " I know my Egyptian history, and this was the title Pharaohs gave to their high priest, Son of God, as the Pharaoh was in the incarnate of God on earth. It is making a bit more sense now. For a Judean Rabbi to declare himself, God would have been extreme blasphemy, punishable by stoning to death. Jesus was only taking an honorary ancestral title given by the Pharaoh and handed down through Moses and the Essenes. The Essene believed their priesthood came directly descended from Abraham, Moses, and the Exodus. It is also true that Jesus also referred to himself as the son of man; this is repeated many times in the New Testament. ”

“ But why this particular Pharaoh ?” asked Richard, “ I did not think they were monotheistic.”

“They weren’t,” I replied, “only from the Pharaoh Amenhotep I to the Pharaoh Amenhotep IV, aka Akhenaten, they were believed to be the first to hold in one God, Aten. Pharaoh Amenhotep I supposedly had a close relationship with the prophet Abraham, as intimated in the Old Testament. Their relationship started the following of monotheism through mainly the influence of Abraham. After the death of Akhenaten, court intrigue brought back polytheism and thus the suppression of monotheism. It is suggested by some authorities that this started the Exodus of Moses Prince of Egypt. Moses was of the line of Akhenaten; he fled with the priests of Aten and the Israelites to preserve monotheism and avoid persecution. Also, this now points out that it was not the Pharaoh Ramses’, the most powerful of all the Pharaohs, that caused the Exodus. There has never been any evidence supporting that Ramses’ was the Pharaoh of the Exodus. The priests of Amenhotep and Abraham brought with them all the precepts of the belief in Aten. Some also say they brought the Ark of the Covenant, the original commandments. Thus, the starting of our heritage in monotheism. The Essenes believed they were the spiritual descendants of Akhenaton, Abraham, and Moses. ”

“Peter,” I suggested, “the outstanding charge is clearly against Imperial Rome. As an internal matter, the Sanhedrin would be expected to be first investigating, charging, bringing to trial, and sentencing one of their Rabbis’. Rome would have had nothing to do with this internal Judean problem. This is a first, nowhere in the New Testament does it mention the charge against Rome. Also, did you see they called Jesus an Essene Rabbi? Many scholars have speculated that he was an Essene, but this is the first evidence that points to it. Jesus was baptized by

John the Baptist, who was an Essene, and his cousin. The Bible does hint at his Essene background when Jesus spends forty days and forty nights in the desert. The Essene community lived in remote desert areas." I added. " Also, could you see the early Church in Rome condemning Rome for the death of its Messiah? Guess who would be the easier scapegoat? What do you think, Cardinal Jean ?"

" This is one train of thought the Church is pursuing; if the evidence supports Jesus was an Essene, then we have a historical trail right back to the Pharaoh Amenhotep I and Abraham. This finding could make the Church look upon the Pharaoh Amenhotep I to Amenhotep IV as biblical prophets or God's anointed kings as were David and Solomon. They developed and nurtured Abraham's monotheism. Monotheism at this time was the state religion. If it had persisted in Egypt, who knows where we would be today? The prayer term amen may have come from these very Pharaohs. Maybe Egypt would have been the Holy See. As for blaming the death of Jesus on Rome, I doubt whether Constantine would have confirmed the early Christian Church as the state religion if they kept to this account. Please, Peter, carry on."

Peter began again.
Priest Annas: Yeshua Ben Dawid, are you not conspiring with your wife the Priestess Mary the Magdalene to join the Canaanites with the Judeans to overthrow King Herod, the Sanhedrin, and lead a revolt against Rome itself?

Yeshua Ben Dawid: Mary is my wife, she has converted, as you know, to the one God. We are lawfully married, witnessed, and you celebrated with us. If her followers come with her to be reborn in the light, would not God welcome them?

"Again, Mary the Magdalene, Priestess of the Canaanites and wife of Jesus," Peter whispered.

"There is much evidence to support this," Dr. John Harris offered. "Her very name Magdalene translates to Tower. In other words, Mary of the Tower or Temple. At this time, it was a commonplace Middle Eastern religion to the goddess Artemis."

 "It is also confirming," I interrupted, "that there is more and more evidence that Mary Magdalene was very powerful within Jesus' ministry. Sorry for the interruption Peter, please continue."

Yosef Ben Arimathea: Thus, yours is the coming of the kingdom of heaven. Not the destruction of Jerusalem and the Temple.

Yeshua Ben Dawid: I come not to abolish the law and the Prophets but to fulfill them and bring you back to Abraham.

Priest Annas: You have said before witnesses that you would destroy the Temple and build it up in three days. Is this not blasphemy?

Yeshua Ben Dawid: If I rebuild to the precepts set down by Moses, to the glory of God, how is this blasphemy? Did not King Solomon build to these same precepts?

 "Did Moses set down the rules for the building of the temple?" Richard asked.

"I think I can shed some light on that subject," Cardinal Jean replied. " If, as some thought suggests, Moses was a true prince of Egypt and related to Akhenaten, he would have known the holy dimensions of Akhenaten's Temple to the one God. King Solomon's Temple was supposedly built to those dimensions. The Essenes believed the Temple in Jerusalem was not built to these dimensions. There is evidence that the Essene Temple at Qumran overlooking the Dead Sea was built to the sacred dimensions of Akhenaten's and Solomon'sTemple. Again, Richard, this is only a theory, but this finding seems to point in that direction. Peter, let us continue."

Peter started back to the translations.

Yosef Ben Arimathea: Yeshua Ben Dawid, do you intend to lead an armed insurrection to destroy the Temple and overthrow King Herod? If so where is your army?

Yeshua Ben Dawid: Mine will be the opening of the heavens, the Lord will smite his enemies, and his legions of angels will bring the kingdom of God to earth. There the righteous will be judged, and the sinful condemned. You know my teachings. Have I not taught openly in the Temple and synagogues where all Judeans come together? I have said nothing in secret. I hold the spiritual kingship from the house of David while Herod holds the corporal kingdom.

"Again, a dual kingship, one spiritual and one corporal," Peter interjected. " Were Herod and Jesus working in support of one another ?"

"There is evidence of this," Cardinal Jean suggested, "and just think between the two of them they could have united all of Judea. A powerful kingdom. I wonder what Rome would have thought of this."

 Peter continued.

Priest Annas: Do you, in any way, propose violence against this council or the throne of Herod?

Yeshua Ben Dawid: He who lives by the sword shall die by the sword. Only the truth will betray you.
Priest Annas: Yeshua Ben Dawid, if I smite you on your face, will you not return the blow?

Yeshua Ben Dawid: I would turn the other cheek, and I would say to you, do unto others as you would have them do unto you.

Yosef Ben Arimathea: I see no fault in this man, surely this is a debate and interpretation of scripture, and when has the debate of scripture been a crime? Is this not the essence of Judean society to debate scripture?

High Priest Caiaphas: Yeshua Ben Dawid, I hold Caesar's coin and Herod's coin, who do you serve?

Yeshua Ben Dawid: I say to this council, render unto Caesar the things that are Caesar's. Render unto Herod the things that are Herod's and render unto God the things that are God's and God's kingdom resides in every man.

Yosef Ben Arimathea: I rest my case.

High Priest Caiaphas: This Sanhedrin council has heard the evidence, and now we must cast our ballet to judge you.

" So the Sanhedrin actually had a vote on Jesus' guilt or innocence," I announced.

" Looks that way," answered Peter, " let's see what else is revealed ."

"They would I believe, convene a Mishnah," announced the Cardinal, "the Mishnah, probably twenty-three Rabbi. This was a very early trial by jury. They traditionally also made laws and judgments."

High Priest Caiaphas: Rabban Hillel take the Mishnah and come back with your judgment.

"You're right on that Cardinal. They did convene a Mishnah," Peter read.

Priest Hedron, Scribe: Mishnah has convened and delivers the verdict to High Priest Ciaphas.

High Priest Caiaphas: So be it, this Mishnah and council have ruled in favour of the Rabbi Yeshua Ben Dawid. I rule that I have not the support of this council to charge and execute this man the Essene Rabbi Yeshua Ben Dawid. There are no grounds to find Rabbi Yeshua Ben Dawid guilty of blasphemy, sedition, or treason against King Herod or this Sanhedrin. The charge of sedition and treason still has to be heard before Rome's Governor Pontius Pilate at King Herods' request. I leave your fate in his hands. We must now hand you over to him.

"So the Sanhedrin did not find Jesus guilty" I interjected, "this should change our understanding of the New Testament. Do you not think Cardinal Jean?"

"Very much so," Cardinal Jean answered. "It will have huge consequences to all Christianity, Judaism, and possibly Islam."

Yosef Ben Arimathea: High Priest Caiaphas, can we not just petition the Governor Pontius Pilate to release Yeshua Ben Dawid as King Herod has found no crime against him?

High Priest Caiaphas: We must obey the King's request as he is now beholding to the Emperor, and Pilate is the Emperor's representative.

Yosef Ben Arimathea: High Priest Caiaphas I ask a boon before we hand over Yeshua Ben Dawid to Pontius Pilate. Yeshua Ben Dawid's family waits outside in the temple precincts, his mother Mary, his wife Mary Magdalene, and his brother James asked to see him before we bind him over.

High Priest Caiaphas: I see no reason why not. They may see him before we take him to the praetorium on the morrow. I close this case.

Peter looked at us all in amazement, "Well, stark quantifiable written evidence that Mary Magdalene was Jesus' wife. This is utterly astounding ."

Cardinal Jean interjected at this point," It has been postulated through the ages that she was his wife. There is other evidence suggesting this. After all, he was a Rabbi; this was the Judean tradition to marry. To be celibate would be condemned in that society, especially for a Rabbi. Celibacy in the early Church was not practiced, and it was not until the First Lateran Council in 1123 that finally forbade any cleric to marry. Some suggest that this was to maintain church property as then it could not be passed onto heirs as an inheritance. The Church has long dropped the idea she was a reformed prostitute; there is no reference to this in any of the gospels. She is recognized as an apostle who many think was held in high esteem, rivaling that of St. Peter. "

"Gentlemen," Richard quietly interrupted, "I think we have missed the big picture. Neither Herod nor Caiaphas condemned Jesus of treason, sedition, or blasphemy. This is the hard evidence that was suggested earlier in Jacque de Moray's confession."

"Again, we could be radically rewriting the New Testament," Cardinal Jean added. "This could also bring justice to centuries of suffering by the Jewish people. No wonder this is so dangerous to some sects."

"Would this not be dangerous to the Church of Rome if released?" Richard asked Cardinal Jean.

"Pope Benedict XVI apologized to the Jewish community for years of persecution. I doubt this revelation would change this," Cardinal Jean added.

"May I ask? Richard requested. "We have met with a little bit more clarity of biblical characters in this trial. There are the Sanhedrin priests, Caiaphas, Annus, and Nicodemus, which we are most familiar with. The one that plays a crucial part, almost as Jesus' lawyer, is Joseph of Arimathea. Who is he, and what do we know about him?"

"There is much legend about Joseph of Arimathea, especially relating to the Holy Grail."Cardinal Jean interjected. "He also, according to legend, spirited Mary Magdalene to safety to the south of France. What we do know is that he was supposedly related to Jesus and one of his followers. It was his tomb that Jesus was buried in. He was wealthy, highly educated, and well-traveled, and as we can see, accepted within the Sanhedrin. To be able to read in those days was rare in the populace. We tend to gloss over that Jesus could also read and was highly educated. This was not a trait of a simple layman, as some tend to portray him. It is stated in the New Testament that Jesus as a youngster astounded the Sanhedrin by reading and quoting from scripture."

"We are not finished yet; there is more to come. What else will we find, Peter, please continue?" I prompted.

"Ladies and gentlemen," interrupted Cardinal Jean, "we have worked away all of the morning, and it is getting on to 2:00 pm. We have not even stopped for a break. May I suggest we continue this afternoon after lunch. Lunch has been planned, let us take a rest and refresh ourselves. We will meet for our meal in the cafeteria."

We were all surprised to see what the time was. The morning had flown by, and although most of us wanted to continue, we realized a break would be the best course of action. Bob and Richard first returned our relic to the safety of our designated safe. We then all proceeded to the cafeteria.

"Also, and I think we will all agree, no talk yet of what we have discovered," Bob suggested.

"Thank you, Bob," the Cardinal added, "I was about to suggest the same if we are all in agreement?"

We all agreed.

The evening was still bright, the warmth of spring enveloped the small courtyard. The one pomegranate tree was in full bloom, wafting the fragrance throughout. Jesus and Judas sat in the shade beneath the tree. Judas turned to Jesus touching his hand.

"Lord," Judas gently exclaimed, "you have been declared as their Messiah. The population of Jerusalem laid wreaths at your feet as you entered the city, declaring you as Messiah. This is as you foretold. The Sanhedrin has advised me they want to present you to King Herod; he is ready to accept you as Messiah. The Sanhedrin has even paid me the King's court expenses for your presentation to Herod. I have their thirty pieces of silver with me. They would not incur such a large cost if they were not certain you would be accepted. It would take us quite some time to collect that sum for payment. King Herod will see us and proclaim you his Messiah. Will you not accept?

Jesus sat leaning back with his eyes closed. "The Sanhedrin has no authority over me. My authority comes directly through the Lord of our Fathers, Abraham, and Moses, as followed by the Essene Priesthood. That, as you know, is our truth. I do not need the Sanhedrin approval and neither do I want it."

"I am with you," Judas gently pleaded, "as is Mary and all your apostles, but we need the Sanhedrin to gain Herod's court. Nicodemus has confirmed your acceptance, plus we have Herod's approval. This is, at the moment, the only way to Herod's court. Herod knows the pulse of the people and does not want to go against them. Herod is no fool. He knows with your approval, he can unite Israel and Judea as in the days of David and Solomon. He also understands that your wife, Mary Magdalene, has brought huge numbers to solidify our cause. Herod also has the ear of Tiberius; we cannot fail.

"Judas," Jesus' eyes held him, "Nicodemus does not speak for the whole Sanhedrin, he is one of a few that supports me. There are many within the Sanhedrin that wish my downfall, especially those tied to the temple money lenders. I have, as you know, little trust in their promises. Herod, I trust more, only because he sees me as a base to expand his power. He knows, with me, he will be able to unite Israel and Judea. He wants to be the new King Solomon. He plays a tenuous position ever since the execution of Sejanus. Sejanus sought him out as a potential ally, but now he is gone. Now, Tiberius and Rome are looking for any evidence of traitors. As such, we must be very careful. If they wish a meeting it will be on neutral ground. From there they can escort me along with the disciples to King Herod's court. If you can arrange it, I maybe willing.

"What would you consider neutral ground, Lord," Judas asked.

Jesus sat thinking for a moment, "Across the Kidron valley at the olive groves. We are all familiar with the place. There I would consider meeting them with all my apostles. Judas, you are one of my most trusted, if you can arrange it there, I will give my consent."

"Yes, Lord, I will see what I can do. I will see you on the morrow, hopefully with great news," with that, Judas left.

Late the next day, it was still quite warm. Judas hurried to see Jesus. They were still at the house the Joseph Arimathea had opened to them. Judas found Jesus sitting outside in the courtyard discussing with the disciples.

"Judas," It was Matthew who saw him first, "where have you been? We have been finishing off our celebrations for Passover this evening."

"I know, please forgive," Judas addressed the meeting, "but I had pressing business elsewhere."

"He always has pressing business somewhere," Peter called out smiling. "Probably has to do with money and how to accumulate it. Right Judas?"

"Yes, Peter, paying bills and purchasing our victuals," Judas replied, " Someone has to look after you and your prodigious appetite."

A roar of approving laughter broke out as Mary Magdalene rose and greeted Judas, "Come Judas and sit with us."

Judas sat next to Mary, in a semi-circle, with Jesus sitting in the middle.

Judas tried to get Jesus' attention, "Lord."

Jesus held up his hand, smiling at Judas, "It can wait a little longer until we are finished here."

Jesus turned back and continued discussing the plans for their Passover.

Judas' attention to their ongoing plans was entirely lost. He was trying to keep his excitement under control.

Mary turned to Judas, " Don't let them get under your skin. Your task of looking after our expenses is never enviable and always under scrutiny. They know little about it. Have you eaten today?"

"No Mary, but I am all right." Replied Judas.

"Wait," Mary answered and was up and away, returning promptly with a mug of wine, some unleavened bread, and a little bit of fish, " Eat and relax a moment. What is bothering you?"

"Mary," Judas whispered, "I must speak to Jesus first. I know, as his wife, he keeps nothing from you. All I can tell you is that things are in place for Jesus to take his rightful place as Messiah. His time has come, and I have been instrumental in setting things in motion."

Mary held Judas' hand and gently squeezing spoke quietly," He loves you dearly and respects all the organizing you have done. I know that you love him and will only do what is in his best interests. You have my love as well. Now drink your wine and eat."

"Thank you, Mary," Judas took a drink of wine, "He is a little worried about this one."

"Finish your food, Judas," Mary encouraged. "The fish is from Peter's boats."

Judas sat and ate his meal and drank the rest of his wine, "I think now he will agree to the compromise I have managed to arrange. I think great things are in store."

"I know, as you do, Judas, that his Kingdom is at hand. Never, since the time of Solomon, have the people of Israel and Judea been more ready to unite. We must tread carefully, Rome has been stung and will lash out at the slightest infraction."

"Jesus does not want violence," Judas insisted. "His message to all humanity is of brotherly love, inclusiveness, and the laws of Moses. This is his calling to bring the Kingdom of Heaven back to his people. Once he is established, all the prophesies will be fulfilled to the glory of God and Israel."

"It is what he always preached," Mary agreed. "Jew, Gentile, Rome, Greek, and Egyptian, all united under the love of God the Father. This is what drew me to him and my conversion to his Gospel. Many of my followers have done the same and united with him."

"Mary," Judas answered, "you have been a major factor in his movement. You have brought huge numbers of your followers to his cause. I feel, Mary, we are truly on the verge of something great and wonderful, the likes that have never been seen or imagined."

At that moment Jesus called, "Judas, come and tell me your news, we have some peace. I have sent the apostles to finish the arrangements for Passover."

"Go to him," Mary indicated.

Judas rose, taking his leave of Mary. She smiled, releasing his hand and letting him go. Judas joined Jesus, sitting beside him.

"What news do you have for me?" Jesus enquired.

"They have agreed, Lord. We will meet at the olive grove in the Kidron valley. The meeting will be tonight, after Passover supper. We will be met by the Sanhedrin and there escorted to King Herod's court. The monies, thirty pieces, will be given to the court's official. We will then be announced and taken directly to King Herod. Joseph Ben Arimathea has also confirmed to me that the meeting with Herod will take place.

Also, Nicodemus has advised me that the Sanhedrin has agreed to this meeting."

"So, you think we can trust them?" Jesus asked.

" Lord, I would not knowingly lead you or any of us into danger," Judas insisted. "I have spoken to the Sanhedrin, Nicodemus, and Joseph Ben Arimathea; all is ready. What would they gain by not following through with this agreement? As I said earlier, they have even paid the court cost, thirty pieces, which I now hold."

Jesus laid his hand on Judas' shoulder, "I know you would not, but there is, unfortunately, no love lost between the Sanhedrin and us. If I am declared Messiah by Herod, their power will be vastly diminished. Who did you speak to at the Sanhedrin?"

"I spoke to High Priest Annas, he agreed to our terms," Judas replied.

"Why not High Priest Caiaphas?" Jesus asked.

"Annas advised me, Caiaphas had also given his approval to our meeting," Judas answered. "He also said Caiaphas was not available as he was at court with Herod setting up our meeting. What do you want to do Lord, shall we proceed with the meeting?"

"Alright," Jesus approved, "go and advise them we will be there. When you come back, speak to me just before Passover supper. Speak to me first; don't say anything to anyone else. If all seems well, we will proceed. Go now with my blessings."

With that, Judas left for the Sanhedrin. It was not long before he returned. As the evening was still warm, Passover was to be celebrated in the courtyard; a long table and benches had already been set up. Most of the apostles were inside preparing, their laughter spilling out into the courtyard.

Jesus saw Judas and beckoned him to come over and sit in a quiet corner outside. They spoke quietly.

"What news?" Jesus pressed.

"All is to what we have agreed to," Judas confirmed. "We will meet Caiaphas and the Sanhedrin at the olive grove, after Passover. From there Caiaphas will escort us directly to the court of King Herod, there we will pay the court official and be taken to the King. He is expecting us."

Jesus bowed his head and thought for a moment, "I am still wrought with indecision and distrust, but we must make our move now. We cannot keep the people waiting for their Messiah. I have prayed long on it, but still have not had the peace that prayer brings me. What do you think my friend, are we ready?"

"As far as the people and Jerusalem are concerned, we are all ready. King Herod knows this and wants the two kingdoms united. The Sanhedrin must ultimately bend to this. If this is not the time, then it will never be."

"Alright, I will announce it during Passover," Jesus quietly replied, "when I pass the bread and wine to you, Judas."

Judas gently held Jesus' hand, "I am ready, and with you, as always, Lord."

"Go then," Jesus directed, "and get yourself ready for Passover."

Later that evening when all the rituals of Seder had finished, and the Passover meal consumed, an atmosphere of relaxed comradery spread through the apostles. Mary sitting to the right of Jesus was conversing with Peter, and Judas to the left of Jesus was in deep conversation with both Jesus and James. Everything was light and friendly.

Jesus smiling, surveyed his apostles, and held up his hand. The table hushed as all eyes fell on him.

"My dear apostles," Jesus announced, " Tonight we will make our way to the oil groves of Gethsemane and wait for the Sanhedrin to arrive. There, as appointed, I will be pointed out by one of you and taken by them to King Herod's court."

Peter rose immediately, "No Lord, who among us would betray you? Do not give yourself over to them. They have always plotted your downfall. Do not trust them."

"Peter, this I must do, all has been arranged," Jesus calmly responded. "It has already been done, and I must follow. My time has come."

"Who amongst us would do this? I will not," Peter remonstrated.

At this point, all the apostles cried out, "Who is it? It is not me."

Again Jesus held up his hand, calling for calm. The apostles silenced, waiting for his response. Jesus then dipped his bread into his wine and offered it to Judas.

"Judas, I have excepted this blessed course as you know. Go Judas, do what must be done." Jesus pronounced, "I will follow."

"Yes, Lord," at that, Judas rose quickly and left the Passover table.

"Judas, what have you done?" Peter called after him, then directed himself to Jesus, "Lord, what has Judas done, what does this mean? Where will you follow?"

At this point, all the apostles were clamoring for an answer.

Again Jesus called for calm.

Jesus stood, addressing all of the apostles, "We will gather this evening at the olive grove, a neutral place, where I will meet with the Sanhedrin and be presented to King Herod. There I will be proclaimed Messiah. My time has come, as I have always proclaimed to you. This has all been arranged, now come with me and pray with me that this is God's will."

Again Peter cautioned, "Lord, I would follow you to the ends of the world, but I do not like this. James speak to your brother, can you not dissuade him from this course of action?"

"Peter, James, I have already spoken," Jesus interrupted, "I have made up my mind. The people await their Messiah, as I have already been proclaimed. For the first time, the way is open; I must take this opportunity. I know the risks, but I also know what can be done. Be with me, Peter."

"I will be at your side," Peter capitulated.

"Then, come all of you," Jesus requested, "We will pray together for the outcome foretold in scripture. If it is now, God will be with us."

Mary moved to her husband's side, holding his face, turned him towards her, and kissed him lightly on the lips, "Let us go my heart. My love and prayers are with you."

With that, all the apostles followed Jesus and Mary to the Kidron valley. It was a quiet walk, with much contemplation amongst all. Mary held Jesus' hand, not speaking as she knew he was deep in thought. What would be the outcome of tonight?

The darkness of the night was soon upon them. It had cooled down; the walk was pleasant. They finally arrived, it was a familiar haunt, all seemed quiet and normal.

Jesus turned to his followers, "I will go and pray awhile, pray with me, that this is the time foretold."

Jesus walked off a short distance to a grove of oil trees, fell to his knees, and was immediately in deep prayer. Mary stayed by his side, letting him have his quiet meditation and prayer.

The disciples moved off in small groups, but could not concentrate on prayer. Soon, they were discussing what would be the outcome of the night's events. There was much loud trepidation.

"Please," Jesus pleaded, "Did I not ask you to pray with me?" I cannot hear my thoughts with this rancor between you. I ask you to give me some quiet, so I may pray in peace. I need all your prayers, that this is the time foretold."

"Sorry, Lord," James replied, "We will pray with you, that God will bless our mission."

Jesus went back to his place of prayer.

Mary gently touched him on the shoulder, "They love you and are greatly concerned for you."

"I know, this is an onerous burden for all of us," Jesus quietly replied, "What if I fail? What if this is just a trap? I wish this cup was taken from me, but it cannot. I am the Essene High Priest, the Son of God. To this, I was born."

"I cannot foretell what is to happen, my love," Mary gently murmured, kissing him, "But this I do see, your message will envelop the earth."

A moment later, Judas interrupted, "Lord, they are here, coming up the pathway."

"Alright, come with me Judas," We will go and meet them. Mary, please stay here until I know it is safe."

Jesus and Judas walked toward their meeting with the Sanhedrin. The rest of the disciples followed at a short distance. As they came closer, they could just make out Priest Annas and his secretary Ben Zebulum. There were others, but as it was dark, they could not make them out.

Judas turned to Jesus, putting his arms around him and kissing him, "Jesus, you do me great honour. Now is your time to bring the Kingdom of God back to Israel."

Jesus smiled at Judas, just as a call went out.

"Arrest that man," the call came from Priest Annas.

At that moment, it was obvious that Priest Annas had come with the Sanhedrin Temple Guard, who quickly surrounded and held Jesus.

"No!" screamed Judas, "What are you doing? This is wrong. Where is Caiaphas? We are to be escorted to King Herod. You promised me; this was all arranged."

Judas' voice was drowned out by the violent melee of Jesus' disciples attacking the Sanhedrin Guard. Peter had drawn a short sword and hit one of the guards' helmet so hard blood was oozing down the side of his face. Other disciples had charged in swinging staffs, as the struggle grew more violent.

"Stop!" cried Jesus as he pushed his way into the throng.

Jesus was now in the middle of the battle and was holding the injured guard, using his scarf to staunch the flow of blood from the side of the guard's face.

Again, Jesus cried, "Stop! Have I taught you nothing? If you live by violence, surely violence will befall all of us. I will go with them. God will be with us."

At that, the disciples melted back as Jesus allowed them to take him away.

"You bastard, Judas!" shouted Peter, "Now look at what you have done!"

It was already getting hot and humid in Arkansas, but the Reverend Andrew Ducane's office was pleasantly air-conditioned that late evening. An overhead ceiling fan wafted gentle breezes throught the office. The Reverend was pleased and relaxed as he reviewed his sermon for the coming Sunday. Last Sunday's sermon had brought in a record take at the church, and as yet, the receipts had not come in from the telecast. Hopefully, this coming Sunday would equal it. The elimination of Jed Cassidy was of little consequence, a man who had killed numerous times and paid well to do it. He was now before his maker to be judged. The Reverend knew all Jed wanted was his money and had no belief in the Bible or his church. Jed Cassidy had been a means to an end to preserve the sanctity of his Bible; if he could, he would have sold the relics to the highest bidder. That was not going to happen.

"I am the new savior of our sacred Bible. If only the world knew," the Reverend thought to himself. "My place is guaranteed in the afterlife. I will sit at the right hand of the Savior Jesus Christ."

He was buried in self-aggrandizing thoughts when his private line phone rang on his desk.

"Reverend Andrew Ducane, yes, no, that cannot be! I have it here; I have not failed you. It was placed in my hands, and I destroyed it! But, you said I had the choice to capture or destroy it. The Vatican cannot have it; they are lying. I have destroyed it, I tell you!" the Reverend repeatedly repeated himself. "Cassidy was successful, he gave it to me, and then we destroyed it. Not only that, but he also eliminated that bastard, Findley. We were more than successful. God was surely on our side. After that Cassidy took off, I don't know where. You know what he is like, very secretive."

Although the office was air-conditioned, the Reverend was starting to sweat profusely, and his hands were nervously shaking. His breathing was becoming short and quick. His collar of office, all of a sudden, was too tight and too hot and so uncomfortable. He reached around and unpinned it.

"I'm telling you I have it and can show it to you. Alright, bring them, what do you mean they are here already?"

At that moment, the door of his office opened slowly. Three men in dark suits, black leather gloves, and dark sunglasses walked in and surrounded the Reverend's desk."

"Where is it?" the first one of the men demanded.

"I have it; I will show you," the Reverend nervously gulped. "I have done the Lord's work. I am the salvation of our holy Bible. I will be remembered forever for doing the Lord's work."

The second man, almost bodily lifted the Reverend from his chair, "show us!"

The Reverend's knees buckled, but he caught himself on the desk. "This way, follow me, I will show you, trust me."

The Reverend's compound, church, crematorium, and sports centre were large, not to mention the cemetery. Behind the cemetery through about ten acres of woodland was the Reverend's luxurious home. The entire complex was carved out of a substantial wooded area butting into Quachita National Forest, quite secluded.

"It's just a short walk over to the crematorium," the Reverend nervously indicated, "follow me."

"Get in the truck, we will drive," one of the men directed.

"It's not far we can walk," the Reverend pointed.

"I said get into the truck," the man demanded.

There was a large extended cab of the black Ford F150. The Reverend was pushed into the back, sitting between two of the men. In five minutes, they were at the crematorium. The Reverend was escorted inside.

"Get it," the man demanded.

"It's here," the Reverend directed them to an area behind the crematorium furnace. He went over to the bench, unlocked a draw and picked up a flat melted misshaped piece of lead. "Here it is, see I told you, I had it destroyed as they told me." He handed it over.

The man looked at it and then threw it onto the floor. "Where is Jed Cassidy?"

"I don't know, he came, gave me that," he pointed to the lead on the floor. "Took his money and left. Drove away, that is all I know."

"We know he came here, but never left the compound. We waited for him, but he never turned up, funny that. His car rental was found nearby abandoned, not two miles from here."

"Do you know where he went? You were his first and only stop when he returned from France."

"As God is my witness, I do not know," the Reverend pleaded. "He is probably back in the hinterland with his militia."

"Bring him back out to the truck," the man indicated.

The other two men frog marched Ducane to the truck.

"Put him into the back of the truck."

The two men lowered the tailgate and pushed the Reverend into the back of the truck. A third man joined them.

"Tie Ducane's hands behind him, tightly." They were directed.

"No, what are you doing?" the Reverend screamed.

The third man bound a chord of thick rope around the Reverend's hands at his back and then bound Ducane's knees together.

"You have one more chance to tell us where Jed is, or we string you up for good."

"Please, please, I had to!" the Reverend screamed out. He was shaking, sweating profusely, "he would have sold it to the highest bidder and contaminated our holy scripture. All we had done would have been for nothing. I had to destroy them both. Please, please, you don't understand, you are wrong. I was successful in doing the Lord's work. We are blessed."

"Now you will shut the fuck up." A gag was place around his mouth and painfully tightened. "We understand quite well; you failed us. The Vatican has the relics; Findley is very much alive and quite well. You eliminated Jed Cassidy; three strikes against you. You have been tried and found guilty."

The third man picked up a long length of rope that was in the back of the pickup truck and slung it over a large live oak bough hanging over the back of the truck. One end was secured to the oak trunk and the other end tied in a hangman's knot was placed and tightened around Ducane's neck. Ducane tried to struggle and call, but the other two held him tight.

"The end of the rope is secured around the trunk of the tree," the third man called out.

The Reverend stood there, almost on tip toe, in the back of the truck.

"This can't be happening," he thought to himself, "they don't know what the do, I am their Messiah, stop, stop!" He tried to yell through the gag.

The truck lurched forward, leaving Ducane dangling in the void. The last sensation, as he tried to gasp for air, was his tongue swelling out of his mouth and hot piss running down his leg.

"Shit, I forgot to give him this," the third man remembered.

"What's that?" his partner asked.

"Thirty silver dollars, apparently his payment from our contact in the Vatican for his betrayal." He threw the pieces under the swinging body of the Reverend. "Let's get the fuck out of here."

We quietly ate our lunch in the library cafeteria, all deep in our thoughts, Jesus before the Sanhedrin. It almost felt contemporary, hot off the press. What else would be revealed?

 Cardinal Jean had arranged an area apart from the rest of the cafeteria crowd. Before we left the laboratory, he and Bob advised us not to speak to anyone regarding what we had uncovered. We all agreed without hesitation.

"It is too early yet to disclose anything before we have all the facts and translation," the Cardinal counseled. "Plus, all the items must be carbon dated, to confirm dates of origin."

To this, we were all in accord; we must cross all the t's and dot all the i's before our discovery is made public. Of course, the Cardinal was right, but this only made us feel we were still in a deep conspiracy.

Lunch was light, as we were too excited to eat. All wanted to get back and finish the translation. What revealing discoveries would we find?

"Alright, shall we venture back to the bowels of the library?" Cardinal Jean prompted.

There was no hesitation. We all stood up almost in unison. All the eyes in the cafeteria turned on us.

Bob laughed, "could we be a little more enthusiastic?"

That broke the ice. We all started giggling like naughty children in Church who had seen something amusing but couldn't hold back. Everybody in the cafeteria was looking in our direction, wondering what was going on. Of course, that only added to the levity. We hurried away, trying to subdue the giggles, which only made it worse. It had now changed to deep belly laughs, but this broke the tension as we ran back to the lab. Soon we found ourselves back in the lab bedecked in our lab coats and paraphernalia.

Peter opened the next copied scroll.

"This second scroll is in Latin, I wonder if this is the second part of the trial under Pontius Pilate," mused Peter, his hands trembling with excitement.

"Peter read, please!" my anticipation getting the better part of me. Then I felt a hand on my shoulder.

"Greg," Cardinal Jean announced, "all will be revealed, take a breath and calm yourself."

"I know, I feel like a child that cannot wait for a treat," I answered, "but I will behave."

Peter smiled at me and started.

Aprils, Dies Lovis XXIII XXXVI Jerusalem, Province of Judea

Provincial Judean Court of the Governor Pontius Pilate. To the Honour of the Glorious Emperor of Rome Augustus Tiberius

"I believe that translates to April, Thursday 13th, about 36AD," Peter translated. "Does this coincide with the church's biblical date?"

"There are several dates for the crucifixion," Cardinal Jean answered. "For all their discipline, science, and engineering, the Romans were terrible in keeping a proper calendar and dating."

"This is it, people, we have the trial of Jesus before Pilate. Surely, this is as groundbreaking as it can be. Will it concur with the gospels of Matthew, Mark, Luke, and John?" Richard asked.

"Let us see," Cardinal Jean responded.

 Peter continued.

Praetorian Scribe Arturus Janius, Jerusalem, province of Judea.

Priest Yeshua Ben Dawid accused before the court of sedition and treason.

Praetorian of Rome Governor of Judea Pontius Pilate and acting Procurator: I have read your minutes of the trial of Yeshua Ben Dawid. If you found him not guilty, why have you High Priest Caiaphas and Annas come before this tribunal?

High Priest Annas: The Rabbi Yeshua Ben Dawid has been brought before you, and this Praetorium charged with sedition and treason.

Governor Pontius Pilate: What is he doing here? Couldn't Herod and the Sanhedrin deal with him?

High Priest Caiaphas: My Lord Governor, the Sanhedrin, did not find the Rabbi Yeshua Ben Dawid guilty and, therefore, could not condemn the Rabbi Yeshua Ben Dawid. King Herod also found no transgressions against his court by Yeshua Ben Dawid but deferred the charge of treason against Rome to you; in this, he knew he had no authority to act on this charge. Herod knew the populace had no love for the Sanhedrin, so again he wants Rome to settle the matter. Herod wanted a traditional dual leadership of Judea, as was held with King Solomon and King David. He as the corporal King and Yeshua as the popular spiritual Messiah. Now that Sejanus is dead and has lost his support, he must defer to you, Governor Pontius Pilate. He does not want to make any judgments at the moment as he feels he does not know if he has the EmporerTiberius's support. We would not act alone without Herods' approval. If we acted solely on the treason charge against Rome and executed Yeshua Ben Dawid, the populace would rise and destroy the Sanhedrin. The Sanhedrin found Yeshua Ben Dawid not guilty and dropped all charges.

Governor Pontius Pilate;   Let the populace destroy you, good riddance, save Rome the job.

High Priest Caiaphas;   I don't think Rome wants an insurrection in Jerusalem. Now that Sejanus has gone. Who does the Emperor support? King Herod thought he had the Emperor's support through Sejanus. Do we the Sanhedrin have the support of the Emperor? What is the position of your Praetorium? We feel this falls in Rome's and your jurisdiction as you represent Rome here in Judea.

Governor Pontius Pilate;   Are you threatening me and this Praetorium?

High Priest Caiaphas: My Lord, it is not my intention to threaten your office. All I am saying things have changed. Those of us that thought Sejanus was the power behind the Empire now have to look to Tiberius, and he will be looking for what he believes are Sejanus's accomplices. We are all walking a dangerous path. We have been advised Tiberius supported King Herod and the Sanhedrin, but that was through Sejanus. We must defer to you, my Lord. If we are destroyed as allies of Sejanus, where does that leave you if we act without Rome's permission? We are trying to support you, my Lord Pontius Pilate.

"If I remember correctly," John added, "Sejanus, it was rumored, was to be Tiberius's successor until Tiberius found out that Sejanus may have had Germanicus his adopted son assassinated. Sejanus was plotting all over the Empire, garnering allies behind Tiberius's back to make himself Emperor. He got a little too big for his britches. Tiberius had him hauled back to Rome under the pretense of a huge promotion; once back, he was executed. This, for a while, threw the Empire in turmoil."

"Yes, and much more," Cardinal Jean added, "he, Sejanus, tried to marry into nobility without Tiberius's permission. He doomed himself. Sorry for the interruption, please continue Peter."

Governor Pontius Pilate: Very well, we shall hear the case of the Priest Yeshua Ben Dawid. Have the accused brought forward.

Praetorium Guard escorts the Priest Yeshua Ben Dawid before Pontius Pilate.

Governor Pontius Pilate: Yeshua Ben Yosef, you are brought before this Praetorium charged with sedition and treason against Imperial Rome. Do you have council on your behalf?

Yosef Ben Arimathea: With your permission, Governor, I will act on his behalf as I have done with the Sanhedrin Council. I was his counsel to this previous case in which the Mishnah council found him not guilty. Also, the Pharisee Nicodemus is present with testimony and evidence proving his case.

Governor Pontius Pilate: Your counsel is accepted, let it be noted.

Council for the accused Priest Yeshua Ben Dawid is noted as Yosef Ben Aramathea and the Pharisee Nicodemus.

Governor Pontius Pilate: I have read the charges against you of sedition and treason against Imperial Rome, how do you plead Priest Yeshua Ben Dawid?

Yeshua Ben Dawid: Silence, no reply.

Yosef Ben Arimathea: The plead is not guilty, Governor.

Governor Pontius Pilate: Are you the King of Judea

Yeshua Ben Dawid: You have said so.

Governor Pontius Pilate: What of your King Herod? Is he not King of Judea?

Yeshua Ben Dawid: My kingdom is the spiritual kingdom of God, not of this world. Herod is the lawful King of Judea. The kingdom of God resides in all men.

Yosef Ben Arimathea: If I may intercede?

Governor Pontius Pilate: Granted.

Yosef Ben Arimathea: Thank you, Governor. If I may point out, it is the ancient Judean custom to have a corporal king that is King Herod, and a spiritual king or Messiah. Yeshua Ben Dawid was to be this Kingly Messiah as King David had Nathan, and Solomon had Zadok. These were all spiritual Kings or Messiahs. It is this the Judean ancient order that both King Herod and Yeshua Ben Dawid wanted to reinstate.

"Sorry, I have to ask, did Jesus support the kingship of Herod?" Richard asked, "Didn't Herod have Jesus' cousin John the Baptist beheaded? I didn't think there was any support or love between Jesus and Herod."

"That was Herod's father," answered Peter, "it was the other way around, Herod supported the spiritual leadership of Jesus and his wife Mary the Magdalene. If this had happened, it would have united Judea and Canaan under one throne. There was great support for a dual Kingship, one corporal and one spiritual, to bring back the tradition of King David and Nathan plus King Solomon and Zadok. Herod's son supported this dual Kingship, it would have made him very popular and powerful, plus it seems he had the support of Sejanus to follow this path. The Sanhedrin had deviated from this dual Kingship. Much to the anger of a greater part of the populace at this time. Thus we can see the support for Jesus."

"Also, to unite both kingdoms of Judea and Canaan," Cardinal Jean added, "would have given Sejanus another strong ally. Please continue Peter."

Peter started reading again.

Yosef Ben Arimathea: Governor, as you can see, this is purely a Judean religious matter. There is no plot against King Herod or Rome.

King Herod supported Yeshua Ben Dawid to be the spiritual King Messiah.

Governor Pontius Pilate: Then why has Herod deferred this case to me? Can he not deal with this case himself?

High Priest Annas: Governor, if I may, you speak for Rome. The charge against Yeshua Ben Dawid is treason against Rome. King Herod has no jurisdiction in such matters. If you free Yeshua Ben Dawid, then all charges will be dropped. The Sanhedrin found no fault in the man. He claims only to speak through God.

Governor Pontius Pilate: Yeshua Ben Yosef, do you speak on behalf of God?

Yeshua Ben Yeshua: Thou has said it with thine own words. I interpret God's laws.

Governor Pontius Pilate: In this Praetorium of Imperial Rome, only the Divine Emperor Tiberius mediates on behalf of the Gods. Do you dare to make yourself above Tiberius Caesar?

"The Emperors of Rome did consider themselves divine, didn't they?" Richard interrupted.

"Yes, in many ways, they did," answered Peter. "The Emperor was Rome's chief priest, and only he could mediate between the Gods and Rome. When the Emperor died, he immediately ascended to heaven as a God. If the Emperor was born of a previous divine Emperor, he was already considered divine. To deny this was punishable by death."

"So, you see, if you tried to usurp the Emperor's divinity, you were tempting a charge of treason," I said. "That was a death sentence, plus with the political situation, Pilate would want some brownie points sucking up to Tiberius. If Pilate thought his position was tenuous, letting this go would put him on precarious ground."

"But to execute such a popular holy man as their Rabbi Jesus would this not cause an immediate bloody uprising?" Richard pressed.

"Yes, but now the blame would be put on Rome with Tiberius' blessing, not the Sanhedrin or Herod. Rome could care less for the populace," I added, "and who was going to rise against Rome? Jesus would not have advocated that. Peter, please continue let's see what else is revealed."

"There were uprisings in Judea," Cardinal Jean added, "but they were subdued with bloody reprisals. Nobody at this time had thought Jesus would not have been the new Messiah. It should have been a peaceful transition. Judea did eventually revolt, and Rome thoroughly destroyed Israel, casting out its populous."

"Shall I continue?" Peter asked.

We all nodded in agreement.

Yeshua Ben Dawid: Silence.

Governor Pontius Pilate: Do you defy the divine authority of Caesar Tiberius?

Yeshua Ben Dawid: Silence.

Joseph Ben Arimathea: Governor, Yeshua Ben Yosef, only claims this on behalf of Herod and Judean law. There is no threat to Rome's authority.

Governor Pontius Pilate: I will decide what threatens Rome. Do you understand your ally and Herod's has been executed? Sejanus is dead; you must show where your alliance is,

is it with Sejanus or Tiberius? Silence will only confirm your guilt. I will give you another chance and my pardon. Do you defy the divine authority of Tiberius Caesar?

"Sejanus is dead. Pilate is confirming this?" I added.

"Yes, you can see the political turmoil," Peter answered, "I know that Sejanus was a rising star, second only to Tiberius. With Sejanus executed, everybody was scrambling to fill the void currying Tiberius favour. Sejanus wanted to jump the gun; some historians believe he was about to assassinate Tiberius and become Caesar. Tiberius found out he had his son Drusus and his adopted son Germanics murdered. So, in a brilliant underhanded move, Tiberius had Sejanus arrested and executed. Sejanus had the army behind him, and he was setting up spheres of support all over the Empire. You can see why Pilate would not defy Tiberius."

"Peter, you have it right on," Cardinal Jean supported Peter's premise. "The Empire was in turmoil at this point. Tiberius was hunting out all of Sejanu's allies and pity help the one that even fence sat. Please continue."

Yeshua Ben Dawid: Silence

Governor Pontius Pilate: Centurion, take this King of the Jews out and flog the insolence out of him. Maybe that will loosen his tongue, but I want him able and conscious when you bring him back.

Pharisee Nicodemus: Please Governor if I may speak to Yeshua.

Governor Pontius Pilate: I will have both of you flogged if you want. I will have no disrespect for Imperial Rome. Take Yeshua Ben Dawid away and flog him.

Sentence of flogging issued.

Richard, "Why wouldn't Jesus just admit to loyalty to Caesar? Wouldn't that have saved him with Pilate's pardon?"

"I will answer that," Cardinal Jean announced. "Everything that Rome stood for was anathema to Jesus and the Judean state. To bring back the spiritual kingships of David and Solomon in the eyes of Jesus and the Judean people would consecrate the relation between God and his chosen people. With this, the Judean people believed, they would triumph over Rome and restore Israel. Jesus could not compromise and betray everything he stood for."

We were all quiet for a moment. The exact tenuous situation of Jesus' plight had sunk in. The New Testament had come to life as never it had in the past. We were now witnessing a rewriting of history. Peter continued reading.

<u>Tribunal Recesses</u>

Governor Pontius Pilate: Centurion, bring in Yeshua Ben Dawid. Has the sentence of flogging been carried out?

Centurion Longinus: Yes, Governor, He is conscious, but not at this point able to walk without assistance.

 Governor Pontius Pilate: Centurion assist him to sit before this court, and what have they put on his head?

Centurion Longinus: The soldiers put a crown of thorns on the priest to mock him as the King of the Jews. I shall remove it; he is no king, Governor.

Governor Pontius Pilate: No leave it; it may loosen his tongue even more. Yeshua Ben Dawid, I ask you for the last time, do you defy the divinity of the Imperial Emperor Tiberius? Do you understand I will set you free if you accept the divinity of the Emperor? Your suffering will end at my command.

Centurion Longinus: Governor, he cannot see you; the blood from the thorns is blinding him. Shall I wipe his face?

Governor Pontius Pilate: Make it quick Rome does not have all day.

"Wait, Longinus!" Cardinal Jean almost yelled out, "This is the same Centurion that speared Jesus in his side as he hung dying on the cross. He is referred to in the Gospel of Nicodemus, and according to this, Nicodemus is present at this trial. This surely is a new huge revelation, Longinus actually existed, amazing!"

"Some accounts," added Dr. John Harris, "state he did this out of mercy, as in most crucifixions the victim had their legs broken to quicken death. Once the legs could not support the body, all the weight transferred to the arms diminishing, terribly, the victim's ability to breathe. A most excruciating way to die."

"Was Longinus not eventually sainted," I added.

"Yes," Cardinal Jean responded, "they say he helped bring Jesus down from the cross and helped clean the body. Later he converted to Christianity. He was made a Saint very early in the Church. Please, Peter, continue."

Centurion Longinus wipes Yeshua Ben Dawid's face.

Governor Pontius Pilate: Answer my question, do you accept the divinity of the Emperor Tiberius?"

Yeshua Ben Dawid: Silence.

Pontius Pilate: You have condemned yourself Yeshua Ben Dawid. I cannot help you. Your sentence for treason against the Emperor will be crucifixion. Do you understand I find no crime with you, declare for Tiberius, and I will set you free?

Yeshua Ben Dawid: silence, no response.

Pontius Pilate: Yeshua Ben Dawid, you have condemned yourself to crucifixion. I wash my hands of you. Centurion take the prisoner away.

Pharisee Nicodemus: Governor, please, if I may speak?

Pontius Pilate: I will allow it, but of what use it will be, I cannot imagine.

Pharisee Nicodemus: I call upon the clemency of Pax Romana. If you called for the whole of the Empire to declare for the Emperor's divinity, you would probably wipe out half of the population. That is why we have Pax Romana, that is why the Empire is great. I call upon you as Governor of Roman Judea for the clemency of Pax Romana.

"Well, this is something new what is this Pax Romana that Nicodemus is requesting?" Richard asked.

"Pax Romana," Cardinal Jean answered, "was a peace the Roman Empire experienced from Emperor Augustus and lasting just over two hundred years. There were civil rights for non-Romans; also, anyone could become a Roman citizen. One did not have to be born Roman. It held together the Roman Empire, and for its time, reasonable peace and prosperity. Pax, Concordia, Pietas, Humanitas, and Copia, in other words, peace, harmony, duty, decency, and wealth were the constants during this period of the Empire. Nicodemus was pushing to apply the very essence of Roman law."

"I guess Jesus was not a recipient of this generosity," Richard stated.

Peter resumed the translation.

Pontius Pilate: that law applies to the Empire and those that live in it, not to the proceeding of this court. I answer to the Emperor, not the Sanhedrin. The sentence remains.

Joseph Ben Arimathea: Governor, I beg for clemency. Is not the flogging enough? He is of no threat to Rome or you.

Pontius Pilate: He is a threat to me as he will not accept the divinity of Tiberius. I would be condemning myself if I did not denounce Yeshua Ben Dawid. The sentence is to be carried out. Yeshua Ben Dawid, you are a traitor and rebel to Rome and have condemned yourself. You are to be crucified as the rebel King of the Jews. I wash my hands of him.

Yeshua Ben Dawid: I say unto you, and to Rome, I will be long after Rome is dust and is just a distant memory, I will be.

Pontius Pilate: Many have said that of Rome, but Rome is eternal. Take him away.

Praetorium Scribe Arturus Janius

The charge of treason against the Rabi Yeshua Ben Dawid is upheld. The sentence is crucifixion.

Sentence carried out on the following day Aprils, Dies Veneri XXIV XXXVIII at Golgotha by order of Pontius Pilate

Governor of Judea Pontius Pilate

Report of the Execution of Yeshua Ben Dawid

After examination, the Rabi Yeshua Ben Dawid, King Messiah of the Jews, had expired on the cross.

The body of Yeshua Ben Dawid on a petition to Pontius Pilate was retrieved by his family Mary the Magdalene his wife, Ya'akov Ben Dawid his brother, Joseph of Arimathea, and his mother, Mary Ben Dawid

Minutes of the trial sent to Emperor Tiberius.

Minutes copied, to be delivered to King Herod and the Sanhedrin.

Peter looked up, "The end. I wish I could say, and they all lived happily ever after. It does feel like a fairy tale, but ladies and gentlemen and your eminences you have it. If this proves to be true or should I say authentic, it will be quite a change to what we have been brought up to believe. And as you can see, even Rome recognized Mary Magdalene as the wife of Jesus. But mainly it was the Sanhedrin that eventually found Jesus innocent and begged Pontius Pilate to pardon Jesus and set him free. Not much has changed from the politics of today to that of yesteryear."

"No mention of Barabbas," Richard inquired, "Nor any great crowds calling for the death of Jesus."

"A lot of scholars feel that it never happened," Peter suggested. "Why would Rome or should I say Pontius Pilate release a known convicted traitor? Could you imagine Pilate standing in front of Tiberius and trying to explain that one? The inclusion in the bible for the release of Barabbas and the crowds calling for the crucifixion of Jesus is a political explanation to appease Rome. Remember, Constantine, had just made Christianity Rome's official religion. How would it seem if Rome was the cause of the Messiah's death? Far better if the Jews were to blame, and that has been their burden ever since. I wonder now what consequences this will have on our relationship with Jewry?"

"But still, I don't understand why no bloody rebellion?" asked Richard.

Cardinal Jean raised his hand, "If you remember there was no rebellion after John the Baptist was executed by Herod's father and not by the Sanhedrin. Herod's son was supportive of Jesus for the dual Kingship; so was the populace. The sentence against Jesus was carried out by Rome, not the Sanhedrin or King Herod. If there was a rebellion in the planning, it was premature not expecting Jesus to be arrested as he had the support of Herod, and Herod had the support of Sejanus. In a twinkling, all that changed, leaving, I guess the populace in a daze. Also consider, if Pilate found Jesus innocent, he would be aligning himself with the machinations of Sejanus. He knew Tiberius would not have viewed this in his favour. After that, it left James, the brother of Jesus, and Mary Magdalene his wife to administer over the Church. There is no mention that either of them had called for a rebellion. It was all but assured Jesus would have been anointed as their Messiah. Don't forget that some of Jesus' disciples were also reporting that Jesus had risen from the dead. The removal of his body from the cross, which was unprecedented at that time, would have supported the claim that he had risen to some of the populace. Surely, this would have quelled any thought of rebellion if Jesus was alive. It would also have saved Jesus'church."

"It is fairly accepted that during this time Pontius Pilate was still worried about his position. There has been a recent discovery in Jerusalem of an inlay step carved to the glory of Emperor Augustus Tiberius donated by Pontius Pilate. So, he was still trying to cover his ass by placating the Emperor," Dr. John Harris explained.

"One other notation," Richard asked, "states one of the family members who asked for the body of Jesus was his brother Ya'akov Ben David. Who was this, do we know?"

Again, it was Dr. John Harris who answered, "I think this was St. James, Jesus' brother who took over the Church after Jesus was crucified. He was later stoned to death in Jerusalem for his faith, that is when St. Peter took over. One other question, how was it that Pontius Pilate allowed the body of Jesus to be removed from the cross? Rome did not intend for crucifixion to be a quick death; on the contrary, it was deliberately meant to be a slow agonizing death, sometimes taking days. Any deemed felon that was crucified was left to rot as a warning to the populace. In my mind, this confirms that even in death, Jesus was still a powerful figure. Who would have such power to intercede? Certainly not the Sanhedrin, Pilate couldn't give a damn about them. Mary Magdalene, although a powerful Canaanite, I don't think she had that power. Joseph of Arimathea, supposedly wealthy, but still, I don't think he had that influence, even though all the Gospels say it was he who petitioned Pilate. It must have been King Herod who worked diplomatically through Joseph of Arimathea; he is the only one that could have had that much influence on Pilate."

"We may never know," the Cardinal answered, "but I think your reasoning, John, is the only sensible alternative."

"After that, where did the body of Jesus finally rest?" I queried. "That is still a mystery. However, Mary Magdalene was said to have seen the risen Christ, according to the Gospel of John. Matthew, Mark, and Luke Gospels say the tomb was empty and Jesus was not there.

"The Bible states that Joesph of Aramathea owed the tomb where Jesus was initially laid. I think his body was spirited away as a condition on the orders of Pilate. I don't believe Pilate would want a martyrs shrine to incite further riots and sedition," Peter added.

We were all quiet for the moment, each with their thoughts as to what had transpired.

Nobody talked until Cardinal Jean spoke up, "This is only the tip of the iceberg. Carbon dating has to come in, stylistic and linguistic studies must be carried out on the writings. Once that is done, then people, we must open this up to the world and invite them in to scrutinize our findings. We are looking for at least another two months for this to come to fruition, just here at the Vatican. The final acceptance or renunciation of these documents will take years. I think now it is time to retire and reflect on our revelation. I have arranged for supper at my apartment at 7:00 pm. We have much to discuss."

That day, after we had gone through the entire translation, Cardinal Jean had invited us up to his apartments after supper, Bishop Pace was also there to greet us. His apartment was sumptuous as befits a prince of the church, but as usual, he was very gracious and made us very welcome. We dined elegantly but quietly. We were all reviewing in our minds what we had witnessed. The effect it had on each of us and, of course, universally what the outcome would be. After supper, we were invited to the Cardinal's sitting room; there, we were made comfortable as wine, cognac, and coffee were served to us.

"A little something to relax us all after what may be the greatest New Testament discovery of the modern age," Cardinal Jean motioned us to make ourselves comfortable and sit. " I called you all here to see what effect our discovery has had on you personally. You, more than anyone, will have been profoundly affected. You risked a lot to bring it safely here. Was it worth the risk? What changes do you see it will have on Christianity, and for that matter, Judaism?"

As we sat there, comfortably, thinking of our reply. At that moment, we were interrupted by a knock on the door. Bishop Pace rose to answer. We were all amazed as to who walked in, none other but the Pope. Bishop Pace immediately went down on one knee and kissed the Pope's ring.

The Pope raised his hands, "Please no formality here, please stay seated, I should be bowing to you. Captain Godet has informed me of your perilous journey to bring your precious cargo here and precious it is. I have read the translations and have no doubts about their authenticity. You have brought me closer to Jesus Christ than I have ever thought possible in my life. I bless you all for it. Now, if I may, I would like to sit with you and hear your thoughts, but I will defer to Cardinal Jean as our moderator."

"Your Holiness, we were about to ask the very question as to how our findings have affected each one of us," Cardinal Jean answered.

"Then please continue," the Pope requested.

Cardinal Jean turned to Peter, "Since you were our translator, I think it should be you to start our discussion."

Peter sat thinking for a moment before he started to express an opinion, "Your Holiness, Cardinal Jean, and Bishop Pace, my dear friends and of course my dear wife, I am an atheist and I hope I do not offend, but I am sure this will have immense repercussions on mainstream religions of Christianity, Judaism, and Islam. To me, I believe what we found has made the figure of Jesus more human. I put him in context with his times, the political intrigues, as a man, not a god. The only problem, will it be believed? I tend to look at the New Testament as an enchanted heavenly tale when in reality, it was heavily political with powerful people such as the Sanhedrin, Herod, Jesus, and Mary Madeline vying for leadership under the dubious eyes of Rome. Most of this revelation cannot be found in any of the Gospels. In the end, it was Pilate showing support for Tiberius as divine, while Sejanus' power play came to an abrupt end, destroying Jesus. I think he, as a man, saw the futility as he slowly died on the cross, calling to God as to why he had abandoned him. If what we have found is accepted, we have both a philosopher and to others a martyred god. The choice is up to the individual, and there lies the rub, one man will interpret God his way and another differently. If that man does not agree with the other, we start all over again with conflict of one kind or another. I think I could love religion if we did away with God. Without God, I think religion would be a spiritual village, and much of the bitterness, conflict, war, and death would disappear. Religions' contribution to humanity at the moment and past has been just the opposite."

"I won't debate your assessment of our findings, but you have given me part of what the world will ask us, thank you, Peter. And you, Greg, what do you feel it reveals to you?" the Cardinal asked.

"I don't know where to begin; only a month ago, I was sitting comfortably with Peter translating a small medieval tome, having no idea where it would lead, but let me start. I have been an agnostic all my adult life, always posing questions, and never really getting the answers I want. I have looked at all religions, but always have come back to Christianity. Jesus or should I say Yeshua Ben Dawid has always been an enigma to me. I am not saying I believe he was a god, but if you tear away everything else, the miracles, the prophecies, and come down to his basic teachings, I can find no fault. He was always loving, forgiving, and inclusive. He may have been our first to promote feminism. He was a man that was married, as confirmed, to Mary Magdalene and probably had children. A lot of what he said, now makes sense to me. I understand why he took the title, "Son of God," and why he wanted to destroy the temple yet build it back up. Jesus the Essene stated he had direct lineage through the house of David and Abraham, to Moses, to the priests of Amenhotep IV, aka Akhenaten. What we have found confirms the entire theological heritage of our belief in monotheism.

The title given to the head priest "Son of God," referring to the divine Pharaoh Akhenaten, was handed down through the Essenes. Pharaohs were considered divine. The temple was not built to the sacred dimensions of Akhenatens' and Solomon's temple as Jesus wanted. It puts in historical context the Exodus. Ramses' connection was always questionable, as no historical proof could be found confirming the Exodus. Now we know it was not him. All we need to know now, did Jesus rise from the dead? If not in body, he certainly did metaphysically. Does it matter? Inclusiveness was what Jesus preached, and certainly, Mary Magdalene was one of his greatest assets bringing in converts from the mother god Artemis plus the God Fearers. The relaxing of circumcision and dietary rules managed to bring together a broad spectrum initiating the start of the greatest universal religion. He would have welcomed everybody, and this is part of the power base he led and left behind.

Does it matter that the divine, or whatever you want to call it, put the puzzle to us only to lead us to his words of reconciliation for all of humanity? In the beginning, was the word, John 1:1. Although the deeds may be lost or totally exaggerated, the words and the meaning are resurrected. Christianity states we are all created in the image of God, making us all equal brothers and sisters in the eyes of God; no one is above another. Is this not the beginning of our democracy? Is this not a cosmic philosophical wisdom and is this what we need today, a new philosophy? Our churches are emptying; people do not want gods but a spiritual way of living. Does not a more human Jesus and Mary Magdalene fit that bill? A real spiritual family. We must recognize that both Jesus and his wife Mary are both co-founders of the Christian religion. Maybe I am starting to love Jesus as the man, the philosopher. Have I found true faith? I don't know, am I still an agnostic? One quote I do hang on to that sums up my beliefs, goes like this; 'I believe the harmony of natural law, which reveals an intelligence of such superiority that, when compared with it, all systematic thinking and acting of human beings is an utterly insignificant reflection.' "

"Whose quote is that," Peter asked.

"That belongs to Albert Einstein," I answered.

"Thank you, Greg, that was very eloquent. An agnostic philosophical Christian, probably a new term, but as the word states, always looking for the truth, and by your quote from Einstein, you feel there is a divine or intellect that directs the universe. And now Richard, what do you have to add," Cardinal Jean asked.

"I was the only one in our group that was attacked. I know there were other deeds of violence, but this was very personal. I have been wrestling in my mind as to the perpetrators and their vindictiveness. How can they try to destroy such works of art and books? I thought this kind of violence died with the Nazis. I know now we must always be on guard. To me, this comes down to radical religious militant white supremacy. The hatred of the Jews, not only did they crucify Jesus, but also betrayed him. This should all change now, like Hitler, he needed someone to hate, to give credence to his diabolical creed. No more us and them to polarize the opposition. Our discovery has only shown the love and inclusiveness of Jesus and his wife, Mary Magdalene. What we have found will completely undermine our enemies who have been trying to destroy us and our find. We have won an amazing victory without violence as Jesus preached. On a more scholarly bent, we have a historical chronology starting with the Pharaoh Amenhotep I and Abraham. The beginning of our belief in monotheism. A long Hebrew relationship, starting with Abraham, Joseph, Jacob, and then the Pharaohs from Amenhotep I to Amenhotep IV, aka Akhenaten. This followed with Moses, and the Exodus as the old line of Pharaohs died off bringing in the new lineage that supported the old polytheism religion of Egypt. Moses, a true prince of Egypt, fleeing with the Hebrew Essene to protect the monotheism of Amenhotep and Abraham. As always, when the new comes in, the old is persecuted. Finally, with Jesus, the direct descendant of this chronology. It is a marvelous unfolding of our religious history."

"Thank you, Richard. Do you think you have it in your heart to forgive these people that attacked you and tried to destroy this?" the Pope asked.

"I hope I can, I know this is the right thing to do, but I am still wrestling with it," Richard confessed.

"Forgive the intrusion, Jean. Please continue," the Pope apologized.

Cardinal Jean turned to Bob, "Bob, we have known each other for years. I think I know what your comments will be. I would still like to hear them, old friend."

Bob smiled at his old friend, "Cardinal Jean, I know you would prefer for me to call you just Jean, but on this occasion, your title deserves its status. We, Richard, Greg, and Jennifer, Peter, and Pat, have been through a harrowing escape. They put their trust in me, and I always gave them the truth. That is my contribution, the truth, and as long as we hold to that everything will unfold as it should. That is where my faith stands, the truth."

"Thank you, dear friend. I hope I always live up to that standard. I know you, Dr. Harris are somewhat a late participant, but I would still like to know your views," the Cardinal asked.

"Thank you, Cardinal. We have history, philosophy, and religion all rolled into one. Do I favour one study over the other? I don't think you can separate them. What events have not been molded by all three and will continue to be so as long as mankind interprets them. Truth, as always, is in the eye of the beholder. I think we have another thousand years of interpretation, and it will be just the beginning. That is my job to teach this and how exciting it will be. I will be as none partisan as I can," answered Dr. Harris. "I know I was brought here as an outsider to see if this would be an open impartial scientific, historical, and theological investigation. You all have, in my estimation, passed with flying colours. This wonderful revelation could not be in better hands. I feel blessed to be part of it. This will be the highlight of my life, and I thank you for my invitation. Before I finish, the one thing I am now realizing is how this Jewish Rabbi and his Canaanite Priestess managed to morph this obscure hinterland religion into one of the greatest international religion, Christianity. Jesus saw his role to restore the ancient religious rules of Abraham and Akhenaten. Through the conversion of his wife Mary Magdalene and acceptance of her as one of his most prominent disciple, she tempered him to make peaceful inclusion his greatest strength. The dietary rules were relaxed and also circumcision; this allowed the God Fearers in and, in doing so, the whole Roman Empire. We must recognize her as maybe the greatest founder of Christianity. I feel this will be the greatest renaissance of Christianity. And now Cardinal Jean, may we ask your thoughts on what has unfolded?"

Cardinal Jean sat back and closed his eyes, "always a revelation like this can be a double-edged sword. Either it will bring us closer together or drive us further apart. You have seen this with your escape from danger. I tend to think it will be the former as it is the truth, but it will take time. Maybe we will be rewriting the New Testament, a new gospel, 'Gospel of Joseph of Arimathea,' or the 'Gospel of Mary Magdalene.' Maybe we will recognize Amenhotep IV, aka Akhenaten, as a new prophet. There has always been a close relationship with Egypt and our bible, Jesus, as a child fled to Egypt. Hopefully, whatever transpires will bring Christianity, Judaism, and Islam closer as children of Abraham. To that, I say the word 'amen,' which again we believe comes from Amenhotep IV. Our findings now will be open to the world, and I dare say will take years to be accepted. If we are children of Christ, then Judaism is the grandparent, but further, the Egyptian Pharaoh Amenhotep IV and the prophet Abraham are the great grandparents prophets of all, including Islam. We must be one family; this is my greatest wish."

All eyes now turned to the Pope. "What are your thoughts, Holiness?" I asked.

"I will answer that, but first I would like to hear from the ladies, Jennifer and Pat. Jennifer, what are your views on our discovery?"

Jennifer thought for a moment, "I am not a theologian, nor am I a historian. I am an artist, and I see the beauty of creation all around me.

Is it divine creation or pure accident? Did God put Jesus on earth, or was his life the sum total of the politic in which he found himself in? Maybe it was both, but it was his time, and he had a profound effect on humanity. The one thing I do hold as a wife is that Jesus loved his wife, Mary Magdalene, dearly. It is time the church honoured her as such. This was the dual partnership that founded Christianity. So maybe I am telling you I believe in it all, an all-encompassing faith of love and spirituality, honouring both man and woman. Maybe it is time we started to intercede on God's behalf. He has given us everything, but we like spoilt children want him to do more. God's true gift to us is our free will; he cannot take away that gift by interceding in all our manmade catastrophes. That's what I think."

"Jennifer, that was profound, God cannot intercede as it would deny the free will of mankind. Hopefully, one day, we will evolve to your epiphany. And you, Pat," the Pope asked. "What are your thoughts?"

"Oh my god, I have not yet come down to believing we are safe here in the Vatican. I still keep looking over my shoulder and putting my hand on a gun that isn't there, and I hate those things but thank God we are safe. We have been in so much danger that nearly every moment, I am praying to keep us safe. I guess dangerous times make us an instant convert. As to what has been found, this will be a matter of conscience to billions of people belonging to the major religions in the world. My conscience is telling me we have a real person, both husband and wife, who tried their best to make the world a better place and that I admire. It is time the church recognized the contribution of women, especially Mary Magdalene. It is time women were equals within the church as Jesus realized and held them in high esteem as working full members of his church. "

The Pope sat there head resting down in his hands, quiet, listening intensely. He then looked up, smiling, and nodding in approval. "Now, you see what my dilemma is. I have heard all your comments, and they have touched me. Your diversification of thought will be magnified one hundredfold to my universal flock. How do I approach them with this new insight? I believe what I am hearing is that now we have a real person in Jesus. My faith has always confirmed Jesus was real, he was the son of God, and he was sent to redeem us. I have heard nothing that shakes the foundation of my beliefs, only confirms them. We may have lost much in the original Gospels, and the church accepts this. We now have an additional true path. We know the truth about Mary Magdalene, and slowly we are trying to exonerate her and bring her to the status she deserves. Again, my dilemma is how we, the church, take this to the faithful. It may take a while, and I may not see it to its fruition, but I think Cardinal Jean will. And I can tell you it is in good hands, as you take this to the world."

"Thank you all; I hope we will all continue to have this discussion many years to come," answered the Pope, "but now I must take leave of you all."

"Your Holiness," I asked, "before you leave, what of the confession of Jacque de Molay, the last Grand Master of the Knights Templars?"

"So long ago, but still it comes back to sting. It is a dark stain on the church, such a power struggle. There was a schism within the church. One Pope in Rome and another in Avignon, each with their kings supporting each power block. Each was pressuring the other with annihilation. The recruiting of more and more troops and troops cost money and who had more money than they knew what to do with, the Knights Templars. They were the bankers of Europe and a lot of the Middle East. King Philip had his eye on the Kingdom of Rome and all its extended kingdoms and territories. If he won these and seated Pope Clement in Rome, all these kingdoms would be his, he could have been the new Holy Rome Emperor, a new Charlemagne, but he needed money to finance this. So the demise of the Templars. They were hunted for many years, as the church was aware of their secrets and hidden wealth, both could compromise the church. In their way, they stayed loyal but distant, keeping their secrets. With this revelation, they must be exonerated. Jacque de Molay went to his death as a martyr. We pray for his forgiveness, and he should be elevated to sainthood. We must ask forgiveness from the Masonic Brotherhood. We are much closer to them today than most people realize. And now with that, I have one more thing before I take leave of your company. I would like to give special thanks and blessing to you all and especially to Bob as he brought you here safely and trusted us to help reveal your treasured find."

"Thank your Holiness," Bob replied, "we have worked closely over the years, and I hope even closer still in the years to come. Old rifts take time to heal, but I think you and I are at that point," Bob took the Popes' hand in both of his. "I think the secrets held over the Vatican can now be laid to rest. I believe now a great historical injustice will be rectified. I thank you for the support."

"Thank you, Bob, but there is still work to do," And with that, he turned and blessed us all. Cardinal Jean rose and escorted the Pope to the door.

As if on queue to break the moment, one of the Cardinal's priests knocked and entered with David Silver CIA. Silver bowed and kissed the Pope's ring, in a quiet voice he spoke to only the Pope and the Cardinal.

Cardinal Jean turned around and announced to us all, "The Reverend Andrew Ducane is dead. They found him hanged from a tree on his parish property. Thirty pieces of silver were found placed under his hanging feet."

"The FBI found him," Silver added, "they were on the trail of your nemesis, Bob, Jed Cassidy. They followed him from the airport to Reverend Ducane's church, but then he disappeared. We don't know where he has gone, and if he is back up in the hinterland of Arkansas with his paramilitary group, chances are we will never find him unless he comes out. He could hide up there for years. We won't give up, though. With Ducane gone and dead men tell no tales, I doubt Cassidy will be any threat; he was just the hired help. If Ducane was still alive, we might have had a lead as to Cassidy's whereabouts. As for Ducane and his betrayal of the truth, he received his thirty pieces."

"Someone is still out there, they know we have the original, and the Reverend Ducane paid the ultimate price for his failure. They still have an organization and are powerful enough to put out a hit. Are we still in danger, Bob?" I asked.

"We will always be in danger. To what degree you must ask yourself. We have dealt them a blow they cannot recover from easily. The Trial of Jesus and the confession of Jacque de Moray are safe. Their sphere of influence is getting smaller and smaller. They are no longer a threat in the UK and have been severely curtailed in the USA. Will they come after us? I doubt it. They will not want to expose what little strength they have left. No, they will wait and probably a long time before they make another move. Hopefully, there will be another group of ordinary citizens as you have been that will take up the gauntlet."

The next day, after a late lunch, we all met in the library science lecture lab. Cardinal Jean had called the meeting along with Bishop Pace.

"Dear friends," Cardinal Jean started, "we now have back all the physical analysis of the Knights Templar article, inventory number 1998. But first I would like to ask Peter, who did all our translations, Peter, in your estimation, did the Aramaic and Latin translations meet with your linguistic approval for the era they were written in?"

"Yes, most definitely, the dialect and the dialogue could have only come from the era of Jesus Christ and that of the Roman Empire. John and I had the same conversation, and after he read the scripts, he came to the same conclusion."

"So you concur, Dr. Harris?" questioned Cardinal Jean.

"Yes, it is of that era, I have no doubt," John replied.

"Good, both Bishop Pace and I agree with your findings. So now, before I keep you in too much suspense, the physical report. I have copies for all of you, and I will let Bishop Pace read the report."

"Thank you, Cardinal Jean. First of all, I cannot say how excited I am about our discovery. You have given me the greatest gift of my life. Thank you, my dear friends. First on the list;

Sample #1, Lead, Plumbum: although hard to give an exact date for lead, probably 1000   AD. The chemical analysis indicates a Middle Eastern origin.

Sample #2, Leather: species sheep, cured in donkey urine, indicating a Middle Eastern origin   Carbon dating 1100 AD to 1500 AD.

Sample #3, Beeswax: pollen matches that of Southern Greece. Carbon dating from 1100 AD to 1400 AD.

Sample #4, Vellum surrounding cedar tube: calf's skin and lime content indicates point of   origin France. Carbon dating 1100 AD to 1500 AD.

Sample #5, Cedar, Cedrus Libani: from Lebanon. Carbon dating 1100 AD to 1200 AD

"So, Dr. Harris, your guess was right," Bishop Pace added, "the cedar was from Lebanon."

"This just gets better and better," Dr. Harris beamed.

Sample #5, Hyslop, Hyssopus Officinalis: Middle Eastern, carbon dating 1100 AD to 1200 AD.

Sample #6, Silk, Chinese, carbon dating 900 AD to 1000 AD.

Sample #7, vellum, (Aramaic trial of Jesus Christ) carbon dating 100 BC to 100 AD.

Sample #8, papyrus, (Latin trial of Jesus Christ) carbon dating 100 BC to 100 AD.

"And one final sample, which is a surprise," Bishop Pace beamed, "which is....."

Sample #9, human hair, brown, Northern European. Carbon dating 900 AD to 1100 AD.

"Ladies and gentlemen," Bishop Pace added, "this last sample #9 may very well be the Knight Templar that stored our relic. Impossible to say who that would be, the Kingdom of Jerusalem lasted nearly two hundred years. What we can determine is that this was probably found and stored in the early years of the Kingdom, either under Grand Master Hugh de Payens or Robert de Craon. It was in this period most of the excavating of what was considered Solomon's Temple was achieved. I thought this would strike home to you, Bob."

"It is humbling," Bob responded, "we have come full circle, even to the point that the Templars may now be reviving the writings of Christianity."

"What is paramount now," Cardinal Jean added, "is all our investigation confirms the authenticity of our documents. Are we now ready to open this up to the world?"

We all looked at one another; there was no disagreement; we were ready. Battle-hardened, you could say.

"We have our list of guests," Richard confirmed, "which has been submitted to the Vatican through Pierre."

 The British Museum
University of Basel
University of California
Oxford University
Manchester-Sheffield Center for the Dead Sea Scrolls
Cairo Museum
The Open University of Israel
Harvard Divinity School
St. Andrews University

"Will the Vatican, Cardinal Jean, support our findings?"

"The invitations are ready to send out, all on Vatican stationery," Cardinal Jean announced. "The Vatican approval has the Papal seal. Now let us start to rewrite the New Testament."

My novel is fictional; all my modern-day characters are fictional. But, I must say, as to my contemporary fictional figures, these are a conglomerate of people I have met throughout my life. How could it not be? My historical people, however, did exist with the following four exceptions, the presiding scribe Priest Hedron, and Priest Annas' secretary Ben Zebulun, that were present at Jesus' Sanhedrin trial. At the Roman trial, the Praetorian scribe Arturius Janius present during Jesus' trial before Pontius Pilate is fictional. The fourth fictional character is Iain McLennan in the fictitious letter written by Charles Rennie MacKintosh.

My historical figures starting with Charles Rennie MacKintosh did exist along with his Glasgow School of Art and his church, the Queen's Cross. The fire at the Glasgow School of Art did happen and is documented. Characters pertaining to the persecution of Jacque de Molay all existed and are well documented. The biblical personage is all taken from the New Testament, mainly the Gospels Matthew, Mark, Luke, and John, with additions from the Old Testament.

My main characters in the New Testament were, of course, Jesus Christ (Yeshua Ben David), Mary Magdalene, Judas, Herod, and the Sanhedrin. I call Jesus an Essene, which was likely as his cousin John the Baptist was an Essene, and he baptized Jesus. The Essene stated that they were directly descended from the priests of the Pharaoh and Moses; this is well documented in one of my sources, 'The Mystery of the Copper Scroll of Qumram', by Robert Feather. The Essene declared themselves as the chief priests to the monotheist Pharaoh Amenhotep. Amenhotep was the incarnate of God on earth; their high priest's title was, 'The son of God', as he served the incarnate God-Pharaoh. Hence Jesus' proclaimed the Essene title son of God.

Was Mary Magdalene, the wife of Jesus? Of course, she was, and it is high time our Christian faith proclaimed this. Not only was she Jesus' wife, but cofounder of our early Christian faith. After she converted to

Jesus' Judaism, she brought large numbers from her faith into Jesus' flock. Her acceptance and followers were in line with Jesus' preaching of inclusiveness. There is much within the Gnostic doctrines declaring this, also the marriage of Jesus and Mary Magdalene as documented in the coded 'The Lost Gospel', by Simcha Jacobovich and Barrie Wilson.

Did Judas betray Jesus? There is much in the Gnostic writings declaring Judas as highly educated and one of Jesus' closest disciples. At the last supper, as described in the Gospels, the disciples were vying with Jesus to pronounce, who was to point him out. Jesus knew that he was to be declared Messiah with the approval of King Herod. Judas, I feel, was to set things in motion for Jesus, but the political environment of Rome came crashing down around them. The Sanhedrin also knew if Jesus was proclaimed Messiah much of their power if not all would be negated. Much of the political machinations of Rome are left out of the New Testament, and it was this tenuous situation that brought down Jesus.

 My novel proclaims the historical line of Jesus the Essene and the Essene sect, who proclaimed direct lineage to Moses, Abraham, and the Pharaoh Amenhotep. The Essene stated that they were the true voice of God through Abraham and the Pharaoh Amenhotep, who embraced the monotheism of Abraham. Moses, a true Egyptian prince, and the Essene brought these precepts to the holy land and later to Israel through the Exodus. Moses was the last of the monotheist Egyptian royalty. The Essene believed the Temple in Jerusalem was not built to the proper holy dimensions set down by Amenhotep and King Soloman and therefore had to be destroyed and rebuilt, as Jesus preached. After the death of the Pharaoh Akhenaten or Nefertiti, the last of the monotheist Pharaohs, the new Pharaoh possibly Tutankhamen, brought back the old polytheism, thus starting the Exodus of Moses and the priests of the monotheism. It was the followers of Moses that later became the kingdom of Israel. This is far more likely than the biblical

Exodus of the Pharaoh Ramses. There has never been uncovered any historical evidence linking Ramses to the Exodus Pharaoh. Ramses was the most powerful of Egyptian Pharaohs and would not have had any problem putting down a minor rebellion, such as the biblical Exodus. Again, this is well documented by Robert Feather's, 'Copper Scrolls of Qumran.'

Did Jacque de Molay dictate his final confession to his friend, the Archbishop of Sens? He certainly had time to do this as he was interned for seven years before his execution. Molay was in continual contact with church officials, and Pope Clement. His original sentence was for perpetual imprisonment. He recanted his initial confession procured under extreme torture. His feet were tied to a brazier and roasted until he submitted to a false confession. He argued his case successfully to Pope Clement, finally having the Pope declare him innocent; this indeed was well documented. In the end, it was King Philip, through his hand-picked Bishops had Jacque de Molay declared a recanting heretic and quickly burned at the stake. This was without Pope Clement's permission.

My novel is not by any means a critical critique of Christianity but rather points out a lot of what is missing in the Bible. What I am trying to point out is the man, Jesus Christ, the Rabbi, and the political era in which he lived. Also, Jesus as a mortal, his philosophy, his teachings of love and inclusiveness that must be the overriding importance of Christianity. Christianity has veered too far from his essential teachings, and if we want a renaissance in this faith, we must go back to the original. The basic teachings of Christianity through Jesus are probably the most loving and gentle philosophies of all religions.

The End

For Now